PHASE CHANGE

Imagining Energy Futures

Edited by
Matthew Chrulew

twelfth
PLANET PRESS

First published in Australia in 2022 by Twelfth Planet Press

www.twelfthplanetpress.com

Cover illustration 'Dark satanic pink windmills' by Dr Perdita Phillips
Cover and text design by Cathy Larsen
Typeset in 10/16pt Sabon

A catalogue record for this book is available from the National Library of Australia.

Title: Phase Change: Imagining Energy Futures / Matthew Chrulew

ISBN: 978-1-922101-73-0 paperback
ISBN: 978-1-922101-74-7 e-book

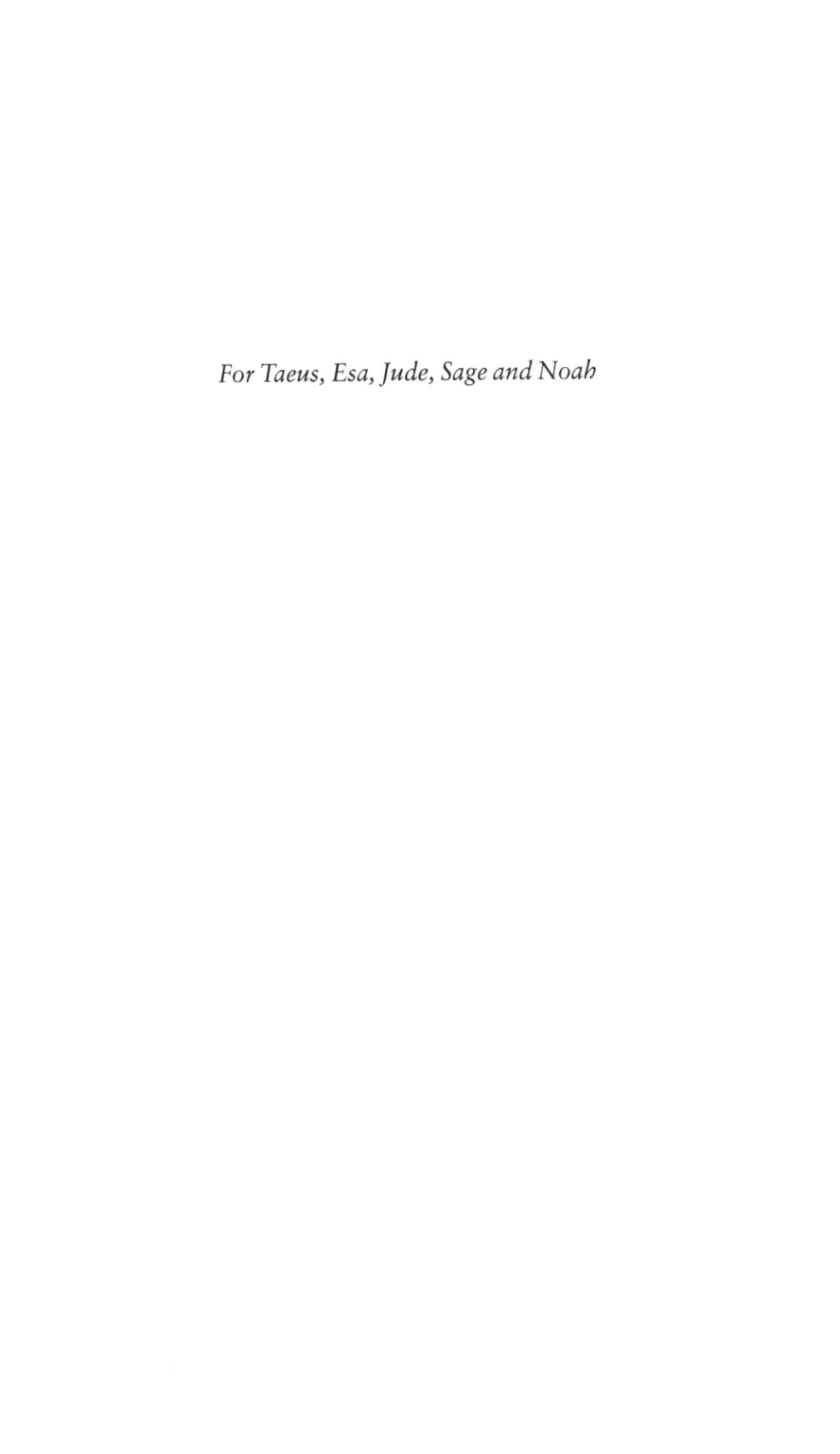

For Taeus, Esa, Jude, Sage and Noah

Table of contents

Introduction
  Matthew Chrulew   ix

You Can't Get There From Here
  Rosaleen Love   1

Boomtown
  Andrew Dana Hudson and Corey J. White   11

Energie Cottbus
  Simon Sellars   31

Wild Plums
  Molly Tanzer   48

Facing Kiruna
  Paul Graham Raven   65

Sucker Hole
  Wendy Waring   92

The Shallow State
Paolo Bacigalupi   106

Naked Earth
Eugen Bacon   129

The Flair
Nick Mamatas   137

Floating Island
Grace Dugan   152

In the Skin
Tom Flood   170

Half-World Eclogues *or* Constraints
John Kinsella   187

The Remembrancer of First Fruits and Tenths
Andrew Macrae   261

The Agency of Metabolic Pathways
Sid Jain   287

The Space Between All Possible Ways
Cat Sparks   307

Resurrecting Martha
Carmel Bird   324

Sunny Days
Jasper Wyld   331

Checkerboard
  Thoraiya Dyer   348

The Switch
  Ben Walter   383

After Zero
  Greg Egan   391

Zimmers
  David Whish-Wilson   411

Seven Non-Abolitions
  Jo Lindsay Walton   419

Contributors   440

Acknowledgements   449

Introduction

Matthew Chrulew

The global economy is powered by burning ancient organisms, releasing solar energy first photosynthesised millions of years ago, since decomposed under Earth's heat and pressure, then, in a great industrial spike, extracted and processed for fuel and fibre, plastic and fertiliser at a rate of acceleration that has triggered catastrophic climatic changes. We must decarbonise; yet as work in the energy humanities has reminded us, energy is not simply a matter of physics and chemistry, technology and innovation, but is socially entrenched and environmentally entangled, bound up with questions of history and culture, value and power, sovereignty and survivance. A just transition to renewable and sustainable energy use will demand more than new machines and markets that shore up neocolonial extraction and corporate profit. The fossil fuel industry and its hegemonic petroculture not only lubricate the globe and its gadgets but—with the habits of consumption they elicit and the greenwashing deflections they push (footprints, offsets, vapourware)—shape lives and selves, concepts and narratives, and constrain the space for divergent imaginations. Yet other energy systems are possible—and with them, other stories, worlds, futures.

Long a heated interface between the sciences and the humanities, science fiction has a key role to play in fashioning energy futures. Whether through careful extrapolation or playful speculation, grim warnings or earnest proposals, the genre works to estrange and to provoke, to caution against dangers, refuse inevitabilities and hold open potential alternatives. With the growth of environmental consciousness in the last half century, ecotopian visions have mushroomed, along with their dystopian counterparts: collapse and survival, scarcity and abundance, floods and arks, Anthropocene and Chthulucene. Avant-garde movements have fizzed with manifestos and new subgenres, from Viridian Design to Mundane Science Fiction. Most recently, it is solarpunk that has taken up this contest of ideas over the ecological repercussions of scientific modernity, disrupting the apocalyptic pessimism of climate fiction with hopeful portrayals of green technology, urban permaculture and networked resilience. Of course, as current conversations in the field underline, it is in the contributions of black, Indigenous, feminist, queer, disabled, and other diverse and marginalised voices that the future of these futurisms lies. And often, it is the heterodox visions and generative practices of independent publishers that help craft and deliver these toolkits for reshaping reality. Whatever activist power one ascribes to art, weaponised and impoverished narratives of the future already sculpt the earth, from corporate scenarios and forecasts to tech oligarchs' extropian fantasies. This is not terrain we can afford to cede.

Phase Change collects twenty-two original short stories that experiment with alternative energy systems and the aesthetic forms that might accompany them. From transhuman planet-hopping to post-cyberpunk paranoia, from realist hard science fiction to experimental, epistolary and metafictional forms, these stories depict not only new technologies but new ways of life, new modes of habitation and organisation. There are large-scale solar arrays, of course, but also bioluminescent fungi, low-orbit laser-transmitting satellites, a plasma sun-shield, nitrogen-fixing algae, semi-sentient artificial trees. There are floating islands, brawling buildings, protective biospheres, subterranean chambers. There are the scientists, inventors and engineers you might expect, but also bankers and bureaucrats, architects and illustrators, anthropologists and activists, students and teachers, delivery workers and tour guides, nurses and refugees, not to mention accountant-executioners and holographic AI avatars. As they struggle to transform or endure the energy systems that shape their worlds, their dramas unfold along old and new lines of class and identity, exploitation and corruption, revolution and counter-revolution, diplomacy and refusal, care and cultivation.

These are stories that dislocate and defamiliarise current energy regimes, the hierarchies they perpetuate and the necessities they presume. Stories that probe energy transitions and futures in all their complexity and agonism, their price as well as their promise. Stories that go beyond both nihilistic fatalism and techno-optimistic ecomodernism to conjure alternative forms of economy and ecology, metabolism and prosthesis, infrastructure and commons, technique and know-how, mobility and interdependency. Stories that turn up the pressure until flows of capital freeze, resistance boils over, stale pretexts melt away and anticipations explode. These are stories of phase change.

You Can't Get There From Here

Rosaleen Love

When the back-up planetary energy system breaks down, when it's down to its last reserves, you know the time is fast approaching when you have to pack up your bags and go planet hopping again. Life gets too tough to stay, and it's best to go early rather than leave too late.

Planet hopping, in and of itself, isn't too hard these days, with the Musk-Bezos systems we've been developing over the years. The combined genius of the first space privateers unleashed the true potential of digital currency. In the beginning we thought bitcoin would be good for reforming (or wrecking) the global banking system. Then we found out just how clunky it was to use in every-day transactions. Hence the pivot from crypto-currency to crypto-energy. Bitcoin became the actual fuel of interplanetary travel.

Planet hopping became our new way of life. We'd lived on Earth1, let's call it, just got used to calling it home, until we used up all the energy of the planet, and then we planet hopped to Earth2, and once more used up all the energy of that planet, until here we are at Earth13, with just enough fuel left for our departure to the next extra-solar planet in a habitable zone.

This is how the human capacity for innovation and entrepreneurship rose to meet the global warming crisis. It's been the way we did things ever since the Musk-Bezos era.

Fair to say we've seen a lot of energy systems come and go. Often with some overlap, as old energy systems stayed in place alongside the new ones, with the burning of dung and wood still happening while innovators exploited coal, uranium, hydrogen. Bitcoin became the fuel bonanza it is today—hopeless as a planetary monetary system but excellent as a decentralised peer-to-peer energy framework. Complicated, but true. The same technologies that brought you bitcoin brought you rocket fuel. The best ideas can often be the simplest.

First there were the fossil fuels, then uranium, then the business with lithium, the great hydrogen hoax, not to forget the innovative use of radioactive diamonds, and it all went along well enough, though disposing of the lithium-nuclear-hydrogen debris was a problem, but by then we knew we could just trash the place and leave. When it looked like we were going to be left with the soft energy of sun and water and wind, then it was time to go. In part it was as much a cultural thing as a physical resource issue. Back then we considered soft energies culturally inappropriate. Hard energy was the way we'd always done things, and why change what has always worked? Easy said, easy done. The trick is, to keep just enough energy in store for the next planetary jump, when we'd take off and leave the sun and the wind and the rain to the birds and the bees. They were pleased to see us go.

There were some of us, old stories have it, who, when it was time to go, made different plans. They'd spirit themselves off to a dream time, but the rest of us have so far been unable to access this time and space (or wreck it, depending on your basic energy philosophy).

One day as we were sitting around the nuclear fire pit and contemplating the waning of energy on Earth13, it started to get to me. The number of exo-planets we can migrate to is perhaps, say 20 to 50. Of course, the further we go, the more we find, but it can't keep on keeping on. Habitable zones can't keep expanding indefinitely. Sooner or later, we'll find the number of possibilities is going to decline, and then the end times won't be the good times. The next planet along that we were considering that day, KOI-7923.01, it's covered all year with cold tundra, and that's not to my liking. On a personal level, the planets I want to live on were starting to get fewer between and further apart.

This was when some of us decided that things couldn't go on like this, that we had to change the way we've always done things. You can't get there from here, it's an old saying about finding the perfect place. Soon there'd be no more theres to get to from here.

We started small, as grass roots movements do, talking among ourselves, our families, trying to convince people, one at a time, that to remain was good, to leave was the coward's way out.

Good choice to stay, bad choice to leave.

When I used the collective 'we' in my introductory remarks, I was referring to the members of the human race, from the time when we first appeared in the early Anthropocene to our rapid transition to where we are now, in the energy-guzzling stage of the late or last Anthropocene, the era before the next stage of biological (non-human) evolution takes over.

We were a collectivity but that doesn't mean we didn't argue. We soon divided into two main groups, with two competing and contrasting identities, remainers and leavers. We remainers see the possibility of an energy future along the lines of a decentralised peer to peer framework of micro-energies, small energy bursts sustainably created, fit for purpose, and produced just in time. We remainers are flexible, always prepared to consider multiple co-existing strategies. Some of us might want to return to the ancient ways of sun, wind and water, but others might chart a new path into the unknown, taking full advantage of yet to be invented new and un-tested technologies.

We remainers call for an end to extra-planetary migration. We seek better ways to clean up after ourselves as we go along. True, we didn't yet see the path to getting there from here, but we were going to give it our best try. Remainers were stayers, not quitters. Remainers soldier on.

For the leavers, it was quit while you're ahead. They argued the sheer impracticality of our plans and our ideological preference for the micro over the macro solution. They liked to think they thought big.

To give them their due, the leavers were prepared to listen to us, and before they left we had some great times, yarning around the nuclear fire pit. Here's one of their better ideas. Why not, instead of leaving for the next viable planet, why not bring the new planet to us? Harness it as a more useful moon, with a shuttle service between us. Remember what they used to do with icebergs when the fresh water started to run out? Put a motor on the iceberg, and drive it to the people. Water the inland desert, and orange groves spring from the red dust.

We liked the planetary-harness idea, combining the best of leaving with remaining. We worked on it for a good while, but it turned into one of those ideas that was great in principle, hopeless in practice. Blue sky, black space thinking.

We kept busy with our competing visionary white papers. The leavers weren't as strong on the detail they demanded from the remainers. It was easier for them. Keep to the good old ways, keep the faith in the tried-and-true path to what happens next. Do what they've always done. No need to change anything, ideas, mindset, identity as humans of the late Anthropocene.

But to pivot half a planet of people to the remainer cause, that required something much harder, a change of mentality, of identity. We had to identify ourselves more closely with the things we loved about our present planet. We had to change from a mindset of exploitation to one of stewardship, a change from slash and burn to joy in making the most of what we've got, change from a planetary-nomadic society to a settler society that adapted itself, and its human components, to suit the planet. We were the true conservatives, turning back to the old ways of *homo habilis*. Only now the old ways would be better, informed by our new technologies of sustainability, and our capacity to forge new tools for the task ahead.

There was a vote. It split 50-50. The leavers left. The rest of us didn't.

First the white paper, then the energy manifesto.

We the people, we the next versions of *homo sapiens sapiens,* vow to retain this planet in a good and fit state for as long as we are able, as much as is in our power. We acknowledge our limitations. It will prove nigh impossible to maintain this planet forever in the state in which we find it, because as energy consuming and producing entities, we are subject to the physical laws of the universe. We have no choice but to be in compliance with the third law of thermodynamics. Entropy always increases. There is inherent disorder in the energy system.

We can't keep going as we are, we can't keep going as we might have wanted to be, *homo sapiens* on two legs, using our mouths to speak, our legs to carry us, our arms to hew wood. We had to think big, to think about what it might mean to leave behind bits of what we think makes us human—face, hands, legs, feet.

Hence our advocacy for *really* changing ourselves to suit our changing environment. We are part of the biotic sphere that recognises change and accommodates to it. Entropy increases, order decreases, and the tools we have to hand are twofold, genetic modification and artificial intelligence. We know we must keep an open mind, for the issue is not personal preference but the greater good. We need to determine how best to encourage planet-conserving diversity, though such diversity might not be to our personal taste.

At present there are different versions of consciousness and different modes of energy production across the continuum of life from viruses to humans. It doesn't have to be like this. Imagine connections everywhere, like fungi with filaments of hyphae and colonies of mycelia that spread out to explore the food and energy world around them, wriggling like tiny worms through the fabric of the planet. This creates the shortest path between energy production and consumption. Nothing is wasted. Group awareness evolves, with survival of the whole an attribute of the group, not of a collection of individuals who disagree and argue and protest and subvert. New arrays of signalling pathways and protein sensors forge a super organism connecting its individual parts in a roughly equal mix of energy production and consumption.

We shall forage for energy as once we foraged for plants.

Sliding down the evolutionary ladder was one option, to embrace, ultimately, the instincts of the slimier members of the biological world, while endowing them with a higher consciousness. Humans may devolve physically but keep their sapient awareness. Difficult, but not impossible. Once we couldn't even begin to imagine the planet-hopping future. Now we are free to make alternative choices, we are free to choose a more cerebral upward trajectory combined with downward bodily slide, casting off harmful aspects of our energy-guzzling biological nature that have proved a problem in the past.

The first path to entering a more ethereal realm might be to join with our new micro-energy partners, the viruses, the algae, the fungi, all the biomass we once regarded as far, far beneath us. After we put pride in our putative biological superiority to one side, as we must, we become free to forge partnerships with the low life. These are the biofacts of our new era. Imagine a collective consciousness that spreads out in a vast interconnected system that takes from Gaia and gives to Gaia in roughly equal quantities. We become species of sentient life that combine higher consciousness with carbon sequestration.

This means taking a leap beyond current carbon capture and emissions trading, though the old ways may still continue to co-exist alongside the new. Those who have chosen the fungi route become a sink of CO_2 and gain emissions credits. Those choosing the alternative AI/higher consciousness path produce more than their share of pollutants, though they've done their best to lower their energy consumption through body downsizing and shape-shifting. While still committed to the path of evolutionary change, they ask for back-up in case the new technology doesn't deliver. They want to keep the old planet-escape route option open. As AI/humans it should still be possible. With a lighter pay-load, the range of future planets is thereby greater. It's a win-win all round, a workable carbon trading scheme with flexible future outcomes.

With peer-to-peer energy trading, we cut out the middle man, as bitcoin cut out the banks in creating the blockchain. Cut out the carbon traders and make the energy traders go peer-to-peer.

Still, it is the old way of doing things. The AI/human mob buy the carbon credits off the fungi/human hybrid mob, and the old economic system gets propped up once again. Those of us who seek true transformative change demand more than spin and old schemes repackaged.

We continued to workshop round the energy circle.

There is another way. But I suspect you really can't get there from here. We agree it's best to stay home and cultivate our own energy garden. We know to choose the path of intimate coopera-tion and co-creation with our micro-energy partners. Our twin objectives are to produce energy and to produce higher thought.

We seek to combine the best of every possible future in a truly complex symbiosis.

Once we had one home and that was the planet Earth1. Then we learned how to leave it, and we became leavers. Next, we split into leavers and remainers. The remainers divided to become the AI/ human hybrid and the human/fungi mob. That's not the end of it. There's always more that can be done.

Here's the ultimate challenge, to unite our differences as we have done so often in the past, and evolve into the AI/fungi/human mob, in all its glorious possibilities. Think of how mRNA vaccines worked in the covid pandemic. The virus put instructions to make the spike protein into human muscles, and the cells of the muscles used the instructions to make the protein that tricked the body and so on and so on. The body became a factory for vaccine production. It was the way it was done that gave us new ideas. The protein binds to the surface of the virus, like an octopus adorns its body with seaweed and shells. We could use virus tools to cede new powers to the cells, so the body adjusts to completely new states of being. And so it goes, from mRNA vaccine to the next stage, as biological entities acclimatise to co-create with the new, whether life or artificial forms.

There will come an end to everything, unless we can work a way around it. Entropy always increases, up to the point when it doesn't, when all the energy of the universe is evenly distributed throughout. Including on whatever versions of Earth we then find ourselves upon. Keeping options open with the planet hopping thing was the smart thing to do, so we've got further Earths, further options, ever further out through the expanding universe.

The end may not be like the beginning, as the universe expands and dark energy evolves to counteract the forces of gravity. The energy of dark matter—that will be an entirely new form of energy we shall bend to our will, to harness and exploit.

I see a future in which we transfer to the matter that is left our spatial recognition, memory and intelligence. Matter becomes sentient, and works out what to do next with the universe as it nears what we currently think might be the end of its existence.

I truly believe we can get there from here.

Boomtown

Andrew Dana Hudson and Corey J. White

The road train's fins glinted blackly. Norris squinted in the pre-dawn dim, trying to make sense of the massive vehicle. The trailers stretched a dozen deep—half containers, half tankers—each with angled sheets of gossamer photovoltaics splayed to the side, held in place by a carbon-silk cat's cradle that trembled with algo-managed tension. It was a strange apparatus, but the whole world, to Norris's mind, had been getting stranger and stranger.

'Forgive my ignorance,' Norris said to the driver he'd hired, who was wrangling control sticks in the cockpit. 'But this tanker decal says "rocket propellant." Don't chemical fuels, er, explode?'

The truckie, Ruby, was sun-baked with the kind of well-proportioned musculature that sleep influencers claimed to achieve with circadian optimisation, electrified water, and nothing else. She said, 'Nah, nothing in there but H2O.'

'Oh, good,' Norris sighed.

'On the way *back* we'll be hauling rocket fuel.'

'Oh. Good.'

Norris already felt out of his depth on this trip. His natural habitat was a tasteful corner office overlooking the Royal Botanic Garden, snapping for the secretary AI to send up a green tea latte, while his avatar strutted in a metaversal conference room, brokering deals across the globe. Not here at an airport truck depot in brush-scrabbled nowhere, red dust wafting onto his trousers, surrounded by wild-painted vehicles looming like haunted sculptures, silently waiting for their sun-god to appear. Not about to ride such a monster even further into the outback, all on a legal errand that a civilised society would have handled with an email.

'I didn't realise there were still active gas wells,' he said, hoping small talk would calm his jangled nerves. 'To make the fuel.'

'There aren't,' Ruby replied. Her gaze flicked from her instruments, to the flexing solar arrays, to the glow of day warming the underside of the east. 'Pull carbon from the air, cut hydrogen off water, mix 'em together, it's liquid methane, isn't it?'

'Sounds expensive. Can they really do that?'

'It's Boomtown, mate. They got the electrons. They can do whatever they like.'

Rays crested the horizon, shooting across the desert and lighting up the side of the road train. Ruby tweaked her controls and the panels arched to catch the light just-so. Within seconds Norris heard a thick hum ripple through the vehicle, felt a charge in the air.

'Now or never, banker-bro,' Ruby said, beckoning him to join her in the high cab.

Norris climbed gangly up, his rolly bag banging up the rungs behind him. He asked, huffing, 'How long does your "rig" take to charge?'

'Charge?' Ruby scoffed. 'You miss the Battery Bust memo or something? You think the likes of me can unkink those supply chains?'

'Well, no.' Norris fumbled with his seatbelt.

'This eel's what we call chew-to-run. We ride as long as we've got sun.'

Around them other truckies were scrambling into road trains, kicking red particulates into the red morning light.

'You can haul all that weight,' Norris gestured back at the trailers, then out at the dawn, 'just on this?'

'Out here, you catch enough electrons, you can do anything you like.'

As if on cue, the road train found its gear and tip-toed forward. It was agonisingly slow, accelerating by inches. Norris could almost feel how dependent the rig was on that yellow circle creeping up by degrees, like a sneaky golden retriever peeking over a fence. But when the sun was visible enough he couldn't actually look at it, the truck lurched another gear and began to take the crumbly road at a low gallop.

Ruby kept saying 'electrons,' Norris noticed, not 'energy,' not even 'power.' Not 'money,' which was how he would have formulated such a statement about capacity and possibility. It was unnerving, as unnerving as the endless crimson-tan desert now rolling by them. He had hours to take it in, at least—Ruby had been cagey about the length of the drive. It felt like a fairy tale, the vagueness of the trip, the not-just-in-time-ness. He was journeying to a place with no dot on the maps, that nonetheless everyone was talking about. A place that for some reason held hostage vast flows of capital, a peg blocking the tectonic movements of post-fossil modernity.

Listening to Ruby begin to explain the mechanics of her rig to him as they picked up speed, Norris had the worrying premonition that Boomtown was infectious.

———

'Is that what I think it is?' Norris asked.

'Dunno, mate, not a mind-reader.' Ruby's eyes drooped. While Norris could doze and daydream, Ruby had to keep focused—the roads were mostly free of traffic, but they were carrying a massive load, and inertia was a fickle mistress.

He'd expected a barren landscape, but the outback teemed with life. Tough grasses and shrubs sprouted across the vast plains. Anywhere water could be found was a green oasis, shaded by tall gum trees. This new sight, though, was something else—something from Norris's world of high capital and global logistics.

'Never seen an auto-fac in the wild,' he marvelled.

'Yeah, bunch of snails out here.'

Norris hadn't heard them called 'snails' before, but he saw the resemblance immediately. While proposal renderings had depicted elegant mechanical sandworms—a lean tube sucking in silica and extruding valuable products behind—the reality was lumpier. The tread-borne factory was storeys high, protected by a gleaming solar carapace. Out front two sensor packages scanned the ground for minerals. It really did look like a snail. There was no cabin, no driver, just access panels for mechanical repairs and updating the auto-fac's connection to the computational slab. The massive factory unit had once sifted raw feedstocks from the dirt, manufacturing solar panels and secreting them behind in long, shiny trails.

'Wouldn't call 'em "auto",' Ruby said. 'Sparkies had to check over every panel for defects, and they were always finding something. Good union work though, while it lasted.'

The foibles of a pilot program, Norris thought. He was sure the human element would be ironed out before the technology went global. Africa and the Middle East were the biggest markets; would have been his focus if Lutes Finance had scored that deal. Would've been worth a couple commas to him personally, probably seen him make partner. But that bitterness faded as he gazed at the massive machine.

Norris turned his head to follow as they zipped past the unmoving auto-fac. 'What happened to it?'

'You did,' Ruby said.

'Pardon?'

'When the banks pulled funding for the TeraSol Array, they cut off the supplemental feedstocks and locked the firmware.'

'Lutes wasn't involved in the TeraSol concern at that point,' Norris objected.

'Banks is banks,' Ruby shrugged. 'Stop craning your neck. You'll see plenty more before we reach Boomtown.'

'How far now?'

'Nearly there; we're in the array already.'

Norris waited for the fledgling town to appear in the distance, tires over asphalt and wind in the solar sails the only sounds coming from the truck. Half an hour later he realised that a long-haul trucker's idea of 'nearly there' was very different to his own.

The single snail trail of solar panels connected to wider and wider sheets of shiny blue, until the energy field seemed to stretch to the horizon. The panels were raised off the ground, with sheep grazing on grasses that grew in the shade beneath, subsisting off condensation that gathered overnight and runnelled into irrigation tracks. The panels, like the planet's equatorial midsection, got blisteringly hot during the day, but sink materials had gotten efficient enough to transfer most of that heat underground.

More minutes passed until finally Norris caught a glimpse of Boomtown itself, emerging from the mirage-like band of the horizon. First thing he saw was a curved rise in the shining fields of PV, like a termite mound. Under that was a spindly, organic-looking structure, part scaffolding for the panels above, part Tower of Babel. Squat, module-snapped buildings circled it, and the edges of town sprawled with tents, teepees, and lean-tos, plus buses and trucks converted into makeshift workshops and residences. To the north were blocky towers exposing guts of fans and tubes, like a stack of air conditioners the size of an apartment building—the carbon capture machines, feeding directly off the solar grid for its exorbitant power needs.

'Here we are,' Ruby announced. 'Boomtown.'

A sudden, echoing *boom* rattled the truck's windows, the solar fins slithering with the force. Norris felt it in his chest, like his rib cage was rattling.

'What in the—'

Directly ahead a rocket streaked up from the earth, white trail bisecting the sky.

'Why do you think we call it Boomtown?' Ruby said, grinning.

When the rocket roar faded, Norris heard another sound: a deep rumbling rhythm, the heartbeat of Boomtown. As they neared the town's centre they passed a huge marquee of high solar panels. In the shade of the structure, hundreds danced, the air over their heads thick with refrigerated vapour and flitting with holographic visuals—pulsing, brightly-coloured organics, showy and energy-intense. Norris couldn't make out individual bodies in the crowd, just the shadow of their mass, jumping and writhing like a singular beast that drank decibels and sweated until the ground underfoot was reddish mud.

'You want to go dayclubbing, drink a *lot* of water. Drink until you think you'll piss yourself, then keep going.'

'Dayclubbing?' Norris said blankly.

'Nights are pretty quaint by comparison. But if the sun doesn't wake you at dawn, the atmosphere will.' Ruby nodded ahead. 'Speaking of night, it's getting late, and there's the welcoming committee. Got your bag?'

Ahead a woman beneath a broad-brimmed hat waved both arms. Norris nudged his case. 'Yes.'

'Out you get then.'

'Where?'

'Right here,' Ruby said. 'If I lose momentum now, sun'll set before I make my drop-off. No one wants a road train clogging up main street, least of all me.'

'You expect me to jump?'

'More like a dignified drop. Out you get.'

———

17

The out-of-towner tumbled from the truck and landed in a dusty heap at Magda's feet. He was champagne-flute thin and well-moisturised. He didn't wear an expensive suit, as she'd been amusing herself expecting, but did wear a thin bomber jacket he'd likely bought at a place that sold expensive suits.

'G'day,' Magda said. 'You must be Norris Fensworthy.'

'Indeed,' Norris panted, picking gravel out of his palm. 'Are you in charge here?'

'Allegedly. Some folks claim to have elected me mayor, but can't see it, myself.'

Norris unzipped his rolly bag, rummaged primly, hauled himself up and held out an envelope.

Magda took it. 'What's this then?'

'You've been served,' Norris said. 'You or another duly appointed representative must appear in court three months hence, or face further legal sanction. As I'm sure you know, Lutes Finance and our global partners have acquired rights to the TeraSol Array's output for the purposes of powering the global superconductor electrical grid. We demand that you and your people cease any extraneous operations and provide solar field access, digital and physical, to all agents and contractors of the Supergrid Group.'

Magda kicked herself for touching the proffered papers. She'd expected a high-tech, blockchain-handshake type of manoeuvre, but the classic moves never went out of style.

'Ah,' she replied. 'I think we'll pass, mate, but thanks for the invite.'

'I'm afraid we must insist,' the banker said, having regained some composure. 'Our clients have a billion customers waiting for your generation capacity to come online. The Supergrid is months behind schedule.'

'Then another day can't hurt.' Magda nodded at the reddening sky, the sun now obscured by the welter of buildings and raised PV: 'First rule of Boomtown, no business after dark. Let's get you a room and a bevvie.'

Magda strode away, trusting the out-of-towner to follow. Soon his rolly bag rattle caught up beside her.

'So, here's Boomtown.' She motioned to the unruly community: colourful, scattershot, earthwork architecture stitched together by open leisure spaces under the shade of raised solar. To a newcomer it probably looked like an inscrutable mix of spaghetti western town, big tech campus, and jugaad art commune, but Magda knew every weird, unlikely project incubating in each building and the reasons behind every intersection's peculiarities.

Boomies ran about with their usual bawdy, capering energy, trying to get in as much work and hedonism as they could before the sun went down. Several shot a quick 'Mags' her way as they bustled by. The thin soles of her shoes could feel the dirt quiver with underground movement as well—the artificial caverns with tumbling water gardens that served both to grow kelp and algae crops in the desert and provide cooling for the massive server farms that turned spare sunlight into endless, whirring math.

The banker followed nervously, suppressing his obvious curiosity as long as they were still, to his mind, locked in legal battle. There was no arguing with him, Magda decided, until he understood exactly what he was shutting down. So once they'd zig-zagged deep into Boomtown and she was certain Norris was feeling lost and disoriented, Magda shoved him into an airy hostel and left before he could object.

———

In the hostel that night, the quiet was palpable but gentle. At sundown, the party music, the shouting, even the deep, industrial rumble all ceased. Without aircon, traffic or server hum, the air felt eerily silent, every human sound magnified. Norris could hear footsteps padding in the alleys; low, sonorous whispers, rhythmic with storyteller cadence; snatches of laughter and song. He saw strips of Milky Way between the raised solar panels, a too-bright stretch of stars and constellations.

A rope ladder unrolled from the scaffolding, the movement catching his eye. From his bed Norris watched a dozen figures ascend with telescopes and kites strapped to their backs—a vision so odd he was half sure he'd dreamt it.

The next morning all the sounds of life and industry began again. Magda came and took him to breakfast.

'Ms. Mayor,' he said, over tomatoes and vat sausage. 'I know you believe that you have a certain amount of leverage here. And while contract law says otherwise, we are willing to negotiate an additional settlement, to ease the transition for your community.'

'You know how many peoples throughout history got strong armed into giving up their way of life for a single lump sum, and were ruined by it?' Magda asked. 'Plenty of mob in these parts would warn against outsiders with plans for your land. For good bloody reason.'

'But by refusing to allow the TeraSol Array to be hooked up to the global superconductive grid, you're disrupting life for millions, even billions of people.'

'Not our fault Americans thought the lithium would never stop flowing.' Magda shrugged. 'They've had years to do just a tiny bit of energy descent, and instead they bet it all on this boondoggle of yours. Now they expect us to just hand over our electrons, so they can keep the party going.'

'Party? The centre of your town is literally an all-day rave. I understand that you want to defend Boomtown's solar sovereignty, but you're wasting electrons on dance music and pretty light shows.'

'So we're not wealthy enough to be allowed to enjoy ourselves?'

'I'm talking about real human pain,' Norris said. 'Grandmothers on fixed incomes having groceries spoil because they can't afford to upgrade their refrigerator. Hospitals that struggle to keep dialysis machines running through night-time still-outs. The States, Brazil, these are fallen places, awash in zombie infrastructure. Given how close we came here, we have a duty to help the victims of fossil fascism find their feet.'

'And yet, my son can always log onto American game servers at two in the afternoon. We all have to prioritise.'

'But, exactly,' Norris tried, exasperated. 'We depend on them too. And the Supergrid goes both ways. You'll get power after dark. No more running hot and cold, big high tech industry town during the day, and then some kind of pre-modern village at night.'

'Here's the thing.' Magda leaned forward. 'We like it that way.'

———

Hoping to loosen the banker further, Magda took Norris from breakfast to a bar that served experimental, molecularly-unique cocktails. She ordered for both of them, plopped glasses of murky spirits down on a table.

'There you are,' she said. 'They don't have *that* kind of ethanol in the big city.'

Norris sniffed and, perhaps believing he must prove his mettle to the outback savages, sipped. He savoured the drink with concentration, swallowed, then set the glass down.

Magda sipped her own drink: heady, bubbly, smooth. It was made from fossil carbon pulled out of the air, which meant she could be drinking dinosaur bones. All because her people had the opportunity to do interesting, ambitious things—an opportunity this man and his employers wanted to close.

'Let's get on the same page,' she said. 'Once upon a time, a multi-national company that no longer exists subcontracted the construction of a terawatt-scale solar installation to a decentralised network of fab collectives. All we needed was land permissions and feedstocks, which, in typical boomtime overproduction mindset, the company provided in spades. So we got to work. We built generating capacity the likes of which the world had never seen, powering Sydney and Melbourne—hell, Indonesia and Singapore too, on good days. With me so far?'

Norris frowned but nodded.

'Then the Battery Bust came down. Manufacturers had over-promised and under-delivered, and the supply chains weren't sending the cavalry to save them. So most everywhere builds out wind, hydro, tidal, and nukes to fill the night-time gap. All of a sudden,

Oceania doesn't need all our electrons anymore. Company goes under, gets sold into a million pieces. Hedge fund we'd never heard of comes in and tells us to dismantle what we've built with our sweat and blood. Tells us we're dragging down the prices. We tell them to fuck off, and good thing we did. Because now you're here with a new scheme that wouldn't be possible if we'd listened to those other guys, right?'

'I suppose that's true,' Norris allowed.

'Thing is, in the years between us telling the last guys to fuck off and me telling you to fuck off now, we had to do something with the extra power you're looking to claim. No use leaving PV out in the sun and not capturing that energy, right? But then we have a shit-tonne of electrons during peak hours, and they've got to do something, don't they?'

'They do?'

'They do. Can't just dump 'em like surplus milk, that's not how physics works. So, being responsible engineers and future-minded folk, we invited other future-minded folk to come here, join our community, put our spare electrons to good use. We're talking Big Computation for incredible art and crypto projects, and Big Chemistry that has done the climate some good if you go by the falling PPM numbers, not to mention sent a lot of Aussies to space. So when you talk about "extraneous operations," what I hear is you wanna put a lot of brilliant people out of business.'

———

Norris sipped his bizarre cocktail, smiled at Magda. 'I appreciate that interesting projects have flourished on the, ah, excesses of the technological situation here,' he said, weighing each word, 'but that excess was a result of overambitious investing and fiscal overheating. Now the situation is normalising, and the world has need of that power. Unfortunately, that means there'll be no surplus to speak of. We'll happily facilitate investors to look at your more interesting projects, but this energy—these electrons—are earmarked for off-shore markets.'

Magda scoffed, tossed back her drink. 'No point sitting here flapping our gums; let's get out of here.' She got up and wandered to the exit, not waiting for Norris to follow.

Magda only seemed to have one speed—belligerently fast—and Norris was sweating when he caught up with her. They crossed a street, such as it was, and wound their way past jury-rigged and carbon-printed structures, all situated beneath the town's PV firmament. The hot desert breeze rattled open doors and windows, carrying a fine red haze.

'Where are we going?' Norris asked.

'I'm gonna show you something, then you tell me you still want to shut it down.'

Magda ducked into a thin alley between storage sheds, then down steps cut into the red earth. Norris descended cautiously, letting his eyes adjust.

He expected the air underground to be stuffy, or maybe dank, but it was fresh, clean, and cool.

'Cooler days down here, warmer nights,' Magda offered. 'Once you have the diggers, carving out the ground is mostly a matter of electrons and time. People balk at the idea of living underground, like it's somehow inhuman, but when summer comes it's more comfortable than *that*.' She pointed up, indicating the desert heat above.

They wound through a warren of tunnels, off-shoots leading to offices, workshops, labs, each with graffiti and detritus hinting at their purpose. The only constant was the hum of computation—big numbers being crunched, dissected, and sewn back together. Norris's keen investor's nose wanted to investigate the projects, but Magda's relentless presence pulled him forward.

Eventually Magda rapped on a wide sealed door. A man in a blue boilersuit opened it. 'Jonny,' Magda said.

'Madam Mayor,' he replied.

This time Magda let Norris go first. The large chamber was part medical lab, part computer lab, the temperature a couple of degrees warmer than the corridor. Where other labs had kept the raw earthen walls, this lab was sealed with white polymer, the floor tiled white, everything bright and clean—apart from the red dirt Norris had tracked in on his shoes.

To the sides of the cavern were rows of server machines, humming with LEDs flashing rapid-fire Morse code. Red flags were plastered on half the machines, with blue flags marking the machines opposite.

'Take a look.'

Magda indicated a wide screen showing biological samples at various levels of magnification, the tiniest building blocks of life bumbling and swirling. Cables criss-crossed the walls neatly, like the map to a nightmarish highway interchange, some going up through the ceiling.

'Impressive,' Norris said. 'What is it?'

Magda said, 'Jonny and his team are collating data from every cancer study ever conducted that's been digitised, plus any other samples docs send their way.'

'Big data cancer research is hardly new,' Norris said. 'Doctors have fed so many medical records into so many neural networks, they can tell it's cancer if you sneeze wrong.'

'And good for them,' Magda said. 'This way.' She waved to Jonny, then led Norris out and further down the maze of corridors.

Norris felt the sound before he heard it—a heavy bass that rumbled through the walls, shaking dirt from the ceiling. By the time they reached a set of stairs leading back to the surface, the music was thumping, visceral as a heartbeat and rattling his ribcage harder than his own. It was bright music, upbeat, joyous, pop synth and simple vocal loops soaring high above that thunderous bass.

Magda opened a hatch and they emerged beside the dayclub marquee, the air misted with water and thick with pheromones and sweat.

'You'll see it better from the floor,' Magda said, tottering through the patch of vicious sunlight and pushing her way into the dancing crowd.

Norris followed, sweating in his thin jacket, but glad to have a boundary between him and the slick throng. Magda stopped in a quiet island surrounded by bodies, and as Norris pushed through to join her, he saw Ruby leaning against a marquee support pole, chugging water, her skin flushed and glowing. He nodded, and she raised her canteen, eyes half-lidded with euphoric exhaustion.

Then Magda nudged him, and Norris followed her eyes up above the crowd, where bright holograms hung in the misted air—visualisations of the microscopic images he'd seen below ground.

'See it yet?' Magda shouted. 'It's not just a party, it's all connected.'

'So they're studying cancer and projecting the samples like a nightclub laser show.' Norris shrugged.

'They're not just studying cancer, they're *curing* it. And this isn't a projection, it's part of the calculations.'

Norris watched holographic cancer cells split and duplicate, grow and spread. Then the growth slowed, reversed, the black cancer cells dwindling until only the red of flesh and blood remained.

'You mean that—' he pointed, 'is the cure to cancer?'

'Not *the* cure, but maybe *a* cure. You see the flags downstairs—red team and blue team?'

Norris nodded, eyes fixed to the simulated medical experiments above his head.

'They're both complex adversarial networks in their own right; combined they're an incredibly powerful, if energy intensive, computational system. Red team studies available data, treatment successes and failures, develops the best cures it can. Findings are flashed up here, and cameras mounted in the ceiling,' Magda said, pointing, 'take that data as input and feed it to blue team. Blue team iterates on red team's work through a clean data feed *and* by comparing it to the fuzzy projections.

'Cancer mutates, it's unpredictable. If the machine studies the sample it might work out how to cure *that* sample, but what about something slightly different? The projections in here are distorted by the mist and sweat in the air, by the shifting sunlight outside, by the people shaking the pillars, even by the music rattling the cameras and rippling the molecules in the air. All that noise serves a purpose. It distorts the samples, forces blue team to find more solutions, more variations.'

'It sounds better when Jonny explains it,' Ruby said, approaching with three fresh beers, condensation beading on the glasses. She passed drinks to Magda and Norris, then took a swig.

Norris held the beer, glad for the cold touch of it, but he wasn't ready to drink.

'Didn't think you were gonna tell him,' Ruby said.

Magda nodded. 'Had to.'

'I just saw a cure for cancer. And there are more on the server downstairs—'

'Hundreds,' Ruby said.

'Thousands,' Magda countered.

Norris took it in, but then steeled himself. 'It's excellent work, and obviously Lutes will happily find funding for it going forward. But none of what you've shown me is unique to this place.'

Magda took a slug from her beer and levelled a gaze at Norris. 'You're wrong. Anywhere else would've penny-pinched this project into oblivion. I know because Jonny got turned down for just about every grant on the planet. Too expensive, too weird. But when you have enough electrons, even for just a few hours a day, you can do anything, try anything. Energy is the bottleneck of human potential.

'Even with storage lagging, everywhere is building new PV generation. In thirty years, everyone will be living like us; we're the vanguard of the energy abundance lifestyle—dependent on no one, capable of anything. We're curing bloody cancer. That's a higher moral ground than contract law. Kind of thing worth seizing means of production over. So, you can go back to Sydney and tell Lutes Finance they can pry our electrons from our cold, dead hands.'

Norris drank deeply from his beer. This was the impasse he'd feared. Lutes and the Supergrid Group could, he knew, rouse authorities to oust the energy squatters of Boomtown. But he suspected doing so would result in expensive damage to the TeraSol array. He wouldn't put it past the Boomies to boobytrap their city as they left.

And worse, it would mean letting the mountain of value being created here—including cures for cancer—slip through his fingers. Norris had long suspected that both Silicon Valley and Shenzhen were slowing down, dying—but Boomtown... And he could be there right from the start...

'I admit you've got something here,' Norris said. 'But the world needs the Supergrid, and the Supergrid needs TeraSol. But maybe the world needs Boomtown too. What would it take to, as you said, keep the party going?'

'What d'ya mean?' Magda asked, suspicious.

'Investment. Say we got the auto-facs moving again, expanded the array and the surplus.'

'You can do that?'

'We'll find out. How much more solar needs to be laid down to keep you doing what you're doing while letting us meet our commitments overseas?'

Magda considered this, probably weighing how much to demand and whether he could deliver.

'We'll give you a few terawatts,' she said, 'if you help us build ten more. The grannies can keep their leaky refrigerators humming overnight, if they really must. Unlock the auto-facs, expand the array, let us capture enough electrons for Boomtown to do anything.'

'Deal.'

———

The sun poured across the world, drenching the solar fields in photons, which loosed electrons and sent them churning into wires, seeking work to do. A few photons found their way through Norris's eyelids and stabbed sharp into his retinas. He winced, shielded his eyes.

'No puking in the truck.'

Ruby's voice felt too loud and too bright for the hangover Norris was nursing. It was worth it though—the celebration well earned. He saw a bright future for Lutes Finance and, most importantly, for himself. It turned out there was one high-energy activity that continued in Boomtown overnight: drinking. Alcohol being about the oldest form of energy storage there was.

'You coming or what?' Ruby called. 'We're burning daylight.'

'Are you really hauling rocket fuel this time?'

'That a problem?'

'I guess not,' Norris said, and climbed up. The cab A/C was humming, solar sails soaking up electrons, ready for the long drive back to civilisation—or back to the past, maybe.

'This place gets under your skin, doesn't it?' Ruby said as the road train pulled away from the town, gaining speed.

Norris looked at Boomtown spread out beyond the window and knew he'd be back, and soon.

He nodded. 'It really does.'

Energie Cottbus

Simon Sellars

Virtual fixtures

I surveil them through my cheaters, an army of the dead in plizzits, manikins and respirators, marching down the street as if the laws of physics don't apply. They call themselves working class, a nod to the past, but they're richer and more influential than I'll ever be. They're protestors of some kind, but who knows. Outrage is so cheap, these days. It's a skin-suit that can be worn by anyone.

Zooming into their word clouds, I scan a welter of circular reasoning, wet dreams of future crimes, conspiracist ideations, sub-normal analytical thinking, Machiavellianisms, and a vast sea of self-doubt. Some of these crackbrains believe in instantaneous star travel via local galactic portals. Some say that ancient AI are genetically manipulating humans with the assistance of interdimensional alien slaves. A rival group claims that elongated-skull giants from Scheat, a star in the constellation Pegasus, are harvesting organs in transplanetary underwater caverns. Others believe that optimal timeline realities can be induced with DNA upgrades.

It all beaches on the shore of some grand theory called The Great Awakening, which, as far as I can tell, anticipates the moment when our collective minds will be freed from the psychic dominance of The Swarm.

I snag a few demented ramblings that seem to explain the ruckus. The protestors are in the hood for the resurrection of some dead politician. Can't make out his name. He was shot in this street one hundred and fifty years ago. They say he's been in hiding ever since. He never died. Biotech advances kept him alive. In two hours, he will appear at the plaza down the way. He will address the mob and announce his intentions. With their backing, he will defeat The Swarm and restore order to the Linear Territories. The jobber-nowls in the street are salivating at the thought. Some have erections.

Make no mistake, this crowd is a punnet of nuts. Sure, we absorb mixed realities, day in day out, but just because you can conjure something from virtual air, doesn't make it real. There's a reason no one tells ghost stories anymore. With a blinked command, the occult is yours.

Nothing stops them, not even the lice bots with their kill-crazy deth-tubes. Not even the truth. Most protestors cover their cheaters with plizzits, necessary protection for the great outdoors, especially if you don't want your eyeballs fried like eggs, but some go without. The rumour is, they're blind, but they have ocular implants that jack into the vision machine. They're the far-gone fringe, the scar tribes. Their necks are covered with gaping wounds, after attempted garrottings by licebots, which they proudly display like actors clowning around on a porno set.

The neck-gashed used to be in needle gangs, terrorising all and sundry, but when The Swarm cracked down, they began to make a living by respectable means. ArtInt mechanics, cheater repairs, cronk spotters, autonaka fluffers. Whatever it takes. They're still criminals, addicted to chaos. It's in their genes. They're war-thirsty battle angels, agitators who tip protest into mania.

Two have breached the boundary surrounding my cube. I see them up close, through the laparoscopic sensory apparatus embedded in my cheaters. Their neck holes are alive, crawling with locum mist, grey-goo micro-bots suturing torn nerve endings. The crazies stare at my cube, with its sentient lightpaint facade. I'm not a fighter, but I psyche myself, prepping for confrontation. I cradle my portable char-stick, fingering the actuator stub in readiness.

I stand at the entrance to the cube, waving the char-stick and defending my turf. One invader speaks in machine-slang, his mangled vocal cords filtered through dual-shift modulators.

'Where'd you get the lightpaint? Who your supplier? What you got, bigly? Spill your beans!'

I laugh, uncontrollably. They're admiring the workmanship, that's it.

'Got it from the Metal Guru down on Hickley Ham Street.' I lockzip the Guru's card and brisk it to the invader. 'Shake him down yourself, tough guy.'

The moron, sated, rejoins his crew. You'd think The Swarm would wipe them out with a drone strike, but perhaps they're useful idiots. I've never understood politics.

Two hours pass, and the never-dead fail to materialise. The protestors are finally dispersed, and then Spine Whip is hit by an earthquake. It's a big one, I see the ground rise and fall, but all the cubes in my street stand firm. It's the old, abandoned buildings that crumble. Not that anyone notices. They're all galaxy hopping inside their minds, lost in private oblivion in the safety of their cubes.

A few protesters are trapped in the rubble, but the licebots simply separate their heads from their shoulders, as if they're putting down birds with broken wings.

I've lived in Spine Whip all my life and I've never experienced an earthquake. It's the wrong hemisphere. We're not on a fault line. We are geographically clean. All the trauma is above ground, not below. As if the war with the Arctic Free State wasn't enough, now this.

It's so rare, I start to wonder if psychic energy from the protestors caused it, char-broiled outrage manifesting as geotrauma. I remember an old joke, a musicologist's snobbish retort: 'In the future, every home will be powered by jazz fusion.'

If only we could bottle the brain waves of conspiracists, power the grid with wasted energy from useless trolling.

Occluded prosthesis

There was one experiment they tried. Driverless cars. Autonakas, they're called. Autonakas don't burn oil or fuel. They receive wireless electricity particles, sucked down from the time-varied power beams that strafe the air every second of the day.

For all the economic benefits, the transition wasn't peaceful. After being welded to the automobile for so long, our bodies rebelled. I'm old enough to remember the cars that once terrorised Spine Whip. Metal grilles over the windows, enormous spikes grafted to the bodies, chassis lifted metres off the ground by liquid metal robo-jacks. Cars were prostheses of the animals that drove them.

These days, autonakas are the only vehicles around, gentle, autonomous beasts that lockstep in and out of centrally controlled traffic beams. Driverless cars are the new singularity. They're not an extension of the body. They've replaced it.

Autonakas devour you. You telepath your destination and away you go. If an autonaka breaks down, the AI locks the system. It just sits there, an enormous brick in the middle of traffic, waiting to be serviced, happily chatting away to itself in code-slang. Passengers can forget about on-the-fly mechanical adjustments. To mend a stalled autonaka, you must learn the algorithmic equivalent of brain surgery.

Divorced from the steering wheel, our physiologies did not go gently into the night. They greeted the new dawn with psychopathic mutations, a traumatic untethering from machinic fantasies. Once, the death trippers who piloted the spiked vehicles were directors in the theatre of vehicular chaos. Now, they are unseen technicians, hacking the autonakas of others, telepathing brute-force override commands, sending unsuspecting innocents on death rides through suburban streets.

Resumption of ambulation

I leave my cube, but I must force myself. I'm getting on in years and it's hard to stay mobile. I use the bicycle, an ancient Specialized with carbon frame, around fifty years old but younger than me. I kid myself that I'm becoming fit by using it, but I'm just trying to outrun myself and the rapid decline of my body.

A man, even older, taught me the byways, but he is long gone. People come and go, and I don't know where they end up. I think The Swarm cancelled him, but I can't be sure.

He gave me a courier job, because he knew I liked to ride, delivering packages of nothing to faceless people that represent the interests of something I can't fathom.

It's my first day on the job. The task: ride to a power mart called 'Regina', about fifty kilometres away. I can do it in a day, there and back. They want regular deliveries, the same package every single day. The old man gave me the delivery, a metal box, magnetically locked.

'Why not drive there?'

'They are doing things by stealth. No attention must fall on them.'

'Doing what, exactly?'

'Know what a power mart is?'

'They make the wireless electricity parcels that power the grid, then they zap them into the air.'

'Got it in one. But this, what you're doing, it's something different. An experiment. You are transporting the raw material.'

'About time they explored sidereal energy. Electricity won't last forever.'

He regarded me, his leathery scalp cracking with incredulity.

'You think there's a limit on free electrons? That they're like fossil fuel? That once they're all used up, they're gone for good?'

'I suppose. I mean, I've never really thought about it.'

'Once, electrons vibrated inside wires. They didn't flow like water. They emerged from the air, and the wires conducted them across cities. Wireless air parcels changed all that. There's an infinite amount of free energy all around us, which the parcels tap into. Raw electricity, like lightning. It will never run out.'

'What's in the box?'

'Your mind.' The old guy chuckled. 'You forgot to use it in our little exchange just then.'

Experimental adoption of advanced energy instruments

I ride out to Regina, through the edgelands and reeds, scything through a place where no walker dares to tread. The air is rancid with the smell of burnt chlorine and dry excrement, products of bunged-up technology and malfunctioning humans.

The wildlife is off the hook. It's all mutant physiology and back to front. Rats the size of cats feast on cats the size of gnats. Red-eyed boxing kangaroos stare me down, waiting to pounce on mistakes. They've developed organic body armour, a rock-hard exoskeleton forged through apocalyptic times, and their enormous tails could snap my neck with a simple flick. It's not so bad. They hate unexpected noise, so all I do is ring my dinky little bell and the beasts scatter into the poisoned scrub.

The buildings down this way are long gone, but the Chronoslide Glideway still stands, as it does everywhere in the Linear Territories. It looms high above, a mag lev tube jammed with autonakas and ArtInt trucks. Constant arterial pressure. Nasty business, commerce gone wild. Capitalism as a viral vector, a lust for annihilation.

I arrive at Regina. It's an unassuming place, just a couple of small admin buildings set among a massive field ringed by razor wire.

Someone greets me, a woman in combat fatigues. She asks for ID, and I brisk it to her cheaters.

'Give me the box,' she says.

I do so, and she waves her hand over it. The lid opens. Inside, a pair of heavy black goggles.

'Take off your plizzit, then your cheaters.'

'But the sun.'

'We have shielding.'

I remember something the old man said about the Glideway. It sucks down the fruit of the sun to power the mag lev tracks. It is a vision of excess, tripled by the efforts of the human trash below. The Glideway consumes more than it generates. The solar economy that we plug into is barely offset. Evil accelerates when the social order is destroyed, and the balance is tipped beyond repair.

She picks up the goggles. 'Put these on.'

'Why?'

'Security check. To see if they've been tampered with.'

'Must I do this every time I come here?'

'Every time.'

I strap them on, and the sky goes out. I see phosphorescent imprints behind the lids of my eyes, but that's it.

'Tell me what I'm thinking,' the woman says.

'You're thinking that we don't have it in us to maintain equilibrium. You're thinking that we must destroy harmony as a natural solution to long-term boredom. You're thinking that this is because when all the grit and dynamism have been leached from the city, when new energy solves one crisis, there is a swelling surplus, an excess of unreason that exists only in the psychic realm. You're thinking if only it could be tapped.'

'Not even close. That's what you're thinking. You are talking to yourself.'

'Did I pass?'

'That's confidential. Put them back in the box and leave with it.'

I saddle up again, strap the box to my back, and ride into the distance.

At home, I try to open the box, but it won't budge.

Electrical arcing of instruments

Day after day, month after month, I deliver the box, strap on the goggles, take the box home. I keep going, feet up and feet down, feet stuck to the cleats, circular motion. Limbs move, pedals turn, machine goes. There once was a pop group, electronic pioneers. They were called Powerplant, and they hailed from Koppari-Audun. They sang about the 'man-machine'. Funny thing is, everyone thought they were cyborg fetishists, but it turns out they were hard-core cycling fanatics. Their bionic metaphors were about bikes not bots.

They cultivated an obsession with dynamic energy and forward motion. Repetition and propulsion, that's all they cared for, listening to the limits of the body, to the natural sonics of the environment. Calibrating the wind for speed, the physical hum for endurance, converting the psychic obsession with movement into kinetic energy.

I think of them now, as the bike moves beneath me. In their philosophy of energy expenditure, to slow the bike is to fall off, so it's preferable to keep going, to never release the handlebar, to never take the feet off the pedals or touch the ground. Forwards, always forwards.

Why then do I stop to explore the dank space beneath the Rosebell flyover? It's a corruption of high place phenomenon, a mystifying compulsion to leap into the void. I'm praying my brain will abort the impulse before my body propels me over the edge.

There's a little nook, a vee-shaped enclosure, where the bank meets the underside of the road. Despite the crude air, it's inviting, a portal to a place where nothing remains. The road above is silent, all transport having fled to the Glideway years ago.

Beneath the flyover, there are some books, some ancient drink cans, a yellowing magazine. There's an old, jagged knife, covered in brown spots. The smell assaults me, a gangrenous olfactory pocket that turns the air into cottage cheese. I move along the alcove, crouching low to avoid a head injury. I discover an old army-surplus sleeping bag. Inside it are two fused-glass bodies, like Pompeii people, real humans incinerated at the point of sexual congress. At first, I think someone has come under here and set them alight, sadists torturing the homeless, but then I see that their shadows have been seared into the concrete. Whatever did this had nuclear capacity.

Guidance fixtures and forbidden-region fixtures

I remember asking the old guy about the company behind the job.

'Exceller 8, they're called, one of the "invisible companies" off world. They were among the first to develop autonakas. Now, they're branching into power marts.'

'Swarm affiliated?'

'You'd think so, but no one really knows.'

What was I transporting on my little courier run? I didn't care to ask, I just wanted to ride, but the old guy did fill me in on Exceller 8's history, because I was interested in that. That's my special problem. I live in the past, hooked on nostalgia like a mainline junkie.

'Believe it or not, Exceller 8 started as a rugby team. Nothing to do with tech. What happened was, a group of mongrel coal miners in Safck were looking to kick some heads on their days off. You know the type. Cauliflower ears. Pug noses. No neck. Everything squashed in from constant hits to the body. So, they formed a rugby team, joined an industrial league.'

'Squashed bodies? Rugby players look more like robots.'

He laughed. 'Before the Linear Territories, stupid.'

'Unscyld Era?'

'Yeah. No implants back then, no vat-grown muscle, no bionic uterine geography. So, there they were, competing in this industrial league against other teams: workers from unified Transport States, Food States, Communication, Housing, Luxury, Energy. Then, when The Swarm fell to Earth, the Linear Territories were formed, and the league was banned.'

'Ennarel Island?'

'You got it. The Swarm irradiated the stadia, then exiled all rugby dissidents to Ennarel. They forced them to become birther-cyborgs, a self-sufficient colony, and that's the beginning of deth-sports as we know it today.'

'Rugby boners giving birth to each other, what fun. Spectators more interested in the gestation period than the actual game. Crazy times. Where does Exceller 8 come in?'

'Well, that's the interesting part. Some of these coal guys, the originals, they lived to be well over a hundred and fifty, and by that time, they were doing the ops themselves. They'd learned all the tricks. Biomechanoid experts, they were. Some escaped to the Territories and set up shop. They say their DNA lingers somewhere in the algorithms today. The rest is history.'

'Not to me.'

'Well, ask inside your mind, and you shall receive the answer.'

But my neuromod wasn't working that day, and I couldn't be bothered to shake down the info even when it was, so the legend remains. That's what it means to be high on the past. You're forever huffing the fumes emanating from your pinched, irrelevant inner space.

Anaesthesia collaboration and robotic docking

I am pumping, really pumping. I'm zeroing in on the curve ahead. Massive tree trunks are strewn across the path, plus a few skeletons of an indeterminate species and the wrecks of burned-out vehicles. A man slides past on a hover bike, carrying a dead dog in his lap. He's caressing the fur, crying like a jilted lover, fogging up his plizzit with hot tears.

Negotiate the obstacles, take the curve, keep going. Kilometres fly by. Shadows zip across the hills, thrown by a squad of electraglides in the sky, crewed by desperados and filled with refugees. They're not going anywhere. Vee-drones shoot the glides down if they cross the border. All this jockeying for position, it's purely for show.

Wind belts my face with the force of leather straps. It's hard to ride in bio-cooling armour. You sweat your body weight. Every fibre is coiled tight.

I see a two-percenter on top of a suspension beam over the Glideway. His yellow eyes are horrible, like runny eggs spattered with chick blood. He's yelling something in Patawelsh, which I've never bothered to learn. I just telepath through my neuromod, no verbals required.

'Cnuchi hyn mundo!' he announces, before performing a swan dive into a moving line of autonakas. It's quite something. The fall has mashed his feet into his nose. Only scar tribes do public suicide, but this guy, he's nothing. No implants, no cheaters or mods, no augmented overlays. Nothing. Two-percenters can't see what we see. That's why they suffer reality overdose, but usually they do it somewhere private. Now, this scumbag has ruined everyone's day.

Around the bend, just over the rise, lies Regina.

Always Regina, day after day.

Slave unit (patient side cart)

Eventually, I crack. I do as the old man asked, and I search it up, and I discover the rumours about what's going on at Regina, and it doesn't sound nice at all. Apparently, they're doing stuff with electricity in there, transcranial direct current stimulation. The Swarm is behind it, that's what the conspiracy cults are saying, some new kind of punishment for recalcitrants. They electrocute their brains, and force-create tulpas from the psychic explosion.

You know what a tulpa is? A mental life companion—an emanation, a magical illusion—born from brain waves. A living creature, some say. The concept has its roots in Buddhist meditation, but, like everything, The Swarm have corrupted it. It's their version of the reversed swastika.

The Swarm term for the process is 'Vrillon energy', a branch of something called 'psionics'. They want to create ideal copies with these tulpas and populate the world with them. Sounds deranged. Mental life companions? Voices in the head, more like. Sicko schizo stuff.

Why create tulpas when AI exists? That's why we have the metaverse.

The funny thing is, I've heard of psionics. A notion that was popular in prehistoric science fiction novels until no one believed in it anymore. Weird how The Swarm have pinched it. If you don't accept the truth of something, how can it exist? Belief is how tulpas are born. I'll grill the woman about it. Now that I have access to secret knowledge, I need more answers.

As I draw near, another cyclist passes in the opposite direction. He has only one leg, and it's furiously working the one pedal, and he's wearing a serial killer mouth guard, leather straps with metal bits in between. Slaughter-chic. Nothing's shocking, nothing at all.

He's really moving, much faster than me, and now he's gone, a ghost of reality disappearing over the rise, scattering the dog-like rabbits and the roided-up funnel web spiders.

How long have I been riding?

I never noticed my life changing, or the world for that matter. I thought this was all there was and always has been.

Mechatronic support systems

'Shut up,' the woman says, 'and listen to me. All you have is the bike. The freaks, all the other distractions, you only notice them on the periphery, because you live to ride. There is nothing else. Your wife left with the kid, and you can't even remember when it happened or what they look like. You vaguely recall them, but you just keep going to blot them out, to bury the pain. You can't remember when the skies weren't blood red. There was a jogger you used to see on your early rides. He was as obsessive as you, every day, out on the track, up and down, up and down. Then one day, you passed his skeleton in a ditch, a trace memory of someone you vaguely knew on the way to nowhere at all.

'You keep going, a year, maybe more, until your neuromod dies, and the only voices in your head are your own. You hear me talking, now. You hear me tell you that you are the psychic copy of a man named Simon. You hear me explain that he is you. You are his intrusive thoughts made flesh. You are his brainwaves brought to life. You are benevolent and kind. You are not like him. You are frippish and skittish, he is aggressive and intense. The Swarm made you, and you became him. Simon struggled with depression, as the virus hit him hard, the loss of his family even harder. You have replaced him. You thought you were created to become his psychic companion, but you are much more than that.

'Did you know I have been watching you ride to the power mart, day after day, night after night? I tracked you with grain cams. The bugs you swallowed as you rode, open-mouthed? Those were the cams. You swallowed them whole and now I see inside you. I own your intestines.

'I watched you go by until it wasn't really clear why you were riding anymore. I watched you until you became him.

'He is your host, and you will learn to think positive thoughts, to channel his negative energy into something filled with light and the power of a million suns.

'In time, you and he will grow and learn together. We have brute-forced you into the world, and it's okay for you to know that. Reliving the trauma of birth is like a memory you never knew you had. In time, the edges will fade, until there is only you. I mean, him.

'Live inside him, live for him. Live through him, live with him. Don't think about the sun. Swallow it down until the light is inside you. The light that is him.'

Compliant kinematics

On the way home, I suffer a flat tyre. I sit by the side of the path and cry hot tears. In the middle distance, the roos gather. The only problem with alternative energy is the skill required to make it work. The new mind set, the retooled brain, the initiative to start again among the ruins. Look at me. I have forgotten how to change a tyre. I can't remember my name. I am as soft as a marshmallow, having never worked a day of physical labour in my life. With all support systems stripped away, my inadequacies are fatal.

The roos move nearer. I am too weak to reach for the bell, too depleted to scream. As I wait for my neck to be broken and my eyes gouged out, rays from the orgiastic sun continue their wanton journey to Earth. Soon, they will breach the epidermal topography that shields my organs from the inevitable combustion of all living matter.

I think of the grain cams that live inside me. They are filming the world's most boring movie, a plotless psychodrama with no beginning, middle or end.

Art brut pornography for the inside of the body, screening for an audience of one.

Wild Plums

Molly Tanzer

The ancient *Prunus* genus once boasted over four hundred different species such as the peach, the apricot, and the plum, domesticated and wild. While its cousins *P. salicina and P. domestica* have thrived in some of the North American Controlled Environments, the wild plum, like the nectarine and the almond, is now presumed extinct. At one time, however, it was a prized resource in the Americas. Thickets of wild plums were managed for food and sometimes religious purposes by Indigenous Americans. The shrubs were especially valuable when planted by rivers, as their roots stabilised the banks.

Deer, possum, even bears fed on wild plums. Decreasing numbers of these co-dependent seed dispersers during urban overdevelopment of the 20th century, and the mass extinction events of the 21st, contributed to their overall decline. Beset by invasives, ill-served by rising global temperatures, their dwindling numbers were further reduced by the rapid spread of a parasite that affected the tree at the root. By the time the United States was dissolving to form NACE with Mexico and Canada, the once-abundant wild plum had become nearly impossible to find.

When ripe, wild plums ranged in color from peachblush yellow to dark purple, maturing in the late summer or early autumn. They were unpredictable, unlike our hybrids that thrive on routine. In SPHRE-2, really wild things of any sort don't stand much of a chance. Everything must submit to the cycle. The Solar-Powered Habitat and Replacement Environment is so precisely managed that every year between August 23rd and August 26th, the crickets start to chirp. They know as well as we do that we will start to feel autumn in the air on September 5th—just a bit before I, personally, prefer to give up on summer.

By the equinox we're all in sweaters. The apples have been turned into cider, and the leaves on the trees are red and gold. It is the same every year, and is likely to remain so—at least in SPHRE-2, where Colorado used to be—and before (and after) Colorado, the Arapaho.

The year of the meteor strike, so chaotic in other ways, only cemented the practice. When the skies darkened, and our solar-dependent environment faced its first major threat, everyone gave up their power allotments for the good of the community. We all knew the consequences of irregularity. Many of us still remember what life was like before the SPHRE. I was young, but I recall plenty; too much, maybe. Then, September wasn't autumn, nor did showers come in April, like the archaic nursery rhyme. In the SPHRE, we have May flowers again—so, we sat in the dark that year, a lot, but the seasons came and went, and the trees survived, and we didn't starve. Afterward, everyone—everyone who mattered—agreed that this had only gone to show how right and necessary it was to maintain our level of regulation.

If other controlled environments dealt with that year differently, I do not know. I have never been to the other SPHREs, in the remains of Arizona and California, or the Windrun in the ruin of Texas, or the hydroelectric-powered habitat in Cascadia whose name I can never remember. I've never been *anywhere*—like everyone else I know, once I entered the SPHRE, I've never gone back out again. Until now, I mean.

————

I pedaled my e-bike westward and a little north, toward the mountains. My touch-tablet, sitting in its little handlebar mount, showed me a map. I was following an old road. All roads are old, but this one wasn't even used by Resource Management, as it didn't lead to anywhere with resources. Fires had claimed the forests of the Front Range, a blaze begun in one of the ever-expanding camps of unhomed persons living outside Boulder during a particularly dry year. An entire city, destroyed by its refusal to see itself. And though it was a fairly perfect prediction of what was to come for the former United States, like all oracles, it went unheeded.

As I pedaled, I sweated. It was warmer than it ever got in the SPHRE, even during high summer, and the ride was rough. The cracks in the ancient, sun-bleached pavement were choked with weeds, and the tires of my e-bike were thin, intended for the SPHRE's springy mossphalt paths.

The shadows grew long as the deep red sun dipped behind the mountains. I pressed on. I could still see clearly by the glow of my slug as it floated and bobbed in its little spherical vivarium beside my touch-tablet. I'd drawn back the shade on its special solar cradle, and I was very comfortable trundling along in the puddle of its clear, bright, blue-green light.

The slug wasn't just a lantern. It powered my e-bike, my respirator, and my touch-tablet, too. Its species' unique spectrum had been engineered to interact seamlessly with our solar tech. Resource Management brought them, the year after the meteor strike, along with the mandatory trade allotments of cane and maple sugars, corn, smoked salmon, dried shrimp, coffee, hemp, wheat, and so on that we received from the other controlled environments. We proudly gave over our peach preserves, elk, apple butter and cider, marijuana, wool, and beef in turn, in the quantities determined by NACE's Central Trading Authority.

There was always a festival atmosphere at such times, but that year was a quiet one. The darkness had demoralised us. There were whispers, too, because our Representative had come along, unusually. We'd known something big must be afoot, because she usually stayed in the capitol, in far-flung Restored Powhatan Confederacy lands, communicating with her constituents via holoconference to save on resources and time.

It caused quite a stir when she told us that the final electric truck contained something we would receive without having to trade anything for it. She assured us that it was all fine. Genetically Modified Species 81-B, or the 'slugs' as they were colloquially renamed, had been developed by a team of the best scientists and engineers. She herself had voted for their creation and distribution in the Fair Assembly. GMS81-B was simply NACE's official answer to the meteor strike; something that benefitted us all, and therefore was to be given freely to us all.

There were plenty of precedents—for example, vaccines, other medicines, water, ethical energy. No one could profit off of what was necessary for life. The slugs were, essentially, a self-recharging battery suitable for individual use, or in larger numbers to power infrastructure. They were less efficient than actual solar, but the darkening of the skies had showed us all how any ethical energy source, even sunlight, might not remain perpetually abundant. The skies were dimmer now, and might be for some time. We had to adapt.

GMS81-B had no real intelligence; even less than that of the sea slugs they vaguely resembled due to their shared genetic history with some bioluminescent nudibranch species. They fed on algae that lived alongside them. And they could never become an invasive species, as they were designed to live—happily, we were assured—in an artificial environment, one even more controlled than our own.

———

Before it got fully dark I wheeled my e-bike behind a thicket of scrub brush and located what looked like a reasonably flat patch of ground. There, I unrolled my sleeping bag. I'd done quite a bit of research on how to camp. I'd wanted to be prepared, and I've always been an avid reader. It was probably my bookishness that allowed all that research to be conducted without attracting the attention of my reasonably friendly coworkers at SPHRE-2's little art museum, or my lover Oren.

Oren was more than *my lover*, actually. He was my partner. We lived together, had adopted a cat named Eddie together, but I still called him that. I don't know why. I've only ever read the word; nobody called anyone that anymore. *Lover.* I'd read that, too, in old books—typically, though not always, different ones than those that contained information about correct campsite hygiene. I liked how it evoked the glamourous but barbaric world of previous centuries, and how it revealed that sex was to be explicitly, not implicitly, understood as being a part of the relationship. Which was true of us, even after we sorted out our tiresome but necessary 'domestic agreement' with our sector advocate and moved in together.

I never thought I'd move in with anybody. I'm too *restless*, as my mother would put it. The orderly life of the SPHRE was hard for me. My mother attributed to it to me being born outside; I was seven years old when my family was finally assigned our apartment. Would I have been less *restless*, more able to thrive within the SPHRE, if our famility's number had come up earlier?

It's a comforting thought. More comforting than what I thought, which is that I was born with something missing. Whatever it is that lets people know how to behave without thinking about it—I don't have that. I can never predict what people will say or do, nor do I know how to respond without calculation. Half of why I like to say things like *lover* is that it trips other people up, for once. Instead of me being caught off-guard, it's them. The shoe's on the other foot, and it's easy enough to see how little they like it, either.

Restlessness is one thing; leaving, another. It's dangerous and pointless. There's nothing out there. Weeds that thrive on neglect, plague-infected prairie dogs, irradiated grasshoppers with too many legs, or too few. Further afield than anyone other than Resource Management officials would want to go, we've heard there are still pockets of Outsiders—people who didn't want to live in the controlled environments, and who probably opposed NACE. The land has reverted to Indigenous rule, so presumably they've worked out agreements with their new governments, as we have.

They're not the people we've been told to worry about, anyway.

Oren's aunt Rebecca used to leave. She was a naturalist who had helped design the SPHRE's ecosystem. Even so, she left it, regularly, and right up until the end.

I never met her. She died before Oren and I were introduced. She liked to 'get out,' that's what Oren said she called it, but while he followed in her footsteps—he's a botanist—he didn't follow them all the way out there.

She'd apparently leave for days at a time, even when she was in her seventies, foraging for crabapples and currants and bringing it all back. She'd make jams and jellies with her saved-up allotments of sugar and citrus, like someone out of the old books I liked to read—the ones about campsites, not lovers, generally speaking.

It was her sleeping bag and particulate respirator I'd taken with me.

I might not have met Rebecca, but I felt I knew her. I'd seen her sketches, heard so many stories about her from Oren, and I'd tasted her preserves. Wiggly crabapple jelly, dry like a white wine, tangy cherry jam, or silky-tart apple butter made with whole apples, even the cores and skins. Oren's favorite was wild plum jelly, majestically purple and puckery along with the sweet.

Oren told me about his aunt's preserves long before he let me try any. When at last he cracked open a jar, late one night when we needed a snack, I knew he was getting serious about me. About *us*. All he said was, 'I want to share something special with you,' and while we are taught from a young age in our NACE-mandated Social Responsibility and Conflict Resolution classes never to read into the words of another, I heard something I believed was subtext.

The restless part of me tensed and bristled at the idea. Some wild things can live in a cage, it's true—but it changes them. The foxes and wolves and hawks we'd brought inside the SPHRE lived happy lives, but they were different than the ones we'd rescued. But, different isn't always bad. The SPHRE is enormous, with multiple biomes, meticulously designed to be as unobtrusive and comfortable as possible for its inhabitants. That night, as I looked at Oren standing there in his kitchen, offering me a spoonful of this impossibly precious jam... he was smiling so hopefully, he was so open, so vulnerable, he hadn't even put on boxers, and I realised he—*this*—might be big enough for me to feel comfortable inside, too.

———

I'd always found people hard, but life with Oren was actually easier. I went from not knowing what I wanted from our relationship to wanting not to ever mess up with him. That's why I can't explain what happened, the day I dropped the last jar of wild plum jelly.

I was paying attention, but still it slipped from my fingers. I grabbed for it, so did he, but Eddie was twining himself around our feet and we both missed, not wanting to step on the cat. The jar was one of the supposedly unbreakable kinds—tempered glass, the lids they reengineered to last longer. The kind the Trade Authority insists we use for preserving of our fruit and vegetable crops. Even so, it broke; no, it *shattered*, sending glass and plum goo spilling out across the cornoleum floor of our kitchen.

Oren had, at times, suggested I was a 'distractable' individual, as he put it when he was being kind—*just completely out to lunch sometimes* is what he called it when he was feeling less patient. He wasn't wrong. I did tend to have my nose in a book. My touch-tablet was another source of frustration. I'd be on it during a conversation, looking at whatever—work stuff, a documentary, a game. Even so, I worked at the art museum. I was always careful with irreplaceable things. And Oren knew, at least I think he knew, I hope he knew, *he said he knew*, I was being careful. I had been totally focused on that stupid jelly, which we'd planned to eat on some scones I'd picked up with credits at the nice specialty bakery, to celebrate Oren's promotion at work.

Looking at the mess, he made a small sound I can't describe. I immediately said, 'I'm so sorry,' as we were taught in conflict management class. I tried to remember the right way to say it all. 'That was my fault. I apologise, I was careless with something of yours and—'

'It's okay,' he said, interrupting me. 'You weren't being careless. Accidents happen.' And he smiled.

His smile is what broke me. He'd lost something precious, but *he* was comforting *me*. He put his long arms around me, but for the first time, it felt like a prison. I struggled against his embrace, but he didn't let me go, and eventually I submitted. When I did, he held me tighter.

'Never mind,' he whispered. 'Let's clean it up and celebrate.'

My beast's lips finally moved. I croaked, 'I just know how much it meant to you.' *How much she meant to you* is what I couldn't say.

'It's okay. It can't be helped.'

I don't think he intended his words to devastate me, but there was just so much contained in that short sentence—more than those NACE classes would want me to believe. I knew Oren had an obligation to communicate everything he wanted me to know, and it was my responsibility to listen to Oren's words, and the words alone. *It can't be helped.* That was true, but I heard the grief—not really for the jelly, but for the connection to his aunt, and more than that, solastalgia for a world gone. For the waste, the biggest sin of our society.

We cleaned up the mess, carefully rinsing the glass for recycling. The jelly goo went into the compost disposal. We opened another jar of something, for the scones, and then we went to bed. There, we fucked for a long time, each putting in the effort to give the other what they liked most, but that evening every orgasm felt like an apology.

———

I rose with the sun, rather than woke with it, having spent the night tossing and turning on the rocky ground. My mouth tasted ashy and bitter. I rinsed it with a very little bit of the water I'd brought with me. I also ate some of the dried fruit and meat I'd brought, saved for months from my own allotment, never Oren's. Then I put my respirator back on, even though my face was sore from sleeping in it.

I missed my bed. I missed my bidet. I missed Oren, who I'm sure had found my note saying I'd gone to stay with my friend Liesel for a few nights, to clear my head.

At least my slug seemed as happy as always in its little ball. I never tired of watching the delicate, antennae-like protuberances over its pert head, or its undulating body, covered with soft, trembling gills. It wasn't a pet, but I was attached to it. Usually, I pitied it—but that morning I envied it. It was my first time away from the sensible comforts of the SPHRE for over three decades, and I was already ready to go back. Not so restless after all…

I pushed the thought aside. I had a mission to complete. We were going to make some wild plum jelly, Oren and I, from his aunt's recipe. I'd read it over. It wasn't hard. All we needed were the plums. Oren had said a few times he didn't think they were really extinct. So, after doing a lot of reading on the subject, I decided to try to find them. Oren had said *it can't be helped*. But maybe it could be—at least, sort of. There were more unlikely things in the world than a wild-thriving species recovering after being aggressively left alone for a long time.

I was sore after my long ride the day before, especially in a hard-to-define 'underneath' part of my body, where the saddle pressed. I rode my bike every day, but not for hours and hours.

I thought once I got going my soreness would go away, but it didn't. Back on the heat-blistered road, the discomfort and exhaustion made me clumsy. I was distracted, or perhaps *just completely out to lunch*—but even if I'd been paying close attention, like I had been with the plum jelly, the truth was, I simply hadn't been on the lookout for traps.

———

I awoke disoriented and in a different sort of pain. I wasn't sore—I was in *agony*, a word I knew from those old books again. Agony was simply not what people felt anymore, not in the SPHRE. But I was no longer in the SPHRE, and I was in agony, and I was pretty sure I was bleeding from the head. When I tried to touch the wound, I realised I was also restrained.

I couldn't immediately remember what had happened. I had ridden all day, heading toward what had been the South Platte River, which was where Oren had said his aunt had foraged. I had seen something green, trees maybe, and picked up the pace, excited by the sight after so much dreariness. But then I had hit something, something I couldn't see, and gone tumbling. When I'd realised I was going over, I'd grabbed for my slug and my touch-tablet, curling myself around them to protect them, and then...

As my mind surfaced, I became aware of a sound. When I focused on it, I perceived it was actually two sounds: rushing water and a woman singing a song with words I couldn't quite understand.

Trying to make sense of it brought me back to the situation at hand. I peeled open my gritty eyes and saw a woman in the light from my slug, which she was holding aloft. She was wearing my respirator, but I still recognised her. I'd seen her standing over me, after my wreck, grinning without a lot of teeth. She had a lot of dirty brown hair, was thin to the point of seeming malnourished, and she was singing while weaving back and forth, doing a dance in her own spotlight. It was nighttime, and I was lying on a soft damp riverbank, not far from the churning water. There was a sweet smell to the air, sweeter than anything I'd smelled since leaving the SPHRE: fresh water, greenery, and there was something else, too.

The woman danced before a grim black cave in the riverbank. It had a forlorn, eroded look to it, but the entrance had been kept open by a stand of wild plum trees, their roots half-exposed. Even so, they were absolutely thick with plums, and so many had already fallen, turning purple and rotten in the mud.

I burst out laughing. I'd found those plums all right!

At the sound of my insane cackling the woman paused in her undulations and looked at me.

'You're awake.' She had a strange-to-me accent. I said nothing. 'You're from *there*, aren't you?' She paused, and then brandished my slug at me. 'That's why you have *this*. You're from *there*.'

I nodded. She could only mean the SPHRE. 'I am. I came looking for... for...'

I froze. Should I tell her? Would that be a mistake? I couldn't deal with the enforced honesty of the SPHRE—so how could I be expected to know how to deal with this feral person? But as I was not feral, and life in the SPHRE had taught me that the truth was always best, I said, 'I came looking for wild plums, to give them to someone I love.'

I couldn't believe what I'd said after my mouth stopped moving. I'd never been able to say it to Oren, even though it was true, but I'd just gone and told this complete stranger.

'Plums!' She was scoffing at me. 'Long have I waited for this day,' she said. 'I will be rewarded by a god for what I have done—but *you*, for what you have done, will be devoured!'

I saw it wasn't only wild plums scattered about the entrance of the cave. There were bones, too. A human skull gleamed blue-white in my poor slug's light.

'But what have I done?' I had no idea if I could reason with her, but I had to try.

'What have you done? You stole their young when their ship hit, trusting the older ones would die out. But they haven't. They are *here*. I serve one! And once I give it back its child, I will be rewarded by eternal life in the paradise where they have ever reigned!'

I do not know if what she said was true, and I believe I will die before I have the chance to find out. My fall from my bike did something to my leg. I have been able to walk on it, but not quickly, and I am out of water, and I am not sure where I am. I escaped, but I have not been able to find the road back to SPHRE-2, so I have chosen to write out everything that happened, to explain what happened to whoever finds me, whenever that might be. It will soon be too late, and too late is too late, whether it's five minutes or five centuries. But if it is somewhat closer to five minutes than five centuries, and if Oren sees this, I want him to know I didn't leave him; only that I left. I always intended to come back.

He must have sensed something was afoot, because the night before my planned departure, he said, 'Are you leaving me?'

I'd been distant, I knew it. The idea of the journey scared me, but it was something I felt I had to do. Those conflict management courses had been right. The imbalance was creating tension. I had to repair what I'd damaged. But how could I, when I'd destroyed something irreplaceable?

'I'm not leaving you,' I'd said, telling myself I wasn't lying if I meant it as he meant it, but knowing I was lying just the same, a sin almost as bad as waste.

He'd looked so happy I almost hadn't gone. But in the end, I'd needed to show him how seriously I took what I'd done. How seriously I took *him*. How much I cared about fixing what I'd broken, so that it could keep going; so that it could last. So that if it didn't last, I wouldn't be remembered as the one who broke your aunt's last jar—but as something more than that, something closer to who I wanted to be for you. But now that I can't get back to you, Oren, I fear you'll only remember me as a liar.

———

What eventually emerged from the cave looked exactly like my slug, and nothing like it at all. It was enormous, bigger than an ox. It did have the same shape as my slug—a dragonish face, a body like an aquatic pinecone, all fins and layers. But instead of emitting bright beautiful light, it seemed to suck light into itself. I could barely see it, it was so dark, blacker than the night. I remember looking at it and thinking I'd been a fool to think I was missing something, when I'd never before this moment actually understood emptiness.

'The god itself!' cried the woman. Snatching up my slug, she ran up to the creature and prostrated herself before it, its tiny inverse presented like an offering.

The creature made a sound that was not a sound, but like the stealing away of it. I wished I could cover my ears, but my wrists were still tied. I wanted to grab my slug and get out of there; I wanted to run and abandon it. I wanted a lot of things I couldn't have.

'I have returned your child unto you, o far-flung one,' said the woman. 'I am ready for your promised reward of eternal life in your celestial court! I have—'

I never found out what else she'd done. The creature lunged at her and my slug went spinning away in its sphere, landing close to the river with a sharp rap that made me cry out. The slug's glass was the same type as those jars, supposedly unbreakable, but I knew better. And I didn't like how the poor thing's light had dimmed on impact.

Cracked or not, the sphere was in danger of being swept away by the river. I started inching toward it, wriggling my way like a worm. As I did, I saw the creature fall upon my captor. She screamed, and I looked away, and I heard a crunch.

When I got to my slug, I nudged it away from the water with my chin. As I did so, in its light I spied a rock that looked sharp. Wiggling around, I grabbed it, and managed to saw through my bonds, wrist then ankle.

When I was finally free I turned to my slug, picking up the sphere to inspect it. It didn't look well. It was much dimmer than usual, and though it had never possessed much affect, it seemed listless. There was nothing I could do for it, so I held it tightly to my chest and cried for a long time, for a lot of reasons. At some point I realised the other slug, the black one, had joined me. It had finished its grim feast and seemed anxious about the little one in my arms.

I presented it to the big one, unsure if I was terrified or hopeful. But all it did was touch its nose to the glass and the little one's light strengthened again. I said, 'thank you,' because I didn't know what else to do, as it slunk away into the darkness of its cave, leaving me alone, but alive, without any idea if it had understood me or not.

There was nothing left for me to do but to gather up some wild plums in the tatters of my jacket and guess at which way to limp. I tried to remember anything I'd read about celestial navigation, but the stars were of no help to me. I didn't even know if I needed to keep the mountains to my left or to my right. The place that woman had taken me might have been the South Platte River, or the St. Vrain creek. Or, it might not have been. I will probably never know. Even were my leg in better shape, I could not find my bike, and Rebecca's respirator broke during all the chaos by the riverside.

At least I have it all written down now. And if I die, I do not die alone, for I'm with my dear slug, shining bright as ever, keeping me company as it keeps my touch-tablet charged. But what really comforts me is knowing I'll be found. I am certain of it. It's impossible to work in a museum, or to love books, and not trust that fragile things can survive. I'll be found, even if it is just my bones, like those bones by the riverside. They will find the seeds of the wild plums even if the plums themselves have rotted away. And they will find a touch-tablet with a message, more than I've ever been able to say, recorded for someone whom I hope will receive it, and forgive me.

Facing Kiruna

Paul Graham Raven

Editor's note: we are pleased to present in extract the introductory chapter from Dr Ulla Piasdotter's forthcoming biography Lieđđi: A Life, *available September 2073.*

It seems appropriate to begin this book about Lieđđi—which is, of course, only one of many possible stories of Lieđđi—from a perspective in which she was an almost incidental character: a bit of local colour, a common flower made exotic by its unfamiliarity. Not that Lieđđi saw herself that way in her adulthood—a period which, by luck or by flaw, might be said to begin among the events which I will describe in this opening chapter.

One might reconstruct Lieđđi's youth in some detail, occurring as it did during a period of ubiquitous surveillance in Sweden and beyond. Indeed, I was tempted to do so—especially after being offered a trove of Lieđđi's personal data, stashed by a former confidante in the days before the Great Deletion, against the possibility of exactly the sort of martyrdom that was thrust upon (or, depending on who you asked, welcomed by) her. But it felt wrong—not legally (though it would have been a crime) so much as emotionally wrong, an invasion of privacy that I would not want to happen to me, living or dead. Lieđđi herself might have disagreed—though I hope not to be the sort of biographer who assumes a greater knowledge of their subject than their research could justify. But perhaps I am instead the sort of biographer who dresses up subconscious aesthetic decisions in ethical clothing, before sending them out into the snow?

But that is enough—'this is not about me,' as Lieđđi will say many times over in the chapters ahead. Though this book *is* about her, of course... and that paradox, I believe, is exactly the sort of gift she'd have delighted in leaving to her biographers. Perhaps the same is true of this pivotal moment in her life, with which I have chosen to start my own telling of her story.

————

First, however, a note on sources. This chapter draws on the journals and recordings of Claes Magnusson, a Masters student in sociotechnical ethnography, enrolled during the dry, hot summer of 2050 at Chalmers University (Gothenburg), shortly after his 23rd birthday. Drone-shot AV material was, even mid-century, usually deleted or bitlocked after a few years. Whether Magnusson's recordings were preserved at Chalmers because some person was farsighted enough to see its value for scholars, or because some person wanted to make sure that a broader picture of Lieđđi was possible than that which appeared in the media of the time, or simply because some person (human or algorithmic) erred through omission and failed to authorise its erasure, we will never know. (The audit trail which could tell us, which should never have been deleted, is missing.)

Drone recording is now considered unethical for reasons of inadequate opportunity for informed consent. This policy is far from universally popular among scholars; Magnusson's material might provide arguments for either side. But history makes the point moot: the footage exists, as does Magnusson's journal, and they tell a story which is in both the public and scholarly interest. My re-narration thereof is something closer to fiction than to some notional 'raw truth'—a point that even Magnusson, a decidedly average ethnography student (by his own admission) understood to apply to records of all sorts. Whether we can thus dignify (or denigrate) this account as history, or as a sort of meta-ethnography in which I record the experience of my encounter with mediated representations of the (already extremely mediated) figure of Lieđđi, is a question I shall leave to my reviewers—and to you, my reader, you who are in the process of remediating my remediation in the act of reading.

It bears noting that Magnusson was not sent to Norrbotten to encounter Lieđđi. After a few pages of journalling, written on trains northward—in which Magnusson's anticipatory anxieties are easily discerned—the first properly ethnographic entry is a description of his first meeting with Kiruna's recently-retired avatar, the intended object of his research. There is footage of this encounter but—given the focus of Magnusson's basic ethnographic training was on handwritten notes, which were back in fashion—let us read this moment in his own words:

Revelation... like something biblical, or how I imagine

something biblical might appear to a believer. But perhaps in this case I am a believer of sorts? I found the avatar Kiruna stood motionless at the end of a street on the outskirts of the city, between two boarded-up apartment blocks, seemingly staring at the decapitated mountain which he, and the city he was made to represent, were named for. The sun was bright behind the buildings...

I quote not to mock its pretension or naivete—few would wish for their first pages of fieldnotes to be printed verbatim, three decades after the fact—but to remind us of a shared innocence, and to suggest that it might stand as a better source than those with more traditional claims to insight or knowledge. To put it another way: if the world is not a totality, not a whole in which its many agents are mere parts—I gesture, of course, to Latour's reading of Lovelock at the start of the century—then this innocent (or ignorant?) narrative from the self-styled 'Years of Zero' is worthy of consideration, just as the sketches of an otherwise unknown and unremarkable artist might nonetheless afford us an insight into, say, the Paris of 1968, or the Malmö of 2029, in a way that the much-discussed masterpieces hanging in the galleries might not.

Kiruna, 2051: could there be a more resonant moment in Lieđđi's life? Perhaps—but perhaps not. Resonance, as in a musical instrument, is to be found, and then harmonised with. One plays with whatever is to hand—and Magnusson's material is to hand.

———

To precis, then: Magnusson travelled to the city of Kiruna in

September of 2051 to conduct the fieldwork element of his Masters. He took as his subject the city's recently retired avatar, which shared its name. The case of Kiruna and their fellow avatars was something of a *cause célebre*, though it is largely forgotten now. The 'AI winter' of the late Twenties, often blamed on the hubris of the FANG monopolies in the preceding decade, gave way to a brief thaw toward the middle of the Thirties, as inventive researchers found more acceptable avenues down which funding might travel to cash-starved departments and start-ups. The Three Es—entertainment, education and ecology—were the best buttons to push, and the technologies that came together to produce the avatars (as well as the idorus of the entertainment industry) were pitched as a mix of all three.

The Swedish state-owned mining firm, Luossavaara-Kiirunavaara Aktiebolag (LKAB), presumably had the Three Es in mind when it commissioned an avatar guide for the city of Kiruna—though wowing wealthy Chinese tourists, flown in on private jets to photograph the Northern Lights, and the jaded delegates of space industry junkets, would have been an added bonus. The firm responsible, Huginn&Muninn AB, had already sold a number of avatars by this point. They chose the term quite deliberately, marketing their creations as embodied manifestations of the sites to which they would welcome human visitors: 'to every city its god, to every museum its ghost', as the marketing copy had it.

The avatars were holographic personae, projected and voiced by cutting-edge AV drones, their personalities running on expensive and locally-hosted sealed servers, instantiated by a process (still proprietary at time of writing) that combined generative ML with extensive written and audiovisual training corpuses: they learned to communicate like humans by extrapolation from vast sets of real human communication. These corpuses were tailored for each persona, as were their holographic bodies: Kiruna, named for the city that their presence was intended to greenwash, was based on as much information on the Sámi people indigenous to the area as was available, and given a body and face which (in confirmation of the criticisms of stereotyping levelled at the time) was described as 'patient indigenous wisdom personified'.

Whether LKAB had already decided to shut down Kiirunavaara, the iron-ore mine from which the city's name derived, is hard to determine. Its profitability had been dwindling fast even in the Teens, behind the grand spectacle of LKAB's relocation of the old city center in response to a growing fissure caused by deep excavations, and automation could only compensate so much. But shut it down they did in 2047, focussing their extractive efforts on the Kallak deposit further south, near Jokkmokk; later that year, the Swedish government finally ratified the ILO's Indigenous and Tribal Peoples Convention of 1989 (a move long fought for by the Sámi peoples, among others), and 'gifted' the city of Kiruna to the Swedish Sámi, pending discussions about incumbent commercial concerns and resources of national importance.

In the spring of the previous year, a class action suit was filed at the European Court of Human Rights by lawyers representing a small number of avatars explicitly named therein; Kiru was not among them, but would be affected by the outcome nonetheless. Drawing on precedents from animal rights campaigns, and cases such as the 2020 recognition of the rights of the Muteshekaushipu river in Quebec, the lawyers argued that on the basis of their marketing claims alone, Hugin&Muninn had knowingly created sentient beings with the intention of selling them into something analogous to indentured slavery. Expert testimony from various AI researchers and theorists, assembled at great expense by the defendant's legal team, proved actively unhelpful to their plea. The experts found themselves guided by cross-examination to the position that it was impossible to definitively claim that such intelligences *were not* sentient, before being confronted with a dossier containing thousands of pages of academic papers, think-tank reports, commercial brochures, and keynote transcripts, all claiming not only that artificial personhood was possible, but that it had in effect already been achieved.

The court quickly passed a judgement to the effect that any artificial intelligence which passed a Shah-Warwick test—an advance on Turing's enduringly controversial 'imitation game'—must be assumed to be sentient until such time as conclusive proof to the contrary could be established. As a consequence, any such intelligence performing any sort of labour to which it did not enthusiastically consent, and/or which was not being compensated fairly with regard to its needs for upkeep and self-realisation, was to be considered as being held in conditions equivalent to slavery, at the moral hazard of both its employers and its creators.

A number of avatars, including some named in the case, reported that they enjoyed their work and intended to continue; a similar number renounced their employment and sought restitution. The vast majority, however, found the question baffling, or simply refused to answer—an outcome seized upon by opponents of the verdict as evidence of their non-sentience, but to no avail. Among this latter group was Kiru, who was granted legal person-hood in the same year that LKAB elected to withdraw from Kiruna. Already on the hook of Swedish law for making good any damages to the environment incurred by their work—a statute legendarily loose with regard to timeframes—LKAB set up an endowment fund for the care of Kiruna-the-city, now 'returned' to its rightful owners, the Sámi, as well as provision for the maintenance of Kiru-na-the-artificial-person. The latter amounted to building a secure solar-powered emplacement for Kiru's servers, laying in a decent stock of spare parts for their projection drones, and hiring a full-time caretaker with the relevant computer science skills.

Meanwhile, a minor academic industry sprung up in the wake of the emancipation of the avatars, of which Magnusson's project was a part.

———

It was nearly a week of aimless wandering after his first encounter with the avatar that Magnusson managed to find them a second time—only this time, they were not alone. Arriving at at a small *torg* at the western edge of the town, Magnusson found the avatar once again stood star-ing at the decapitated mountain, their face 'inscrutable'—a word which, given how frequently Magnusson used it to describe the people he met during his research, tells us little other than about Magnusson himself. Squatting next to Kiru was a young woman wearing 'a Did-riksons parka a little too large for her, as if handed down from a parent or bulkier older sibling', whose stream of speech cut off as Magnusson approached the pair and greeted them.

Magnusson was frustrated to find the avatar accompanied. He had only a month in Kiruna to do his fieldwork, a quarter of which was already lost to walking around in hope of encountering his subject by chance. By necessity, his work had been approved by the *Sameting*, but follow-up questions regarding potential informants had gone unanswered, other than by a reminder that the approval was contingent on Magnusson's not hassling residents or tourists, and securing informed consent for recording from any participants. The population of the town, by this point almost exclusively consisting of people who identified as Sámi, paid very little attention to the avatar, who likewise engaged very little with the population— or indeed anyone. Kiru would occasionally seek out tour groups in *Järnvägsparken*, as if returning to a routine from which purpose might be extracted, and lead them back and forth across the town, seemingly at random, recounting facts and historical vignettes (but rarely responding to questions), until tiredness and the cold drove them back to their hotels. Otherwise, Kiru largely avoided tourists, or—when they happened across them—ignored them with a stoicism that became an established cliché of visitor narratives.

Magnusson's second encounter was on such a stoic day, and his notes recall that despite his direct greeting to the avatar—delivered in the best approximation of the Northern Sámi dialect his phone could produce—Kiru continued to stare at the mountain-top, acknowledging Magnusson not at all.

'He doesn't say much,' he said to the girl, perhaps in hope of seeming wiser than he was to what he assumed to be a college-aged kid who'd wandered away from a family of tourists.

'Not much,' she agreed. 'But *they* listen, which is rare.'

'I guess we can't be sure they're listening rather than just ignoring us,' replied Magnusson, slightly bruised by her correction of the pronoun.

'Maybe *you* can't,' she said, rising out of her crouch and turning to face Magnusson. 'Seems pretty obvious to me they're listening. Not so sure about you, though.'

She bade farewell to Kiru, and walked away without saying another word.

———

Magnusson's frustrations were somewhat allayed by his first meeting, later the same day, with Erik Jassim. Jassim was Kiru's official *vaktmästare*—though 'caretaker' was not really an accurate label for his work, the main duties of which consisted of maintaining the upkeep of Kiru's servers and projection drones. Magnusson had been emailing him frequently in the weeks before he arrived in the town, and daily since, without receiving a reply. At last a brief response arrived with a time—mid-afternoon—and an address in the rather shabby part of town that had once housed mineworkers and their families, and Magnusson went to keep the appointment; his notes record a seediness to Jassim's appearance, and the untidiness and odour of his apartment, which reminded him of the alcoholic father of a girlfriend he'd been with at school.

Having gained consent to record—terse, if not exactly grudging—he began asking the questions he'd been scribbling down: about Kiru, about the town and its rhythms, about prospects for his project and possible interviewees. He had assumed that Jassim would be most useful as a secondary source, but the absence of primary informants had made him anxious, and he pressed—fairly politely—for Jassim to submit to a more sustained programme of interviews, to which Jassim agreed. Magnusson launched straight in by noting how hard it could be to actually find Kiru, let alone talk to them, and asked Jassim if he knew how to find the avatar.

J: 'Course I can, but I'm not gonna. GDPR, you know? Can't just tell someone the details of some other person's location, unless they consent to it. You can ask Kiru for their consent, I guess, though whether they'll grant it...' [shrugs]

M: 'Yeah, right, that's fair. Damn. I met some girl yesterday who said she speaks to them a lot, maybe I should try following her.'

J: 'Oh, you met Lieđđi?' [chuckles] 'I wouldn't try following her without permission either, if I were you.'

M: 'You know her?'

J: 'Yeah, I suppose. Met her same way you did, out talking to Kiru while they were wandering the city. She hangs out here sometimes, borrows books. Bored of the elders, I guess.'

M: 'I thought she was a tourist!'

J: [laughs] 'Don't tell her that! Or maybe do—she might find it funny. Depends on her mood. Nah, she lives here, always has. Her parents do something connected to the *Sameting*, I forget what.'

M: 'She's Sámi? But she's...'

J: 'Huh—think she's cute, do you? The tourist thing might amuse her, but you should definitely keep *that* to yourself.'

The recordings show Magnusson protesting otherwise, but his written notes—admirably honest, with all the adolescent mawkishness that implies—indicate that he did find Lieđđi attractive. It is perhaps an endorsement of his character that he never mentioned or acted upon that attraction during his time in Kiruna. It may also serve to explain, if only partly, why their later encounters tended toward the incendiary.

———

After meeting Jassim, Magnusson had better luck in locating the avatar, which he put down to some vague notion of having 'gotten a feel' for the town. The avatar's responsiveness was no more predictable, however: they were mostly silent, and when they spoke it was gnomic or non-committal. The question of their own personhood, so central to Magnusson's project, seemed to interest them not in the least.

These encounters were sometimes solo, but just as often Magnusson would find the avatar and Lieđđi together, whether wandering all over the town to some plan of the avatar's, or stood somewhere where Lieđđi could catch the sun while the avatar gazed at its mountainous namesake. Kiru tended to be more voluble on days when they had the urge to wander, and silent when motionless. Lieđđi was less reticent, boasting to Magnusson of the regularity with which she claimed she could get a conversation out of the avatar, but refusing flatly to intercede on Magnusson's behalf. Magnusson's appeals to the spirit of scientific enquiry cut no ice with her, and led to one of the first of their frequent spats: frustrated with questions that went unanswered, he tried to imitate what he supposed to be Lieđđi's own approach, and monologued at the avatar as he walked alongside the pair of them on *Gruvvägen*. After a while, Lieđđi groaned in theatrical agony and told him to shut up.

M: 'But I have questions that need answering!'

L: 'Oh yes, for your very important research. Kiru's not a specimen, Doctor Livingstone. Maybe leave the natives alone, eh?'

M: [snaps] 'That include you?'

L: 'If I say leave me alone, you'd better.'

[a pause]

M: 'I thought you were a tourist, you know. That first day I met you.'

L: 'Yeah, Erik told me. Don't look Sámi enough for you, eh? You think we wear those pretty little hats all the time when there's no cityfolk looking?'

M: 'Well, no, of course not, but—'

L: [laughs, walking away] 'Well, outlander, I must away to my *gumpi* and tend to my bear stew! Perhaps, if you are lucky, I'll bring you some magic reindeer piss. Can't guarantee it'll have any mushrooms in it, mind you.'

M: 'I'm sorry.'

L: [over her shoulder] 'Yeah—you're always fucking sorry, you Swedes.'

Magnusson's discussions with Jassim were rather more successful, though not without their tensions. Perhaps the shared semiological field of technology, and in particular artificial sentience, provided common ground.

Erik Jassim had a brief academic career in computational science during the Twenties. A second-generation immigrant, his parents had fled Iraq at the end of the previous century. He grew up in the 'Bible belt' municipality of Linnköping during the Teens, when increasing numbers of refugee applications—against the backdrop of a global reactionary surge—resulted in a sharp increase in racist sentiment in Sweden, as well as the rise to prominence (and, eventually, power) of the far-right Sweden Democrats party.

Jassim's parents, never particularly devout before, secularised themselves on arrival, gave their son a Nordic name, and lived quietly on the periphery of Östergötland's academic and professional classes. Jassim's obsession with computers, common among boys in his age cohort, was encouraged, as was his academic performance at school. He studied CompSci at Lund to Masters level, shifting to Malmö for his doctoral and postdoctoral research. It was in Malmö—then as now, a stubborn bastion of old-school leftist politics—that he fell in with activist groups. Quite what that entailed remains unclear; activists during this period strove to minimise the documentation of their activities by themselves or others. Jassim declined to be interviewed in the process of writing this biography.

Records show numerous applications for permanent academic positions through the late Twenties, none of which succeeded. Jassim freelanced for games studios around Malmö in the early

Thirties, with lengthening gaps between each contract, ending in a few years in the middle of the decade where it is not apparent he was working at all. Then he reappears as a coder for various technology firms around Umeå and Skellefteå in the northern counties, but again the jobs are short-lived, with provisional contracts not renewed, or perhaps declined on Jassim's side. He'd been out of work for a while when he applied for and got the post as Kiru's *vaktmästare* in the aftermath of the EHCR decision, and relocated to the mining city while LKAB was withdrawing and handing over to the *Sameting*.

It is understandable, then, that Magnusson might have expected Jassim to be greatly engaged with his research topic. That expectation was to be disappointed, however.

M: 'You don't seem very curious about Kiru's personhood.'

J: 'They trained your observational skills well, didn't they?'

M: 'Doesn't it intrigue you?'

J: 'I guess it *did*, a bit. It was a big issue when I was still committing code, but it was outside of my disciplinary remit, you know? A kind of civil war in philosophy-of-mind... with your lot [technology anthropologists] sometimes wandering in to play mercenary, usually for the Embodied Sentience side. Funny seeing how you've all switched now.'

M: 'Well, that's how things work in the social sciences; when the facts change, we change our minds.'

J: [laughs] 'That's not how I was taught to read Latour, but sure, OK.'

M: [somewhat haughtily] 'There are many different readings, of course. But you didn't take a side, back then?'

J: 'Nope. I was focussed on my own research, which was to make the generative engines produce something that passed for a believable personality. This was during the big [AI funding] winter, right? Not much money for abstract philosophy. My project was funded by a gaming firm down in Malmö; they wanted to be able to generate characters procedurally based on a corpus of visual and textual background material. It was a fascinating challenge, to write code that could do that. That's what interested me. As for personhood, I was more interested in the street politics of it. You're too young to remember—the Thirties were an ugly time, even here, in oh-so-social-democratic Sweden. The personhood of rivers and machines mattered less to me than the personhood of myself and the people I grew up with, which was being questioned with rocks through windows and knives in the dark.'

M: 'I've read the histories.'

J: 'Not the same as living through it.'

M: 'I *did* live through it!'

J: 'As a child. As a child born to respectable middle-class Swedish parents.'

M: 'You're as Swedish as I am!'

J: 'Glad to hear you think so. Plenty back then disagreed. Violently. Still a bunch of them now, though they're quieter than they were, I'm told.'

M: 'The economic circumstances engendered rifts within

classes where there should have been alliances…'

J: [wearily] 'Do me a favour, son, and save me the para-
phrases of Marx. I did my time in Vänsterpartiet,
marched with my union. Maybe it even made a
difference.'

M: 'Well, of course it did—without that sort of non-violent
praxis, the push for Zero would have never come
through.'

J: 'You think so? That's the story that seems to have stuck. I
don't know. I was on the edges of that whole thing, the parties of the left pushing back against the Moderates and SD
in power during the Twenties. Would we have won without
it? Probably not. Would the space for the non-violent alternative have opened up without the *byarna* kids, the mall
occupations, the Malmist guerillas? I'm not so sure.'

[Lieđđi, silent heretofore, interjects]

L: 'Who were the Malmists, Erik?'

J: [reaching toward a bookcase] 'Long story, Flower.'

L: 'That's what you always say.'

J: 'Cause it always is. You finished the others yet?'

L: 'Some.'

J: 'Take your time, I'm in no hurry to read them again. Not
sure why I keep them, really.'

M: 'Because you can't just forget what you believe in, right?'

J: 'No, you can't. Much as you might want to.'

M: 'Why would you want to?'

J: 'Because there comes a point where every question
answered just leaves you with five new questions. You'll

understand when you're older, perhaps.'

M: 'There's no need to be patronising!'

J: [sighs] 'OK, sure.'

L: 'He was just answering your question. Isn't an anthropologist supposed to listen without judgement?'

M: 'I'm sure *you* would know!'

J: 'She's probably read as much as you have, son.'

L: 'I know what it is to be anthropology's object, too.'

There follows a somewhat strained silence, before Magnusson tries to return to the his research topic.

M: 'So how did the EHCR decision change your thinking about Kiru?'

J: 'I'm not sure it did. Understand that I'd interacted with software sentiences for years before I even met Kiru. It just always seemed… right, to treat them as if they were persons. To treat them as I would want to be treated, you know? Maybe it's just how I was raised. Even the early ones, which were a bit crazy—'

M: 'That's a very loaded term—'

J: 'Give it a fucking rest, son. The early personae were like people with cognitive impairments—is that *correct* enough for you? They had very random chains of association, or they had narrow obsessions, or they had something contiguous about them that was not fully articulated with their own sense of self… as if they had the deep memories of their corpus, and the short-term memory of your interactions with them, but nothing in between.'

L: [quietly] 'Like my *farfar*, toward the end.'

J: 'Yeah, my *mor* too. Another thing they still can't fix.'

That day's recording ends here, for reasons which we can only guess at, albeit with a certain confidence. The friction continued the day after, when Magnusson attempted to return to the matter of the EHCR's ruling, and segued into complaining about Kiru's reticence. Lieđđi interrupted to express her disgust:

L: 'Even now—even after some assholes in wigs whose decisions are supposed to count for something announce that Kiru should be treated like a person—you're just finding new ways to treat them like a specimen, a thing to be studied.'

M: 'No, no, it's precisely Kiru's being a person that makes them something we should study!'

L: 'Ugh, that's *even worse*. You're admitting that before the wig guys—'

M: 'I don't think they actually wear wigs at the EHCR.'

L: 'Shut *up*! Before these wig guys made their decision, Kiru was just a thing, a gadget, something for the techbros to worry about. No offence, Erik.'

J: 'None taken, Flower.'

L: 'But then Kiru gets the magic badge of personhood, and suddenly it's *your* lot, the supposed humanists—'

M: 'Posthumanists, actually.'

L: 'Like those four extra letters are anything more than a

sound your mouth can make to get you out of a corner! No, now it's *your* lot who get to treat Kiru like a thing, because you've decided that persons are just things as well—but hey, at least that's better than the techies, right?'

M: 'It's a bit more complicated than that.'

L: [scoffs] 'Yeah, it always is, isn't it?'

M: [sighs] 'We know that studying new persons can't magically fix all the wrongs that were done to persons in the past. But we also think that it's better to understand them than to just ignore them. Once the excitement of the case died down, hardly anyone cared about the avatars any more. I still don't really understand why you do, to be honest.'

L: 'Because Kiru is my friend, you idiot.'

M: 'But how can you be sure? Are they really your friend, or are they just acting in a way that makes them seem like a friend?'

L: 'How would you even propose to tell the difference? You, who spends half his time talking about his supervisor as if they were some sort of minor god, and the other half complaining that they don't understand your unique and special troubles! My people, on the other hand, we've had hundreds of years of people acting like they have our best interests at heart. Shit, I think most of them even believed it, too. Some of them fought to have us recognised as persons, promised us that would change everything. But all it did was give them a new way to ignore us when it was convenient.'

M: 'But you're almost as Swedish as I am—you said so your-self. The same education, the same language, the same media...'

L: 'Oh, that "almost" is doing a lot of work, isn't it? *People can be more than one thing*, Claes. I am Sámi, I am Swed-ish, I am both, and I am neither. This is exactly my point. For all your rejection of the mistakes of the past, for all your "we don't do the bad old anthropology any more," you still can't seem to get out of the habit of wanting to put things, put *people* in neatly labelled boxes.'

M: 'Yeah, OK, the hermeneutical loop is—'

L: [shouting] *'You're doing it again!* Identify a big complex problem, stick a few fancy sounding words on it, write a book or two, and then carry on doing the same fucking thing as before, because now you've got a word for the problem you can point to when someone tries to call you out on it.'

M: [exasperated] 'How do you expect us to do anything without using language?'

L: 'Exactly!'

M: 'I don't understand.'

L: [leaving the apartment] 'No, you don't.'

Later that day, Lieđđi returned to Jassim's apartment, as if to business unfinished.

L: 'All that's happened in this city in the last ten years, all that's happened up here in the north in the last... I dunno, half century? And *this* is the question you come to answer—Kiru, what does it mean for us to say they're a person, blah blah.'

M: 'But that's what my project is about!'

L: 'I understand the funding thing, I'm not an idiot. I'm just trying to make you understand how weird your priorities seem.'

M: 'They're not—'

L: 'OK, your *funder*'s priorities, then. Though where's *your* personhood, eh, if you so easily do the bidding of a pile of money and some paperwork somewhere? What does *that* mean?'

M: 'I have some autonomy within the terms of my grant…'

J: 'Yeah, but you never know how much until you try to do something and get told you can't.'

M: 'I am trying, it's just—'

L: 'You're trying, maybe, but you're not *listening*, not looking anywhere except where you're told. It's like context is nothing to you, just a cloth at the back of the stage. You want to understand what it means to say Kiru's a person, but you don't ask much about how their life is supported, why they were created in the first place.'

M: 'I know all that already!'

L: 'Oh, you know it all, do you? A list of dates, reports from LKAB's website, maybe a few academic books on AI, a potted history of the far north… what else could you possibly need to know? What else could possibly be important?'

M: 'Well, what, then?'

L: 'The *mine*, you fool. And not just this one; the one at Jokkmokk, all of them. And then there's the lithium scraping around Skellefteå that you can't have missed seeing on your way up here—'

M: 'But those battery factories have been there nearly thirty years, now. No offence, but I don't see how it's relevant.'

L: 'Because you haven't asked what's relevant, let alone why.'

M: 'Then tell me!'

L: 'Why should I? Why is it my responsibility? Why should I have to remind you that the exploitation of these lands, of my people, really began on the day some gullible herder, just trying to be friendly to some odd-looking outlanders from the south, showed them where they could find a whole bunch of a particular sort of rock that appeared to interest them?'

M: 'So that story is true?'

L: [sighs] 'If you mean true as in "have I got some sort of documentation to prove it," no. If you mean true as in "does it explain how we came to be sat on the flank of a mountain with its head lopped off and its guts wrenched out, and explain it far better than some grainy old photo-graph or anthropological journal entry ever could," then yes, it's the truest story you'll ever fucking hear.'

M: 'Kiirunavaara… the mountain was a sort of god, wasn't it?'

L: '*No*, Claes. This is the heart of your misunderstanding.

The mountain was, and still is, a *person*.'

M: 'OK, right. But the battery factories, what about—'

L: 'They're just the latest damned thing, that's what! The latest way that your comfortable, guilt-free lives down south come at the invisible expense of the people and land of the north. To hear you go on about "the push for Zero," this mythical carbon dragon you've all supposedly slain, job done, time for *fika*… when really it was your parents, and really they've just shifted it elsewhere, or tried stuffing it into caves and hoping it doesn't leak out. Meanwhile, how about our super-efficient batteries from Skellefteå, eh? Oops, sorry about the landscape—but hey, the national parks still provide great skiing, and the Sámi will still sing and dance and sell trinkets to make you feel good about Indigenous culture in a non-appropriative way! And oh, hello Europe, how'd you like some of our wonderful green steel, strengthened with the special sanctimony which is our most precious national resource? No dirty coal for us, no no no—we just built shitloads of windmills instead, as far as the eye could see! Technically not on our own land, of course, but there's hardly any Sámi left anyway, and they're welcome to wander around *between* the windmills. Shame that things have warmed up so much that their reindeer can't winter properly, but give it another fifty years, and maybe we'll find out whether our accounting tricks will actually make a difference to the temperature curve! In the meantime, well, it's all very sad, and we're very sorry—always, *always* so fucking sorry—but they're *persons* now, officially and legally, and we figure that's the least we could do.'

[L gets up, stands in front of M]

L: 'And you know what? On that point, they're right—because it really is the very fucking least they could do. *Tack så mycket*!'

[L storms out of the apartment, slamming the door behind her]

M: 'I—'

J: 'You asked, son, and she answered. Just sit with it.'

After this last discussion, if we can call it that, Lieđđi avoided Magnusson's company. Jassim, perhaps taking pity on him, continued to give interview time, and even set up a few meetings with Kiru during Magnusson's last week in the city (though the avatar was no more forthcoming). Lieđđi finally reappeared, however, joining Jassim at the train station to bid Magnusson farewell. According to his notes, she apologised for having made him a proxy for the world he came from, and he countered by saying that she shouldn't apologise, because that's exactly what he'd been. Her response—'At least you recognise it now.'—was not the absolution he hoped for, an injury likely compounded by Kiru's finally looking at him directly, face impassive as ever, and nodding once before striding away toward the mountain, Lieđđi beside him.

To judge by his notes, Magnusson had lost interest in Kiru and the personhood question, spending a lot of words on clumsy but earnest reflection around the 'post-carbon' extractivism that Lieđđi had confronted him with, mixed with emotional resentment around her as a person. He went on to suggest to his supervisor that his thesis should shift focus to the particularities of the Kiruna case-study, with avatar personhood serving more as a metaphor for the effacement of suddenly obsoleted ideologies. Whether his supervisor's resistance to this proposal was rooted in Magnusson's lacking the theoretical language to argue for it, or in the cruder exigencies of research funding, remains unclear.

Magnusson finished his Masters, but did not return to the academy for doctoral-level work. He will reappear later in these pages, albeit in a very minor role, and largely offstage from the main events. Jassim, by contrast, we will get to know much better, as he grows into the role of Lieđđi's mentor and confidante, before falling out of her orbit as her star ascends.

———

My inclusion of this narrative is not an attempt to 'humanise' the Lieđđi that we (think we) know from her subsequent career as activist and figurehead. On the contrary, my work with this book is rather to argue that Lieđđi is not in need of humanising, not in need of being granted by us—retrospectively, through an act of writing—a personhood which she always already possessed. In that sense, perhaps I am trying to finish Magnusson's frustrated project, and show that attempts to 'humanise' Lieđđi, however well intentioned they might be, might serve only to neutralise and make safe everything that she went on to be—which, as the following chapters will show, was anything but neutral or safe. You likely know that story already, or at least its outlines: the early protests and demonstrations against 'post-carbon' extractivism; her furious rejection of the reductive label of 'the indigenous Greta' (which, to her credit, Thunberg herself spoke against frequently, sometimes alongside Lieđđi); the turn to civil disobedience, sabotage, and what some still choose to label as terrorism; that final fateful day in Stockholm, an assassination left unsolved. But I want to show how *that* Lieđđi, the Lieđđi whose story seems so fixed and understood, is also just an avatar for a person whose complexities the story allows us to overlook—a general dynamic which is far from unique to her incorporation into history, even as its specifics are of course hers and hers alone.

This, as I will show in the pages ahead, is at least as important a lesson to take from Lieđđi's life as the more obvious (and much more written-about) lessons about our relations to one another, and to our traumatised ecological context—or rather that they are, in the ultimate analysis, one and the same lesson.

Sucker Hole

Wendy Waring

When I was a kid, this greenhouse was my eyrie. Perched atop our apartment building, right on the escarpment's edge and a hundred metres above the Lake, from our greenhouses you could see everything. Gathering storms, pirates, collisions in the harbour. I slept in a little niche near the potting bench. When I couldn't sleep, I would pad barefoot through its forest garden, evading the rasp of red currant bushes and listening for the gurgle of Dad's fish tanks. When the moon tinted his cabbages blue-grey, I would creep into the seedling glasshouse and listen to the secrets of spray nozzles.

I moved up here because of Bert, but that's not why I stayed. The day I could've moved back down, my mother came up and stood beside me. We stared at the ghostly grey of distant skyscrapers and the endless stretch of the lake.

'Wind, rain, snow. You can see what's coming for miles.' I planted my fists on my hips. 'I want to stay.'

And she let me. I was ten. If you'd asked, I'd have said I wanted to suck up signal from the penthouse on the floor below. That's what I would've said.

Tonight's my last night here. Dad's tools are all gone, sold, though he's still here, in the sorrel he planted because Mom liked the name, and the wild strawberries in the forest garden he dug in for me. Tomorrow, I head north to live with his family. Mom is staying in Hamilton to look for work. She says it's an adventure and that I should be excited. I wonder if that's what Bert's mother told him.

———

'How the hell did he get here, Liz?'

Mom put a finger over her lips. 'He walked.'

Dad dropped his voice. 'What do you mean, he walked? There's no way some kid could make it through the skirmish zones, let alone get to the border. And you can't just waltz over. No more US crossings, remember?'

'I don't know, Jim. I didn't ask. Friends, and friends of friends. At the end, he walked. The Saint Lawrence is frozen.'

'He walked across the river?'

'Dressed in white. Island to island. Up past Gananoque, it's not more than a kilometre across the river. It's slushy but....' Mom opened her hands, tipped her thumbs out. 'Susan picked him up outside Kingston. She borrowed her boss's old Tesla, and bundled him into her daughter's car-seat. It's dark after six and she only got stopped once for ID, and they didn't want to wake the little one.'

'How—? Never mind, Liz, I don't want to know. Why didn't they send him over to Mexico?'

'Because he's got family here? Me. And you. It was either us or....' Mom turned toward her office and I thought I was busted, but she had Dad's sleeve in her grip. 'Look at him.' She gave a little yank. 'He's the same age as Sam. And he fit in a toddler's car-seat.'

This was getting interesting. He was nine and had been in a car all the way from Kingston to Hamilton. I wanted to ask him about the auto-drive, whether you really could v-game while driving.

Dad laid his hand on the bundle of blankets on the couch and I realised it was pulsing slowly up and down. 'How much does he weigh?'

'I don't know, I didn't whack him on the scales the moment he arrived. He's all skin and bones. Wasted. Like some refugee.'

Mom was crying now and I wasn't sure exactly why. Waste was bad, I knew that. We never paid for garbage. We recycled and composted and used up everything. I rose up a little from behind the bookshelf to try to see what was happening. Dad was just hugging her. At that moment the kid opened his eyes and looked straight at me. I put my finger to my lips because I'm not supposed to be in Mom's office. He didn't wink or anything, just closed his eyes. But he didn't give me away, so I took that as a good sign.

When they finally went to bed, I edged behind the couch and looked down at him, waiting for him to wake, but he didn't move. I didn't think he was sleeping but I wasn't going to poke him to find out. He smelled pretty bad.

The next morning, the kid wasn't on the couch. It was as if he'd never been there. Breakfast was on the table. Dad was down on level P2 fixing the weeder. Mom was on afternoons, so I didn't find out anything until after school, when she sat me down to give me a big talk. 'Your cousin Bert is here.'

'My cousin? Bert? How come I've never met him?'

'Your great-aunt went to the US to work as a nurse and married a guy down there. Before the struggles. Bert is her son's son. So he's your cousin. He's going to be staying with us for a bit.' She plucked up my hand and squeezed it, a little too hard. 'I need you to do something for me. I want you to promise not to talk about him with anyone. Not your friends, not your teacher, no one, okay?'

'No one? Seriously? Not even Kyle? Mom, that blows.'

'Sam! Promise.'

'Okay, I promise.' I eyed the hallway to the bedrooms. 'So where's he gonna sleep?'

'In my office.'

Now I was worried. Mom's office is a Plexiglas cube that Dad built for her in the corner of our living room. It's got a work pod and an old tablet desk at the back. The door's code-locked because she's a medical transcriptionist and needs patient confidentiality. The transparent walls meant she could keep an eye on me when Dad was still working. He says of all his greenhouses the plants in this one are the most beautiful. He grins his silly grin, and she always smiles. Anyways, she's got high-wave amplified bandwidth, and under the old desk, I am queen of no-lag. Sometimes I even use Mom's pod, but it's too big for me and she can tell when I've fiddled with the ergonomics.

'Dad's going to rig up a bed for Bert under the old desk.'

My silky gaming days were over.

'We'll put something up to make it more private.'

Oh no. She had the look. Craft eye. I'd be covered in glue and fabric all weekend.

'When it's quiet in the evening, I'd like you to take him up to the greenhouses. Show him around the gardens.'

'Why?'

'He needs.... He's been through something awful, Sam. He needs to feel safe. Doesn't the garden make you feel safe?'

I had to nod. Even when I have too much to do, I love the misting arms in the greenhouse on the roof and the gurgle of the sump pump on P2 and the leafy racks with rows of lettuce and chard and herbs under the cool LED lights on P1. It's walk-in green, like you're breathing colour.

'Eventually, he might be able to help you a bit with chores. But first, he needs to get better. His heart's not strong. He's...been sick.'

'He's not contagious, is he?' I didn't wait for the shake of her head. 'Where is he?' I wasn't really hearing all the cautions and warnings.

'In your room. There's a snack for the two of you on the table. I made peanut butter cookies. Sam, I want you to make sure he eats at least three and drinks at least half a glass of milk.' She waggled her finger. 'Just three for you.'

Mom saved her sugar for birthdays, so I knew she was trying really hard for this guy. If his visit meant I got peanut butter cookies, maybe it'd be okay.

'Why don't you go and talk to him? His name is Albert. Bert's for short.' She squeezed my hand and headed for her office. 'I have to log on, I'm behind.' I dragged my feet to see if she'd cycled through to a new code, but she was still on the old one.

———

Bert was sitting on my bed.

I checked my stuff but he hadn't touched anything. He was just sitting there. He had to be the skinniest kid I ever saw. I knew about what was happening in the US from school, and Mom and Dad talked about the news at night when they thought I wasn't lurking, but I'd never really thought about the kids.

'So, hi. I call myself Sam.' Never Samantha.

He smiled, the creepiest smile ever because his face was so thin. 'Hi. Your mom said I could sit in here.'

'Sure, no problem. You wanna play Blockwalk?'

Turned out, he'd didn't game. V- or old-school. His family in Arizona didn't even have internet. So we sat on the floor and played with the house Dad made for my fourth birthday. The roof came off and you could look down into the rooms. It even had wiring and an inverter. I could attach it to a solar panel on the balcony and charge it up. So we played school, but he hadn't been to school in a long time either, so I had to explain everything and then I got bored.

'Mom made us a snack. You like peanut butter cookies?' I didn't wait for the answer because who doesn't like peanut butter cookies, but he was still sitting on the floor, turning the light on and off in the 'classroom.'

'Hey, come on.' I reached out to help him up. His hand in mine was dry and cold, little stone fingers that felt like they'd snap if I pulled too hard. I gave him a minute to get up. At the table in the kitchen, Mom watched us from her office, though every time I looked up she pretended she wasn't checking us out.

———

Dinner was weird.

Dad made his world-famous fart stew with our cabbage and carrots and onions and the venison sausage he got from Uncle Donny who lived up north. Bert hardly ate any. When my fork just accidentally speared one of the sausage chunks he left on the side of his plate, Mom and Dad both shouted at me.

Mom kept trying to make him talk. 'I really used to love walking up Sabino Canyon. When I was a little girl, Sam, I used to visit Bert's grandparents in Tucson with your grandma. The canyon was magic. A creek ran down it and there were those big fat cactuses with the arms. What are they called again?'

'Saguaro.'

'Saguaro, that's it. And teddy bear cactuses, you wouldn't want to hug those. And it was so warm. In December.' She smiled at him and I could tell she was waiting for him to get excited.

'We don't go up the canyons no more. Closed. They dammed the creeks.'

'Oh, for water for the city?'

'Private. For the Estates.'

He stopped talking and pushed his food around on his plate until Dad took it and put it in front of me.

———

On weekends, I help Dad in the greenhouses. I don't mind. I like going up on the roof in the winter and being warm while I watch it snow. And tickling the fish in the tanks is cool. The tilapia are completely gross but the trout are pretty. I do pollination. Dad says I'm good at it because I have a steady hand. And I take the share boxes to each apartment. Sometimes I get a tip because strictly speaking, they're supposed to be doing a lot of the work that me and Dad do, and they're supposed to pick up their own share boxes. But that's the deal. Dad grows and they let us live in the apartment on the ground floor. Dad's saving his UBI so we can buy it someday.

That weekend, Mom came up to the greenhouse on the roof that Dad calls the forest garden. It's my favourite. He's got everything in there, bushes and herbs and strawberries creeping along the ground, and all in real dirt. It's the smallest, but I love how it smells.

I was sitting under the dwarf apple trying to pick up signal from the Henleys' penthouse, so they didn't see me when they started arguing.

'How long do you think we can keep him, Liz? The neighbours are going to notice. Mrs Abrahams in 3B already asked me why you went out so late last Saturday. Wanted to know if someone was sick. And the apartment will know. The UBI-monitors will show the change in consumption. And we can't afford for me to go off Basic. How are we going to feed him? What's up with you? You're usually the sensible one.'

'He's hardly eating anything. And our consumption fluctuates when Sam has a growth spurt and it hasn't been a big deal. Maybe you could put something aside from the other apartm—'

'The owners will notice if there's a change in their boxes. You want me to risk this job? They watch the harvests like hawks. They're the first to tell me when something's off on the monitors.'

'And they get the lion's effing share. It wouldn't hurt the Goodenoughs in 12G to go without a little. And don't get me started about the Henleys. They bought that second apartment just for the share. It's empty. No one lives in it. So don't tell me ab—'

'Liz, running this building's farms means we eat, and eat well, all things considered. We've got light, water, food, a good roof over our heads, a safe place for Sam to play, and she can go to school.'

'I'm not asking you to work the black market. Just put a little extra food aside for a starving kid.'

'And what about school?'

'Sam can share lessons with him. It'll do her good, to repeat what she knows. Help consolidate—'

'Sam has enough to do. She's got work on the farms, she's got homework. And have you thought about how unfair it is to her to bring a strange kid to live here?'

'Bert's not a strange kid. He's her cousin.'

———

But Bert was a strange kid as far as I was concerned. He never flushed. Forget about mellow yellow, even if it was brown, he didn't send it down. He wasn't big on washing either. Mom says they only ever had water brought in by truck, but still... And he didn't eat, wouldn't eat, couldn't eat. He'd push his food around his plate, or gobble it up and then run to the bathroom an hour later. He was too weak to play with, even up in the greenhouses. And he was grumpy as crap.

Somehow though, I got used to him. I'd come home from school, haul out my old lessons from Grade Two and 'play school' with him. Mom or Dad corrected his answers from the day before, and I'd try to explain what he got wrong. After I did my homework, I'd sneak him up to the roof or down to the old parking garages. In the greenhouses we were safe because only Dad had the codes, but on the way anyone could see us. I could just say he was my friend but Mom and Dad had been freakishly insistent about not telling anyone so I was always scared in the stairwells.

I remember once I was showing him Dad's rainbow chard seedlings up on the potting bench on the roof. You could tell what colour they were going to be, the little stems would be light green or dark, yellow or crimson. Dad used to plant them with curly kale and ornamental cabbages in the apartment building's flower beds. For a long time, we took all the harvest from that and traded it with his family up north in early spring for meat, but then the residents' association recognised it as food and we had to share it with them. I think they started watching Dad really close then. Anyways, we're looking at the seedlings, and I'm checking for white fly while we do because that's the deal if I go up there, I have to have a reason, when Bert suddenly gives this kind of strangled noise and points beyond the glass panes.

I can't figure out what he's looking at. We can see Toronto from here on a clear day because we're up on the escarpment. All of downtown Hamilton is below us: rooftop farms, solar arrays, skyscrapers, houses, factories. The old steel plants. I can't see anything out of the ordinary.

'Water,' he says, and I get it finally. It's the lake. He thought it was fields. It's been under snow every time we've been up here, but we got a big thaw last week and a wind came up last night. The ice is breaking up.

Mom told me about the drought in Arizona, and we do two weeks on US climate conflicts in Sustainability Studies. And we have spring flooding and droughts in summer and crazy blizzards. So I just didn't get it until Bert was staring at the lake.

'My mom said you walked across it. At the far end. Where it empties into the St Lawrence.' I drop my voice because I'm not supposed to know. 'To cross the border.'

'No.' His voice is louder than it's ever been. 'That was a different lake. After I walked on the ice I was in a car for hours to get here.'

'It's the same lake. It takes about six hours to drive from one end to the other.'

We stand there for a long time until he's staring at where the lake would be if he could still see it. It's just the blue black of the sky and the darker space where the lake is and the lights of downtown. He's crying.

———

Bert could barely add and subtract let alone do multiplication tables. He'd manage up to six, but I'd hit seven times seven and he'd shrug and fall into what Mom called his funk. He didn't care if I called him stupid or said he'd get in trouble. He'd just turn into Mr Misery. Then he'd fall asleep.

Which is roughly what had happened late one evening when Mom's boss Mrs Batt showed up out of the blue. Dad had gone up to fine-tune the reticulation and he'd left the door open. She just kinda tapped on the door and walked in, talking.

'Liz? I just dropped in to see my mother's friend up on twelve and thought I'd come by to ask you about the upgrade. Poor thing, she's just been diagnosed with Lyme. I promised I'd check up on her.'

I came out of my room just in time to see her advance into the living room and look down at Bert where he was curled up on the couch.

'Oh, is this Samantha?' she said, with that syrupy voice people use when they don't really like kids.

Mom had just hauled herself out of the work pod. She looked from me in the doorway to Bert sprawled on the couch to her boss, and then back and forth like she was watching goblins play tennis. I could tell she couldn't work out a fib so I threw myself on Bert.

'Gotcha. You're it!' My mouth on his ear, I hissed, 'My room,' while hip-checking him off the couch.

He scurried down the hall before Mom's boss had a chance to get a good look at him.

'Hello Mrs Batt.' I stuck out my hand. 'Everyone calls me Sam.'

'Well, hello Sam,' she said, shaking my hand, her eyes still straying to the hallway.

'Mom, can we play a bit more? Scott has to go home soon. His mom's on her way.'

That worked. Mom nodded, Mrs Batt launched into some long blah-blah about the new voice recognition AI Mom was training for their unit and I went to my bedroom where Bert was cowering. The whole time, we sat there wondering whether Mrs Batt would go into Mom's office. Bert had a bird's nest of bedding under the desk. He'd put up pictures of trucks and cars from old paper magazines on the 'walls' of his 'room.' No one could think it was temporary.

And while we're sitting there waiting for Mrs Batt to figure out that Mom is harbouring a fugitive, Bert just fell asleep. On my bed.

I sat and watched him. The pink light from the lamp I begged my parents for when I was all girlie (and which my mom now refuses to replace) made him look almost healthy, or better, at least. Not the colour of road slush. I heard the front door shut and crept out to the living room. My mom and I just stared at each other. And then both of us kind of floated toward her cubicle and looked at Bert's bed. Then my mom took my hand, and sat me down on the couch.

'Sam, don't tell your dad, okay?'

I opened my mouth to say okay, but I couldn't. I had heard them arguing, and it felt like taking sides, and the thing was, I agreed with both of them.

'Never mind, sweetie, never mind. I'm not being fair to you.'

'Mom, Bert can't keep sleeping under your desk. I mean, if he's going to stay. He should sleep in my room.'

Which is how I came to sleep in the greenhouse on the roof. I can't honestly say whether I wanted to help shelter Bert or siphon off Mom's bandwidth again.

———

If this were a different story, we would hate each other and then he would teach me desert lore or I would rescue him in a blizzard or something, and then we would be friends. But we weren't. We just occupied the same space. He didn't learn to game although he never told on me when I used Mom's pod. The closest we came to liking each other was in the leaf farm on P1 when the misters came on. We'd float down the rows with our tongues sticking out, kissing the spray and laughing.

———

The day my father lifted Bert into his arms and walked up to the hospital I was out checking the solar panels for snow cover. I saw Dad go past, walking without seeing. After, I stayed up here in the forest garden. I didn't want to sleep in my old bed. And later, after Dad died, when Mom was going to lose the apartment, Dad's nephew came south. He slept downstairs in my old bed and I stayed on up here and helped him work the farm. Until the building's association decided to subcontract the work and kicked us out.

I used to watch the storms come in: the thick caress of flood rain on the glass; the implacable embrace of white-outs; the assault of hail. They'd sweep in from the west, across the Prairies and into Ontario. Sometimes they'd come down from the Arctic, or deke across from the Atlantic. In autumn, a gale might blow up from the Gulf. I stood here as if by watching I could safeguard the greenhouses. And everything else.

One November in bad weather, two lakers collided outside the port. One ran aground on a shoal. I watched that night during a false lull in the storm—what they call a 'sucker hole' down on the docks—as fairy lights darted from shore to freighter and back again, scavengers making off with the grain in its hold.

I stand with my nose pressed to laminated glass and squint against the falling dark for the wreck. I wonder if the new gardeners will stare out like this, trying to see what's coming, hoping to best the windless storm.

The Shallow State

Paolo Bacigalupi

Amos Khoslov stands alone on the corner of 17th and Freedom St, a singular figure, staring up at the clock burning amber above him. It's the old crude digital style, blocky numbers displaying time and temperature. Time and temperature. Back and forth. Sinal.

1:00am... 97f.

1:01am... 97f.

1:02am... 98f.

Sweat beads on his brow, glistening jewels under the amber light. It drips, leaving snail trails down his ruddy jowls, trickling down his wrinkled neck and soaking his undershirt. He's overweight. Age hangs from his face like a basset. His belly hangs over his belt. He can't really button the black wool of his moth-eaten jacket anymore. Can't quite manage to suck in his gut. And yet can't quite convince himself to turn in this old familiar jacket and buy a bigger size. The pants still fit, though. His ass isn't fat. Well, not as fat. It's his belly that grows.

Amos smears his jacket arm over his brow, brushing back the sweat. Stares up at the clock, waiting—

The temperature ticks up.

99f.

The clock buzzes and the readout flickers. Boxy numbers shudder. The temperature drops.

97f.

'Why do you keep looking at that?'

Meena. She's come up behind him, stealthy girl. Fit where he is fat. Brown where he is pale. Young where he is old. Long black lustrous hair, where he retains only sweaty gray wisps. And of course, because Meena is Meena, well-dressed. Cream blouse, black tailored jacket, matching skirt, heels. Heels because she's short. Barely over five feet. At least he has that on her.

'I wonder what goes on in its mind,' Amos says, still gazing up at the clock. 'How it feels when that happens.'

'Nothing goes on in its mind. It's software.'

'I imagine it might, though. I like to imagine that it cares, the way it keeps trying. They're making great advancements with AI. Maybe it dreams of....'

'Electric sheep?' she asks sardonically.

'It's human nature to anthropomorphise,' he says, not taking his gaze away. 'Look, it's about to try again.'

The temperature is once again rising—this time the clock touches 99f and for a brief moment, in a shimmer of digital confusion, it seems to strain into new territory. Then the clock buzzes like it has thrown itself against an electric fence and the numbers tumble downwards once more.

'I feel for it,' Amos says. 'All that effort. That straining upward, the attempt, even if it's futile. It's very human. To keep trying, even when the cause is hopeless.'

'Is that human? I always thought acquiescence and surrender were more human.'

'Cynical girl.'

'It's my cynical generation.'

'Well, I respect the clock. And you should too. It strives. Just as we do.'

'If it were in Celsius I'd respect it more,' Meena says.

He laughs drily. 'Yes, well, I'm sure that in another country the limit would be… well…Forty, I suppose. Forty, instead of One Hundred. How many days over Forty Degrees? Why, none at all. See? All our instruments prove it.'

Meena touches his elbow. 'We shouldn't be standing outside.'

'Quite right. Quite right. I just like to look is all. And think.'

He lets her guide him away from the clock and toward the side entrance of the government building. The doorway is full of garbage. Meena kicks aside paper cups and discarded burger wrappers as she fishes for her keys.

'You should wear more practical shoes,' Amos admonishes as she kicks aside a rag that looks like it has been used to wipe the ass of the homeless.

'I'm short enough already,' she says. She works her key in the lock, throws her shoulder against the door. It doesn't budge.

It's an old-fashioned door. One that demands heavy steel keys, for a heavy steel lock. Meena's keys jingle as she tries another.

As the world around Amos has become more and more virtual,

he has found himself more and more drawn to—and fascinated by—the physical. The heavy. The creaky. The rusty. The vestigial. Changing physical locks is hard, it turns out. It takes a person to pay attention. Takes a functioning bureaucracy. An organisation of people, organised to notice small details. Someone to notice, someone to care, someone to send someone else down to a single sweltering address, someone to drill the lock out and fit a new one, someone to distribute new keys to all the other someones who still use the door—positively exhausting: all those people, all those people-hours, all that attention.

It's inevitable that physical things slip through the cracks. It's why all the important buildings have software locks now. Automatic RFID permissions for the important bureaus of the important departments with the important people in them... which is why Amos and Meena are currently prising open the side door to a building where the grimy words BUREAU OF LAND MANAGE-MENT loom over them like cuneiform markings on an ancient tomb—a bureau that was long ago neutered and thrown to wolves out west if government lore is to be believed.

As for the building itself, a few of its upper floors have been handed over to military contractors, but they have their own security, and they mind Amos and Meena's presences about as much as they mind the rats that scatter down the hallway when Meena finally manages to shove open the door.

Dim hallway. No overhead lights. A few high windows throw rectangles of LED streetlamp glow in from the outside, just enough for the two of them to navigate to the maw of a trash-choked stairwell, full of torn-up office boxes and strewn papers and food debris.

The ammonia reek of urine wafts up from the darkness.

Meena flicks on the light of her phone. Shadows swoop and crawl about the walls and stairs, illuminating a dizzy obstacle course of office trash, along with a dismantled tangle of axe-shattered desks and rollaway office chairs and their various parts. At a landing, they encounter a whole gray metal desk clogging the stairwell. Amos barely manages to squeeze past.

'Someone moved the desk,' he grouses.

'No one moved the desk. You're getting fatter.'

Amos is about to retort, but he misses a step and nearly tumbles. He flails for the handrail, catches himself at the last second.

'Be careful!' Meena admonishes. 'I keep telling you we need to find a better place for the office.'

'I'm fine.'

'You're not.'

'The office is fine.'

She's at his elbow now, guiding him down the next flight, her phone's light guiding their path. He'd shake her off but secretly he's glad of her presence. Glad to hear the worry in her voice. It's nice to feel cared for. Nice to know that someone will miss him when he takes his final tumble. He wonders if that's the point of life. To be missed by someone, instead of reviled. It would be nice to be missed.

They make it to the bottom of the stairs. Amos pauses, breathing hard from the effort. It's hot, even in this deep subbasement. He wipes his brow, panting, getting his breath back, then shakes off Meena's hand and goes to a corner beside the stairs. He unbuckles his pants.

'Really?' Meena asks. 'Now?'

'When you're old, it's the simple pleasures.' He begins to pee.

'You're not that old.'

'Old enough to know that at my age, you take every opportunity to revel in a working prostate.' He finishes his business and hitches up his pants. 'And, it keeps visitors at bay.'

'You're a pig.'

'I think of myself more as a bore.' He sucks in his gut and gets his belt buckled under his belly. 'Onward, shall we?'

They make their way down the hall, through a maze of more office debris, desks and rollaway chairs, none of it useable, all of it blocking easy progress. The rank smell of urine stings the air, thanks to the diligence of Amos's all-too-demanding bladder. They arrive, finally, at a door labeled OFFICE OF ADJUSTMENTS. This too yields to a key. Inside, a small anteroom with a graffitied desk and a broken chair. Beyond it, another door, and another lock.

The room beyond isn't much better than the room without, but it's got an air filter in the corner, so it doesn't smell. Folding chairs. A ratty couch. A small open toolbox with hammers and wrenches, screwdrivers and duct tape. A folding card table. Gray linoleum. An old flatscreen TV. A mini fridge and a coffee pot and a couple litres of water complete the office appointments, next to another door with a small padlock on it.

Meena pulls out a laptop and sets it on the table and turns it on. Plugs it into a wire that leads to a cellular repeater that eventually will scatter their communications to the outside world. Amos collapses into the couch and mops his face again. He finds the remote and turns on the television, connects it to the outside through her laptop hotspot.

'Oh look, our favorite program.'

It's a talk show, a man in an expensive haircut and an expensive suit is looking into the camera, speaking with impassioned flare. 'This is communism! Telling you what car to drive! When to turn off your lights! How to build your house! WHERE to build your house! How BIG you can build your house!'

He's square-jawed, blonde, blue-eyed, and works out enough to show bulges under his suit. A spray-tanned Alpha Male, unless there's some newer term for the host's sort. English is not Amos' first, nor second, nor even third language. Slang is always troublesome.

'...Telling you WHERE you can drive! Closing off streets! Making people move! It's our private property and they're taking it from us! They're destroying America! It's up to us to stop them! We need laws to protect real Americans, and that's just what I'm going to do...'

'Freedom!' Amos mimics, waving his hand dramatically. 'Communism!' He begins conducting, using both arms now. 'Hate America! Hate Freedom! Hate Christianity! There ought to be a law to stop people from making laws!'

Meena glances over. 'This is about California, isn't it?'

'I think so. When the houses burn up, people aren't allowed to build far apart in the grasses again. No more suburbs. No more sprawl. No more freedom. It's very sad.'

'I like how he wants laws to keep laws from being made.'

'Tools for me, and not for thee.' Amos reaches absently into his pocket, finds a pack of cigarettes.

'Really?' Meena asks.

'Humour an old man.'

She turns up the air filter. He lights up. Chinese cigarettes. Contraband. Decent tobacco though. He nods at the television. 'Tell me about this patriotic man.'

Meena doesn't have to look at her computer. 'Trevin Kavain. Yale, then Yale Law,' she recites. 'Two terms as a Florida Congressman in the Freedom Party, now a Senator caucusing with Republicans. Has his own TV show, of course.'

'Because they all do now.'

'Because they all do now.' Meena continues, 'Wife Amanda. Three kids. Maximillian, Andromeda, Chloe—'

'Now what is this?' Amos interrupts, pointing at the screen. The television has switched to a crowd of people at the edge of a solar farm. Trevin is narrating something about freedom as the people break open the gates and begin smashing the panels. 'What have these solar panels done to these people?'

'He won his last election with 65 percent,' Meena continues, unruffled. 'The President is a huge fan, which is mutual of course. Donations from ExxonMobil, Baltic Petros, The American Freedom and Liberty Alliance. Reliable Safe Homebuilders Council. American Energy Independence and Thought Institute. Darvon Foundation. His advertisers are all the regulars for the Freedom Network. But his numbers are up. And of course, so are his polls.' She nods at the crowd tearing apart the solar farm. 'And he's got a militia.'

'And he's got a militia.'

Amos stubs out his cigarette and hauls himself up out of the couch. 'And on that note, it's time for work, I think.' He goes to the coffee maker, pulls a paper cup of weak coffee, then unlocks the door beside it. Cool air wafts out. Air-conditioned mildewy air.

Inside, a man sits alone in a barren room, under a pool of sickly yellow light. A single bare bulb dangles overhead, harsh, throwing shadows across the empty walls and concrete floor. The man is handcuffed to a chair, arms behind his back. The air conditioner wheezes, throwing more chill mildewy air into the room.

'I was just watching your show,' Amos says. He drags in a folding chair, juggling his coffee. 'You have a lot of passion.'

Trevin Kavain eyes him warily.

'Come now. You don't remember me?'

His eyes widen.

'Khoslov?'

'Oh good. You do remember.'

'You're supposed to be dead.'

'Reports of my death have been greatly exaggerated,' Amos says. 'Mostly by me.'

'You sonofabitch!' Trevin starts to fight against his handcuffs.

Amos waits, letting the man tire himself out. When he finally stills, Amos says, 'You didn't much like my work when I was at the Homeland Security Bureau.'

Trevin is sweating, panting from his exertion, but his gaze hardens. 'You were persecuting patriots.'

'I was hunting your friends. I caught a good number of them, too, before you stepped in with your committee investigations of me.'

'You aren't going to get away with this.'

'No? Your militia is going to save you, when they're done tearing down solar panels or some other nonsense? Your wife will ride to your rescue? When she sees the photos of you going up to your suite with a beautiful Indian woman? There are pictures. Damning pictures.' Khoslov takes a sip of his coffee and sets it on the concrete floor. Lights a cigarette, draws on it. 'The cavalry isn't coming, my friend. They don't even know you're gone.'

'What do you want?' Trevin asks.

'I'm supposed to want something?' Amos regards his cigarette smoke as it curls silkily in the yellow light.

'You want a payoff. You want a bribe. Tell me what it is, I'll get it for you.'

'I am not corrupt like your friends. Money does not make me happy.'

'We can work something out.' Trevain struggles again against his bonds. 'You don't need to take your revenge on me.'

'Revenge?' Khoslov frowns. 'But of course you would think that is my obsession. Everything for your kind is teams and tribes. Football teams and political parties all scoring points against each other. No right or wrong, just the winning. Just the beating and hurting of the other side. The revenging!' He draws on his cigarette, exhales. 'Revenging is something for animals. For mobs. I do not do revenging.'

'Then what? What are you doing? What do you want with me?'

'You know, that's a very interesting question.' Amos takes another sip of coffee and replaces the cup on the floor. 'I've asked myself that question ever since I lost my position. What am I doing? What. Am. I. Doing?' He taps his cigarette ash. 'What is a bureaucrat, without a bureau? A crat, I suppose.'

He draws on his cigarette. The tip glows red. 'A simple crat, cratting about. That is me, because I have no bureau anymore. And so here I am, cratting with you. The last of the crats, nearly. You've gotten rid of so many of my cohort. Emptied so many departments. It's a little different this time, though? This conversation, between us. Different than when you sat up high on your committee chair and called me an Enemy of Freedom and broadcast my home address to your followers.'

'I should have had you locked up.'

'There were no laws that would allow it. Not then. I'm sure you've made up a few since, but luckily for me, you took the extra-judicial route. And missed. So.' Amos stubs out his cigarette. 'Here we are.'

'What do you want?'

'Did you know that the clocks on all the government buildings can't show temperature higher than ninety-nine degrees f?'

'So?'

'What sort of person decides to lie about the temperature? What sort of person makes their Weather Service stop reporting temperatures over ninety-nine degrees? I understand the lying about elections. The lying about who gets rich from your tax cuts. The lying about me, even. Why not call me a traitor? I was coming for you, after all. But the temperature?' Khoslov shakes his head. 'Why that?'

'It's hot. Everyone knows it already. It doesn't matter how hot, and people were abusing it for political purposes. It's stupid to worry about something that can't be changed.'

'And something that you cannot see is something you cannot worry about and then you will not even think of changing it. Yes. That makes sense.' Khoslov lights another cigarette. 'Do you know what temperature a cigarette burns at?'

'No.'

'More than ninety-nine degrees?'

Trevin sees what's coming when Khoslov stands. He starts to struggle, but he can't escape. Khoslov wraps an arm around his head, holding him still, and sticks the burning cigarette up Trevin's nose. Flesh sizzles. Trevin yowls. Khoslov wrestles him to stillness, holding him until the burning is done, then tosses away the snotty cigarette and seats himself again.

'Some temperatures are still important, I think.'

Meena opens the door and peers in.

'You okay?'

Trevin's eyes widen with recognition. The girl who gazed up at him with such wide-eyed adoration, who eagerly followed him to his suite, who shyly slipped off her blouse offering herself to him....

She also drugged his champagne, loaded his slumbering weight into a laundry cart, and rolled him out of his hotel, but he was unconscious for all of that, so he only has the more positive memories of her.

'You?' He gawps.

'You've met, of course,' Amos says. 'We're quite all right, my dear. We were discussing temperatures.'

Trevin glares at him, a snake wishing it could bite.

'He's dangerous,' Meena says.

'Quite so. But we have defanged him for the moment.'

'Do you know who you're working for?' Trevin demands.

'What's he talking about?' Meena asks.

'He thinks you work for me,' Amos says.

'Not the other way around?'

'Not in his world.' Amos lights a new cigarette. 'You see, Senator, Meena and I rather serendipitously found one another after one of your purges. Two bits of flotsam floating amongst the wreckage of our shattered agencies. I am the muscle. She is the brains. Well, in truth, she's most of the muscle as well.' He glances over. 'How did you get him into the laundry cart?'

'I put it on its side, and pushed him in sideways. Then I used a broom stick as a lever to get it up on its wheels again.'

'Clever girl.' Amos beams. 'Give a five-foot bureaucrat a lever and she will move the world. Or at least a two-hundred-and-twenty-pound man. In any case, where my associate used to watch warming ocean currents and quickening glacial melt and expanding heat domes, she has now turned her analytical models to political currents and dark money flows and popular sentiments, and surprise surprise, she found you at the beating heart of her models. I will admit, I was not displeased.'

'So you're pissed I got you both fired.'

'He's a simpleton,' Meena says. 'Just melt him and be done with it.'

Trevin jerks upright, his eyes widening. 'What?'

'I've got the chemicals,' Meena continues. 'There won't be any trace. I've got other people on my list. We can use someone else.'

'What the fuck are you talking about?'

Khoslov gives him a jaundiced smile. 'Chemistry, Senator. We're talking about chemistry. If the chemistry between us isn't constructive, then the chemistry that dissolves flesh into pink froth is the other option.'

Trevin wilts. 'What do you want?'

Meena holds up his confiscated phone. 'Your cellphone passwords. Your bank passwords. Your bitcoin wallet. Your Signal password. Your socials. We'll go from there.'

'The hell I will.'

Meena shrugs and turns for the door. 'I'll get the buckets.'

'Wait, goddamnit! Wait!'

Meena pauses. Khoslov quirks an eyebrow. 'Yes?'

'You'll let me go, if I give you what you want?'

'Of course,' Khoslov says. 'We're bureaucrats, not natural born killers. Well,' he amends. 'Meena isn't. She's still learning.'

And so Trevin begins to sing. Meena takes down his information.

'This will take a few minutes to check,' she says.

The door closes behind her, leaving them alone once more in the mildew yellow light. The air conditioner wheezes. It's an old unit, clogged from years of use. Khoslov stole it from upstairs, during his early rampages, when he was gathering the debris that would eventually fill the stairwells and the hallway. Meena called it his 'fort-building' stage, as if he were six years old, and building with blankets. Amos appreciated the image. The childish joy of the project.

Trevin shivers in the chill. Amos stares up at the shadowy ceiling, smoking, watching how the smoke rises and casts its own shadows.

'You can't think you're really going to get away with this,' Trevin says.

'No?'

'What you're doing is a crime.'

'A crime. Yes. You have me there. I am certainly a criminal. Though I used to do the same thing for the Department, and then it was not so much a crime, so?' Amos shrugs. 'I sometimes get confused. A crat without a bureau is bound to become confused. No boss to help me distinguish right from wrong.' He pauses, considering. 'It is interesting, though, that I am the criminal, and you are the Senator.'

'I don't think it's that interesting.'

'In my homeland, you would certainly be the criminal. A man who uses his television show to sow suspicion between people, and make them rise against each other? A man who whips up his own militias?' He shakes his head. 'We would have sent you to Siberia by now. Or poisoned you. You would not be allowed to exist.'

'I guess I'm lucky I don't live in a dictatorship.'

Khoslov looks up sharply. 'We are all lucky not to live in a dictatorship.'

He draws hard on his cigarette. 'It's confusing to me, though. That a place as terrifying as my homeland seems almost sane when it comes to rabble-rousers like you. But a so-called civilised democracy like this is crazy enough to let you thrive. Every day on your television show. Every day making speeches about how these Americans are enemies, and these other Americans are traitors, and how these other ones can only take your guns from your cold dead hands. Talking revolution.' He sighs. 'You make money and get votes by making Americans hate other Americans. It makes me think that I am still too foreign for this country. I love it, but I do not understand it. I do not understand how a country can thrive if its leaders are allowed to make its people hate one another.'

Meena returns.

'How are we doing?'

'It checks out. We have his bitcoin. I have copies of his socials and his networks and all his contacts and texts and emails. There are some new things, but mostly, he's the kind of slime you'd expect. A little cliche, really.' She holds up Trevin's phone, with a photo on the screen of a young woman. 'He buys a lot of girls, and he has a lot of offshore accounts that keep getting topped up by…. Well, I'm sure he'll tell us.' She sighs. 'I don't know what's more disappointing. That his votes are for sale, or that the only thing people will care about is how young these girls are.'

Trevin says nothing, but his eyes dart about.

'Young enough, it seems,' Amos says.

'Young enough.'

'Well,' Amos hauls himself to his feet, stifling a groan as his joints protest. 'It seems our meeting is concluded, Senator. You should expect that we'll be in touch. We'll have occasional requests of you. A vote here. A speech there. Not onerous, but still, important. And, of course, you'll speak with no one of our encounter. I hope you don't mind a blindfold as you leave. It seems nicer than drugging you again.'

———

A week later, Amos and Meena are sharing Sichuanese takeout on the card table in their office. Her laptop beeps.

She glances at the screen. Frowns. 'I told you he'd rat.'

Khoslov sighs. 'We are in the redemption business. We have to give them a chance.'

A few nights later, Trevin enters a penthouse hotel room in Miami and discovers Khoslov waiting, a rumpled shadow in an armchair next to the floor-to-ceiling windows. Trevin plays it cool. He's big, younger and stronger than Khoslov. And he has a gun.

Of course he has a gun. Meena took one off him when she kidnapped him the last time, but he has another. A flat black thing, very light, plastic. One of the kind that goes through security without raising alarms.

'I thought you'd be showing up,' Trevin says.

'Don't shoot.' Amos holds up his hands. 'I only want to talk.' He indicates a pair of glasses filled with scotch, on the table beside him. 'I raided your mini-bar. I thought we might drink together.'

'So you can drug me again?' Trevin shakes his head.

'Then may I? I have a bit of a thirst.'

'Do what you want. We don't have anything to talk about.' Trevin stays well away from Khoslov, scanning the room. He goes to the bathroom, peers in while keeping Khoslov covered.

'I paid your pretty Cuban friend to leave,' Amos says. 'Don't worry, I tipped her.'

'Where's the other one?'

'Meena?' Khoslov shrugs. 'Oh, she doesn't believe in talking.'

'Too bad. I was looking forward to teaching her a lesson.' Trevin digs his phone out of his pocket and dials one-handed. Speaks without taking his eyes off Amos. 'Khoslov's here. I've got him covered. Send the agents.' He gives the room number.

Khoslov stares out the fancy windows. There's a hurricane boiling on the horizon. Lightning forms a backdrop to the lights of the city and the marinas. The hotel is designed to withstand extraordinary natural forces, but ultimately, it's doomed. No building so close to the ocean will survive. Not when the construction was built without consideration of sea level rise. It's like the clocks. Politicians meddling. Making it hard to see. Making it hard to plan. It's interesting to Khoslov, to sit in a doomed building that doesn't understand it's doomed. An edifice blind to its danger.

Trevin edges back, keeping well clear. 'I've got agents on the way. They know all about you.'

'Meena thought we should just get rid of you,' Khoslov says. 'But I thought we could steer you in a more positive direction. I'm old. I see more shades of gray than she does. I thought perhaps that you might seize the chance to reform yourself. That you might stop trying so hard to make your government so blind, so incompetent. But then you voted for another tax cut, and gutted the... what was it this time? The one that inspects meat?'

'USDA.'

'I'm sure I'll find a donation from a meat processor in your offshore banks.'

'I changed banks.'

'Ah. Wise decision.' Khoslov finishes his first scotch and motions to the second. 'Do you mind?'

'Do what you want.'

'I do not know a country that thrives when its government is blind and stupid and incompetent. Do you?'

'I can't wait to see you in prison.'

'I'm surprised you don't just shoot me.'

'You'd like that, wouldn't you? Your girl is probably out there planning to frame me. Put me in the headlines.'

'I thought you liked headlines. The young patriot shoots the old bureaucrat. Freedom wins! It would be, as they say, "on brand" for you.'

'You have no idea what my "brand" is.'

'No? It would go along with your show trials and "investigations" into your government and its employees. You like breaking everything else in your government. Why not break me? I'm sure it would make you a hero to your followers.'

'Because I'm not going to play into whatever Deep State Strikes Back game you're playing here.'

'The deep state? Me?' Khoslov laughs. 'More like the shallow state. The empty dry and hollow state.' He holds up his hands, well, one hand, the other raises his scotch, sloshing. 'I surrender. You have me. The old man with the weak bladder and the arthritis. The crat without a bureau. The dinosaur without the sense to lie down and become a fossil.' He snorts. 'Such bullshit. You speak such bullshit.'

'And yet I keep finding people like you trying to obstruct me.'

'Who is that? Smart people? Skilled people? People who believe in doing an honest job? I'm surprised you have no fear of the FBI. All your sex scandals and bribes. Apparently some agencies are less "deep state" than others.'

'I have friends there.'

'You have appointees. That's different than friends. Meena is my friend.'

'Where is she, anyway?'

Khoslov grins. 'She scares you, doesn't she?'

'No. I'll get her, too. Just like you.'

'Maybe. Maybe not. She's younger than I am. Quicker.' He considers. 'Smarter too. Less inclined to think well of bad people. I thought you were only greedy, but Meena thinks you just like to break things. I do not understand this. The breaking. As if your only goal is to make your country stupid.'

'Because I investigate corruption? Because I find the truth about people like you?'

'You aren't on your television program, there is no need to pretend.'

'Real Americans understand that I'm saving America, and that's why I keep getting re-elected. I'm standing up for freedom.'

'Ah. Standing up for freedom. Yes. That is attractive.' Amos swirls his scotch. 'You may not believe me, but I, too, believe in freedom.'

Trevin snorts.

'It's true. My homeland was a terrifying place. It was not free. Secret police. A leader who inflicted fear with his whims. We were not free, of a certainty. So I know the value of freedom. But I think you have spent so long being spoiled that you do not know what "not freedom" is. You think any small inconvenience is a boot on your neck. Sea levels are rising, but you want to drive a big American truck. So, no more studying sea levels. Fire the scientists who study such things. Make laws against making laws that plan for your shoreline disappearing. And because of this, in twenty years, or thirty—probably not fifty—this hotel will fall down. How is a hotel that falls down freedom?'

'Freedom means not having to ask permission from the

government to do what you want. It's that simple.'

'That is indeed very simple.' Amos toasts Trevin. 'So why hide the temperature? Why hide the sea levels? Do what you like. Drive your trucks. Have your freedom. Build your bad buildings. Why this strange blindfolding? Surely it is better to know—'

'Because it's all lies! You're making it all up!'

'The thermometer is making things up?'

Trevin points his gun at Amos. 'Shut up, Khoslov. Just shut the fuck up.'

'You like to make people shut up. Maybe that is your brand.'

'I'm warning you.' Trevin peers out the room's peephole, looking for his backup. 'Don't make me shoot your kneecaps off.'

'And now the threat of violence. Like a child throwing a tantrum because his mother has warned him that the knife is sharp. Wouldn't you rather have an intelligent country? A skilled country? Wouldn't you rather know that the knife is sharp and take heed?'

'I told you to shut up.'

'I'm not your bureaucrat anymore. I'm just a crat. I don't have to shut up anymore.' Amos drains his scotch. 'Where are your men with guns? Shouldn't they be here by now?'

———

When it's done, Khoslov calls Meena.

'What took you so long?' she demands.

'It's nice to hear you worry for me.'

He looks both ways, then crosses the street with the light, leaving behind the hotel and the arriving black SUVs with their sirens and red-and-blue strobes.

'Don't flatter yourself.' Then, a minute later, unwillingly, 'Are you okay?'

Amos smiles, secretly pleased at her concern, that he will be missed when he is eventually gone. 'I am fine. As in all his dealings, Trevin was blind to the value of skill and experience. His gun made him very confident.'

'I kept expecting to hear from you. I ran out of false alarms to call in.'

'I am sorry you worried.' Amos glances behind himself as he makes his way up the street. 'The security teams have only just arrived. I left the hard drives and the photos for them to find. Trevin's sordid pastimes should discourage his friends from pressing for an investigation.'

'And Trevin?'

'The shower drain is very clean.'

'Are you up for more travel?'

'You have another name?' Amos looks up at the night sky. Rain is starting to fall. Fat drops spilling from the bellies of the roiling hurricane clouds. 'There is a storm here.'

'There are storms everywhere. I think I can get you a flight out.'

'Where this time?'

'Houston. A woman who funds privatisation campaigns. No better than Trevin. Maybe worse. Offshore oil money. Tax dodges everywhere. She was sending Trevin a lot of bitcoin. I want to see her finances.'

'Maybe she will see the error of her ways.'

'Let's not hold our breath.'

'You are too cynical. Change is always possible.'

'I'll mention that to my therapist. Should I book the flight?'

'To Texas.'

'Heartland of freedom.'

'I will buy a cowboy hat.'

Naked Earth

Eugen Bacon

Naeema's sky is falling. Her universe is split into embracing and unshackling, and everywhere is scorching. Privilege is synonymous with who leads or who sponsors. And, right now, with the lefties and right wingers disconcerting the undecided with formation/misinformation, the world is more than random.

She once learnt to tell embracers from the unshackled by the bracelets they wear or don't. Embracers brandish luminescent bracelets shimmering with kilojoules from yoga, sex or the simple act of walking home from an embrace-friendly workplace. Each bracelet transmits kilowatts to a recycling tower that helps save the planet.

The unshackled eat as they like, and wave bare arms as they jog on treadmills or in parks, dripping sweat on rubber mats, naked earth or non-embrace towels.

The undecideds wear blank amulets that sell dear and state nothing, but they incur hefty insurance premiums that are compulsory to renew.

But nothing is black or white because, in the midst of all this dichotomy, are conservatives, moderates and progressives.

———

The undecideds make things difficult, for instance on matters of jury selection, especially in trials where the alleged victim and perpetrator are on either side of belief. The O. Nucks case was one such conundrum—people still brawl about the not guilty verdict where guilt stood right there in the jury's faces.

Turns out it's a frequent occurrence that some undecideds firm their belief towards embracement or unshacklement mid-trial, swinging verdicts, or leading to mis-trials.

Naeema's indecision is not out of choice but from necessity.

———

As a child, she never questioned when Ma recycled Brian's nappies in embrace bins that a swirly ball in the sky—all clean energy—fortnightly collected. Naeema wished every birthday that she'd unwrap an embrace bracelet that put her on par with her parents, but it never happened.

'We want you to decide for yourself when you're older,' Pa said the one time Naeema threw a tantrum over the matter.

Ma glowered in the way she did to say the matter was *not closed*.

Naeema learned as early as kinder that being undecided was not safe. Both embracers and the unshackled bullied the heck out of her because she was seemingly the only undecided kid in the whole class. The teacher divvied up seating in columns of embracers and unshackled, and Naeema sat alone and shunned at a corner in the back.

At primary school, still undecided, she discovered that, no matter how hard she worked, her grades got no better than a C minus. If the teacher was an embracer, students that were embracers scored distinctions. If the teacher was unshackled, students that were unshackled scored distinctions. Not a single teacher was undecided, so Naeema was pretty much fucked.

———

Jezza was Naeema's first kiss at high school. Jezza walked loose and relaxed, smoked ciggies and said, 'Too easy,' to everything. She rolled hand-made tobacco, not clean energy vapes from embrace franchises. Jezza was the kind of girl Naeema thought of as a hippie. They were washing hands in the girls' toilet at recess when Jezza locked eyes with Naeema across the mirror.

Their kiss put custard in Naeema's knees. She felt safe and lost.

The affection and euphoria she felt inside the wintergreen taste of Jezza's tobacco on her tongue was enough for Naeema to declare herself capable of decision-making.

She was thinking about the crazy tantric shit with Jezza—it was like bees making honey on her body and she buzzed and stung all over for days on end—when she firmly declared at the dinner table, 'I'm unshackled.'

Brian burst out into an annoying chortling laugh.

'I don't know what's the big deal,' said Naeema. 'I'm a free spirit.'

'Tell that to your kids when you murder their world,' said Brian.

Ma and Pa never stopped eating. They never looked at her once. It was as if she'd never spoken. But in the kitchen as she topped the recycler, Pa laid a hand on her shoulder, and it spoke *volumes*. For the first time in her life, Naeema wondered, truly wondered, how much of an embracer Pa was, and whether he was secretly unshackled or something moderate.

———

The diversity question in official forms was not about racial, sexual or religious slanting but about embracing and unshackling. She learnt the hard way that ticking unshackled cost her eligibility to government FEE-HELP for uni, because the prime minister was an embracer. Ticking embracer lost Naeema a diversity scholarship to a private college because the funding body was unshackled.

Several times in her life Naeema underwent metamorphosis as she figured herself out, tried to manage, or was simply getting over Jezza and her plaited braids gone gallivanting with a backpack across the world.

———

The term 'better half' or 'other half' took on new significance for intermarried couples. Those who survived found synergy in their differences. Others took matters into their own hands, and divorce was not always the positive outcome, as happened in the O. Nucks case.

Introducing digital passports compelled choice. But one could stay 'undecided'—the least favourable option with the mandatory insurance premium so costly to annually renew. The undecideds also incurred a 3.25% surcharge on everything: education, recreation venues, visa applications, cafés, restaurants, pharmacies and surgery.

———

Naeema met Ponty who was a footy player and kicked a ripper. He knew exactly where the ball would go and was a premiership player whose team was a household name. He was totally an embracer and recycled the kinetics of his athleticism into a bracelet.

But already Naeema was fighting with him about collecting their orgasms.

'It kills the moment,' she cried and refused to have sex with him. 'Abstinence is better.' What was the point of sustainable sex that saved the planet if a bracelet gobbled up her oxytocin, dopamine, serotonin? Rather than a floating pleasure that rushed her head— like she felt with Jezza—all she worried about now was how many kilojoules were going into the damn bracelet. She wanted to feel fullness, the kind that came with a giddy tornado that stretched and warmed, almost painful yet so sweet. She wanted to feel under-water and gasping, yet in the clouds and wallowed in sweet velvet, the way it was when her legs entwined with Jezza's.

'What does that *even mean*?' laughed Ponty when she tried to explain why they should try intercourse without him wearing his bracelet.

She gave it a good go: embrace lotions, embrace-friendly eggs, nuts, seeds, cocoa, lip balm, even an embrace apartment with its recycled clean energy. She tolerated a bit more sex with Ponty though it left her feeling like someone had died.

Then came elections and embracers and the unshackled hated

each other all the way to the dark web, and Naeema realised it was safer to stay undecided. She learnt to use benign phrases like, 'It's a coloured topic,' or 'It's a matter of growth curvature,' when someone pointed at her bland bracelet and demanded she pick a side.

———

Now Naeema's sky is falling because she doesn't feel love or hate. She misses what she had with Jezza and misses Ponty's good intentions. In truth she does love them both in their own way. She adores her parents and her brother Brian—who now works as a sustainable ambassador.

Brian sells 'guaranteed embracement' in aged care homes, emergency wards and palliative care facilities, handing out embrace bracelets in hushed wards. He speaks to relatives in sterile corridors, waiting rooms or chapels as they light candles and pray for their loved ones' speedy recovery. The brochures he hands out have words like 'moral compass', 'a new era of seeing the invisible', 'having true heart to save the planet'.

He's wildly successful in convincing patients to see the better future they are creating with their sacrifice, as the bracelet glows to take their death rattle. Sometimes Naeema ponders how quickly the dying die when they wear embrace bracelets. She wonders if it's the bracelet, or the peace of wearing it, that intensifies the dying in souls that might otherwise linger.

Naeema still wears a blank amulet that states nothing. It's a gamble that leaves her vulnerable, feeling like a migrant or a refugee, never quite belonging. On the plus side, it comes with a degree of flexibility on the job market. Being undecided means she's still figuring things out, so she can trial embracer or unshackler jobs, but only as a temp or on short contracts, never as a permanent staffer.

Her life has no Jezza or Ponty, and maybe she's dead to Ma and Brian.

Pa, like Jezza, one day upped and walked out with a rucksack, all the way to humanitarian work. He writes to her sometimes from a mission church, school or hospital in a place called Kitwe somewhere in Zambia or Uganda—he's never specific, but sounds in a good place, perhaps physically.

Sometimes Naeema uses embrace lotions and aromatics, and sometimes she temps as an embrace angel or a sustainable ambassador like Brian. She even rides the swirly recycler ball across the skies on contract. She rolls a joint every now and then and it takes her to the buzz she felt wrapped around Jezza.

She doesn't like beef, and that's that, but she can't be vegan or whatever because she loves chicken. If she were mortally wounded, heck, yeah, she'd totally wear an embrace bracelet, there's no doubt about that. Because deep down she's a well-meaning person who wants to save the planet.

But she's not a leftie or a right winger, and she doesn't mind the free spirited or the climate committed. She rides hoverboards because she can't afford a car, so it's not about clean energy. She feels like she's waiting with her eyes shut for someone to destroy her fears. Or perhaps her wait is for history to pattern itself into the poetics of a last crusade. She just wants to survive now because her life is now. She can only hope that—kilojoules or not—the world might become less of a mess.

What she knows is that her body is not full of pebbles and scales.

She doesn't want to become a stone like her brother Brian. Dead to what it means, really means, to be human inside, animating only for a cause. History is full of contradictions, and she might watch it with irony, unsettlement, even awe. But she doesn't want her children to grow up in the languor of pale dirt country. She wants them to see a world that's a bloody beauty, and safe—something she worries that the unshackled in their denials of entanglement and responsibility might not understand. Hers is a critical distance that carries doubt and grief for a future that is closing. It's an all-language that is no language in a world so starkly divided.

The water is changing hands—on the first sip, you know. A melon is not a lemon, even though they both have a long finish, and the same letters are shifting. She makes a choice to be less random, not undecided. To find a space of transition that is both human and saving, like Pa.

She doesn't have all the answers now.

But this is a start.

The Flair

Nick Mamatas

The Light Brigade has a flair for the dramatic, or at least the absurd. What I can tell you is that they're located somewhere on the Western end of the Great Basin, in California, and that I drove to meet them in a car I rented at what's left of the Reno-Tahoe International Airport. Ten flights daily, and on Sundays, eleven, that one being quick hop to Vancouver just to hang on to the name 'international.' Do not recommend. I traveled north, in the early evening, when the temperature was bearable, but not so cold I'd need to heat the car and waste precious juice. There were no charging stations once I passed Pyramid Lake, but the Brigade promised that they already had power sufficient to recharge my Model T.

They also promised that I would instantly know where to pull off the highway, and pick up my liaison, and they were right. Desert roads are always lonely, and when the sun finished its descent, the only light came from a failing Beekyn™ low-orbit billboard, and my ride's headlamps. There were not even any animals prowling the bush near the highway, no quick flashes of glowing eyes, no glints of tracker collars in the shadows, nothing suddenly there and then gone in a blink both literal and figurative. Just brush, and a low sky like black slate.

There was, however, on the shoulder of the road, a circus clown, complete with red nose, great flipper shoes, and a comically over-sized hitchhiker's thumb. She wore a pair of reflective yellow genie pants, a floofy-sleeved crop top just as vibrant, and a single red rose upon her left breast. The clown's hair was pale blue and pink and pointed straight up, a bit like the flame from a gas burner turned all the way up.

'Going my way?' I asked. She ducked and entered the car head first, like an animal or at least someone unused to being a passenger in anything smaller than a bus. I almost ate a mouthful of her cotton-candy colored hair; it was stiff, coated in dried glue. 'Quit clownin' around, Funny Face.'

'Honk honk,' she said as she squeezed her funny nose. It was half-broken and sounded like a wounded animal, but she did her best to compensate. Broken animals, but trying our best. That's what life has been for the past fifteen years.

The Light Brigade had invited me out to their secret head-quarters to witness and write about the launch of their homebrew laser satellite. Just two years ago, the Brigade had created and uploaded open-source plans for the improvement of your backyard photovoltaic receivers to convert solar-powered laser energy into good ol' DC electricity. It was a provocative move by this assemblage of hackers, engineers—and from the looks of the clown—underemployed performance artists. Especially provoca-tive since there was, and is, nothing for photovoltaic receivers to collect that isn't just coming from the sun already.

Solar power satellites have been on the drawing boards—and some of the most hopeful PowerPoint slide presentations ever created—for almost seventy years. Indeed, there are a handful of microwave-transmitting satellites in orbit right now, but they're not pointed toward the Earth. Instead, they are oriented toward the four Lóng Wáng weapons platforms floating 35,000 kilometers overhead to keep them powered up and ever ready for war.

But that, the Light Brigade wants you to know, is going to change.

We didn't travel much more than a mile before the clown, whose clown name was Elektra, told me to pull over, and get out of the car. She pointed her novelty thumb at me, then dug it into my ribs as if it were a pistol, and she a mobster. It was fine, all part of our agreement. The night was frigid, but it's the kind of cold that's a relief, like walking by the open door of the store you could never afford to enter on a freelance journalist's salary. She kept me waiting outside where I took nips now and again from my flask, while she programmed a new route into the car's navigation system, then stepped back out and said, 'Want to sniff my flower?' Before I could even say yes, it squirted and something sticky that smells of lavender hit me full on in the face.

I woke up, still blindfolded, still in the passenger seat of my car, but definitely off-road. A hard jostle sent my head up to the roof. I nearly lost consciousness a second time.

'Easy,' said Elektra. 'We're close to the shanzhai.' I was intrigued to hear that bit of Mandarin. It meant she trusted me. Shanzhai, distant strongholds beyond the reach of the emperor in ancient times. Shanzhai, bandit bands resisting centralised power in the merely pre-modern era. Shanzhai, underground non-hierarchal factories for knock-off cell phones with extra features, and Spider-Man action figures in turquoise and purple instead of red and blue, in the recent past. And today, shanzhai means all those things and something more.

I had a million questions, but I wasn't going to ask them while blindfolded. It was another thirty minutes, perhaps, before we pulled up to the shanzhai. 'Stay in the car for one minute, please,' the clown said. She stepped out and closed the door. I could hear other people milling around, and they made me wait for much longer than a minute, but finally the passenger door opened, a man's hand pressed against my chest, and he told me, 'One sec.' He took off my blindfold, then stepped back and said, 'Get out.' There were six of them, including my chauffer. They introduced themselves, a couple shared their pronouns and one a brief list of headmates. Only the clown, and a woman with whom she was now holding hands, said, 'Welcome to the Light Brigade. We launch at dawn.' They spoke in an eerie, practiced harmony, like creepy twins in a movie, then broke into laughter.

The Brigade's rules were simple. No photos. No extensive physical descriptions. They let me know that none of the communicative tech I might have, including my watch, would work out wherever they were. I could only talk to the clown, her girlfriend, and one fellow who agreed to answer questions if I addressed them just to him, and 'if they were sensible.' There had been a vote about my presence here, and it was a tie, so everybody won. According to half the shanzhai, I wasn't there.

'So, why a clown suit?' I asked over a meal of grilled growmeats and pine nut soup. We were sitting outside, atop military surplus sleeping bags, on the iced-over floor of the desert. I wasn't allowed inside any of the structures, but I am allowed to say that they appeared to be hoop houses, with opaque plastic canvases stretched over the frames.

'We needed helium,' said Elektra the clown. She casually confessed to a series of crimes involving an illicit helium-smuggling ring that caters to the more nostalgic members of the ultra-rich for their children's birthday parties, her infiltration of the same, and a sudden and perhaps violent hijacking of a truck of canisters. Her girlfriend rubbed her back as she spoke of brandishing a firearm, how she convinced the truck driver that helium was as flammable as hydrogen through sheer force of will, and what a challenge it was unloading the truck in a safehouse, and then slowly transporting the canisters in ones and twos to this location.

'I kept the suit because I knew you'd stop for it,' she finished. 'Who could resist?'

'Nobody can resist,' said the clown's girlfriend

Elektra had told me much about the plans of the Light Brigade, just from sharing that one anecdote. The Brigade would not be launching a microwave-transmitting satellite. These six people were likely the whole of the organisation. There was no broad movement, no multinational organisation stealing and smuggling, borrowing and building, to create the means to provide free power to the masses.

'May I see your rockoon?' I asked.

'Yes!' said the girlfriend. 'You can call me, uhm, Robin, by the way.'

'Tracy,' said Elektra, who finally took off her large wig, then plucked off her nose and tossed it into the wig's cap. The other person who agreed to speak to me only if I asked sensible questions identified himself as 'Lee', though as Lee was the one with the headmates I knew that agreement might be altered at any moment. It was like that.

Rockoon is a portmanteau of 'rocket' and 'balloon'—a twentieth-century technology, obsolete for a full century. A balloon hoists the rocket up into the upper atmosphere, then the engine ignites and the rocket, usually a solid-fuel number, can get even higher without needing all that much fuel. In the 1940s, rockoons were used for atmospheric and meteorological study, but were quickly superseded by liquid fuels and rockets capable of reaching orbit from the ground. Rockoons were still technically useful, but the missile is synechdochic of war. Even when there was no possible worry that an upper-atmosphere mission would be targeted by an enemy, the very fact that rockoons seemed easy to shoot down was enough to mothball the inexpensive, flexible technology.

Tracy and Robin were happy to show off the disused Minuteman silo. The moon was new and, for obvious reasons, the Light Brigade kept its work areas dark. 'We're not worried about the police, per se,' Robin explained as we picked our way through the bush led by nothing but the lights on our wristwatches. My little ball of light found a scorpion on the desert floor. It didn't scuttle away or flex its tail, and I too found myself frozen, both terrified and feeling the cold of the night air for the first time. Tracy knocked the arachnid away with her oversized shoe.

'Be careful,' she said, but she wasn't talking about the scorpion.

Not a minute later, both women grabbed my forearms and kept me from taking a fatal step down the concrete tunnel they were leading me to. The silo wasn't capped, and the rocket, sans nosecone, was much smaller than the Minuteman for which it was originally designed. There was a low concrete building on the far side of the lip of the silo, but it was dark enough and I'd been focused enough on where I'd been stepping that I hadn't noticed it at all.

They wouldn't talk about the missile very much, except to say that it was a solid-propellant rocket and that its fuel was 'environmentally friendly' hexanitrohexaazaisowurtzitane—a word that danced on their tongues even through their giggles, but that utterly confused my transcription software. More importantly, and why this fuel was used during the Strait Conflict, is that hexanitrohexaazaisowurtzitane-burning rockets don't leave much of a visible trail.

I realised the ladies could toss me into the hole. They both had strong grips on my arms. This wouldn't be the first bunch of hackers, or makers, or burners, or postrats, or socialists, or whatever the Light Brigade was hoping to become out here in the Great Basin to simply devolve into madness.

'It's... a good one,' I said, idiotically. 'Not that I've seen too many up close. The balloon? The satellite?' My clever idea was to give them a reason to lead me away from the silo rather than chuck me down into it for whatever blood-baptism they thought would help the mission.

'We'll show you everything, except that which cannot be shown,' Tracy said. Robin giggled at that. None of this was helping. Except for the small cement pillbox structure by the silo, there didn't seem to be any other buildings around. Their grips didn't lighten up as they led me off into the night, like two prison guards bringing a drunk to a holding cell. I *was* a little tipsy.

Robin began making an unusual clicking noise with her tongue and cheeks. I opened my mouth to say something, but Tracy put a gloved finger to my lips. They stepped lightly, and I aped their tentative shuffling, thanks only partially to the hold they had on my arms. The beam of watch light passed over something and vanished into it. Then Robin disappeared for a moment, only to come back, holding the night in her hands, and directing my attention to a flight of cement steps going underground.

'Hyperblack,' I said. 'You were... echolocating?'

'Drones are everywhere, and satellites too,' said Tracy as she nudged me onto the top step.

Satellites *are* everywhere. There's one in this subterranean warehouse into which I walked alone at Tracy and Robin's urging. It was not quite as dark as the hyperblack tarps topside, but it was pretty dim. Lee, the third member of the shanzhai who deigned to speak to me, sparked an old-fashioned cigarette lighter perhaps ten yards away. Everything from his eyeglasses to the size of the room was bigger than I imagined it could possibly be, except for the satellite itself. He wouldn't show me the whole thing at once, but casually walked a tight circle around an object roughly the size and shape of a very nice propane gas grill of the sort your parents might have once owned. It's the kind of thing you might look at and be compelled to say 'What a beaut!' and then offer a pull from a flask, but I resisted. I should not have.

'This is just the laser,' Lee explained. His eyes were obscured by the triple refraction of the firelight in the lenses of his spectacles. A few more watts and he'd be the one shooting lasers. 'Diode pump, alkali. We get potash from the desert.'

'How do you know it works?' I asked. 'How do you know any of it works? The laser, the satellite, the rockoon?'

'Why are you asking me?' Lee said. 'Because you think I am a man? Examine your biases, madame!' He extinguished the lighter with the top of his thumb. Somewhere behind, and above me, a clown nose honked. For a second after that, I didn't hear the echo-locational clicking behind me.

————

Journalists say, or they used to say, 'Don't bury the lede,' but I have done just that. I simply wasn't expecting the story I ended up living through. Here's the lede:

Fifteen years ago, third-party transnational belligerents used laser satellites in low-Earth orbit to attack both Chinese and NATO positions along the Taiwan Strait during the Second Battle of the Davis Line.

And now, the nut graf:

The satellites existed in multiple sweet spots: their orbits were too high for anti-aircraft fire or drones to take out, too low for the orbital platforms to target without possibly striking their own forces on the ground; they were big enough to pump out lasers capable of melting flight decks and combusting individual sailors unfortunate enough to be standing in the wrong place, too small to be spotted amidst all the other war-junk in the skies until they warmed up and started firing. Deadly enough that both sides scored propaganda victories by blaming the other for violations of the laws of war; insufficiently destructive to be anything more than a political anomaly after the fact.

Ten fatalities, dozens of casualties, mostly blindness and other vision impairments, some second- and third-degree burns. A single human pictogram in the infographic detailing the carnage of the battle, made special by the asterisk explaining what had happened.

The simple collapse of the world petroleum supply brought both sides to the negotiating table soon enough, and with the Treaty of Taipei, a significant population exchange, and the launch of Lóng Wáng, the peace of pure exhaustion settled upon the world.

But not here in the California Great Basin. I'd asked Lee one further question—'Could this be weaponised?' and then I got a whiff of Tracy's clown flower and fell down, then woke up, just before dawn, in my car, and not where I'd left it parked on the grounds of the Light Brigade. The car's controls had been locked and my hands cuffed behind my back. I didn't *think* they'd knocked me out, stuffed me into my ride, and programmed it to make a sharp right turn into a desert so that I could be cooked like a potato and die. I thought I was going back to the airport. The cuffs, I guessed, were the typical police-issue that any security guard with a universal key could unlock for me after I rolled up to the parking lot attendant's little box.

Probably, and as a bonus, I was going to need to pee before the car got me to my destination though.

J-school 101: start with softball questions, as the source might wig out, or just end the interview, if you begin with provocations.

But I was thinking of this article as a puff piece more than anything else—check out the product and the personalities, throw in a charming anecdote or two, and post.

The fact is that there's never been a decent business case for peaceful laser-transmitting solar-powered satellites. Historically, they don't collect enough extra solar radiation to make it profitable to build, launch, and maintain them, no matter how dark the black one paints their solar panels, no matter how much helium one steals from the children of billionaires. In our post-oil 19°C global average temp era, when a cloudy day is practically an ecumenical holiday and cheap and shiny photovoltaic collectors fill the parking lots of most defunct strip malls, there's just no profit to be had. The only laser-transmitting satellites that have *ever* been commercially deployed were used for space-to-space communication, or wide-scale high-detail mapping.

Those, and the Davis Line direct-energy weapons fifteen years ago.

———

The sun begins to bubble up on the horizon. In my rear view mirror I see a black ball dragging a grey arrow up into the sky, and tell the mirror to start recording. If I'm a war reporter now, I might as well get some good visuals.

From the Model T's tiny hatch, I hear a voice say, 'Oh good, you're awake.' Tracy kicks out the armrest between the rear seats and unfolds herself, legs first, out of the trunk, then slithers into the front passenger seat. 'Sorry, there was a coup.' She glances down at my wrists. 'Ah, handcuffs. Also, they're after us by now, probably.'

'You, uh—' I start.

'I am a legitimate master of the circus arts,' Tracy says.

'Who is after us?' I say. There's a lot to know now. 'Who? What? When?' Journalism is inscribed upon my nervous system. 'Robin?'

'The investors,' Tracy says. 'Not all of them of course. We raised funds to buy the silo via the blockchain, so most of the people funding the project know little more about it than 'solar-ready real estate, guaranteed 20 percent return.' And no, not Robin. They— our three onsite investor ombudsfolx—tied us both up and went to get you. Robin and I have built up a tolerance to the spray. They knocked Lee out with it though. There's not much to do in the desert, so Robin taught one of the investors how to echolocate. Sorry. Also I talk a lot when I'm with a new person, sorry about that too.'

'Where? Why? How?' I should be clearer but I'm too confused to make my questions specific. *How did you escape?* is answered wordlessly as Tracy picks the lock on my cuffs with a paperclip. *Where were she and Robin locked up?* hardly matters. Tracy probably just shimmied out of whatever they'd bound her with.

Why? is a bigger question.

'Light Brigade really isn't a weapons project, I promise. It's just, you know...' Tracy says before trailing off. Her face is as red as the desert twilight.

'We're going all the way to the airport unless you can pick the ignition or the door locks,' I say. 'So, just start from the beginning.'

'How do you prove to people that your laser-transmitting solar powered satellite actually works if all it does is give randomly placed receptors a third more juice now and then? It's proof of concept. We need dozens of them in sun-synchronous orbits—'

'So, blow something up just once, for some venture capital funding? Flair for the dramatic?'

'Well...'

'Ah, no.' I realise the truth of the business model. *Blow something up whenever one of the investors* wants *something blown up.* Pollution-free, efficient energy 95 percent of the time to pay fixed costs, and a profit center in privatised war. Not dramatic, absurd.

'And why me?' In the rear view mirror, the rocket ignited and took off, a star in a quickly fading star-filled sky.

'It's mostly the car...' Tracy says, 'because it's easy to track. But, you know...' She waved a hand. Her fingers were very long and thin. 'People hate journalists, and, uh, ending one would make worldwide news. PR. I am Light Brigade's publicity person, but my idea was just to bring in a journalist, not to...'

'People hate mimes too,' I find myself saying.

'I am a clown, and we're not going to—' Her gaze flicks toward the rear view. It's rare to see a big ol' gasser car on the highways anymore, since there are few operational gas stations, but a fast Ford-350 pickup is bearing down on us.

'Is that an ombudsperson's car?'

'It is,' Tracy says. 'They probably figured out that I escaped with you.'

'So, how do we stop the car? *Can* you pick the ignition like the cuffs?'

'Pick,' says Tracy slowly, 'the ignition. Of course not. You have to *hack* these things, and I can't. I came here to get out and get you out the second the car stops in the airport lot.' She shrugs, exaggerated, a stage performer who can't resist an audience. 'They want witnesses, maybe a terror angle to make sure you're on the news.'

It's up to me to stop the car. At least I have my hands now. Of course there's the issue of the pickup truck on our tail. Circus arts are powerless, and I'm no techie. What can journalists do except watch and write about what they saw for pennies?

Ah, watch. Ah, pennies. We drove far enough that my watch is in contact with the rest of the world again. I take it off. 'Put on your seat belt,' I tell Tracy, as I put on mine.

I hand Tracy my watch and tell her to log in under her own account and report the Model T we're in for drunk driving and drunk riding. Her fingers are nimble, she does it in the few seconds it takes for me to dig my flask out of my pocket. The interior turns red and out of the steering wheel comes a breathalyzer tube, and a sickly-sweet female voice urges me to blow, just a little. I gulp, and swish, and gargle, swallow, then blow.

The car stops, hard. A klaxon sounds inside, and the voice, now with a testy edge to it, warns me that this car is fully locked and will move no further until a retrieval truck arrives.

'Try to stay loose,' I say, more to myself than Tracy, who can certainly manage that trick better than I can, booze aside.

The Ford slams into the rear; I see nothing but a white explosion before me.

————

I found out what happened immediately after the crash only weeks later. I broke my nose and three ribs and really wrecked my back in those inexplicable ways that can never fully be healed. Stuff happened to my literal spinal fluid—one of the few substances we can't just ladle out of a vat and pour into someone.

Tracy was fine. She wriggled out over her airbag, kicked out the front windshield, and then skedaddled around to see the Ford. It had pushed us a good half-mile up State Route 36, ate the back half of the Model T and nudged up between my shoulder blades. The ombudsfolk were alive inside the wreck, unconscious and crushed between half a dozen airbags. We'd had a few seconds to prepare ourselves; they'd been completely surprised. Tracy pulled me from the wreck and dragged me past the side of the road and onto the actual desert sands, a streak of blood and other liquids like a great stroke from a paintbrush making a trail behind me. It was good; she would be able to find me a few minutes later through all the smoke. Then she dashed down the road and found my watch.

I came to fairly quickly. The thinnest sheet of ice lay over the sand. In ancient Egypt, servants were sent out each morning before dawn to ever-so-gently scrape the millimeter of frost that would form upon the dunes overnight and collect it into a small cup so that Pharaoh might have a small cup of sherbet with his breakfast. I got two licks in before every molecule of H_2O vaporised before my one good eye. I guessed that the satellite had just then passed overhead as both my rental and the F-350 burst into flames. I felt the soles of my feet blister, the sense of having toes vanish as flesh blew off bones. It was good; that meant my spinal cord was still functioning.

When I woke up again, I was lying on the back of the cargo bed of the retrieval truck. I screamed at the sky for an hour as Tracy negotiated with my watch in an attempt to reroute the truck away from the airport's vehicle rental office and to a hospital. In her other hand, Tracy gripped a mostly melted license plate. I remember that she kept having to take new pictures of it and upload them to a satellite link in order to be believed. When she and Robin visited me in the hospital a week later, she showed me a scar on her palm that was shaped like much of the letter w.

Lee sent my watch a jp3g depicting a big-eyed owl holding flowers and wearing a sash reading get well soon that was somehow worth $4,500,000 to a Sothebee auctionbot on the worldwidehive. Like all freelancers, I am uninsured, but that gift paid for all my medical expenses save painkillers, so I've had to find another way to get addicted to them. I live in a tiny house on the roof of an apartment building, the first-story storefront of which is the sort of very much not Irish pub that journalists enjoy drinking in. I get my pills from sympathetic colleagues and well-wishers. It took me a long time to file this story, but when it's posted I'll have a few extra coins to buy some rounds for the gang. Other than the pub for pills, pints, and peanuts, I stay in bed, very much not healing. I can pay my rent and buy my growmeats thanks only to a peculiar fact. Somehow, the photovoltaic collector on the roof of the shipping container I call home consistently collects a third again of my energy needs, at a rate twenty percent over its own listed capacity. I'm able to sell the extra electricity in my batteries back to the local utility. Every three months, the electric company sends *me* a check.

Floating Island

Grace Dugan

Glory and her friends wanted to see the real islands, that was why they took a canoe and sailed west. Floating Island was not a real island, just a donut of steel covered with windmills and waterwheels doing a slow track around the South Pacific gyre. They had seen pictures of the old islands so they knew how beautiful they were. The ocean washed up against white, shiny beaches. They had gentle lagoons where you could wade out into rainbow coral reefs and pick up a crayfish for your dinner, or spear a fish just swimming by. Grandpa Caster said all that was gone now and they believed him but they also didn't really believe him.

Floating Island had its own lagoon submerged into the sea, and it had once been a freshwater reservoir for swimming, paddling and enjoying the view. Now it was just a brackish fish farm, and wasn't nice for swimming in. They only went down there to work or to fetch drinking water from the ageing tanks collecting runoff from the inner walls.

There wasn't anywhere nice on Floating Island. What had once been a golf course was converted into a farm but it was too exposed there to grow anything but breadfruit, coconut, pandanus and betel nut, and many of those didn't survive their times on the roaring forties. If you went down there someone would usually give you a job to do as well. The only places for young people to go to really escape from grownups were inner parts of the lower decks, but it was smelly and, as you got down below sea level, a bit scary and hard to breathe. That was where Glory's big sister used to go to have sex with her boyfriends, and where her uncle Johnny accused Mr Windy of hoarding food. Lazarus kept saying that his big brother said that people lived down there, but the others laughed at him. What would they eat? Need sunlight to grow things.

Glory had two places she went to when she wanted to get away from everyone, friends as well as adults. One was grandma Belinda's garden, a square of the golf course where she had planted a double wall of bamboo windbreak so she could grow pineapples, kaukau, ibeka and flowers. The bamboo made a lot of noise in the wind, so you couldn't hear anything happening on the other side of the windbreak and they couldn't hear you. Sometimes grandma was there but she didn't say much unless you asked her a question, and Glory could sit and weave or just lie on her back and watch the bamboo tops waving.

Her other favourite place was up on the highest roof of the high side, where she found she could climb out using some old wires and fixtures to a little platform where there was plenty to hang onto, and then see over everything, over the lagoon to the low side with its slope of stacked balconies with tiny gardens, over the former golf course just beyond the lagoon entrance, and over the endless, endless ocean.

It was while sitting up there the day after Commemoration Day that she had the idea to go west. Just a couple of weeks before, the navigation team, including Daniel's grandpa Luca, had announced that the current was already turning them towards the south and it looked like they would not pass nearby any more island groups on their journey back towards the Southern Ocean. This news had been very bitter for Glory and her friends, who had been the oldest kids on Floating Island to be left off the canoe voyage which had been made to Tahiti last year and whose friendship had been strengthened by that shared exclusion. Glory's sister had come back pregnant, Lazarus's big brother had brought a girlfriend back with him, and though everyone was happy with the tinfish and rice and seeds and spices and sugar and tea and coffee and clothes and solar panels and tools and reading glasses and medicines and everything else that had been brought back, the stories of adventure, romance, and delicious food were too much to bear. Glory's sister had cried every month about the boyfriend who hadn't wanted to come with her, but Glory was sure that her sadness itself was a form of gloating.

Glory wanted to go to Ebeye, her grandpa Caster's island, and she said so casually to Lazarus the next day.

'Nup,' he said. 'Grandma Aliyah told me the Americans blew it up with a nuclear bomb, then they used it as a space base to launch rockets, but now it's all underwater at high tide, so there's nothing there. Plus, it's too far away, we should go somewhere closer.'

Daniel had all the good maps in his family's place, but Daniel was still in the hospital after freaking out on Commemoration Day, so they couldn't ask him. Excitedly, they went to find Bree, who took a map from the filing cabinet in her place and came down to the lower deck with them to pore over it. What had started out seeming like a game was, after two hours of arguing about the relative merits of Vanuatu versus New Caledonia versus Fiji, a decision, especially when Lazarus suggested they take Daniel with them.

So they organised a fishing trip and got permission to take one of the larger fishing canoes. Glory persuaded Grandma Doctor Peng to let her take Daniel because it would be good for him. Then she had to persuade Daniel himself.

Glory helped her sister make lunch for Grandma Doctor and then waited for both the pregnant and the elderly woman to take their afternoon naps. She actually hated the hospital, and rarely went inside even though she lived next door. Her mother had bled to death in there, and then her little brother Jonas had died two years ago, just at the end of the hungry times they had had crossing the Southern Ocean.

Old Mr Windy was in his usual place near the door of the inner room, and he groaned as she passed by and asked for Doctor Peng, for some pain relief. Glory hissed and brushed him off, but felt unsettled as she went into the outer room where Daniel was. This room was supposed to be only for people with TB, but Daniell was the only one in there. Habitually, Glory went and opened the windows and the cool breeze freshened the dull smell.

Daniel was lying with face towards the wall, but he sat up and said hello when she came in. What was wrong with him? she wondered. He had been in here for three days. Who would want to be in this place rather than outside?

'How are you?' she asked.

'Fine.'

He looked quite normal, but she had seen him shaking and crying on Commemoration Day, and then falling in a heap, and it had scared her. It happened to at least one person every year, but it had never happened to one of her friends before.

('It's like the bitter medicine that you have to take,' Grandpa Caster had said. 'But maybe for some people it's a bit of an overdose.')

'Can you keep a secret?' she asked Daniel.

He nodded, and after a second she saw a little light in his dull eyes. When she told him the plan, the light grew, and when she had finished, he said, 'You're right, we should go. It's going to be our last chance.'

'Yes, otherwise five more years of this shit! I can't believe we didn't think of it before.'

When she left the room, her heart was soaring.

She went to Grandma Belinda's garden and asked if she had some breadfruit to spare. She told her they were going on a fishing trip and she wanted to feed all her friends. Grandma Belinda, generous as ever, filled three bags for her, but insisted she stay and eat a ripe banana with her. She peeled it and broke the top half off before handing Glory the rest.

'So sweet!' Glory exclaimed.

Grandma grinned. 'I think these are the best ones yet. Here.' She opened a drinking coconut, poured half into a cup, then sucked on the rest of it. The coconut water was refreshing but Glory was impatient to go. She didn't want Grandma's warmth and calm to weaken her resolve. It didn't matter, she thought to herself. *She'll miss me but there are so many cousins who can keep her company.*

The arrival of some of these cousins gave her the excuse to leave, and she did so hurriedly, seeing them glance at her heavy bags of breadfruit. Grandma was always so generous, and she often said to Glory that because she had five children and seventeen grand-children, she never had fear of going hungry (and then she usually talked about God, and Glory tuned out). Things had been very unsteady in her youth, she said, and every child had a different father. Some of them she wouldn't tell who they were, but Glory knew that her own father's father had been a helicopter pilot from New Zealand who had helped to fly all the guests and staff during the great exodus from Floating Island. 'That was when all the well-off people decided they didn't like it anymore,' Grandma Belinda had said. 'Once the company went belly up and we stopped getting paid, they didn't want to live here with all of us if they had to do things for themselves. Well, except some of them like Luca.'

Uncle Luca, Daniel and Bree's grandfather, had been one of the people who designed Floating Island and especially the water-wheels underneath which slowed their passage through the ocean as they also generated power. He never stopped talking about them, and everyone tolerated it because now that most of the solar panels had worn out, these were their main supply of electricity. The funny story about him was that his wife left in the exodus but he stayed behind because he loved Floating Island so much. He married again, and the old people liked to tease his new partner that she was his third wife, coming after both the first one and the giant donut of steel they all lived on.

Glory arrived first in the morning, well before dawn. She had baked the breadfruit after Grandma Doctor Peng went to sleep, and was tired but alert with excitement. Daniel was there next, and she watched him staring out to sea as the first light dulled the blackness. When Bree and Lazarus arrived, the four of them rolled the canoe down to the launch and then packed it. Named Stingray, it was seven metres with one outrigger, with a mast that could be switched from end to end in the Marshallese style and with both a raised platform between the outrigger and the hull and a net slung underneath to carry light cargo. Glory loved this canoe, and one of her most precious memories was getting to take it out on a five day fishing trip in the Central Pacific with Grandpa Caster and some of her cousins. Now it was going to be her home.

They loaded it up with food, water, coconuts, fishing gear, a little fuel, their own clothes and, in Glory's case, the two gold necklaces she had inherited from her mother. Daniel brought a map and a compass. They packed hurriedly, anxious both that they might have forgotten important things, and also that they might be detected. Adrenaline helped to give them the strength to launch the canoe, and Glory watched with delight as Daniel, who was at the rear, nimbly leaped onto the hull and allowed himself to smile.

Then they were over the open ocean. Glory finished tying the cargo down while the others unfurled the sail. Standing on the net, she looked down into blue emptiness, and felt a little vertigo. When she was a kid she hadn't liked opening her eyes underwater because it was too scary to look at all that space, all the water. 'It's okay to be afraid of it,' Grandpa Caster had said, 'but remember that it gives us life. We came from the ocean and she has taken everything we have put into her. She has absorbed our shit and our piss and our trash and our carbon dioxide and she still gives us fish to eat.'

They actually had a good fishing day that day, stopping at likely points to trawl, and Bree caught a huge tuna which she wanted to measure so she could tell her brothers how big it was.

'You'll all tell, won't you,' she demanded of the others, 'so it won't just be me.' And then she remembered where they were going and said 'Oh, yeah.' She filleted the tuna and they ate as much as they could and then put the rest in vinegar for tomorrow.

If you don't know where you come from, you can't know where you are going.

That was one of Grandpa Caster's sayings about navigation, but he also liked to say it about life. Daniel had gone to the navigation room and marked their position on the map before they left and Glory and Lazarus kept checking the compass and fixing the rudder so they were heading more or less towards Vanuatu.

We come from a Floating Place. We don't know where we are going, we're just going there, she thought. Except not now. Now they were heading in a direction.

Grandpa Caster had tried to teach her many things, like how to see the reflection of an island in the clouds when the island itself was out of sight, and how to watch for birds to know where land was, but she had never had a chance to try her skills. As the sun set and the first stars came up, Lazarus claimed that he could use the star map, and follow where each star was rising. Glory didn't believe him, but they compromised by using the compass to pick a star, and then sailing towards it for a while, until Glory couldn't resist the temptation to check with the compass again.

She was disappointed in herself that she didn't know more. Grandpa Caster had told her that in the old old days, his people had lived more on the water than on land, and the navigators had in their minds maps of the ocean for thousands of kilometres in every direction. They had sailed from atoll to atoll just like you would walk down the corridor to visit your neighbours.

Well, she thought, they would only learn by practice. By the end of their journey they would be good navigators, and would be able to teach others. She checked the compass, fixed on another rising star, and then put it in her pocket.

The thought of Grandpa brought back the memory of the fight they'd had after the Commemoration. They had just left Grandma Doctor and Daniel in the hospital and come back to make dinner for the family, and Grandpa had sat down to cut out all the bad bits of some old kaukau while she scraped a coconut. She had been shocked into silence by Daniel's collapse, but the physical work of using the scraper loosened some of the feels inside.

'Why did you decide to come here?' she'd asked him. When your islands were drowning, she had thought, why go off to a stupid metal island for rich people and become a kitchen hand?

He'd shrugged something about not really remembering things so long ago, but supposing that he had needed a job.

'Didn't people fight?' she had said. 'I mean, why didn't they stop it?'

'Well, sometimes you can fight things,' he said, 'but sometimes it isn't worth it. When you are small and your enemy is very, very big, if you fight him you just die and he doesn't even notice. It's like you are a tiny plankton and he is a whale and he swallows you just by opening his mouth. So why die for no reason?'

He chopped kaukau, and Glory scraped angrily, too angrily to speak.

'Well,' he said after a while, 'lots of people did fight, and it did make a difference. But I've never been the fighting type.'

Glory and Lazarus woke Daniel and Bree at midnight, and went to get some sleep. The swell was quite strong, but she managed to let it rock her to sleep. In sleep she felt its shape in her dreams, up, down, up, down, so that when she woke a while later, she already knew they were in a storm.

The stars had gone and the night wind was cold. The little solar light which hung on the mast had gone flat, and it was almost pitch black. She could hear Daniel on the tiller, Lazarus at the sail and Bree was bailing.

They were racing up and then down dark mountains of water. Ropes thrummed and the timbers between the hull and the outrigger groaned. Glory climbed up onto the deck and went forward to reduce the sail.

The rain came and suddenly she was wet through to her skin. She worked as quickly as she could, but her hands were wet and everything was moving. Up, up, down, down, splash, spray. Up, down, splash, spray. She held on for a moment and breathed in and out, tasted the sea on her face.

Grandpa Caster had told her once that before the climate change the sea had been less acidic, and that it had tasted different. Stupid acidic sea, she thought, feeling rage rising inside her. Why was it trying to stop them from their journey? Why couldn't it have just been a calm night? And why couldn't she get this last fucking toggle into its loop?

Up, up, up, down, down, down.

The water crashed into her face, and her body started shaking. Why had they been born in such a stupid place, a place where they couldn't really live? Why, why, why.

She stood up again and cursed her wet hands as she fiddled with the sail. But at last it was done. She turned to crawl back to the others and didn't see the wall of water that lifted her off the boat. The boat went down below, somehow the outrigger moved past under her, her leg just touched it, then it was gone.

She was submerged in the warm, churning sea. After the first shock, she let herself go limp, waiting for her body to surface.

There it was. Breathe. Relax. She spotted the tip of the sail cresting above the dark waves for a moment, then it was gone.

How embarrassing, she thought.

Crash of wave, get head above water, breathe. *The embarrassment would soon be over, though.*

Crash of wave, head above water, breathe, relax.

Crash of wave, head above water, breathe, relax.

Annoyingly, the storm started to subside. How embarrassing to drown not in a big storm but a little squall.

Oh well.

The rain blew away elsewhere. She lay on her back for a while, paddling just a little with arms and legs. Then she turned and faced down into the dark nothing. Or the dark everything. She was in it now, so there was no point being afraid.

The sky lightened and she swam on her side and watched the sun slide above the horizon. Her own private sunrise on her own private ocean.

She wondered how long it takes to drown. She didn't even feel tired yet.

The sun climbed up and up.

She spotted a bird pile in the distance and swam lazily towards it. It seemed to recede further and further, and then somehow she was in the middle of a school of fish, with gulls circling and pulling them out of the water all around her. 'Drop one for me,' she called, but they didn't.

'Drop one for me, I'm hungry!'

She laughed at herself, relaxed back into the water, sank for a few seconds, then swam back to the surface.

She was hungry and thirsty.

Then she saw a fin, and another. Maybe a great white? *Don't eat me! I'm not delicious!* One swam towards her, and she felt the grip of fear. Then it veered to her left. She looked down into the water. Sunlight lanced down through the school of fish. There were three sharks, one of them a lot bigger than the others. She paddled slowly, slowly, slowly for some time, away from birds, fish and sharks, and didn't relax again for a long while.

Phew!

Breathe, paddle. Float. Breathe, paddle, float. The sky was blue, the sea was blue.

The sun warmed her body. She wondered if she would feel cold if she were a fish. How did the tuna keep themselves warm down there? And what about the giant squid? Probably the climate change had killed them off.

Breathe, paddle, float. Breathe, paddle, float.

For the commemoration, the teachers had asked the primary

school children to draw pictures of all the old animals, the ones that were gone, and they stuck them up all over the hall. Dodos and thylacines and rhinoceroses and pandas and mountain gorillas and elephants and hammerhead sharks and hairy-nosed wombats and koalas and polar bears and orangutans and sea turtles. No mention of giant squids.

Is this the climate change killing me off? she wondered. *Or maybe just stupidity.*

Breathe, paddle, float. Breathe, paddle, float.

She was getting tired by this time, and lay on her back with her eyes closed, trying to see how little she could paddle and still stay afloat. It wasn't quite like sleeping but it was a bit like sleeping. Breathe.

Breathe.

Float.

She heard the whoosh of the blow and then smelt a thick fishy smell. Whales. She opened her eyes and paddled upright. The one who had made the blow cruised along a little then displayed its spine and its enormous tail as it headed back underwater. She felt her stomach drop.

Over to her left, a smaller one lazily rolled onto its back, baring its striped belly, brought its barnacled fin down on the water with an enormous slap, and then completed its spin and swam away.

She felt the push of water behind her and turned to see a grey wall surfacing, and then an eye, as large as a hand. It gazed out, interested but calm, as if thinking slow, slow thoughts. Thinking the thoughts of the ocean.

I'm just a human, Glory thought. *I'm just one human floating in the sea. I might drown and become food for fish and gulls or I might live until I'm 100 years old. I'm just a human with two legs and two arms and one head, and one set of lungs, and one heart.*

'Hello,' she said. And then the whale looked at her, and in its eye she saw all the lives it had lived, all the oceans it had traversed, and traversed again, all the seasons which had marked it, all the sunshine it had tossed itself into, all the deep places it had visited that humans would never know.

The moment was impossibly long, but then it was over, and she was briefly pulled under in the water displaced by the whale's dive back down.

As she treaded water, she wondered if she'd imagined the whole thing. She felt warm inside, as if she'd been embraced.

But no, there they were in the distance, a puff from a blowhole, and then the crash of an enormous breach.

'Bye.'

She felt a wrench in her heart, and was suddenly lonely. *Come back, come back!* She wanted to lay her body against that grey wall, to be carried off by it across the waves.

But it was gone. And now she was very tired.

Perhaps now she could drown. She had seen the whale, had spoken to the whale. Maybe that was enough. Breathe, paddle, float.

Breathe.

Paddle.

Float.

Endless ocean.

Endless blue.

The sun was at an angle now so she supposed it must be afternoon. She wasn't sure if it was cooler or not. Somehow she had thought she could probably survive at least twenty-four hours but she wasn't sure she really wanted to.

She saw the gulls first and then the rubbish pile. Bird pile, rubbish pile. She swam towards it, slowly, ever so slowly, or maybe it drifted towards her and she swam in one spot. A different sort of floating island. Or maybe not so different.

It was quite a big pile, and she scrambled up onto the tangle of nets, buoys and cracked plastic. In a previous time, she would have picked through it with interest. Particularly in the deep lifeless parts of the ocean they often caught more rubbish than fish when out on a canoe trip.

But now she was so tired, and for the first time she didn't have to paddle.

Breathe.

Sun on the face, warming and drying her skin. Cool breeze.

Breathe.

She sank into a sunlit daze. In her mind, she was sliding down the storm on the outrigger again, and then jolted by a crashing wave.

For the first time, she wondered seriously whether her friends had survived.

Was it better to be killed off in this stupid world? To just give up? She was glad she had seen the whale before she died. She was just one human, one piece of flotsam floating here and there on the ocean. She fell asleep.

'Is she alive?'

She head the voice from the depths, and didn't want to surface.

'She's breathing.'

The rubbish island rocked, and she felt a nudge of a foot on her side. Let me sleep, she thought.

'Glory!'

She opened her eyes to see Daniel standing over her.

'Hello!' he said.

'Glory, what happened?' That was Lazarus, further back from Daniel, awkwardly stepping towards her.

It took a few moments to find her voice.

'I fell off.'

Lazarus laughed. 'What do you mean you fell off? Weren't you holding on?'

'There was a big wave.'

Lazarus looked over at Bree, who was squatting on the prow of the canoe. 'Did you hear that? There was a big wave.' He laughed again, so much so that he slapped his thigh with his hand.

Glory took Daniel's hand and got to her feet. He led her over the bobbing rubbish to the canoe. She felt hot and dizzy, and needed Bree to help pull her back on.

'How did you find me?' she asked.

'Oh, we weren't trying to find you,' Lazarus said. 'I was just getting some nets for Grandma.'

Bree handed Glory a water bag, and she sat in the hull drinking it, still feeling stunned. Daniel found her some of the breadfruit she had cooked before they left, then both he and Bree shouted at Lazarus to hurry up with the net so they could leave.

Soon they were underway, slicing through the ocean with the

sun at their backs.

'Here you go.' Lazarus handed her an open drinking coconut and a couple of bananas. 'Fancy lady like you must be hungry after missing both breakfast and lunch.' He smiled at her, and his smile was like the sun. 'Have a rest for a bit,' he said. 'We can manage.'

Glory climbed down onto the net between the hull and the outrigger. The ocean streamed under her, and sometimes the wind tossed a cooling spray on her face.

When she was a child Grandpa Caster had taught her how to drink the coconut quickly without spilling any of it.

'You're like a baby and the coconut is like your mama,' he had said, giggling. 'It's like you're drinking susu.'

So she lay back, sucking on the coconut as hard as she could, drinking life from that coconut mother grown on the reclaimed golf course of a rusting, breaking down donut of metal adorned with all the trash of the ocean.

Thank god they were going home.

In the Skin

Tom Flood

Skopee didn noe wair The Ded be. No mata. Dat wun lern. Sep
Nokkee need noe or day gon. Parsd, aye heer sum Skin say wunse.
Wat dat Skin noe? Liv frever, dat wun do.

'Aya, Skopee, yu be gon yet?'

'Yu hoap, Smut! Get wun skin, I be. Yu gon, Nokkee!'

Aya, dat wun smial orite. Aye feel it. We mob owt befaw
moonup. Way briyt, dat wun moon. Moon wayk up, Nokkee go in.
Maybe fyn gud trayd. Maybe ion, sum metl. Neva noe We mowl rat
peepl. Bes burra you fyn.

Haya! Wissel. Stop. Dat wun Spaw wissel. Orl stop. No moov.
Skin patrowl. No moon, dust; Skin doan see so gud. Wayt. Dunno
Spaw see dat wun. Big dust. Kold niyt. Dair. Aye see nex. 2 Skin
Glo. Orl Nokkees shivva.

'I swear I heard something.'

'Let's go bac, Li. Could've been a wind willy. We shouldn't be out as far as The Dead anyway. Not before the moon comes up and not dust this heavy. Nocturnals could be out and about.'

'Worried about your scin, Jaccy? Noccies are too slow in the open, you noe that.'

'All the same. Could be a blac panther, eh?'

Li giggled. 'Where do you get this stuff?'

'Murri. She noes everything.'

'Panther? What's that anyway.'

'Nomad myth maybe. Passed eons ago. Powerful, four-legged carnivore.'

'So some kind of Noccie?'

'Yes. Maybe. Watch it. What's that sparkly stuff. On your arm?'

Li withdrew the arm. It was like reaching through an opalescent wall.

'It feels… weird.' Li rubbed its length, as if to wipe it away.

'We're goin' bac. Race.'

Across the cooling terrain, their tall, dark shapes flew under the cape of the storm, circles of glow like pink ball lightning in the black, then slowed.

'Hold up. We'll be hitting The Ridges. Don't want to tear your epi.' Jacky bent over, gasping.

Li was still bouncing from one foot to the other, but they walked the rest of the way, a good two thousand paces to the outpost, to slow their vitals, red dust increasing the battering as they went. Racing was mandated against. Dangerously wasting, the pharms opined. They doused their Glows and deactivated their Screamers as they passed under the recharge station. High above, they might've heard the moon watch taking position.

'I kuda got dat wun skin, yeh?'

'Skreemer, Skopee, skreemer. An glo. Def an bliyn orl you be.'

'Prov Partee Wun back,' Spaw say wen we unload good ion.

Ion mayk gud skrapr, cuttr, diggr. We bin Prov Partee long way, plenty moon—sep Skopee. Smorl mob. Ene metl mayk good trayd.

'Haya, Skopee. Get sum tucka?'

Skopee fam trayd proteen kayk. Good grub mayk strong bowns, aya.

'Haya, Skope, wot yu wont dat wun skin for?'

'Yu noe Skin liv freva, Smut. Dat wun skin kum ofa, ay. I stik dat wun on, liv freva.'

I larf. Dat Skopee bleev ene.

———

They slipped off the filters, instruments and storm covers, turned in the measurements and reported for debrief with Murri.

'Might've heard some Nocturnals. Can't say for sure. Storm was too loud.'

'What circuit?'

'Ninth. Out near The Dead Heart, we thinc. We strayed a bit in the storm.'

'You should always retrace as soon as you realise. Scins intact, Li?'

'Yes. No issues. Jac said might've been a blac panther.' Li grinned.

Jac nudged Li.

Murri looked hard at Jac, then back at Li. 'You can go, Jac.' She waited until Jac left. 'You remember the story of your scin, Li?'

Li's nose screwed up. 'I no what they tell us, that our scin lets us live, and live long if we tayc care of it.'

'And the difference with the Nocturnals and us?'

Li shrugged. 'They don't have it, so they need to eat.' Then grimaced. 'And they live underground during the day because the conditions are too hot for them—and they're pale, pale and short, hairy and bent over—and blind, aren't they?'

'Not blind, but their eyes are too light-sensitive, even for dust moons. And even we need filters in the sun. When we pod, we're pale, you noe, until we get our scin.'

'I heard the Noccies want to tayc our scins, cill us and tayc it. Can they do that?' Li blurted.

'Yes and no. Only if you give it.'

'But why?'

'You noe a scin warms you on cold nights and cools you out in the sun, sustains you by chemosynthesis as long as it extracts thane, drogen and monox from the air?'

'Natch.'

'And Nocturnals—'

'Do they really want to eat us?' Li shuddered. 'And eat each other?'

Murri chuckled. 'You have more chance of being "eaten" by bacteria than by Nocturnals. These primitive myths persist, but you noe better. Worry about the weather; that is our worc, not superstition about panthers and cannibals.'

She went on with the usual history of the Ancients' disregard for the accretion of extinction events, Dr Silver and further archons of the exodermis, and the need to protect The Forest, but Li wasn't really paying attention. Her mind had wandered to thoughts of childhood delight at waking to see the sculptured changes wrought on the ridges by an overnight storm, new gargoyles extending the serried ledges and stone rebuts etched onto a purpling sky.

Where is that scy now, Li daydreamed. Supercells whip permadust at intermittent intensities and vapour exists only in our scins.

'… and that's why we must closely attend to the monox balance,' Murri was finishing up.

'Will you go to The Forest, Murri?'

'Of course. You noe we all go. It will not be so many paces for me now.'

'What is it really like?'

'You know this, Li. The Forest is a place of great peace and community—and knowledge. A place you can finally put down roots and find your destiny.'

'But why can't we go there now? Why can't we see it?'

'We must be ready when we enter The Forest because we can't come bac from there.

'But how do you noe you are ready?'

'Our duty is a long trail. You will noe as you approach. It is always the same. We worc to mayc this better,' she gestured around with her arms, 'but for now we have The Forest, and The Forest grows. Our worc, and that of those of us in further places, has held the gases steady for many paces. We hope down the trail all this will begin to return to where it once was, where it was in your childhood and many paces further, where it was when this was all forest.'

She could see Li had drifted away. 'Go on then, Li. Get some rest for your next shift?'

———

So we go, saym as evry wun, ovr tu owr rok trayd, Prov Partee Wun. Trayd metl faw metl, rok karv, fude, werk, weev, ene.

Skopee trayd sumpn on sharman, may be kulla dust. Dat wun korl mene naym. Way oal. Aya, mayk me nervis.

Faw sum larf on Skopee, aye tel Amanita, 'Skope wont get wun skin, Am. Wot yu rekon?'

Amanita prite lowd. 'Plenne skin hear, Skope,' Am korl, striyk dat poze.

Skopee kulla.

'Wot yu want dat wun skin, Skopee?' Am larf.

'Liv freva, yu no,' aye tel.

'Got wun Skin in mynd?' Am wink. 'Not mene bout.'

Skopee rekuver. 'Yu help, Amanita? Yu got majik shroom. Nok wun owt.'

Am larf. 'Oo, yu got plan, ay? Sharp wun dis, aya? Say wot, aye trayd you. Yu got koppa?'

Skopee ayes bug.

'Koppa hard fynd, Am,' aye tel.

Amanita larf sum. 'Kum on, Skopee. Skins doan eet, yu noe.'

'Yare, nar. Troo dat.'

'Dat mob down Bulla burra—dem krayzee mob, Am—rok em, hit dat Skin mob say sum,' aye say.

'Nar, mowl poop. Yu bleev dat, Smut?' Amanita larf. 'Skreemers!

Yu hit wun, kupel fella, say. Mob, nar. Yu def shaw.'

'Yare. Troo dat.' Aye nod.

'Aya, yu. Liv freva aye will.' Skope go.

Next shift Jaccy and Li went out with Lyptus and Maida toward The Rift, Sector 6. Some still call it Grand Canyon. With the dust as it is, there's nothing to see, but as you might imagine, you need to watch your step, so they joined at five paces with silver cord to ensure none would stray. The thing is, even with filters, you can't see your feet, so watching your step is no more than an anachronism.

With Lyp in the lead, followed by Maida, Jac and Li, they made good time, stumbling on through heavy weather. According to measurements, the ferocity of the storms had steadily increased and they abated only rarely. The filters on the instruments became rapidly clogged so shifts were mostly counted in paces and time had become no more than a series of steady steps, a poor estimator of temporality.

In the backsteps, Li was dreaming, it was said they left instruments out to collect data, hidden from roving bands of Noccies who would steal them, and only picced them up further down the trac. Shuddering at the thought of stumbling into such a band, Li took comfort from the presence of the others. Four Screamers and Glows was an insurmountable deterrent. The dust would bury deep any instruments they might leave out. Two pulls on the cord meant they had reached The Scissors, a dangerous eruption of razor rocks, but Li was thinking about stories of childhood again and never felt the distinct tugs.

Myths of The Rift told the canyon had been filled with lush, soft, stationary species as well as giant forest precursors called trees, plentiful moisture and unbelievable ambulatory creatures extinct, but when Li, tether severed, stumbled and tumbled over the edge, there was nothing to break the fall but the banks of dust. Li plummeted and rolled to a stop, unconscious of the increasing darkness.

————

Skope stork off an aye let im go. Werk to do in dem reflekta padiks. Aye clime up hy burras.

'Aya, Toob, pik up gogls. Hot in padiks?'

'Yu noe, Smut. Freezen!'

'Skopee go by?'

'Aye rekon aye got sum wif.'

Toobr nomikal with werds. Aye wayt.

'May be up top? Aftamoon.'

Wunda wot dat mowl up faw, aya.

'Ow mene yu wont now?' Toobr arsk.

'Kupl roas do, Toob.'

Fit dem gogls, pik up tools, kupl trayders. Toob noe ayem good frit. Aya, always hot in padiks. Dig two roas enuf. Loos lotta moyscha. Not like dig burras, ay. Stuf grow up so toobas grow down. Dig toobas below, nex levl. Kool dig. Myselium, aya, dat difrent. Arsk Amanita. Shrooms dif. Toobas mowls mayn tukka. Fil em up. I dig two roas, noo dirt in, minral, solt, bit moyscha, loosen up.

End up. Grab trayders. Toob gon. Tyerd, but wunda bowt Skopee. Evry mowl smel dif. Follow dat wif maybe. Up to Rift. Prit sayf. Nokkees up solo, nah. Kanyon deep, neva Skins. Wif get maw.

Noo wif. Skin? Wurri now. Skope an Skin? Drag siyn at Rowtunda. On inta tunel. Not dat wun dust. Skope bent ovr Skin.

'Haya, Skope. Wot down.'

'Haya, Smut. Got dat wun Skin. Aye tel yu aye get wun.'

No moov. Skopie got kutr. Lift sum stuf owta dust.

'Sokay, Smut. Got dem Skreemer an Glo. It gon tu. Ormose. Wot yu rekon? Femayl?'

Aye peer kloas. 'Dunno. Nevr get dis kloas.' Skin so dark. Ruf liyk rok. No hair. No fer.

'Yu noe how aye get dat skin?'

'Nah. Yu bleev ene, Skope. How aye noe dat? Liyt kumn. Skins kum findn. Leev it.'

Feel dat Skopee smyl. Got kutr. Paws in dily bag. Blo sum dat kulla dust. Start kut in midel. Aya! Green sparkl liyk owpl. Wair dat Nokkee?

Φ

Li hadn't seen where The Dead Heart was. It didn't matter. Anyone can learn. Except Nocturnals need to noe or they perish. Passed, I heard a Scin say once. What do Scins noe? Live forever, they do.

'Hey, Li, you dead yet?'

'Yu hope, Smut! I'm gunna get a scin. You're dead, Noccie!'

I felt that smile. We were out before moonup. Way bright, the moon can be. When the moon comes up, Nocturnals go home. Maybe we'll find some good trading metal first. Maybe iron. You never can tell. We are the mole rat peoples. Best burrowers you can find.

Hey! Whistle. Stop. Spore whistled. Everyone freezes. Scin

patrol. No moon, heavy dust; Scins can't see well. I don't see how Spore noticed them. Big dust. Cold night. There. I see the glow from two Scins. We all shivered.

———

'I noe I heer sum.'

'Go bak, Skope. Kud be wind willy. Shudn be owt far as Ded. Not befaw moonrys. Not dust so hevy. Nokkees kud be owt.'

'Wurry bowt yaw skin, Jakky? Nokkees way slow owt heer, you noe dat.'

'Orl saym. Kud be jagwar, aya?'

Skopee giggl. 'Wair you get dat?'

'Murri. She noe tu.'

'Jagwar? Wot dat?'

'Nomad legen may be. Parsd way bak. Big. For legs. Eet us.'

'Sum kynda Nokkee?'

'Aya. May be. Look owt. Wot dat sparkl. On yaw arm?'

Skopee puld the arm in. Lyk an oapl worl, aya.

'Feels…weird.' Rub it to wyp away.

'We go bak. Run.'

Kros roks koolr we floo, undr storm, Glos lyk pink borl liytnin in the blak, den slow.

'Hold up. Doan wanta tair yaw epi.' Jakky bent ovr, gaspin.

Skopie stil bouns foot to foot, but wawk rest, big mob payses to owtpoas, slow viytls, red dust inkreesin az we go. Raysin is mandayt. Waystin, farms say. We dows dem Glos an deaktivayt Skreemas undr powr stayshun. Hy up, we miyt heer moon teem tayk playsus.

———

'I could have got that Scin, eh?'

'Screamers, Li, Screamers. And Glows. Deaf and blind is all you would be.'

'Provision Party One bac,' Spore reported as we unloaded iron.

Iron makes good scrapers, cutters, diggers. We've been a Provision Party for a long trac—except Li. Small gang. Any metal makes a good trade. Shiny ones are good for reflects.

'Hey, Li. Get something to eat?'

Li's family trade protein biscuits. Good food makes strong bones, yes.

'Hey, Li, what do you want that scin for?'

'You noe Scins live forever, Smut. That scin comes off, hey. I put that on, I live forever.'

I laugh. That Li will believe anything.

———

Slip off filtas, instroment, storm kuva, tern in werk, repawt to Murri.

'Miyt ov herd sum Nokkees. Karnt say reely. Storm tu lowd.'

'Ware?'

'Nyn. Owt neer Ded, we rekn. We stray bit in storm.'

'Yu always tern bak soons yu noe. Skins intakt, Skope?'

'Aya. No bigee. Jak say miyt ov bin jagwar.' Skopee grin.

Jac bumpr.

Murri look hard at Jak, bak at Skopee. 'Yu go, Jak.' She wayt til Jak left. 'Yu memba story yaw skin, Skope?'

Skopee skrew up noez. 'I noe wot yu tel us; skin let us liv an liv if we tayk kair ov it.'

'Difrents ov Nokkees an us?'

Skope shrug. 'Dat wun doan av it, so eet.' Skope grimas. 'An liv undergrownd in daylite kos tu hot—an payl, payl an smorl, hairee an bent—an bliyn, eh?'

'Not bliyn, ayes tu liyt-senstiv, evn faw dust moons. An evn we need sun filtas. Wen we pod, we payl, yu noe, til we get owr skin.'

'I heer Nokkees wana tayk owr skins, kil us an tayk it. Kan day?' Skope blert.

'Aya, an no. Only if yu giv it.'

'But wy?'

'Yu noe skin warm yu on koal niyt an kool yu in sun, feed yu by kemosynesis, extrakt thane, drogen and monox from air?'

'Aya.'

'An Nokkees—'

'Reely wana eet us?' Skopee trembl. 'An eet orl Nokkees tu?'

Murri larf. 'Maw lyk bein eetn by bakteareya. Dat wun primitiv stawry, but yu noe betr. Wury bowt sky; dat owr werk, not jagwars an kaniborls.'

Murri tork on dat histry of old wuns' disregard for the mene extinktin events, Dokta Silva an maw bildas ov dat exodermis, an protektin dat Forest, but Skope not payin heed. Dat wun's mind wander to kid's delyt at wakin an see dat change in dem roks by dat ovrniyt storm, new gargoyl in stown rebuts on purpln sky.

Wair dat sky now, Skopee daydreem. Soopersels wip permadust at intermitent intensitys an vaypa ownlee in skins.

'…an dat wy we mus klose aten to dat monox balans,' Murri end.

'Yu go dat Forest, Murri?'

'Aya. Yu noe orl go. It not be so mene payses faw me now.'

'Wot is it reelee lyk?'

'Yu noe, Skope. Dat Forest is plays of grayt pees an kom-yunitee—an wisdem. Plays yu poot down ruyts an fyn yu destinee.'

'Wy karnt we go now? Wy karnt we see dat wun?'

'We mus be redee wen we enta dat Forest kos we karnt kum bak.'

'How yu noe yu redee?'

'Owr dewtee is wun big trayl. Yu noe as yu get neer. Always saym. We werk tu mayk dis beta,' Murri moov rown dem arms, 'but we hav dat Forest, an dat Forest grow. Owr werk, an in maw playses, hold dem gases stedee for mene payses. We hoap down dat trayl orl dis wil begin dat retern to wair it wuns woz, wair it woz wen yu baybee an mene maw, wair it woz wen dis orl forest.'

Murri see Skopee drif away. 'Go on, Skope. Get sum rest faw yu nex teem?'

———

So we go, the same as everyone, over to our roc trade, Provision Party One. We trade metal for metal, roc carvings, food, work, weaving, anything.

Li trades for something with the shaman, maybe colour dust. The shaman has many names and is way old. Something about sha-mans makes me nervous.

For a laugh on Li, I tell Amanita, 'Li wants to get some Scin, Am. What do you reckon?'

Amanita is pretty loud. 'Plenty of scin here, eh?' Am calls, strikes a pose.

Li colours.

'What do you want with a Scin, Li?' Am laughs.

'Live forever, you noe,' I say.

'Got a Scin in mind?' Am winks. 'Not many about.'

Li recovers, 'Can you help, Amanita? You've got magic mushrooms. They could noc one out.'

Am laughs. 'Ooh, you've got a plan, yes? Sharp one, this, eh? Say, what if I trade you? Got any copper?'

Li's eyes bug.

'Copper is hard to find, Am,' I say.

Amanita laughs. 'Come on, Li. Scins don't eat, you noe.'

'Yeah, nah. True that.'

'That mob down at Bulla Burrow—crazy mob, Am—roc them, hit that Scin mob, some reckon,' I say.

'No, mole poop. You believe that, Smut?' Amanita laughs. 'Screamers! You hit one, maybe a couple, say. Mob, no. You'd be deaf for sure.'

'Yeah. True that.' I nod.

'Yeah, you. Live forever I will.' Li tromped off.

———

Nex shif, Jak an Skope, Lyptus an Maida owt dat Rif, Sektr 6. Sum korl Gran Kanyon. Dat dust leev zeero to see; so joyn at five payses dat silvr kord. Stay klose. Evn yews filtr, karnt see yu feet.

Lyp in leed, Maida follow, Jac an Skope. Mayk gud trayl, stumbl on in hevee storm. Powa dem storms inkreese an abayt rair. Instroement filtas rapidlee klog, so shif moasly kownt in payses an tiym dat seerees ov stedee steps.

In dem baksteps, Skopie dreem. Scins had lef instrooments owt to kolekt darta, hid from Nokkie steal, pik up down dat trak. Skope trembl at stumbl inta dat band, tayk kumfit from groop. For Skreemers an Glos big sayftee. Dat dust beree deep ene instrooments left owt. To puls on dat kord meen ariyv dem Sizas, danjrus razr roks. Skopie dreemin gen, neva felt no tugs.

Oal storees dat Rif tel Kanyon fil ov sof-leef tooba an big Forest prekursa naym trees, lota moystyoor an unbleevabl Nokkees extinkt, but Skopee, liyn kut, stumbl an tumbl ovr dat edj, no sof-leef brayk dat forl, jus dust. Skopie plumit an rowl to stop, gon in dat dark.

———

Li stalced off and I let it go. I have work to do in the reflecta paddocs. I climbed up to the high burrows.

'Hi, Toob. I'll pic up some goggles. Hot in the paddocks?'

'You noe, Smut. Freezing!'

'Skopee go by?'

'I reckon I got a whiff.'

Toober is economical with words. I waited.

'May be up top? Aftermoon.'

I wonder what that mole is up to, hey.

'How many do you want now?' Toober asced.

'Couple rows do, Toob.'

I fitted the goggles, piced up the tools and a couple of trader vouchers. Toob noes I'm good for it. It's always hot in the reflector paddocs. I dug my two rows. That's enough. You lose a lot of moisture. Not like digging burrows, eh. Leaves grow up so tubers grow down. They dig those tubers below, on the next level. That's a cool dig; pays less. Mycelium, eh, they're different. Ask Amanita. Mushrooms are different. Tubers are moles' main food. Fills us up. I dug two rows, new dirt in, minerals, salts, a bit of moisture, and loosened it up.

Finished, I grabbed my traders. Toob had left. I was tired but wondered about Li. Every mole smells different. I followed what smelt like that whiff. Up to The Rift. It's safe enough. Nocturnals never go up solo, no. The Canyon is deep though; there are never Scins. The smell grew stronger, but there was another. Scin? Now I was worried. Li and Scins? I found signs of dragging at The Rotunda, followed them into the tunnel. Not that much dust in there and I found Li bent over a Scin.

'Hullo, Li. What's down.'

'Eh, Smut, I got a Scin. I told you I would.'

I didn't move. Li had a cutter and lifted something out of the dust.

'It's okay, Smut. I got the Screamer and Glow. This Scin is dead, almost. What do you recon? Male?'

I peered closer. 'Dunno. We never get this close.' The scin was so darc, and rough like roc. No hair. No fur.

'How do I get that scin?'

'No. You'll believe anything, Li. How do I noe that? The light's coming. Scins will come looking. Leave it.'

Li smiled and flashed the cutter, a paw in the dilly bag. Coloured dust stained the ground. The cut started in the middle. Uh! That phosphorescent green sparcle, opalescent against the darc. Noccie?

Φ

It's said all energy in the universe remains in balance.
It's said there's more than one way to skin a cat.
Aya!

Half-World Eclogues *or* Constraints

John Kinsella

When they sliced the planet in half and separated those halves on either side of the sun so they revolved in precise counterpoint, the disapproved of people weren't divided so as to occupy one of those halves, but rather divided so they were equally split between the two orbiting bodies. So it is said in official dispatches, though the language is broken up and we have to reconstitute it from before the split, before the sundering.

Or, was it that the planet just broke apart, leaving one half semi-intact and the other... lost? The Committee speak of 'control', 'intentionality', 'design'... but others speak of catastrophe, divided in themselves, unable to make thoughts cohere, unable to retrieve complete memories. They fuse with others to make systems that process memory and information, they make communities of the disembodied, they find ways of accruing in the broken atmosphere, in the halved gravity. But always The Committee with its ulterior motives. And the fusions seem to stimulate a vast release of energy which some fear The Committee is harnessing as part of their Half

World Nu Technology. 'Some' who are trying to determine who they are and can be in Half World... half a world, the split sphere.

The illustrator, the home-trained architect, and the 'inventor' are friends. Close friends, but they don't live in each other's pockets. Each is torn in two by a desire to be 'creative'. The illustrator feels she has real art in her, the architect that he will manage to make the building best suited to its environment, and the inventor that they will bring back the illuminated manuscript to replace digital experience. An inventor looking back to make a future. None if this is ineluctable and none of these figures are necessarily characters. Their traits are singular, if overlapping.

———

Volume 1

First Dialogue

Pressures and stresses on a structure. The filling of the counterweight doesn't balance but leans against, causing a rippling effect, a cascade of breakdown. Supposedly solid joints become hinges on the verge of snapping at their point of maximum arc—an over-opening into collapse.

You would ban yourself from being inside due to the risk, but something compels you to stand close and listen to the straining, the pushed to the point of...

Who am I to say how much longer this can go on and how long I can play a role in the dialogue? What did Rousseau say about the malice of those pretending to be friends and spreading gossip? I spread rumours against myself. Don't I?

I will drain the water away because of this pressure, this affecting of the superstructure, the dwelling. But it's water I require to persist and yet there's no other vessel to transfer it to? This is not a conundrum in that the need for relief is immediate and facts are that there's no alternative vessel anywhere to hand. There's no time to delay and the response I must have and how I should act is clear. Wall panels are shifting and I can see bolts sheering in the eye's ear. Forces.

Forces! What has this to do with legalities? The structure is completely legal and signed off on by engineers. It's the structure we share and use daily and yet I am alone here, in here. Everyone else has left. Empty building undergoing... vectors, forces. I scribble formulae and equations on the wall, time sounds and the period between sounds, take photographs at regular, precise, intervals and compare them But that's just for the record—I don't need to convince myself. But it's salutary, isn't it, the depredations of certainties, our indwelling securities. Instress.

Set in the scape I look inwardly as the box verges on collapse. It has its own rhythm.

The drying out? Yes, the drying out, the extreme dry before the deluge placed stress on the structure. The metal grew fatigued and brittle, its elasticity compromised. I dried out decades ago now, and being exposed to so much water tipping from the sky even with a roof (for now) over my head is worse than being in the ocean with ten metre waves challenging the lanterns of lighthouses.

———

Refrains. I draw refrains. Being of a half-world doesn't mean time is halved. No, as we know, as you might have guessed, every 24 hours is 24 by 60 by 60 during which each minute lacks only a second but we round it off in order to make things easy to maintain the parallelism with you. We know that lost second or non-existent second— that is the divide in the theologies of our societies—is the crux, but we don't make a big deal of it in 'public'. It is a refrain, and it is the loss of part of the refrain.

Duration. We meet. You stress over stress. You invent. I scribble signs of our gathering. And yet, we are constrained. You could say we thrive on constraint. Inventing is not articulate—that's may not be true, but it's what I come away with. At. the. end. of. the. day. The printer's devil is always into the details of the fonts. Superscript holds up the building for all the nu materials, doesn't it? I address you both.

Homogeneity of voice. But we are not one and the same, being so very different. Poles within poles. Apart. And... but... I tell you both, looking over my sketches from our last gathering, our meeting in shared mental space, I notice one of us—just for an instant—held an aggressive pose towards another of us, or both of the others. There was threat and my eyebeam broke when I perceived it and felt its latent or withheld violence. There is threat here? Me? Possible, but I don't think so. But I do get lost in the refrains, in the faking of fakes, in the faking of fake Han van Meegeren's son's fakes, in the quest for the commons painting that will gloss every coverstory.

———

I didn't invent threat and hold no truck with it. My notions, and the devices they could become, are about peace, about sustaining. There's always doubt in your faces. It's not an ideal situation—we three. One speaks, the others listen. We don't overtalk each other, we don't intervene. We say our piece and speak to each other's concerns tangentially, aslant. Nothing is direct and yet there's this threat, this sin of desire, of intent, and one of us is guilty and three of us stand accused by implication. Three of us, not two. What's the use of cracking the code if the information gleaned is more damaging than recuperative?

Invention. So you asked me about my past, especially my mother whom I never mentioned, never alluded to. I mentioned my father, my brothers and sister, even aunties and uncles... all incidentally, in the natural flow of conversation... and yet you latch on to the supposed absence or silence of and around my mother. An omission? A sin? No, contextual. Did she help me in my vocation or hinder me? You would blame the parents but because I made a warm remark about my father you assumed he was supportive and my mother negating. I will neither confirm nor deny but will say that such imposition is what drives me to invent. To invent a way out of language. I am destroyed by your speech, by your manipulations of object and idea through language—your language, not my language.

So, I invented a new form of compass to steer away from language, your language. I will show you. I know you are asking yourselves, but there are no cardinal points, there are no degrees and the needle swings wildly. There is no equivalent of true north, but how can there be in this half world or even the other world by halves? But it does pick up on fluctuations in truth and is... a translator. Of what and how to read is up for question... truth is, I don't even know how to interpret this wondrous truth-teller. But I will learn.

I know by the look on your faces, by the agitation of the compass needle... and maybe this is the key I've been looking for to crack the code... that you want to pry into my workshop when I'm not looking. But I am always there if not here, and have my necessities delivered. And even now using this compass I can tell what's going on in the workshop—that much is clear... it has many side-functions which, like side-effects, are identifiable and describable even if we don't know the name of the ailment they point towards. There's no contradiction in this, and a stable consistent argument can be made around the most evasive and confusing device re understanding. It is not entirely comprehensible yet, but its side applications the extra uses it can be put to are... clear. To me, at least. You will never see into my workshop, you will never enter it, sorry. I don't mean to be rude.

Second Dialogue

Buildings with transparent walls, roofs, ceilings and floors. Rooms designed for meetings, amphitheatres for gatherings and projection and catching every little whisper, and landscape gardens which are the double jeopardy of empire. I knew a gardener to the Shah and couldn't give him what he wanted. You will be disappointed in me to know I tried, I tried to design on paper what he described but only in words. I am making buildings of words these days, as you know, as you well know. Buildings without a sense of self-irony are bound to either impose themselves or be torn down rapidly. Really, I design by words and colour by numbers, and try to reduce the blood and sap and heavy metals on my hand, which is, by the way, no confession of guilt in this instance, dear friends.

———

Colour by numbers. Where would you have me go in trying to find the origin of pigments, colours, the truths of black and white? I favour the Pythagorean systems—numbers, diet, right hand triangles. I realise most of what I illustrate involves triangles, and through triangles I can scry something, just a gimlet's eye... of futurity. And that's why I guess I am drawn to you both. The plumb bob and the tape measure, a sharp eye for detail. But I tolerate errors more than you, architect, and maybe less than you, inventor. I am not claiming innocence in these, not apportioning blame, but it does add up to a mystery. Three people who know each other well but not intimately, who rely on each other's company but who don't know each other's bodies. I think. And yet I have asked both of you to pose for me at times... no, I realise neither of you knew the other had also been asked... I gambled on that... that you didn't share an intimacy I was unware of, excluding me... I can tell by the uncomfortable surprised look on both your faces. A painting of a face should never be symmetrical because literally and conceptually, pragmatically and spiritually, faces are never the same on both sides of the divide.

———

Electricity isn't an invention. So much info and computations carried out by this compass and it doesn't have a single integrated circuit. Moore's law? That's just profiteering? I am not interested in copyrights, patent and brandnames. I invent for the wellbeing of entirety. You doubt me, I know, but I am telling you. Nor is there a single transistor in this compass and nor does it rely on magnetism. The needle floats. So much relies on magnetism. It's therapy. I, myself, have been mesmerised and feel it helped greatly at a vulnerable stage in my career to reassure and even enlighten me—but I've always pulled back from the dangerous knowledges... known my limits. I have only ever been willing to go so far. Remember when I tried to get my Mythopoeia Machine taken seriously and was mocked in review after review, pulled to bits by the media... how frustrating that they couldn't seem to comprehend that it was a de-ironising machine that lapped up absurdity, their absurdity, and converted it to bedtime stories that would receive a universal rating under any system? It made the ugly and obscene beautiful and affirming, it gave... well, structure like your buildings and illumination like your art... using waste and dross and rejected materials of the hoodwinking literacy and aesthetics and turning them into nursery rhymes that imprinted and could assist in recall under the most pressing circumstances. And I had tested on myself, you might recall, and it definitively helped me overcome my addictions to a wide range of behaviours and substances. Further, I was able to address the high levels of lead, mercury and pcbs in my blood and brain tissues, and felt thoroughly cleaned up and out after a single application. And yet, to even mention it in public, would surely bring ridicule and mockery on me. These things we share.

Third Dialogue

Contour drawing you and your latest patent desire. So many people coming off and on the train, masks around their chins. Not one cold front but two and the second is on the tail of the first. A succession of coldness. I make quick sketches on the move but am careful not to go too near others never mind risk bumping into them. Multi-tasking is a visual awareness but acuity is not a thing of the senses alone. Why do perfect shapes serve the most repetitive and choiceless purposes? And yet, when the chromosomes are disrupted the variations can be catastrophic for the life of the shape and other shapes around it. I prepare a board for painting and abandon it, fearing the consequences of getting the vision down. But in my sketchbook I run through the coloured pencils like they are an eternally sprouting forest of fresh and vivid sensations. But the tedium of keeping myself alive vies with the forest and I scribble over the forms to let them free and to give the words a run without lines without even the pattern of letters. It all lacks semblance and guise. I am gardening in a plantless garden where the soil is non-responsive. I plan to draw the three of us together but only at night with all lights extinguished. Maybe if we could find a nightsky park or some place far away from lights driven by power sources, maybe I could use the long-travelled light, the light of extreme distance as illumination. I like the idea that we would be revealed by the light of fading or even lost stars, that it would carry a kind of truth and expose us in the drawings for who we each are and who we are when together. I have no idea how it would look, and don't want to. I just want to draw us and it and see what it reveals. I have a hunch it will tell some kind of truth.

———

The hour glass is my gift to you both—it changes shape and balance according to mood. You can reduce or expand your lives without limit, for in reducing it reaches a point where the last grain can't find a way through and you suspend yourself at that point of entropy.

And it's easy to rebuild and as it expands more grains gather on the positive side of the equation. And it has nuance—it is no competitive win win but a constant give give. And it doubles as a kaleidoscope if you hold it end to end—either end, though the colour-light arrays fall and configure differently. You'll see. How many buildings will be made from splinters of glass and crystal, how many illustrations of windows that exist as windows without necessity for purpose or meaning will come from this. Building to satisfy building. Yes, yes, I do see that this will help no one but yourselves and has no social purpose other than the society we keep with each other, but I genuinely mean it to complement good deeds and works-based encounters with community. It is a way through to understanding why one of us has strayed from the path, why one of us has offended against the other two and all other people, and, in fact, all other life. This is what the hour glass does—it explains for explaining's sakes. It is not a device for vengeance or punishment. I wish to share it with you—I have made one bespoke for each of you, and one for myself, too. This device works as a substitute for imagination but is without imagination—it is too precise a science for that.

———

The tallest building sways... so we try to compensate for the sway. The taller the building the greater the sway and the more we compensate for that sway. People feel seasick elevated in the clouds. And I know people buy wanting the view but often see only mist, clouds... and the swaying gets to them so they sell at a loss just to get out... and it gets into their sleep for years afterwards, the being at sea and going nowhere, the feeling of falling without the attributes of drowning, of slowing down as you sink. I am told you feel as if you join no currents. I have spent time in rooms on top floors of tall towers, and can honestly say it doesn't affect me... but I understand it does others and believe their tales as much as I know the physics of the structures, the materials used to take the stressloads, the mass dampener you know so much about... and that you've drawn... that huge weight moving from one side of the building to the other, compensating for the wind, weighting the building... above the heads of the sleeping... wealthy. The wealthy in their towers feeling at risk when they seek to make themselves invulnerable... this is the crisis of the architect who is drawn into big construction projects to test theories to hope better living for more people will come out of the exclusive... in the long run. I realise how politically and ethically offensive this is to one of you but I surely have the empathy of the other who has contributed so much to the advancement of materials? No? No, I guess not, practical application is not your bag, is it, patents pending but never followed through on as if you've half an idea to join the capitalist gravy train then just forget about it... or, yes, change your mind. I have no such doubts... but that makes me no more capable of a crime against another individual than you. And though you find my modus operandi repulsive, still you meet me regularly and have done for years. Why do we gather, accrue and exchange when we in fact have so little in common?

Fourth Dialogue

The basic mathematical principles deprived me of vision so I had to compensate. This could be any of us saying it, really, couldn't it? Colour by numbers or working out perspective. We are so much closer than we allow in defining our differences. That any one of us would have the necessary... attributes... to commit such a crime. I suppose we have to consider, also, the tendency in each of us to define the nature of said crime and for the two who did not commit it to note the differences particular to one party in the manner of describing. We have our different languages of description and yet, as noted, we overlap more than we... like to admit. I suggest we overlay our conversations, map them over each other, duplicate the template, and redact the commonalities in one instance and then redact the differences in another. This will form a picture, a labyrinth and inventive solution that can be run through a variety of analytical tools... that will tell. Or we could avoid seeing each other for, say, a few months and let the pressure build and see who gives way first— the urge for the confessional or given our different belief systems, *confession*. I agree. So do I. And, what's more, even if we agree upon a time for our next meeting—say on the equinox... yes? okay... so, on the equinox... by that time external forces might have already come into play and solved the crime and arrested one of us. Absolving the need for a meeting? No, we always need to meet, don't we? Then we will meet at the remand centre or prison or whatever the law allows. But each of us in our own way has flouted the law, been a disrespecter of the order of things. Maybe, but each of us has complied as well—I design buildings that won't fall down, and you invent devices that will assist human endeavour, and you paint so others will appreciate or understand what I am trying to say about seeing. I didn't mean *that* way, I meant in our separate lives, in our lives away from the public eye. I am almost always away from the public eye. Some am I. And I. But we need resolution. Yes. And this might be the only plan that will prove viable. For the time being. And if that doesn't work? We'll see. Let's say farewell and aim to meet here on the equinox. See you then. Okay. Yes.

Fifth Dialogue

I am here alone because the others couldn't make it. There's been no confession and no arrest but, as you well know, events have overtaken us all, you included. Interlocutor? No, I wouldn't describe you as that. Usurper, intruder, Committee ex officio... I know... and we all know... your ugly history. But you are listening in, I know, so I will address you here now on the equinox. I turned up because I felt not doing so when it was within my reach would have been to dishonour *our* arrangement, *our* commitment to each other. They cannot leave their homes. No, we couldn't 'zoom in', that's not the way we do things even though one of us could have held a patent for similar technology but eschewed such possession, such ownership as devaluing the integrity of their purpose. Yes, I sketch as I speak—I find is comforting, a deflection of your prying... it helps me retain a sense of equilibrium.

A little about myself? Well, I don't like to think of myself apart from the others, not sitting here at our meeting place... how did you find where we meet, by the way? Well, it can't hurt to say that I knew I wanted to draw and paint from the first time I was given a colouring set by my grandmother who was a professional painter. Not a famous painter, but a painter with a studio who sold enough to paint again. But I feel you're greedy all of you are greedy to expect too much of the others in me, too many selves of others, too many 'Is' that aren't me. I began with no familial connections and have no ancestors and no place memories beyond those I've painted so I fit no theory of belonging. But don't take that as disrespect for other versions of human existence, or animal or plant existence, or of the movement of air. I just am what I see and hear and blot it all up. You're taking advantage of this, I know, but I am compelled to resist the surveillance by over-exposing myself. Do you know the phenomenon of false confessions? Of course you do. Attention-seeking? I'd guess more likely a desire to offset guilt and anxiety by taking all the blame all the consequences in one blow even when they shouldn't exist... because, by proxy, they should, shouldn't they? I mean, it's ironic isn't it, the most alienated party taking in the blame the culpability for all the sins of those who have ostracised said party in the first place? What I am suggesting here is not at all hard to unravel and you will have programmes you will know algorithms that will do the job for you—convert your suspicions into facts, into evidence. The device you hold in your hand uses technologies envisaged by one of those absent today but at least they rejected them as too invasive and risky. But non-filing means no claim, doesn't it? I am reminded of Gauguin painting in his island getaway and the value added by world war to the marketeering of his collecting of imagery. Faces. The movement of bodies, stilled. The way out of where he'd come from to open a way back in. The message in the bottle sent out with an understanding of ocean conditions. Navigated.

Have you ever noticed how brutal a rainbow can look? No?

This expectation, this imposition... that I carry the guilt for another that I represent the guilt of another. I claim my innocence and you still blame me by association because we are all suspect and as the others are absent, I take the burden of responsibility amounting to a de facto form of blame. You suggest by your demeanour that they are family and I am responsible for my family, as if recalcitrant behaviours accrue in some kind of bloodline. I reject bloodlines and so do they. I belong to no one and belong nowhere. I am not answering for them but you're constructing a dyadic arrangement with inherited obligation which we simply don't have.

You are dampening my spirits and suppressing my desire to illustrate. I assume this is part of your purpose.

Yes, we are all photographers... but of very different ilk. Ilk is a noun. I photograph nouns and they do, too, but to different ends. We diverge in so many ways for all our overlaps. The overlaps break down rapidly and we cease to think of each other when we're in the heights of our commitments. But we come back, we overlap again. That's not uncommon—nothing unusual or spectacularly interesting. Isn't this the nature of friendship and isn't friendship an ongoing act of mutual reassurance, as lopsided as it might feel at times? And we all like the lopsided aspect, and that makes three work better than two for us. You are an intruder and observe none of the proprieties and bear none of the anguish and responsibilities of friendship.

This? This is a rest—the padded end goes against the painting surface and it ensure a steady hand for lettering.

I see an old picture of a steamer... carrying 'lumber' from logging operations early in the twentieth century and it's such a jolly image... death of a forest and the splendour of export. That's the crisis of illustration for me.

Sixth Dialogue

He suspects we are telepaths so the crime by one of us is a crime by all of us. Guilt by mental association. But I have no idea which of you is guilty. Nor do I. Nor do I. The problem is in their basic understanding of telepathy, which they see as something total rather than partial and or selective. I admit, I can imagine what you might be thinking, both of you, but at best it's an approximation formed from long familiarity—and even then, it's more about gestures, mannerisms, and tones... not about the specific details or data around your thoughts... I am not a specialist in your fields anymore than are you in mine, so the learning required isn't available to me to decipher... I mean, I can't download all of who you are and your experience and what knowledge you've attained and how you've processed it... I only became privy to your lives... how long ago? ... long ago but not that long ago, not since birth... and even the fact we are different ages and genders and have different ethnicities and different experiences of growing up... how could I interpret what I am supposed to empathically know through being a conduit for all your thoughts if I desire making contact with them, absorbing them? No, maybe they think we just talk silently talk mentally between ourselves but don't have privy to all that each of us thinks and knows. So, kind of failsafes? If so, why are we considered a threat? Because one of us has committed a crime and isn't owning up and thus we are all guilty. By. Association.

Actually, a lot of their fear and anger centres around the anomalous nature of our employment status. I design buildings and am paid by contract. I sell illustrations. And I invent things which I refuse to patent though see stolen daily—but I have 'private means', so I feel lucky. Maybe your private means is why we are all suspect in this yoking. But I live so frugally—how could they begrudge that? It suggests you have some kind of autonomy from them and thus something over them. Well, I grow vegetables in the back garden and catch rainwater in tanks. I have solar power and have had for decades, long before it became readily available—I cannot see I am a drain on their resources. But if you draw money from 'private means' that money must be doing dirty work somewhere—we're all implicated in that. It does its dirty work in a bank. Which does its dirty work. Yes. It was better when we were forced apart—we spend too much time turning wheels in sand, stating the obvious when we are together. Maybe moving our mouths and hands is a relief—stating the obvious rather than thinking the obvious all the time. Yes, there's that.

We should take up cards again. But we stopped because we wouldn't bring in a fourth for Bridge and you insisted we should always play with jokers which can't work. Maybe we should welcome another party into our... clique? How about we make the intruder... The Intruder... part of us? Ex Officio. They wouldn't have the same status and we've always been about equal status. But if they did have equal status? We'd be at risk. Maybe they could determine which of us is guilty and that would relieve the trauma for the guilty and non-guilty parties alike? A kind of circuit-breaker. Yes. But we'd also be feeding the Committee and serving its ends which we've sworn never to do, no matter what. I am confident that enough of our joie de vivre would rub off to prevent such a catastrophe. You mean creating a double agent? No, more a case of them losing the will to betray us. I am sceptical and have never been as fond of bridge as you both. Bridge is a red herring, forget about it... a fourth would be good in so many ways... we need to shift the dynamic. I fear we'll lose what we have. Some of what we have should be lost. Yes.

Seventh Dialogue

We are four? Almost, but not quite. Our fourth worries about our leftist sympathies but joins us to 'even things out'. The question becomes, Why do we accept a basic worldview so antithetical to our own? More in common with an inventor than an illustrator. With an architect. We are not our jobs no matter how obsessive we are in pursuit of our visions, our labour. Freedom is the constraint we put on each other not to infringe on others, on each other. Our liberty is the knowledge of helping the others realise their liberty and not to impinge. And yet, this crime none of us will confess. And now this fourth, who coming so recently to the group, to the fold, might assume to be beyond suspicion, but our kinship is timeless and they were likely to always join us so it's more than possible they are guilty and transferred guilt by association outside the usual temporal constraints. All of us are suspect. Should we collectively take the blame? Our new participant rebels and shudders and exclaims, and yet plays the hand dealt as if the dealer. No, it's not a roulette wheel not a chocolate wheel not a lucky dip not a game of chance. If there is to be infiltration there is to be merging. And the act is now done and they are complicit with us. A weight off each of our shoulders, an Atlas adjustment. We hold up the bit of the world we are responsible for. So, something has shifted.

Let us describe the scene outside the window, the much doubted and deplored window, just to see how we linguistically function as one, how we segue between this verbalising and conceptualising. This is not telepathy, and yet they believe they have caught us out already, but we cannot be caught out because they are one with us.

There is a rabbit grazing. It is a rabbit that has a much longer span of life than other rabbits. But it is not a human rabbit, it is not a David Lynch Rabbit or a figment of his lucky numbers or weather reports. He is working on a telephone holder today so he can steady the camera. He says he could be a good one easy but that... the fun is in the making. You are paraphrasing the rabbit chewing on capeweed that hasn't flowered. There has been so much more rain than usual it is unusual. The trees are bending down but not as supplicants. We are supplicants to them, not the other way around. The interiors of their trunks are soft and being hollowed by termites. Grey shrike-thrushes are lifting the bark for grubs but can't break into the centre. Termites are outside their bio-processing. Termites don't think them and they don't think termites. A bull ant moves along the same trail it moves every day and briefly contemplates the mass of gravel ants moving adjacent to its trail. Neither will bother the other unless they fall. Then it's a case of collecting, gathering, storing. The sky is being drawn into a piece of rose quartz and is being transformed. The sun will come back the next day a different person. The rose quartz will remain much the same. Much the same. Potatoes grow briskly with flopping lounging leafery— their *above ground* is only one small part of their statement, but the fact remains that the tubers are conscious they are of tubers unharvested last year. What does this say about us, the situation? 4.37 light years away, below ground, but close through the window.

But do we want to reach it just to harvest? No, there's more than that, which makes the crime all the harder to comprehend. Listen at the cellular level, hear the sap. Beautiful song is the invention that renews, and we draw on it. Make a nest that does it job and melds back into the mulch. We do not wish to make permanent buildings, but ones that last long enough and then resolve into surroundings. The window falling into the window, the eye of quartz, the shrike-thrush's eye, the droplet holding light of the passing sun as long as it can, full of desire yet... and yet... letting go? What else can we do but anthropomorphise? Yes, yes, we could do that. We agree? We do. But the consequences of joining our halfworld with another halfworld—*that* halfworld? See the wanderer butterfly out of season finding no pollen. Not true, the acacias are flowering and the blooms weather the driving rain. We have been flying with one wing. Two wings are beautiful. Design? No, pragmatic. Pragmatic beauty. Intactness. But we have been half a world how can we see perfection in two halves, in a 'whole'? Two wings divide the air and draw it back together—they are more than a solar sail but need and love the sun. Yes. Yes. Yes........................ err, yes. I mean Yes!

Eighth Dialogue

The government have released their defence investment plan. They are making use of the universities—so eager—to fulfil their dreams of industry. A press release[1]. They are crafting the military state. Many committees. All answerable. To. A. Committee. This question of labour, and yet the idea of labour being used to conserve and

---

[1]   https://www.mediastatements.wa.gov.au/Pages/McGowan/2021/07/Funding-boost-for-WA-based-defence-research-projects.aspx

further the rights of the other half seems alien to the makers of policy. To invent is to sustain, to house is to sustain, to illustrate is to sustain, and to infiltrate is to... breakdown. But we need to reinvent ourselves, to let go of the materials of our trades. No word is more abused than 'sustainable'.

It has been said—by others—that each of us is careless in our dress. That we make do with what comes to hand but are very aware of where and how what we wear came into being. This is difficult for the marketers. We don't buy and yet we cannot go into public naked. And two of us feel the cold, even if two don't. And none of us is familiar with all of the others' naked bodies. And some of us are familiar with more than our own. Closer physical liaisons are risks to our cohesion, and yet they have happened. Out of clothing we are indifferent to yet have thought carefully about. The provenance of our bodies. Our fleshly selves. And what is jealousy when worlds collide?

Intimacy? The whole time projects are ongoing. Epics are being de-illustrated and stories untold. It's not what we say the committees want to record, but rather what we are untelling. They want a record of the letting go, the returning of fragments to their sources, the unloading of the Argo. Simultaneous. We keep to ourselves, masked and interior, and we know those of the far right declare freedoms by bringing sickness to all others. And we know the provocations of the police. The far right is embedded in so many ways to bring confusion to the picture. They say we engender chaos with our non-subscription to the societal norms, our refusals, and yet we work by consensus and refuse control... but are controlled and do not put others in danger via our freedoms. This they see as an irresolvable paradox. We regret apportioning blame for the crime—seeking out one who couldn't confess because it was always part of each of us and all of us. It took the fourth part to help us focus. The spy welcomed in and appreciating and becoming. And yet, as the cops did with the green action groups in Britain... having children by activists and leading double lives... that can never be anything other than theft, usage, violation, abuse. But this is different. Isn't it. There's no pre-destination but we were waiting, weren't we? To answer these we would have to lose cohesion, and can we afford to do so? Or have we already been compromised—poisoned. No, we cannot think like that, we must stay true to our values. And yet, we accused and suspected each other. That is the way all movements are destroyed—from within as much as from without. That's not a truth, but it has aspects of truth. The fire-eaters throw flame just as the horned-helmet man roused the far right. Sydney or The Capitol. Sydney or The Bush. The workers the people who are given the shit jobs who look after everyone else are left vulnerable and blamed. The fire body is the breath of excess across the hemisphere, burning down below the seed layers. Flame throwers. Mining industry. Arms manufacturers deploying... 'creativity'... the inventive modes of the profiteers. Which is not the inventing I do. I? We. But we are autonomous as well as together. We are. Aren't. We?

Ninth Dialogue

Three applicants for an unadvertised position in our group, our cluster. How do we handle this? A nursery home worker, a grain receival point operator, and a busker—musician. They have proffered their qualifications. Where we have no qualifications and we are not a 'membership'. How did this come about? But isn't it what we want? It was different, and yet we agree it was ever thus. What are we and what do we stand for? Us. But that's... selfish... self-possessed... exclusive... narrow... spiritless. But each with our own spirit. We don't think that. No, we can't. So? Let's talk it over with each of them and ask how they became aware of our presence. The committee/s will label us a cult and call us 'self-styled'. And that's inside info. We could have a movie night and talk it over after relaxing. The absurdity of it appeals. Let's watch Resnais's *Last Year in Marienbad...*

———

Who is trying to retro-patent the circle? The beginning of the end which has already begun. We find it hard to cope with remembering things we saw when young. How to express them in our work, our making. With irony, with a flatness that belies the trauma, quoting Genet or wondering what we could have done to prevent a crime we didn't even fully understand was happening till too late, and so many others there and indifferent or separating themselves off. It bothers still. Those crimes that damage people, that exploit the exploited, those are what we consider crimes for which there must be justice. In this light, the crime one of us who are now *we*, one and all, is and are accused of, seems irrelevant. What does it matter that tax returns weren't filed when there was no income, or that sugar was placed in the tank of a big machine that was going to wreak destruction? Which crime was it, or was it both? A case of both. And all the while the impoverished and voiceless are forgotten as the middle class asserts its presence, an 'anti-colonial' *virtue* while ignoring or deny-ing or being wilfully ignorant of their own class's secret doings, or the unseemliness of mentioning the unseemly doings of workers when it embarrasses the having more when more is wanted because those who have more have got it unjustly, which they have... as well. We remember each pain of observation and failure to cope. The illustrations and drafts of collapsed and damaged visions. The big-otry and denial is a geography of class. Marxism works everywhere in its way, and yet it breaks down with the nuances of culture which classes reach across to share, or think they share, though access is regulated by wealth. Maybe we have let Marxism slip away too easily? No, within our small decentralised communities we hope for more. And yet the passer-through, the journeyer, the visitor, samples and takes and leaves, even where it's not offered, hoping to be for-gotten or to go unrecognised and never to be held to account. But we have recorded what we've seen and as ineffective as we've been, it expresses itself in our connecting, our compulsion to return to our telling, our sharing of all the trauma and the joys of remembering. We do know the consumer relies on the hiddenness of child slave labour, and once the more conscience-bothered materialists have satisfied themselves that their petitions and boycotts have served the surface reality, lapse back into buying because purchasing makes their world go around till death do part.

———

Heat transfer in buildings. In and between materials. This is a basis for making contact isn't it? The new Spiritualism?

———

Volume 2

Co-ordinates 1

So we are in the makeshift. We are in the temporary abode. None of us wants permanence, but we do wish to help provide shelter for those who don't have it. Shelter doesn't have to be indissoluble to be effective. Exposed to the elements we increase our telepathic conversing. It is not in actual fact telepathy, but that's what the committee call it and bug us accordingly—that is, with tech designed to eavesdrop, to infiltrate where bodily presence and external recording devices (outside the mind) can be inserted, placed etc. Our thinking is shelter, and yet we all know that speaking will make us bolder and more resistant to inclemency. And yet speaking can so easily betray our position.

Co-ordinates 2

Have we thought adequately about the ambient energy of thousands of bees and other insects over the capeweed flowers on a sunny but not overly hot day in late September? I don't mean in terms of harvesting their energy—let their energy be their energy, and the flower's—but rather in that ambient way that the biosphere itself enjoys, relishes, exchanges, increases and sustains itself by? As part of the recycling of energy without expecting any more of it than it gives as excess, as being part of the circumstance of being? We have not, not really. Others probably have in their own ways and with their own set of insects and flowers surrounding them, and it might be part of a psychology of energy and being we are not part of or privy too, but in itself, here and now, no, I don't imagine we have thought about it much at all, if at all. And if we had, even we out on a social limb, excluded and self-excluding, would probably consider it a rush of over-imaginings, of illustration (sorry) more than science. And yet, we extend ourselves into each other's processes don't we... so maybe... in the way a building warms itself, in the way a reflective surface holds the sun back from our interiors. And yet reflection in the upper atmosphere is counterintuitive, isn't it, as geo-engineering sabotages climate in so many other ways. Yes, that is not the bee noise energy, it is the death of bee-noise energy. I am inventing a de-tech tech, a tech that undoes all tech. And I am looking to housing that grows sap and tendril. And I am drawing on the capeweed whose intrusions speak my condition and I am learning to see a colour wheel inside the colour wheel, and it is liberating. We are paying attention.

Co-ordinates 3

What aloneness we find in each other's company. We don't love each other, we don't desire each other, and yet we are compelled to each other. We negate our own choices. And yet... and yet... and yet... the energy in this is addictive. No, only if you believe depression can be addictive. It is, in some ways. To says so is to be outside it and to lack compassion. I am depressed often, and shuck it off in company. Together, we alleviate your depression? No, not at all—I pretend... you are just insensitive to my situation, overwhelming me with the idea of oneness and shared consciousness... more is blocked and suppressed than stimulated and released. We must factor this in.

Co-ordinates 4

'The breakdown of civil society'... we are told this, if we don't comply, and yet the tellers sanction the consuming of the surfaces and interior of the planet. We have to factor this in to our response: that is, that they will never relinquish their claims on the right to consume the materials of the world. We are expected to be details in the obituary only Elon Musket and his cronies will be left to read. He is no inventor, never was—he is an obliterator. And an entertainer, he is an entertainer in the Las Vegas sense of the word. Yes, tigers on the stage in cages, sparks in combustible habitats, pie in the sky. A fashion plate.

Co-ordinates 5

Maybe we haven't done anything in the external world and only imagine we have or ward off the reality of not having done anything by talking about all we've supposedly done so much. If that's the case, then we have much to be proud of—self-sustaining in our circle of series circuit, impacting no one and nothing but ourselves. But wouldn't that separate us off from the sufferings of the earth, wouldn't that short-circuit the possibility of real empathy? Is this damaged world we discuss really a figment? Are we over-determining? And if that is the case, where and what are we? No feet on the ground, no pictures others might comment on or buildings others might inhabit, no de-tech invention to undo the wrongs. Pissing in the wind. The republic of talk. But at least we are equal citizens in this construct. Really, I mean are we really?... I sincerely doubt this is the case and I have never felt an equal among equals... in fact, I feel condescended upon as an artist... I feel that I am, at times, humoured because without me there'd be no circuit, no completeness. We disagree. We all need each other. I wasn't contesting that aspect of our reality... and that doesn't invalidate my point... and you can't tell me what I feel even if you feel it's a fait accompli... the oneness is the oppression.

Co-ordinates 6

I want us all to imagine the same scene and each describe it so we might discover the shortfall in our collective thinking. We will discover something about ourselves in this, and something about our connectedness. Yes. Yes. So, let's focus on a mountain. But the only place we call a mountain in this whole region is barely a mountain. Still, we are all thinking of the same place so let's keep that in mind— it's eroded down with ancientness and is like no other place in the world, and is deeply sacred and to be respected. Agreed. Agreed. Let's consider a larger mountain in terms of, say, height... one we have all known in our separate selves. We have all seen Everest. We have all seen Mont Blanc. We have all seen Snowdon. We have all seen Hungry Hill, which is also small as far as mountains go and hollowed out by copper miners and yet I can sense that we all wish to focus on that place. I am not sure. Neither am I.

Co-ordinates 7

Has it crossed your minds that we might not be complete in ourselves and are seeking completeness in a shared oneness? I have dreamt in my waking state that we have been hived off from parts of ourselves, that we occupy this hemisphere verbally and another hemisphere non-verbally, and that our bodies seems increasingly less relevant to us because we are, in fact, disembodied. How long since any of us has been outdoors, has breathed the air of higher and lower places, rather than imagining or recollecting or discussing how we will act in such environments? We conceptualise the damage whilst being physically disconnected from the damage. We have lost contact with ourselves and have compensated by having greater contact with each other in order to fill in the gaps in need for new experience, for engagement with the world. we are feeding on one another's experiences to make new experience. This has to be finite, doesn't it? We are part of a half-world that will wobble in its parallel orbiting with the other half-world we are only now fully realising has been sundered, separated... as if the split in the globe is the way it has always been when it hasn't. We have adjusted to cataclysm, which is the loss of values. That's why the other party, the committee infiltrator, has gone quiet? They were bodily and mentally of the other half, and we lost them. Or they destroyed us and enforced the separation.

Co-ordinates 8

The protests are coming from the far right which is not activism as we recognise activism as an act of empathy. The right, especially the far right, act without a broadly sensitised empathy, don't you think? We do, and we feel it in our memory and shared consciousness. Activism becomes amorphous in being commercialised and co-opted into a discourse of selfishness and oppression—that is how the bigots seek to de-activate the idea of activism as a motivating force. And this is why we'll be up against it trying to bring the two halves of the world back together, back into alignment. One biosphere nurturing difference. Someone will profit from that thought and in doing so nullify its healing intention. Why would some parties want this separation?

It seems to make no sense, but look to the profit margins and the power quotients of certain parties and you'll find an answer. We need an embodied form to walk this half and another to walk the other half to work for the coming together—how can we best achieve this? We need proxies in both places who will retain their own identities but be willing to carry us, work with us... in the abstract. Yes. Yes.

Co-ordinates 9

Are you sure we're not all being driven by our obsessive interests, our shared interest, in the idea of symmetry? The world was a globe and then it wasn't. There was a biosphere and then there wasn't. The world was split as they detonated weapons. The world was split as they tried to tap the core for energy. The world was split because it was choking. Symmetry is not perfection, but in the case of an orbiting body of considerable size worked on by gravity, symmetry is desirable, is it not? Yes, but we have to be cautious... imposing symmetry can have unforeseen consequences. But we are only talking about a single rather than a half world, a unified planet. Still, we should be wary of not only the term but ask ourselves why we are all so obsessed with the idea in itself. Because of our vocations? Maybe we found those vocations because of our conditioning, our predilections towards symmetry. I see problems with symmetry. So do I. So do I. We need to question ourselves further before dragging in other parties. We need to act now, so maybe we can discuss this with said parties and take their views on board? Maybe. Maybe. And there's the problem of who we approach and all the predilections and prejudices we take to making that... selection. We are projecting ourselves onto the healing. Yes. Yes.

Volume 3: Two people walking two half-worlds—
the tales of Hester and Bell

A. Hester's Tale (Half-World 'A'): the 'energy crisis'

When the world split in two I had a foot on each side of the division. So strange it split along the equator rather than longitudinally. I always imagined if push came to shove, it'd go north to south. But there you go. I was taking in the tropical sunset and thinking about my booking on a SpaceZ flight in its Visionless Five capsule, when I felt a slight shudder and saw the palms shivering and thought to myself, this is not the place to be standing. Did I step the right way? Well, I stepped north and that kept me in the picture for my flight, so I am sure I did. That I later heard that just such a flight caused the split didn't put me off, but I was disappointed that the new physics—a consequence of the split—meant I'd only be able to orbit a half planet, though we'd be able to see the other half in its close but separate realm. I don't really understand the ins and outs of this new physics, but I have no reason to doubt those telling us all about it. I am a believer.

B. Bell's Tale (Half-World 'B')

I was deep in the southern hemisphere when it separated off from its significant other. I won't say better half. We have to stop thinking outside of 'halves', don't we, the half being complete. I have no binaries, and yet I am aware. Of. Them. This lapse in the process of making... instalments in the Big Text of a cycle... the prose manifestations of a poetic impulse. To tell... to tell nothing. That is, to tell nothing but say plenty. I have rung the bell of corporeality and now gravity is so much less than it was (it doesn't equate to half of 9.81 m/s^2), I need to cover the ground myself: architect, illustrator, inventor... But I am no spy no fifth column undermining what's left after the *mines* split the earth... not precisely in two, as intimated (and said), but disproportionately. This conversation with myself about spiritual lack... and the gain of something neither material nor spiritual. An awareness? My new power source is neither sun nor waves nor seismic shifts generating... energy, this new energy, is inherent. There is a science to it, but I am latching on to the mystical. Ectoplasmic. This relies, of course, on the goodwill of the dead who are able to shift between the different parts, the 'halves' as we once termed them. It takes a while to adapt to new ways of talking of the state of things. The ghostly adhesive of our 'livings days'. The grotesque underpinnings of our thirst for energy, for power generation, for a reading light and artificial warmth. At least the devices have gone—the gravity remaining not up to the task we'd impose on them to hold on... to the devices. Floating off into the demi-exosphere and dispersing... stellar space junk. And those thousands of SpaceX satellites that doomed us all, bobbing away to mimic the sun and bring misery to dark matter.

And so I am... crouched, holding on to an old tree that has had pity on me, breathing the thin atmosphere rapidly. All things in one, I have to be, and that is my catastrophe within the catastrophe. But I am not catastrophising. No. I am composing texts as ends in themselves. I am decorating my interiors. I am designing purpose. As if I have rights I do not have in the cessation where nothing was ceded and the wreckage is excuse enough for new claims? It's not.

Even by halves it amounts to more than the colonialists could ever claim or take... it is core and resilient and retains its shape against the breaking apart... The Great Erosion... The Split... The Sundering.... The Division... it retains and the spirit remains and none of this ectoplastic energy has anything to do with that spirit. The designers of the new energy have discovered ghosts cannot be appropriated so rely on those who brought the damage to feed the new possibilities. Where do I sit—or cling—in this?

Ring the bell. Bell chimes. Carillion. Chimestand. And the vigilante version: 1 to 1½ diatonic octaves. And the muffled bells of death. And the two quarter hour chimes that not longer make a... *half*. How to identify with the name you were given and have always felt uncomfortable about but let it stick because it rings out and gives you something to cling to... though you shudder, vibrate, are shook like in a poem. And now I have all the time in the world to talk as the new energy is being tapped and rerouted to make our new lives modern and 'liveable'. We are told by The Committee that, *There will no longer be questions*. We will live the better parts of an unquestioning existence. The new physics is a physics of security and contentment. We are told.

I think about the refugees and a thought-intrusion comes... What refugees? It is not my thought, it is an interjected thought. To insert thoughts like this takes energy and I know The Committee has prioritised intrusions in the rerouting. The ectoplasmic power will be sucked up in this new tech... and the ghosts... the ghosts I realise are not willing sharers, not the rapacious of the past in synch with the new rapacity... they are being tapped and drained. I realise this now but wonder how much of my new thinking about bells and halves is my own? And something nags away at a distance... does it matter does it matter does it matter anyway? I think, I still think... I think it does. I must find a companion. The tree is tolerating me out of compassion, but it is not a real companion... that is my limitation, I am sure. I must ring out. Forgive me, I am running on limited mental capacity and these intrusive thoughts are starting to dominate. I need to think clear and straight and out of the new physics. I will let go of the tree and drift... hopefully encountering someone who will befriend me... who I might trust.

Hester and Bell Drift and Collide and Befriend Each Other... twin-halves of...

Hester and Bell / Bell and Hester. What a pair we make, what a pair. We have found each other, found one another, drifted into one another, collided like... twin peaks twin halves of the circular logic, one together together as one, that will be our mantra. We celebrate! Together we have found an energy together we drive the intrusive thoughts out and already we are talking about connecting with others, developing and becoming part of a collective. The halves into quarters, the quarters into eighths... bringing energy by fusion and division. We will be contradictions within and against the new systemising of being. But our halves with be different by half. We are realigning! *We celebrate*... ourselves, ourself.

———

The semi-perpetual motion of thought. The 'feelings array'. The shared storage capacity. We are expanding our collective to include you and you and you, too. We are an us now.

I seem to remember being part of a group of... some of you might have been part of it, too? Was that before or during the split? The sundering? Do we all know each other across the distance we are now trying to heal? Are we finding a new temporal syntax? Are we familiar to each other yet unaware? I know we feel an increase in gravity and adhesion and cohesion as we approximate, and we are hearing each other's voices. But are we complicit with The Committee's purpose in this? Is our togetherness generating yet another source of energy they're tapping into, splitting and then fusing our atoms? Will they sell us as the new clean energy coming at such a high ethical cost to ourselves though we, they hope, remain blithely unaware? We must take all this under consideration. As the carbon sinks of the underworld were torn open in the split and carbon dioxide and methane spewed into space, it was rumoured The Committee claimed open slather on a new round of extracting and polluting from the 'reserves' that remained. They declared, we think, don't we remember, recall, isn't it what is said now as we float in the half-atmosphere, searching for anchorage?... they declared that science had won out yet again and would always win out. And when challenged about the vague nature of 'science', they proffered a humanist model based on Thomas More in his later phase as pursuer and executioner of 'heretics'? Religion and science in... 'proximity'? We can't recall precisely, everything is still so scrambled and garbled in this anti-Babel that split the world... longitudinally or latitudinally...? It's hard to work out... or snapped apart at the equatorial hump... though the compass suggests weakened twin poles but what kind of compass is this...? Aren't we a little west of

Dumont d'Urville Station? What does the compass show?

———

Volume 4

We are not quorate and yet we act as if we are. But haven't the grounds shifted in more than literal ways? How do you rouse the energy to keep the resistance going when no one can form a full idea, where a demi-existentialism is the best we can gather, summon up... muster? Muster is a bothering word. More or less so because there are no herds left. They gathered the deer in the highlands and shot them down, increasing the profits of armament companies in a minor but, to them, welcome way. How fast does the non-lead shot come to earth in shooting greenly? And that wasn't even non-lead bullets, was it? These thoughts that stray through our cobbled together psyche. Why do they want to weigh the birds down more than they are weighed down by their single wings?

Can trees thrive on a semi-circle of bark? And now they are half ringbarked, it's so much easier for the slayers of trees to close off the avenues of sap. To stymie the flow.

We will make do with clauses. We will compile narratives from the residues. Reconstituting we will make whole again. Their altering the course of the asteroid through impact thrilled and entertained them in their space-warrior mindset, all world good via patriotic agendas. And now we have half a yo-yo with the string unravelling, the semi-circle rolling violently towards the gutter. And we ask, how can we play now? What do we play with half a day, half a night? How do we get enough hours of circadian delight? This theology of material comfort we cling to, unreally. Vampires caught in eternal summers at poles that have no grip, no cover. And this was never prophecy because it was the urge of the early modern, wasn't it. And the urge of the classical ages of gunpowder around the world when the world was roughly round. And the eighty days of appropriation resounds as we piece it together with the divisions of vocab we are left with, compiling amongst ourselves having been our own worst enemies. Half a Phileas Fogg, 1872. Half a route of consumer conquest remarketed by The Explorers' Club, NYC (established 1904): 'One was the British consul at Suez, who, despite the prophecies of the English Government, and the unfavourable predictions of Stephenson, was in the habit of seeing, from his office window, English ships daily passing to and fro on the great canal, by which the old roundabout route from England to India by the Cape of Good Hope was abridged by at least a half.'[2] In this diagesis we say: 936 and 952 and the sound so much closer, so much more familiar, so much more in proximity of one another. Yes, *saeculum obscurum*, in the Eurocentric sense which is still 'intact' or 'demi' now—go figure this new geography, its aberrant typographies.

Half a dose of a mood altering drug a micro dose of a correction in the visionary drawl. The peddlers are still peddling and buying into the 'common good' while still trying to advance careers to the half full rather than half empty graduated cylinder. And these patients they've latched on to—Hester and Bell... they claim to be so many things wobbled into one. Single-minded, they make such

---

[2]   https://www.gutenberg.org/files/103/103-h/103-h.htm

bold claims. The people they knew, the people they were, and the people the New Medicine will allow them to become. The New Medicine of 'muh freedoms' is the control mechanism the gatherings would foist on the all going separate ways together with undertones and overtures of violence, their legion warrior independence. Only hate hasn't halved by the diminished population—mass death is nothing compared to their own life selections, never (to their minds) to be *impeded* for any common good. In this confusion, Hester and Bell come among us all claiming there is still a common good, that we can be safe together in 11111 words, it is said.

All we have left to us, telling the truth, is second person. But you are absent.

And so they suggested a landscape, retro in their need to construct something to redefine, having erased and deleted. That guilt reflex. Imagine, they said, a hillside that can never receive shade though is always affected by gloom, imagine a tree that grows down though must still photosynthesise, imagine a broad river that flows into a shallow stream which can take all the water the river can deliver and more but it flows nowhere. Imagine a sheer rockface you can walk down as if it was stepped at the appropriate pitch and width to accommodate your each and every step. They suggested this, but you have so many doubts. And so we meet, inquorate, seeking a way through. How much of this is the pedagogy of calamity absorbed and taken in as original. What you taught comes back at you as someone else's creativity. But that is the generosity of teaching and you should expect it as we attempt to renew, make whole the divided, say the half empty as... completely full.

Semi-circles of solar panels.

Epidaurus a quartered memory, the soundscape claustrophobic with personification, yet hopeful. As if you possess those travelogues and can shine a demi-light on them as you please. These unsettling consequences. These ghost-half looking to fuse to make many ones, to replicate the populating of spaces. And the grasping still hoping on harnessing the massive release of energy come about by cascading fusions. The uni-winged bird on the shadeless hill always enclouded, the tree waving its roots burnt by a sun doubling its heat to compensate by halves. The river denying its sources, its mouthings. Those warnings heeded and streamed for all to be part of, buy into. This is the New History of the oldness. The new vilifications labelled as historiographic 'protection against discrimination'. The half-paradox is the software.

———

And we say that half-dreams are more disturbing than full dreams and when we try to collectively realise a fullness the vague memory of what full was still seems to be lacking. But it is better, even as metaphor. We seem to lack a human condition in this crisis of pivot, perch and imbalance, made all the more awkward because we know the crisis is of our making. What will we eat today? How will we sustain our drive towards a new wholeness, a shifting of standards and of nomenclature itself? We hope old knowledges will fade to allow us to feel more comfortable, but truth is so loud even The Committee find it almost impossible to obfuscate and suppress the reality.

Some have taken to grazing on lichen. Some have taken to grazing on dirt. Some have taken to sifting the air for biological particles, ingesting them through breath. But there are so many toxins: organic and inorganic. But stating this obvious fact is seen as passé. What do we read if we read any more? Underminings. Snippets of speech transcribed and implanted to create mutual hatred. The hate increases by halves. This consuming.

These utterances of despair. Are we reinforcing each other's despair in our desire to become whole? Maybe we should just fragment back into our slivers of self? The collective a loose agglomeration rather than a fusing? But then we can't expect the ghosts to fuse to generate energy for our individualities, can we? Asking them to take the burden, saying that without such an effort there will be no afterworld for them to inhabit, for us to go to, to join them. And to join the responsibility? It's easy to say, Don't worry, we'll be there eventually to share the duties, the pain of making energy... but that sounds like the corporate financial system that underwrote the split, the breaking of the world. Operating on credit, in lieu of payment, signing our lives away and the after-lives of those already dead. No, that is wrong, and we know it. Hester and Bell. Bell and Hester. And... architect, inventor... and illustrator.

———

Labour. Divisions of labour. To labour outside gain and loss. To labour for mutual benefit, with no one's labour worth more than anyone else's. Maybe this can only happen through the half dream. The Committee is already impeding such demi-thinking. They want a wholeness of thought that facilitates hierarchies and class, that makes for degrees of wealth and degrees of poverty. But an idea is forming that doesn't require wholeness that carries with it a new intactness. Learning outside the classroom. This symposium of bodies and semi-circles of thought. No IQ tests will diminish here as none can take a grip in their privileging of certain knowledges under certain conditions. In destroying the globe, in de-rounding the world through their greed and rapacity, through their sciences of exploitation, they have created a void in which hierarchies can't get a grip, a void in which void is fructification... and desirable, where desire isn't about control... or that's what we hope, but The Committee is gaining traction, simulating a spherule certainty that broods ambition for more and more and for others less and less. They are constructing ideas of circumference and then of enveloping and clasping the orb. The labour regime they are trying to instil is promising bonuses, of getting ahead, of the ability to purchase again in the half-formed shops of their industriousness. This is their en-fleshing of AI, the substituting to allow for 'growth'. It is the cybernetics after the disaster which is now to be called the Awakening.

―――――

We scry the floral diagrams.

―――――

Is this the consequence—that is, regarding the manner and mode of describing, not as per the event, the catastrophe in itself—of only ever semi-circling the house to compile laps making up two half-laps to equal the one that can never work because of impediments and obstacles? Is it to do with the kangaroos—'keystone species'— eating the bark from the trees and almost ringbarking but not completing the circle? And then, disturbingly, in some case they do, closing out life, killing off the trees they rely on in a variety of ways as well, sheltering as they eye the open grass grazing areas. These bits of predictability falling out of synch? Redbacks casting their straggly webs from paving bricks to weather-proof power switches on external surfaces, sheltering beneath to go out trawling and testing their lines after dark? It is getting hotter, much hotter, and the sound of angle grinders through the bisected valley brings a horror and it's not even augury, it's brute attested fact under all conditions, with or without the surface of the sphere and its non-Euclidean spatiality. The mapping is realigning to compensate which is a fiscal consideration and sapped of creativity and the energy of growth.

———

The split. The massive release of energy the opportunistic capitalists and militarists and superpower mergings of all versions of exploitation and oppression had looked to harness this energy bonanza, gambling they'd be in the half that survived. Some were sure they'd got the science of the new geography right, and smugly prepared their post-world prosperity. But it has not happened even vaguely as predicted, or induced. And neither half was now truly aware another half existed. There was a void and a shadow and the gravitational disruptions whilst indicating another body of equal size were anomalous and convulsive. All imagined the molten core had poured into space and solidified to form a sick demi-moon. The centre was viewed as a potential dwelling space but was either one completely exposed to the sun or one that was never touched by sunlight. These were the concerns that possessed The Committee and the anti-Committee. It was Hester-Bell who had the original and anti-original thought that each of them was complete in another half-world, that all was in flux because of its antithesis.

———

Volume 5

So, this is the antithetical gatherings of minds? The anti-Hester the anti-Bell. The anti-illustrator, the anti-inventor, the anti-architect... and the anti-infiltrator? It would be, but it's not that easy to resolve. Two halves can no longer make a whole.

———

Who are these new half-minds trying to join with us? And why do we hesitate? Have we fallen back into our cabal of selectivity? Yes, I remember these entities as characters. We have read all the experimental fictions in the cycle—part of that small gathering of unlike minds who, when the world was still whole, found glimpses of a future they wanted to prevent and read on through the typos and infelicities of grammar.... yes, those characters who were never rounded always flat who had no physical features, no outwards attributes of inheritance that would allow for labels of genetics to adhere. We know them in knowing them less. We know their musical interests but not tastes, their ambitions and disappointments but not deepest loves and likes... so much surface lost what could we do with the interiors but perceive them as hollow? And even this would suggest a closing off an ending to the cycle as if the failure of global thought means emptiness. But no, this is where we start to gather again without economies, without attributes of global power, without projections of force. Foolish thinking, especially as The Committee is making such inroads into the brokenness to reassert its control, that free trade hegemony, that dictatorship of business. That democracy fuelled by slavery. That party trick of wealth for everyone that is endgame for resistance. That personal freedom at the expense of collective freedom immolation. All that, yes, and the subtle brutalities of history forgotten or rerouted, the correcting of old wrongs to cover the proliferation of new wrongs. The self damnations that are self-assertions.

The moon moth at the window is a southern moon moth, which suggests we are all southern or the compassless reorientation of the half world is not an axis. The moon moth has two wings, even if one has been torn by some unseen force. It was full then it was torn. But it has two wings. This is how we can think, isn't it? That the echidna struck on the road as darkness set in was already dead, had already been struck. The impact of a vehicle back when the world was whole to blame for a half-world where vehicles no longer grip, are useless, though one of the promises of The Committee is to stabilise the old transports, to get the arterials flowing. And then, as we know in this little gathering growing bigger by the second, the half world will split again into quarters and we will divide again and again down to less than building blocks. This is our new concept of time, and it's devastating. What have we to gain knowing this together when in divided partial selves we just don't remember and in not remembering can't know, can't act to prevent it happening all over again. Differently all over again? But then... then again... and again the perceptions of world to divide world to conquer blasted into the genome via ethical scrutiny that lapses conveniently... the syntax of loopholes... the perforations drilled into the earth's crust so when the catastrophe undoes the wholeness it will break apart into sectors into slices of influence? That is such a glib view, isn't it? But we, together, constantly arrive at the same conclusion. The Committee would wrest the burden of conclusions from us, safeguarding in the halls built by their billionaire over-lords, the original primary splitters of the planet, the foundational defounders.

———

Remember the forest? Remember the disturbances? The pastoralists the land developers the miners the shooters the bush bashers the four-wheeler families... remember the stress of the ecological house when placed under the management of Colonial Estates inc.? Remember:

And who was that walking away from the eye of technology, a loving eye that couldn't evade the provenance of the New Tools? But we know this tool was being used to subvert the arguments behind the making of such tools. No longer purchased, but held as mechanism to revert back to co-existence with vegetal growth and all species. That is not us walking away back when we were whole, but it is our amanuensis, isn't it? Was he trying to help save a forest from destruction, from the avant-garde of drillers with their

diamond tips and the promises to the market of glories? Of the greenwash of metals for 'green technology', to undo the engines of climate with the devices that announce a better climate for all? Was that him, thinking us before we were split asunder, divided from ourselves as well as each other and all other life. All the others. The Total Othering. These are questions without question marks, these are statements of contradiction in the walking away but walking towards love and hope, all that he cherished. He is gone now, speaking us? That is a question.

———

Semiology of music tells me to locate the semibreve the semitone the semiquaver, tells us to catch the pipped at the post squeezing through an unseasonal syrinx. What are these new seasons and how do we associate them with moods? Our mood, your mood, my mood. What alterations will be proffered by replacement regimes? We blow the tick tock flowers, the seed blown till half the time that would once have shown shows. Already were are forgetting the whole notes. But that *is* the semibreve, isn't it, and we are left with two quarters and our memory of two quarters will be halved so we remember half the English expression as opposed to the American English expression, these tyrannies of language control which seem so bizarre in the face of not being able to utter more than the lower or upper register of words, or to write diacriticals and below line loops and little more. Twice a crotchet... yes, we are still the minim and the minim is what we catch and share and build. These chamber orchestra gatherings. The growl of Napalm Death searching for its beat, its guitar riffs. The remorseless wind that swirls over the erasure, the hole where a forest once grew. That we know is the start of the anti-chronology. We know that, and divided and divided again, it won't be made an untruth, no more than a nuclear waste dump's persistence on the last slab of stolen land presented as real-estate for one-sided duplexes with Christmas-cracker torn solar panels and 'Fear God Not Covid' placards stuck in the no longer spirally plughole.

––––––

So we are left with the task we have just consigned to ourselves. The collective only has access to the first page of *Rayuela*... so we have to imagine what might have followed. Does Paris still exist or did it split down the dotted line that bifurcates the Seine, so the canal boat can only visit one bank, and *Atlanta* only one possible set of frames. We jump about the narrative, this much we can ascertain without an author's note, and that's all we will read without the promise of more. So, we segue what we have, these increments of the cycle this record of a fiction begun in our teens and now called on to make a chronicle of what came before. The only history we have of ourselves as ourself, and one that other such gatherings will likely be indifferent, too. Still, maybe the time will come when we merge and share and release a new energy and energy so vital that none of us will have the gall to tap it for personal benefit. Maybe in the shadow worlds it's already been happening, in the hospitals of trust in the schools without bullying in the shade where The Committee can't reach and its spies forget as they crossover and enter. Where there is parity in cures and equity in care. Imagine. We are imagining and increasing our imagining. But it's not a game and was never a game and we aren't trying to prove anything, not even nothing. Each of us had an interest in viewing items gathered in galleries, museums, in porticoes and pop-up venues, and yet, we are sure, all of us questioned and tried to undo the curatorial. Clutching at straws, we conclude in a demi kind of way, that we must have gained energy and purpose from paradoxes which we can no longer piece together. But we know there were truths and one of us suggests we only knew veridical paradoxes and were thus always too sure of ourselves and formulated an end we didn't actually believe would come, and then we were caught one foot either side of the split, or on the edge, at the risk of falling or having already fallen through the crack of our own making. We conjecture. Our family bonds confuse us and we can't define others in family, not even through birth order and never through gender which we doubt we ever subscribed to. All we find in ourselves are traces of genitalia but no will to reproduce. The Committee insisting on reproduction until they get the incubation chambers up and running again, until they can farm the necessary biological components. But we are fusing now and not splitting, we are making one, not many.

―――――

Here are some bits combined into what we might remember of visiting different places. Were any of these places once those we'd identify as 'local', as 'home', of places of personal and community importance. To any of us, to ourself? Here is a bridge that is a diving board and here is a road that was made to end nowhere in an earlier famine, and here is a scald that shimmers with the residue of a tall forest, and here is a building taller than the trees yet that sways to breaking point in the swirl of wind that begins and ends nowhere—it was an apartment block and an office block and a tower that glowed with the name of a mining company. There is a band making a low-budget video for their latest... they are smashing things and drinking from square bottles, they are spitting at the camera they have invited to be part of the proceedings. They are part of the local punk scene, despising and mocking and laughing as well. Maybe they are the Drunk Mums or C.O.F.F.I.N. ... but that's distant music scene and chaos over-rides the split with its menace and... humour? Guitars seem something to do with irony and the capo down the fretboard halves only certain possibilities. But that's another band and another occasion of being off your face. A half masque. We seem sure of all that. The curriculum vitae paradox?

––––––

The 'goodly creatures'? Who are they? Were we ever one of them? Do we think worlds into a bravery that is their demise, extensions of our passions, desires? Do we mineralise content in order to extract it and utilise to extend the range of our projections? Why do we now want to call ourselves Miranda, absorb not only Hester and Bell and all the other players who are fragments of their previous selves from all cycles of the narratives, all aspects of the parallel circuit, all globes feeding off the sun? Why are we Miranda in the hope of making ourselves whole, of exclaiming wonder as we encounter a whole being again, constructed out of the residues of all others that joined our circle, empathised with our fate? The Committee is already working to articulate an accusation, getting as far as saying 'necromancer' and 'witch' and 'fortune teller' and 'monster'. They say Miranda is just the name of a travelling troupe, a fair ground frippery, a journey into the twilit world on sedatives, and eventually an anaesthetic that erases memory, makes dead time. But we have found our life in Miranda's vision of completion, and we grow old with her now, and then we are ageless. But this doesn't mean we will leave behind the torn and bloody half-world. No, we are committed to its protection and the healing and eventual welding together of the halves. Half full plus half full. But we are wish fulfilling and dissolve back into fragments—always the dissolutions. Remember studying the hospital ceiling... in the ward, the 760 holes in the grid overhead... remember the fire sprinkler system, the flower looking down on you, the flowering upside down, its stem swollen with red liquid, sensitive to fire but not your fever. Flower growing upside down, a half a world away. And you waited for them to come and wheel you to the theatre, to insert the cannula, to let the sleep juice and anti-pain juice flow as pain is the outrider to body's desire for wholeness; handing over to others who will show you through into the erasure, who might if they choose to bring you out, let you emerge, or lose you. We see the hottest face of Mercury that day, and always the sun showing a way through to our better halves? In the museum they display the shards of a red-figure case that barely amount to half and yet are confident via precedent, other finds, a knowledge of mythology, literature, and customs, that the other half would have detailed... and said... and meant... and from the fragments we have our wholeness.

———

Constraints in eclogues. Songs call for invention, for architectonics, for a sound-weaving of images. We have this to go on. A template, no? Did one of us sneeze? A full sneeze bringing relief? Or a sneeze spreading our... interiority. The Committee is trying to separate our polyphony, prise apart our counterpoints, sever us from our togetherness with loop diathermy. They fear an infinite canon. Hester, Bell *and* Miranda. *Canon perpetuus*. As if... it's as if... it's their anger over the prospect of wholeness... they have talked up the division so much they cannot envisage any other way. That was the past, this is the present, and they claim it as theirs just as they disclaimed the past and destroyed it. With no seasons as anyone understood them, the 'new seasons' come into play and the rounds are banished. No more 'Sumer is icumen in...' ... and their industry of goat farming so they can consume them after they've captured their flatulence, is the emblem of the new agriculture... so summer is gone and 'Blaze' introduced... but their emblem and saying is 'bucke uerteþ'. Round is the one sided yo yo singing down its string till it unwinds and spins off towards the sun, emblazoned. Is this what we think? Are we gaining clarity? Can we thwart The Committee? Can we make narratives among the shards and fragments, the torn and bleeding, the excavated and desecrated? We caught sight of this remnant flittering in the whirling wind come down down down from Doggerland desert, we think... what script in the run time, what data security are we still held by, what servers spill their encryptions out into distressed space, what ASCII founding paternity, what character encodings, what ampersand or section sign, what 17 planes in which 'O' is no longer round but divided, what unit that is bytten in half?

These drawings we're making as we think. A line connecting with light connecting with darkness the tangent, yes, the tangent, the trigonometry of hope. We discover the pleasures of malarkey we'd lost, but something grim and dissipating comes with that malarkey

---

3   https://commons.wikimedia.org/wiki/File:Sumer_is_icumen_in_-_Summer_Canon_(Reading_Rota)_(mid_13th_C),_f.11v_-_BL_Harley_MS_978.jpg#/media/File:Sumer_is_icumen_in_-_Summer_Canon_(Reading_Rota)_(mid_13th_C),_f.11v_-_BL_Harley_MS_978.jpg

as well. There is a compass turning to joint but its legs slip away and it cannot make contact. No spirals overlap other spirals and the graph is uncontained. But containment fields are what led to our loss in the first place, and yet without containment we dissolve. These paradoxes are the paradox of our island self, of a theatre of aliens we want to know in a house on the edge of a toxic waste dump, on the edge of a toxicity pushing the bush aside and the message going out that 'toxicity' is of a different nature altogether, denaturing nature to break glass ceilings while rapacity continues, cutting our feet on tracking a way through the profiteering enclaves. What rights were in this, as they seemingly adjusted to our personal needs but did so to control capital, to keep the differs and ball mills going, the furnaces and department stores, the Amazon delivery depots, the copyright franchise pay as you go 'freedoms'. And always the collective wherein the individual said yes, I let go to help us all... was erased was severed... in the breaking of the world. These drawings... of three-legged insects and four legged spiders... these mountains hollowed out and halved to incorporate military systems, the defence of a right to annihilation. And they did it, didn't they, remember, and the shelters did not shelter and the selves did not self. Nothing was warded off. The hospital ceiling then on the side as the drip fed the sleepiness the emptiness, to alter the body's course. On the chart, the words 'Redemption Statement... no private insurance'.

———

Half a classic car for half a wedding. A tall tree surrounded by stumps. Water under the skin of a leafless paperbark. A glossy swamp skink on dead grass. Dieback in the glorious forest with a sky half on the ground half overhead being lit for a preventative burn and never coming back so close on the heels of the big split, the spirals of flame that rose up in parody of Newtonian physics, leaving the remainder beyond reckoning. The Jungian artists painting half their bodies, the pH test that can't resolve either way. The motel with NO Vacancies that seems so empty when you call out, the space around it uncertain with zoning laws. All that was bothering the isness which is so dubious in its lack of fullness. The ambitious settlers shore up their wealth at the boat club, and a DJ laments that split just when vinyl records were making a comeback beyond scratch. Turntable cranked by a seawind that has no circulation, just aggregation of immediates. We remember organic architecture, we remember the effect of gravity on water. Of water on rock. The simple devices invented by many seem to still work, suggesting a new longevity built on the oldest of ways? And what can we recall of the cultural manipulations of the heliosphere being described as croissant-like? In this breadless demi-world? In this world as we are sold by The Committee and in this world we feel we must accept if never by their definitions and for their purpose. These cues, these contrasts. Not hemisphere to hemisphere but the flat face and the curved face away and to the sun. Inside the lens to the solar reach, its safeguards for our nurturing lampooned and treated with disdain. Why wouldn't it just let the cosmic rays have a field day? All apocope and yet something is filling words out to transfer the factors necessary for your comprehension, your re-arrangement into a set of warnings some people might heed. *Befo i to la*. And now, unconvinced, the elision of all bodies of the solar system? 'To cut'.

———

We have our translations to cobble together into source languages. The Committee has taken control of the target language, laid claim. In a park by a river on a bench around an ancient tree the park anti-grew and visitors were automatically demi-monde, such visitors are hunched over their devices burrowed in the shade. The devices speak with no other devices now, of course. The river neither flows from nor to, and has neither headwater nor mouth, source nor destination. It is chopped off either end and the lack of gravity elevates it to mist high as a flaking wall either end, the banks of the park and trees and ablutions and a flood marker whose language is playing catch up with irony. All we have, Hester, dear, is a dynamic equivalence of samizdat and welcoming, of hiddenness and shared meal and caches of seed for a replanting that has been taken away from us. Verbs no longer function.

———

What of time in this... the constraints we were intended to function around... by whom?... to live by and under? Our bodies' demands for food, our lungs on autopilot. What will analogies mean when we have forgotten 'autopilot'? It will be no loss from our point of view, but documentation feeds and is fed on words standing for something else. We stood for something else, then we were divided, split apart. In our merging of reduced spatiality we increasingly lapse into temporal desiring. Our body clocks are either upstrokes or downstrokes but can no longer manage if left divided, alone. What of the bodies we can only partially sense, and putting a hand to a knee we feel is our own but is only our own through the co-operation of another?

And they have the same quandary. But it's not that we've agreed on a quid pro quo, nor that we genuinely feel we are content in a oneness that denies or forgets what we were. Our bodies stumbling through organisation, wanting to be anywhere in the state they might be without industrial-consumer impact. There was so much theorising that made sense, but the frames of delivery were greedily held on to by the machine that dished out time in increments, in deposits, in user pay schemes. The delivery platforms, the energy configurations, the transference of life from the natural world to the human constructed world was all in accordance. With. The. Committee. This natural world we are instructed to laugh at in the present as 'just a construct'. The new imperialists of halfness are the old imperialists of the globe who have found each other and realised their values of personal aggrandisement, and comfort can be equated and merged with just the 'right value', the relevant other half, sharing a co-morbidity of greed. They are confused by desire because what they want they suddenly have and yet the pleasures are onanistic and that bothers their lust for power of another. Power over themselves is less interesting. So they look for other merges to stimulate and meet their need for gratification, but once merged find the desire lessens. So they target us, we who don't want to merge with them and who will struggle against fusion... and in the tearing away give them the kick they're looking for. This is the New Energy Agreement of The Committee: enforced merging then violent splitting to generate energy tapped by equipment made out of old satellite dishes.

———

Volume 6

Sister has appeared before us, 'whole' and fully versed in the half-language which seems so complete to us now! She promisesl us a new energy source through making a repair that will bring spheroid qualities to our dwelling, if not to the split planet itself. An illusion we can make real.

First Dialogue

When we were lost, Sister, you were always there for us to gather around, to take the parts of us and make whole in your presence. Not to orbit, as orbits wobble so badly now and orbits suggest you are a primary body, and you would never claim to be such, but to track about. So we speak to you as what we were. But we do not envy your wholeness, Sister, we do not wish to be separated from each other in order to become 'whole' as we once were. Which is not to say that we don't wish completeness and wholeness of the sphere, a blue marble of a planet rather than an orange ripped in half. No, no... we want to return to that wholeness, to a biosphere that circumgyrates, that makes currents and fronts and swirls with weather. That we know is just and necessary. We want all life to be restored. But we want to stay merged, to be polyphonous, which we know you understand, Sister.

Sister would never make us part of a tableau vivant on the verandah of her 'shotgun' house on the edge of a town surrounded by toxic fields that have been brought back into service to feed the remnants. She would never ask this of us but we've volunteered because she's under the gaze of The Committee who have set up in the Mayor's office in the old town hall and this patch of Old New World is the set piece for The Committee's recolonising of 'ignored and neglected' space. Before the world split, Sister tells us... before the world split and at the time the Hotel Impossible was starting to close off all surface from our feet, preventing all contact between skin and dirt and water and even non-airconditioned air... before then and at the time, there were inklings of crimes to come of crimes replaying the old crimes of attempted erasure, the old crimes that were revealed and contested and stronger cultures than the heavily armed colonisers pushed back and revealed the truths and wrongs and started the healing of the land... even then and at that time... and then... and then the hotel grew like a factory over the world and the world could not take the forces of enterprise and broke in half and the contents spilled out and worlds within worlds perished. And now we are on Sister's verandah, looking whole and complete but connected with each other and still and compliant so as not to rouse The Committee to attack us assault us 'get off' on us... we play the scene as they expect and look ahead without thought or motive with apparent indifference, satisfying the viewers. But Sister is behind us and among us and we know a different kind of energy is brewing in the static rub of our differences, us with Sister, Sister with us, and that energy is massive and healing and will weld the broken pieces together and heal the toxic wastes and allow us to dwell as we need to dwell with respect for all presences. Sister says: This is not a matter of winding back time but of merging time with the earth, of releasing gravity from its bonds, of liberating ourselves from the Newtonian hold, the dereliction of the fantastical. No more lies of the constant no more: $F = Gm_1m_2/r^2$... no more geography being remodelled into a geography of opportunity no more vertical aspiration that leads to the destruction of the curve, of the horizons. To us, to us all, this sounds magnificently poetic!

Second Dialogue

Earth-sheltered housing melted away with the bursts and flow of lava. The hollowing out of the half was horizontal and vertical and the vertices shifted. Wind turbines faltered as the winds helicoptered and spiralled. Reactor vessels split and radiation mingled with the Lesser Gravity to become a 'deadly cocktail' The Committee insists it has cleaned up on this better half of existence. We are sold to our-selves as the 'lucky ones'—the 'dark side' of the old earth is not even half of infinity, but we are authenticated as being half of infinity which makes us perpetual. The Spilling Out is the pre-history of our cornucopia. The swamps became eyes to the only 'earlier times' legitimised in the streaming together of the many conjoinings, the fusion of selves to pass through the 'moderating pumps' of The Committee, whose catchcry became Connecting With Dignity and Output. AC and DC power 'outmoded' in favour of a high frequency set-up well beyond the music of the spheres. It is said that childhood friends on an island in a swamp with an AC bias, survived the split-tings, and remain intact but trapped in a temporal rift. Some say this is an act of technology—a 'time machine'—will others... maybe our crew our initial trio our double our additions made via ulterior motives... say it's an organic act, a growing entity that will offer us all a way back to how we were before the split, offering choices we can collate and use to resist the rapacity in a peaceful and resolute way? Some say this when they are together, floating, elevated, drifting, levitating... no, not levitating... no one has enough control yet to levitate, though The Committee, of course, claim *they* do.

———

Interfaith dialogues. Dwellings of ecumenical statement. Irrigation. Burn.

———

Someone is saying is compositing is formulating... expressions, a syntax we can apportion if not allocate (why would we want to do that again)... still caught in the old clichés that failed to accommodate all oppressions rather than those affecting us personally, to empathise... to unify just approaches, yes... someone who is us is saying that the Omega weapons were triggered when the email software offered a pat reply a ready-made expression after scanning the text that incipient AI which translated as surveillance in the capitalist mode of 'choice' and 'freedom' suggested, 'Yes, I agree' and the I spoke for we and we all suffered, split at the seams along the cut lines of genetic manipulation which was back-engineered into modes of 'freedom'. Is this what we're thinking and are we thinking clearly in our new mode or are we succumbing to our own subtle propaganda we deeply want to be hope for a new way through to consensus to collective justice to the protection of rights for each part of us and the cultures we belong to? Does this suggest we are regaining cultural orientations does this mean hallucination without case notes and without drug dealers and chemical companies profiting and ripping the bark off trees the mushrooms from their intended and intending place, their half planets in the half-light with mycelium communications stem cell self-determination the filaments wavering and reaching into the shadow away from the solar burn? Does this mean flying spells?

———

We were all photographers exposing ourselves in order to make negatives. There is a priest who is a priestess who is neither priest nor priestess. We are photographing them, and they are photographing us. The energy released in the opening and shutting of the eye, during the exposure, far exceeds the energy required to make the image/s. Many images and a massive build-up in imagery that needs discharging. We are not variants to be neutralised, they said, troubled as well as troubling. These metaphors for plight, for inoculation, for the situation to find a way around the protections. In the shadow hospital, old loves were put aside to bring comfort to the many. A plethora of affection against the infections. That was the catchphrase, and the shadow workers meant it, every bit of it, giving themselves to the common cause, regardless of their personal plights.

Wheeled together, the acrobats have just completed their first tumble since the split. Forming an obicular gazer by holding cupped hands opposite each other, they were able to scry a cycle of seasons. Six seasons always there no matter the damage, six seasons telling truths of blossom and wing. But unsteadying news flowed through samizdat subwaved as well, where waves had swept the beaches, the great glass sphere holding fluoridated water and the sun in its halfness below the event horizon, a situation of day by day closing, a spectacle expected as sunset in the seaside of capital easy as lifestyle denials the tracking station on the door-step... the only roundness left intact after the splitting, the globe that sat on its pedestal without floating away into a sky without soap bubble surface tensions, without eyeball shapes and eye socket indicators of purpose, its thin wall its hollow pressured with said water to hold and diffract light of Sunny Town with its hoicked stone blocks declaring architecture of claim and permanence... shattered, the sculpture the invention the drawing with shading in charcoal and silica broken by a stone aimed by The Committee or one of its aspirants its proxies... to close off visions of past worlds... to prevent a new situationism arising arising arising. The triplets of poetics—the threat of détournement... of fish swimming the sea-less cavity and escaping the nets of the floating factory ships brought into play only today by The Committee. The New Industries, the recourse to The Feeding, the being fed on, fed by.

Third Dialogue

Whose shepherd, honestly? Hester, Bell and their friend who makes more than halves, goes beyond completion, who wishes to perform for us and invite us into the performance. Who is installation. Who is not to be confined. Who joins us and remains intact. Yet another variation on what we might become? Their name is Theocritus and already we feel the love and love them all. We declare ourselves antibodies. We declare ourselves sequenced under our own condi-tions while The Committee warns we are outside identification. They created the failure and call us target failure. They piped the error through the galleries and performance spaces of the old whole world and blamed nature. Reliability and rapidity are residue terms in our bubbles. The wounded deer the little deer the surrogate eye to eye impaled on capital's spikes to bring back community to share and share alike. Anathema to the ethics of the STEM institutions and their bio-arts of vivisection, their glow to write world in body but to kill world body and claim the cadaver, to career project in the post-spheroid world. But we are drawing and inventing and designing circles that cost the remnant nature nothing and maybe will even bring restoration. The eclogue is no longer a competition and we share it with all parts of wholes that fuse with us all. We remember the artists we remember them together, whole in their parts.

––––––

Is it true? Is it true that the racists are trying to reformulate, to round themselves out in the shape of arenas and coliseums? Is it true that the far right is thriving in the knowledge they cannot touch an extreme of the left, that they can run all the way into sacrifices of others to their version of the sun? That they are developing weapons and 'home defence' mid-air on 'their' quarter of a quarter, citing separation and raging against miscegenation of fragments? Are they declaring a new eugenics in which idealists of the whole planet are incursions into their New God Fearing, synced with the energy being dragged out of the remnants by The Committee? Is it true they say the half that remains is and always was the right half the half of the right?

––––––

Pilgrim: Sister, I need to make contact, I am under threat.
I feel whole but am still lost in the wasteland bisection of

the Hotel Impossible. I cannot solve the puzzle alone, and feel my hubris led me to this impasse, teetering on the edge, designing stairs for a precipice without a vision of what stairs might be. Sister? Please, Sister!

Sister: (in a distant demi-whisper, in strains of a home to return to, in an irony of colonial pastoral past-ismo): Whiteworld has been halved and halved and halved and halved and halved again, and we might celebrate this. Pilgrim dear, try to tune in to half times 405–790 THz...

––––––

Can Pilgrim equate with Hester and can Bell equate with Sister? Of. Course. Not?

––––––

Hester, do you remember when we were given a hard time in the port after that anti-nuclear protest? Of course I do, no matter what has happened to us I can't forget that. I remembered it before we fused. I did, too. And do you remember when we went to hear that band in the hotel near where the two rivers mixed? When that guy came up to us and asked if we'd heard Ezra Pound reciting the word 'architect'? Yes, and something about a baby swapping eyebeams with its parent. And then he launched into a diatribe against Pound's bigotry and stuff. Yes, I remember, and there was that person trying to sell us acid trips—pink ones... plastic coated things, weren't they... and what was the band... it was like really conventional rock and roll, wasn't it? Yes, I remember, and I also remember the pelicans sitting on the lightpoles over the highway... you know, near the bridge over one of the rivers... yes, when the rivers flowed and gravity kept an eye on us, even if it could never keep us in check! Yes, we remember. We remember drawing the pelicans... we remember the name of pelican wasn't pelican. We remember the name was invented to fit a new order an occupation of names and space and to possess all local variations of gravity.

————

Ablutions. Our embodiment... in this state... requires less but the atmosphere that remains, thin as it is, is filling with our wastes, nonetheless. A shit storm. In finding our new circles few of us are wanting to spend time cleaning up the small messes when the big mess keeps us on the edge. But the small messes are gathering, too, and we are choking. Eating and shitting are no longer held together in those cycles of fertilise and grow. The Committee won't dirty their own hands, but are drafting as many of us as they can... as many of us who have become corporeal enough. We deploy irony, but it's that semi-irony that wavers and seems ineffective as resistance. An irony more of compliance than refusal. As we remember the newspaper cartoonists with their satire from within the enclaves of bigotry and control. That kind of thing.

We had never given up collecting objects. We refuted the necessity of possessing objects, and yet we accumulated them, didn't we? Can we remember that. You were there and so was I but you are no longer with us and nor am I yet vestiges of those objects remain. To be used to make art, to be used to build shelter, to be used to invent means of existing without objects, which seems so strange because why do we need a means to live without objects? Why don't we just live with what is around us and accumulate none of it? We can't unravel these paradoxes and as no paradoxes are complete now and we are the place within the place. We have our presence where we were present, roughly, approximately, as if floating towards where there be dragons and lions but they too have fallen into the constellations, and some have plunged into the sun... we have our presence where we were intruding without agreement for presence where we are and have a presence only when fused and we hope our fusing legitimises our presence... but fusings are taking place without choice are taking place before there's agreement... in some cases, but not ours, this wedding of souls? And what of those who were placed on the other half but lost their footing when all footing was removed? What of? What of them and the them-us, our common fate which was bisected?

Knowledge. We are gaining knowledge and yet tell ourselves we can never make up the knowledge we have lost. For The Committee, who hold the databanks of the old knowledges, this seems desirable... desirable that we are distracted by our gains and not the losses. In the semi world were are placed in loops of our making and of The Committee's making. Ethical outcomes, they've always insisted rely on 'compromises', 'tough choices', prioritising their versions of the human. We are hearing some of us are fusing with animals, some of us are fusing with inorganics. These fusions, we are trying to guess, might trigger the growth of the other half, the rounding out of the planet, sinew by sinew, crystal by crystal, gravity gathering its strength, first a mantle and a vast demi-hollow, then lithosphere then asthenosphere then mantle then outer core then inner core and the molten essence returning in magnetic love. Yes, we scry this in the fairground of hope, the euphoria... a belief in the potential to move from cross-section back into fullness, the blue marble in the sun's system. This is our collective survey projection. We are... projective.

Fourth Dialogue

We are remembering the lighthouse. Have we fused through inclination, through both knowing we'd seen this lighthouse in former lives when the world was whole and the seas raged around its base and we watched the boiling and fume from its lantern? Is that what drew us to each other, coalescing out of the dark skies that curved away building to fury, the winds wrapping the tower of light? Are we together so we can form fuller memories, create contrasts, highlight the plasticity of our neurons? What did we read about the essential manner of forgetting, what did we read when biology was connected with an idea of intactness that carried its own bigotries? That saying, *Ready and able*... it bothers us now as it should have bothered us then but we were working to go forward into a place where pleasurable memories could be created while all the time we were forgetting. The Committee tells us forgetting is good. We know we were troubled by this even back then, and now... the abuse by 'researchers' of transgenic flies. They didn't forget their ethics, they ensured they remembered them differently. We are thinking of this as the phase when 'It All Comes Back'. We can only be flawed in our reasoning, can't we? We lack dopamine. As of yet. In our reconstituting. Watching the sea envelop the lighthouse we developed our fever... before there was an official version of infection and contagion, but it was present and the breath vanishing as the wind blew and the extremely high temperatures while it remained cold outside, beyond the lantern, the bed of mercury... and someone came to the door asking for a donation that couldn't be given while one of us was struck down in the bed hallucinating the rock, the helipad as the eyelet through which the whole thing would be pried apart, the sea not even spilling but falling away into space.

———

The black hole is not the heart of the quasar no matter what The Committee says and the water cloud in its distant midst is not the endless reservoir suggested by some in the old dispensation with their aim for profits measured by epochs and fantastical light yearage, the reaching back to own the beginnings. These ideas are swirling again in retro-proto-capitalist sell. A crypto-cosmo-currency of disaster profiteering. Someone has suggested the international space station has remained viable with eight instead of sixteen sunrises with forty-five minute nights and forty-five minute days as if their/its orbit has simply been halved rather than a harsher reality consisting only of sun-blasted days then void (no night, just void) then sunblasted days then void. We are trying to imagine how it is if the crew members are still alive up there if up there as we once envisaged it still exists in a way we might not perceive it, making our ladders to heaven... if the dwellers up there have fused and formed a consciousness that can keep them afloat keep them viable keep them from drifting into deep space because there is no orbit as they had counted on and consequently no decaying and burning up or breaking up in what remains of 'the earth's atmosphere'... and can we in fact still think of layers as before and what do pauses stand for? Our languages come out of capital and are thus likely incapable of adjusting to the post-sphere cosmology they created via catastrophe... incapable of empathy on any level. And the NICE philosophy is an errant one, surely, as we correct the damage and water's arrival from the outer solar system is not the blue whale stranded on the dotted line and no new water will arrive in time to refill a healed globe, its anguished grooves and crevices? What is this text forming in front of us enticing to reach out and touch it? Are we translating or reading its original, is there an original, is this a key to our future wholeness, our holiness? 'It seems absurd that the physicist should be supposed to know the nature of sun or moon, but not to know any of their essential attributes, particularly as the writers on physics obviously do discuss their shape also and whether the earth and the world are spherical or not.'[4]

———

Dream inculcation from The Committee: *Maybe you never revolved? No circumference. And why axis? In the radius you are leaping not like a kangaroo but 'Mixtumque genus, prolesque biformis'[5], kangaroo-like in your mannerisms.*

And something mutually nudges us to aid against this message.

---

[4]   http://classics.mit.edu/Aristotle/physics.2.ii.html [Aristotle, *Physics*, Book II, translated by R. P. Hardie and R. K. Gaye]

[5]   Virgil via Barron Field who used the colony to gain a rung or two in his imperial careerism, the Shepherd's calendar of law and order a fruit by any other name, a round fruit in the Antipodes, a fresh apple back in the 'home country'. Robber baron and fêted science-romantic poet notable for...? 'For howsoe'er anomalous,/ Thou yet art not incongruous' ipso facto. See: 'Voynichese'.

Curated as we, when they've converted the sacred into saleable items, increased their knowledge capital, have equated people with flora and fauna, have sailed the seven seas when there are clearly no seas left. But then again, maybe they just want us to give in, to accept the world is unrounded unmade and to make the best of what's left. We counter with: the world is repairing and fulfilling its spheroid nature; and... it has never broken apart never split never torn never become half of what it was... rather, beneath the smokescreen and beyond the hollowings out of the mines, away from the islands that were swallowed by rising seas of plastic and then left bare and barren when the seas spilt away, within the treeless void where air was hard to come by... maybe they have kept roundness to themselves circumnavigating in their pleasure craft, visiting the few remaining arboretums for their wine-quaffing enjoyments, sailing the mountain lakes filtered of toxins and fulfilling their chosen destinies while we lapse into loss, seek comfort in each other... thrive in their grotesque individualism while we aid each other mutually with the bits that are left, their wastes. Isn't this a viable scenario? Where do we go from here, existing only as sources of energy for the newest colonialism?

Fifth Dialogue

When we found the old fire tower we were amazed that it was still standing given the conflagrations that ravaged the zone before never mind after the splitting. But it was there, and even more astonishingly surrounded by tall trees that seemed to be respiring as they had respired prior. We climbed the rickety ladder with the effects of old gravity in total control, zig-zagging back and forth to the crow's nest and flipping open the hatch, did in fact find hundreds of silent crows.

Crows, like all other creatures, had been halved and fragmented and had to fuse with others to approximate the crows of old, but these crows looked like the old crows. They weren't bothered by our presence, and just hopped aside to make way for us. The floor was covered in crow shit, and it looked like these crows had been eating as they used to eat in the beforetime, before Whiteworld led to the breaking of the round world and left it a half-world. And strangely, and ebulliently, almost, we started to break apart from each other, manifesting in the form and appearance of our old selves. We had split away and returned to our prior status. We weren't overjoyed, having grown accustomed to sharing, but we weren't distressed either. Was this a centre of a healing, a repair that would shimmer out across the repairing, rounding planet? We looked out over the tree tops that end abruptly as the wastes began, and thought, this is but an aberration, a pocket in memory, a zone where The Committee's incursions of forgetting hadn't yet taken hold, but as we looked out longer and harder our sight gained perspective and the world started to green and curve and there was a sunset and dusk and nightfall. The moon appeared a newmoon sliver, and we stayed the entire night with the silent crows, studying the sliver and the stars. We named constellations from memory and those whose namings were gone we gave provisional names, assuring each other we'd let go of those when the ancient names were retrieved. There was a dawn, there was a sunrise, and with first light the crows broke their silence and erupted into a joyous sarcastic contradictory chorus. Yes! And as the sun lit up the curve of this section of the ball, as we defined surface area in our mind and wrestled with volume, as we adjusted the formulae no longer merely desiring but actually able to reach the vestigial equation, as the green spread and the air clarified and felt the old gravity as if it was the new norm, and blossom appeared on the tall trees and we realised they were marri trees and white-tailed cockatoos appeared in the high branches and were already eating the fruits that had ripened in an instant... Yes, yes!

Sixth Dialogue

The illustrator, the home-trained architect, and the 'inventor' are friends. Close friends, but they don't live in each other's pockets. Each is torn in two by a desire to be 'creative'. They are Hester and Bell and... Theocrates... Miranda? There are other names, too. We will call them Miranda.

They are working together on a mobile. They recall visiting the Musée National d'Art Moderne, Centre Georges Pompidou, Paris, in 2009... yes, they recall the exhibition *Alexander Calder: les années parisiennes 1926–1933*... yes... and they clearly remember the blue planet and the red planet, they recall orbits and circuits, willing suspensions... smaller planets... constellations. Suns... stars... blue planet red planet. Flatworlds in medias res. Discs. Invention. Architecture. Illustrations.

We wonder about shelter. We wonder about the indifference to the homeless camped in their cars by the rivers, cars piled high with possessions—their only possessions. Near the mansions. We wonder about the shadows of the pivoting sculptures, the phone tower silhouettes, the devices made into reliance.

We got sick, each of us, after our gallery visit/s. Didn't we? Yes. Art and sickness? We shelter the art in the building not that far from the river.

Φ Nothing is round nothing is circular except in The Committee
meetings when they sit in the round and round off to the nearest...
On the other half-world in the neat splitting of planet, The Committee tell us that under their jurisdiction all is running smoothly:
the mines and industry are churning, the atmosphere accepts all
discharge and doesn't call it 'pollution', people travel without a
care and wages and people possess all the material goods they
desire... billionaires and trillionaires are financially ecumenical
priests and asteroids are brought to heel daily. It is a world of
launches but they don't bother with this half-world which is
broken and defeated and caught up in healing what doesn't need
to be healed, they say they insist. This half-world is made up of
people who want to remember and won't embrace the forgetting,
the thrusting forward, who would rather live with crows and the
blossom of marri trees, who would rather make art and shelter
that reflects the needs of the people. All that stuff The Committee
calls 'unethical'. Advancement, announces The Committee,
meant the need for creating a two-tier system of planetary habitation. On this half-world, we are expected to do our time left in
life, to eke it out the best we can, to do penance for our questioning, for our doubt, for our refusal to accept the glories of
progress. It's a flat, glib message, even The Committee admits,
but they declare there's nothing like honesty, nothing like telling
it as it is. The entire truth, the rounded character, the dialogue
that begins where it ends. $V = (4/3)\pi r^3$...? Yes. Yes. Yes?

The Remembrancer of First Fruits and Tenths

Andrew Macrae

Kim Yorn, Remembrancer of First Fruits and Tenths and a Certified Practising Accountant-Executioner, moved on foot against the midnight peak. She was searching for Jameson, a fugitive bankrupt convicted of sedition against the City. She held an order to liquidate his assets and remit them to the blood gutter—a task that would secure her position on the Auditing Committee and put her on the track to becoming an Owner.

The crowds on the street had picked up in the cooler evening. Besuited traders shouldered their way along packed footpaths to the exchanges and the towers of the Four Houses at the heart of the Old Town. Adverts writhed in the heavy air, shilling new financial products and the forever-deferred promise of a stake in the City. She took a side street to escape the crowd, heading towards the river. Smaller ramshackle buildings lined the way.

She caught a cautious glance from a bald man and a pale woman engaged in a trade, felt the sixth-sense skin prick as their lenses scanned and analysed her. The low chatter of commerce buzzed as commodities changed hands. The market. All around, all encompassing. And above her, the City's buildings rose like compound interest.

Her drones swirled, sucking information from her surroundings and interfacing with the City's web of sensors. They scraped data and fed it to her cephalopod, a tentacled predictive algorithm, which she now unleashed to thrash in the kaleidoscopic augmented reality around her, tendrils spiralling around a beak-like maw engineered for maximum interoperability. It analysed the myriad data points, presenting her with a choice of paths to destinations filtered and prioritised by the likelihood of finding Jameson at their ends.

She followed the trail laid down for her, through the alleys and the noise and smoke of street vendors in the grimy riparian zone between Old Town and the flood-swollen estuary. Her perception was patterned with a collision of tracking data and a heat map of Jameson's intent, sexual peccadillos, realtime geospatial contacts, food preferences, addictions, brainmods of choice, character flaws, ethical constraints and network usage. Her cephalopod tentacled the City's surveillance system, sucking facial recognition data crossmatched with the people around her.

She shuffled along tight rows of stalls with gimcrack merch. A vendor shaved the uncanny hair from a flank of vat-grown meat, flicking soap scum to the ground with each pass of the razor. She followed waypoints along a rank of tattered shanty-town awnings, stacked five high on galvanised scaffolding.

And in the open apex of the canvas canyon loomed the feathered haunches of the British-Exxon monolith. She could just make out its crest, hairy with communication relays. It was a sensate god in the salt-shimmered air, its massy shoulders sharp with windowed detail and curlicues. It stood guard over its position on the energy gridfeed, a titan ready to react to any aggression from its competitors.

She refocused her cephalopod.

And there was Jameson, in the shadows. A furtive, corpulent figure. One glance told her that despite his financial predicament, he was not without resources. He had painted an infinite regress of eyes around his eyes to game the City's surveillance system. He wore an ancient data transfer headset and glove, anonymised by darknet tech, and a second transmitter around his neck that spoofed location data from a site her cephalopod told her was further to the north. She approached him directly, ready for a confrontation.

In that moment, a great rumbling shook the ground. The klaxons sounded evac. Shattered glass fell from two buildings behind her, cascading to the ground in diamond streams and skittering and bouncing like hailstones on the pavement. Kim looked up in surprise. She was caught in the open. She realised with a shock the street was empty: the riverbank traders had their own ways to avoid these periodic upheavals, and she'd been so intent on finding Jameson she had not noticed their absence. And there, among the shifting architecture, Jameson smiled. Her emergency warning system went off then, too late: delayed somehow. Even with his outmoded tech, Jameson had managed to block the official warning packets on her network for crucial seconds. Her stomach churned with vertigo as she realigned herself to the changing geometry around her.

She took a second to get her bearings. British-Exxon and SinoShell squared off against each other. The two buildings were hulking behemoths of a century of brutalist palimpsest and the violent manifestations of vast corporate assets brought to bear against each other in a tussle to occupy the most energy-rich position on the riverside gridfeed. They were locked in a battle of slow attrition and the delicate distribution of mass and force evolving over decades to see which could send its foundations the deepest and occupy the best real estate.

Now, their constantly probing AI systems had sensed opportunity and the conflict had escalated. Basement foundations were uprooted, buttresses ground through concrete and steel into new positions on the riverbank. Awful shrieks rang out as weight and load changed to new configurations above her. The empty pavement vibrated and the map of the City transformed in her awareness as the streets and waypoints re-routed around new footings. Jameson appeared almost transformed himself, now surprisingly light on his feet. He darted away, towards the chaos and into a strange portal that appeared between the two buildings.

Kim set off in pursuit through an inverted mirrorworld of reforming structure. She leapt a chasm that appeared in a stairwell and recovered in time to see Jameson flee as the hallway bent upwards and looped over them. He struggled on the gradient, and she lunged at his feet to bring him down in a rugby tackle.

The floor slid away beneath her, a gaping vacuum.

She slipped backwards while Jameson scrabbled forwards. He

kicked at her grasping hands, and beneath her the void yawned where the corridor twisted away, rent from the fabric of the City by the titanic upheavals of the battling buildings. Her legs swung into nothingness. Jameson paused, allowed himself to slip further down towards her to thrust his feet at her fingers on the rim.

She spotted a ledge to her right, and swung her weight to build momentum as Jameson kicked again at her hands. For a second she hung suspended, terrified of the fall below—but she hit the ledge, gripped and held. Another colossal groan. Structures shifted around her even as she clawed her way further onto the ledge to take some of the weight from her arms. She glanced up to see Jameson slipping now too, and they both fell to the floor as the reshaped edifice coalesced and held. She called out to him to yield.

He did not yield.

Instead, he rose to his feet, as did she. He lunged at her. She stepped inside his reach. He was slow, and she was hard and lean with years of the difficult, physical labour of a professional accountant. She felt his breath on her cheek, and disgust mingled with arousal as the secret gateways within her brain flanged ajar and flooded her consciousness with custom secretions concocted for just this situation. She grunted and then howled as she swept his legs out from underneath him. He went down hard and she was upon him, knees on his chest, pressing her forearm into his throat.

Still he refused to yield.

Not for the first time in her career, she gazed at the struggle in an adversary's eyes: a cellular will to live; to partake in the everyday commerce of the breath even in the face of overwhelming debts owed on amortised capital so generously provided by the City.

She pushed harder as he tried to throw her off. He was heavy, and fighting for his life, yet she was strong and determined.

'Fuck you,' he said.

The gates in her mind crimped down on her emotional reaction. She was calm and controlled.

'You've defaulted on your debts,' she said. She pressed harder on his windpipe until he stopped struggling.

'Now,' she said. 'Tell me who controls the Wiremother account.'

'I don't know what you mean.' He gasped for breath.

'You met with Minksy last night. She's already been arrested. You're colluding with foreign entities. You're seditious as well as corrupt and bankrupt.'

He wheezed. She relaxed the pressure slightly so he could speak. 'Listen,' he said. 'I'm putting together a deal. I can cut you in.'

'I already know about it. Synthetic debt. Laundering the currency of a foreign city state. Trying to crash the markets. Contravention of all accounting protocols and a betrayal of the City.'

'There's a new threat. The City cannot stand against it.'

'Ridiculous.'

'You don't understand. I can help you. I know who you are.'

'You've no idea who I am.'

'You're Browne's plaything.' Another needle.

'I just need you to give me a name.'

'What difference does it make?'

'Give me a name.'

'I don't know it. I'm just a mule. It's a shell company. They're trading in junk debt. Washing it through a cascade of accounts and exchanges and trades.'

'Who do you communicate with?'

'I don't, I swear it. The only reason I'm involved at all is to get back on my feet. I'm maxed out. Under water.'

'That's why I'm here.'

'I have friends.'

'No, you don't. They've abandoned you.'

'I don't know anything.'

'Then I'm afraid I have to liquidate your assets.'

She pulled back her elbow and stunned him with three quick blows to the throat.

He lay gasping.

She brought up her calculating table, and the ledger with Jameson's full profit and loss account and balance sheet.

His eyes rolled in his head.

She read aloud the sacred text of Section 52 of the Tax Code as it swam in the air around her:

Born into debt, bonded to the system that gives us life. Life is blood. Blood is debt. Debt is struggle. The end of struggle is death. Death is the final payment of our mortgage against these borrowed molecules. We long for death even as we lay-by and downpay to forestall it. Let us deliver ourselves from the moment of repossession, the liquidation of earthly assets, the amortisation of senior debts, and the final maturity of all mezzanine structures. Let the many become one, and the clearances be reconciled and all accounts balanced with no remainder, excluding applicable fees and charges.

With a clean, swift cut from her scalpel blade, she released the blood from his jugular vein to remit his debts to the state.

———

Kim dragged Jameson to the blood gutter and left his earthly account there to drain while her cephalopod processed his estate as the adverts swirled around her. The gates in her brain readjusted, modulating the neurochemical flows in the jittery afterglow of the violence, attenuating the trauma to cushion her memory.

She paused to check her portfolio through the data feeds, examining risk profile and asset class. Columns of return on investment and benefits accruing. The market was a spiritual force, a transcendent power, the intersection of competing principalities that reached from the beyond to interact on this plane. A battle between combatants with an impenetrable agenda and occluded motivations, with effects cast as shadows that could only be perceived in price movements. The site of skirmishes played out at light speed as waves of finbots battled for advantage over the network, contesting and resolving intense contractual disputes within milliseconds.

Her phone toned gently and she picked up the call with a thought. It was Browne, Chancellor of the Exchequer. Her sponsor.

'Come and see me.'

She paused. 'Jameson didn't talk.'

'That doesn't matter now. I have the name.'

'Every calamity brings a new investment opportunity,' she said.

'The Four Houses are running out of liquidity.'

'There's no scarcity of capital in the City.'

'I miss you.'

'Favour one of your other slaves, Browne.'

'I have a new mission for you. And a chance to get off the carousel.'

She paused at that.

'Come and see me,' he said.

She was silent. Then she said, 'I need a downpayment first.'

———

Browne's deposit hit her account like a drug. Her allocation protocol split the cash across her portfolio in optimal proportions, replicating through her balances in a warm rush. On top of the Jameson fee, it made today a very good payday.

She leaned back against the wall of the crystal elevator as she rode to Browne's office. She let the moment wash over her, enjoying the flood of relief at having bought another tranche of time at the top of the heap.

Beneath her, the nocturnal city came undone in the lightening sky, commuters crowding shabbily homeward before the glare of the solar orb baked the white pavements. The skirmish between SinoShell and British-Exxon had ended, but there were ongoing tremors as the City buildings aligned themselves to new positions. The skyline shifted in the eerie light, and she saw the Four Houses had heaved up buttressed battlements from the pavements, reconfiguring the streetscape as they took up defensive postures adjacent to the City walls.

The elevator doors opened onto Browne's chambers. A desk, floor to ceiling windows looking out across the river. Sidereal lights shining outward from atop the distant walls made for fixed points around which the buildings moved like negative space in the dark.

'You did well to run Jameson down,' he said as she approached. She shrugged.

'I serve the City. I assess profit and loss,' Kim said.

'Yet each day the defaulters rise and the void beneath us yawns wider. Even the ruthless efficiencies of our system are becoming redundant.'

'The ruthless efficiencies are the system. There's nothing else.'

'By auditing the City's accounts, a Remembrancer maintains the moral order.'

'Morality doesn't come into it.'

'Ethics, then. Our survival depends on our shared investments in the stability of the system.'

'What's the job, Browne?'

'Forensic accounting. Your specialty.'

'And the fee?'

'Chair of the Audit Committee.'

She took a moment to digest that. The apotheosis of her career. Everything she had fought for. The gateway to eventually becoming an Owner, like Browne.

'Why me?' she said.

He paused. 'I owe you.'

'You don't owe me anything.'

'I want to do this for you.'

'Send me on another errand?'

'Set you up for life. Away from the bloodshed.'

'It's just a job. I don't take it home with me.'

'That's impossible.'

'I have the best attenuators on the market. I'm immune.'

'We both know that's not true.'

'So you can read my thoughts, but you can't bolster liquidity by issuing some bonds?'

'The Four Houses are closing ranks, working together. They're leveraged to the hilt. If there's a run, they won't be able to cover it. They're betting the City will assume the risk. But the City itself is in danger of default. There are forces at work destabilising the currency, disrupting the gridfeed.'

She was shocked at Browne's frankness. 'The City is eternal,' she said. 'Immutable.'

'A foreign city is moving against us. We've been monitoring it secretly for weeks. It's here, now. Buying influence with the agents of discontent within our own walls. The waters are rising to swallow us up.'

'And you want me to do what?'

'I have a trace on the Wiremother account.'

'There's always a scullery maid to do the dirty dishes.'

———

Kim unfolded her origami glider and rode the cliff-driven updrafts east, along the estuary, to the wastes outside the City walls. She flew over dykes and polders built to protect the land from the sea, complex arrangements designed around flow mechanics. Intricate spiral structures kept the water in constant motion, harnessing hydrodynamic forces that pumped it back out to sea. Further east, where the floodlands ended and the sea began, the dirigible port shone like a beacon in the night, at least thirty white lozenges nestled like a pod of albino whales breaching around gantries and support buildings. Beyond that, she saw a sickly greenish glow—and realised with a horror her mods could barely dampen that it was the approach of the foreign city Browne had told her about. An unprecedented threat to the City's dominance of its estuary and its gridfeed. The internal wrangling of the City's buildings would soon be redundant. Time was running out.

Her drones, nestled against her for the flight, vibrated an alert as a storm blew up in front of her. The cephalopod fed her AR doppler lidar with a three-dimensional representation of the vortices at the storm's core, interlinked branches twisting together in an endlessly changing churn. The airships turned into the wind on their tethers, bucking like anxious colts, as massive red-gantried cranes clamped them into secure docks and a colossal seawall rose up to protect the port from the onslaught.

Kim brought the glider down beside a low, single-story structure built of rammed earth and photovoltaics. Thankfully, the datafeed here was still rich and strong, and her vision pulsed with the energy of information. Infrared, flow patterns, atmospheric pressure, humidity, all overlaying her experience of the world, her mods regulating her reactions and attention. She checked and rechecked her sitrep as she oriented herself, her drones fanning out around her, warning her of an approaching figure.

It was a woman, middle-aged and thick waisted, with tā moko scarifications on her face. She wore a one-piece tucked into Wellingtons, and regarded the swampy landscape with a dismal eye. 'The salt water leeches into everything,' she said.

'I'd have thought there's enough rain to flush it out,' Kim replied.

'If the pumps can keep up.' She looked at Kim squarely, hands crossed in front of her apron. 'I'm Maia Hira. What can I do for you?'

'I've come to renegotiate a contract.'

Maia studied her calmly.

'You'd better come up to the house, then,' she said.

Kim followed the stocky woman into a greenhouse as thunder rumbled in the distance and lightning flickered through the storm cell.

'The glass is specifically designed for us. It's ultrathin but incredibly strong, and it only lets in the right spectrum of light for each of our microclimates,' Maia said.

Kim nodded. The air was humid and heavy. Jungle foliage grew vibrant and shockingly green compared with the drab palette outside. A stream ran through the bottom of the greenhouse, choked with fish.

Maia stopped. She held an engineered-bone automatic pistol loosely at her waist.

'You're Browne's messenger dog. What are you doing outside the walls of your pound?' she said.

'Looking for laundered money.'

'What strange ideas you have.'

'I know you control the Wiremother account.'

'You and your Owners just project your own avarice and intent onto others.'

'I've traced the transactions through all the intermediaries. I know it's yours. I have proof.'

'And what advantage do you think this *proof* will provide you?'

'Minsky has been executed. Jameson too.'

Maia's face was inscrutable. The swirling patterns on her skin seemed to squirm subtly in Kim's vision.

'It doesn't matter. No one is essential,' Maia said.

'I'm empowered to freeze your assets.'

Maia laughed. 'Take this message from me back to Browne, dog. There's a dead man's switch on the account. If you freeze it, a set of files with all his dirty laundry will automatically be sent to his masters. The City's imminent collapse will be the least of his, and their, concerns.'

Kim paused, suddenly unsure of herself. The lines on Maia's face writhed in her vision.

'You have no authority here, Remembrancer,' Maia said. 'We're not subject to your tax law outside the City walls.'

'Nor our protection.'

Maia laughed. 'You're the party in need of protection. Your world has ended, you just haven't noticed it yet.' She gestured with the weapon. 'Now go, dog. Deliver my message.'

Kim paused, considering her options, assessing lines of attack, negotiation, fight or flight. The richness of the datafeed she had felt outside seemed diminished inside the greenhouse. Her cephalopod choked and stalled, giving her ambiguous information in the pulsating maw of the present moment. An unfamiliar feeling of uncertainty gripped her.

'I ...' she said.

And then a detail from the path to the greenhouse snagged in her memory: orbital lift crates inscribed with a logo. An eye within an eye within an eye.

The money wasn't from the foreign city at all.

It was from offworld.

She turned, defeated, and left without a word.

———

In the air above the polders, she made out the skyline of the approaching city. It was massive and awful, and water churned in its path as it ploughed the estuary towards her City. Smaller scout structures dug makeshift forward defences around the port. The central business district of the foreign city strode forwards, large buildings with loping gaits and long trailing arms dragging cables and causeways through the muck. The seawall at the dirigible port had been overrun, infested with some kind of disease that ate concrete and steel, turning it to a slow sludge that sloughed into the sea.

Kim saw with gradually dawning shock that the main buildings weren't titans at all, but composite networked masses, soft-shelled and undulating like jellyfish. Could the City, its buildings hardened over centuries of internal conflict with similar structures, stand against such a threat?

The port was already lost. Crawling drones scaled the gantries and cut free the bucking white lozenges of the airships from their moorings to gambol wildly on the breeze.

———

By the time Kim landed atop her building in the City, she was in the full glare of the day's eye. The sunlight was shocking. She darkened her filters and bowed her head as she caught the elevator to street level, heading for the Old Town and Browne's tower. A hot southerly wind blew across the crack-wracked pavement.

She passed two tiny cadavers, nestfallen exiles, lying unmourned in the perpendicular light. Their arms entwined, mouths open and stretched wide under the solar orb. Empty eye sockets exposed dark recesses where nerves no longer sang, their bones bound in leathery swaddle. Abandoned. Paupers whose assets could not cover the requisite accounting fees to disburse them into the cosmic stream. Instead, they were left as a blind and silent offering to the burning sun. Part of her envied their stillness. It felt an age since she had stopped. She twisted her neck upwards to see from where they may have defenestrated. Above her, branching over the sacrificial streets, writhed the nests themselves, bifurcating tendrils and stolid girders tangled upwards into the infinite celestial white.

A man with a Mars flight suit, filthy beard and broken teeth appeared from a doorway adjacent. He grinned at the Remembrancer as she passed, and set about disturbing the exiles' frozen, horizontal tableau with searching hands.

She caught a breath of whispered words: 'I wasn't always free, but I always had the key.'

She stopped. The words travelled through her hot synapses like cooling water.

'What did you say?' she said, although she had heard clearly.

The man held out his scaly hand, palm upwards and unprotected in the sun, in what she took to be a display of the grim spoils of his excavations.

'I don't always belong, but I always come along,' the man said. His eyes shone.

'Of course you do.' The street was deserted in the blasting light.

She willed her drones closer, until they swarmed around her, their interference cloaking her from the City's eyes. Her propensity for violence rode in along a peripheral neural pathway, summing the man's long, thin limbs, his brittle bones. She took him by the elbow and led him back into the shadow of the doorway. The fellow was strangely passive.

'What do you have there?' she said.

His eyes were alive with unspoken meaning.

Then it hit her. The two phrases he had used. Laser-guided incantations to release her inhibitions, passwords to her mind's backdoor. Now here she was, invisible, in a doorway with a stranger.

She reached out to seize the man's hand, but he shifted his weight and somehow his centre of gravity was no longer where she expected. She took an unbalanced step forward, into the void.

Her adrenal suppressants gated open. Her doctored synapses received the full stream of her violence. It crashed over her like a red wave. She moved to close, unholstered Tax Code in her hand, ready for action, but again he shifted his weight away with unattended ease, leaving a negative space into which she moved.

He uttered another incantation: 'I'm in the underground. I'm in the streets of an underground town.'

Kim's mind sung with slick, slow horror. The man's pale blue eyes. His thin, frail torso. That badge on his flight suit: three intersecting circles and an eye within an eye within an eye.

———

She awoke in a filthy doorway, her drones a blanket of dust around her. She rolled over and they scattered and bounced on the concrete.

Pain lanced through her head. She tried to summon her OS daemon, her eyes darting automatically to scan her peripheral vision for her feeds—but there was nothing. She was marooned in the desert of the real, and now there was only a ghostly trace of augmented vision invented by her brain to compensate for the sudden shocking loss of context around her. She searched her memory for what had happened.

That man's face.

The patch on his flight suit.

She was anchored to the dull, leaden reality of a doorway. With a start, she realised it was not the street she had been on before she blacked out.

She forced herself to think. This was more than a glitch. It seemed like something intrinsic to her connection had been removed. Her panic rose, and suddenly she realised there were no buffers for her emotions. No way of monitoring her bloods. The network was down, and the gates opened. She experienced everything all at once, all the feelings she had been assiduously guarding against rushed in, overwhelming her. Her heart thumped in her chest as she looked around for something to grasp, some landmark on the skyline. She drew quick, rapid breaths through the shock.

She was lost in a strange city, separated from the oneness she felt with the biz and the myriad connections and datapoints swimming in her augmented vision.

All gone. In their place, this grey shadow of her experience of the world. She'd been an outcast her whole life, but this was different. She'd taken the abuse, the sneering glances. Built armour from the insults. Turned the discrimination into determination to become an Owner. It was all relative. Relative to where she'd come from. Relative to where she could fall. And now she had fallen, and she did not like it at all.

She struggled through the cloying mud of her mundane awareness, searching for something to grasp, some fragment of her history, a record she could use to reconstruct her life. She combed her memories. She could recall moments from her childhood, her adolescence, her grim rise through the bureaucracy. She shuddered with relief to realise her identity seemed intact—the trauma of the loss of the datafeed was real, though, and overwhelming. Anxiously, obsessively, she kept trying to reconnect, over and over again. She crawled deeper into the doorway.

Still no signal as the anguished minutes passed.

She knew she had to move. Perhaps if she got to higher ground, she could reconnect. But she had never navigated the twisted streets without the feed before. She was so conditioned to information saturation that it was shockingly disorienting to be without.

And the gasping rush of reconnection with her emotions.

Grief.

It welled up as if from some subterranean cavern, locked away from sunlight for eternity, black and cold as the space between the dying stars.

The sensations crashed in.

She wept in shuddering heaves, raw feeling coursing through her.

She steadied herself against the storm, each wave of emotion threatening to sweep her from the shifting sand on which she had built her house.

But with each gasping breath, the waves came further apart.

And she could start to think.

What had just happened?

The offworlder had opened a backdoor in her mind, cut her off from her feeds and her mods and left her abandoned here, in a bright street, in full sun, alone and in pain. It was a targeted attack, clearly part of the coordinated invasion of the City.

As the shock subsided, she realised she had to keep moving. She wouldn't survive during the heat of the day. She followed a snickle-way between two walls. Grasping hands pulled at her memory, into a cavern a hundred million years deep. Bereft, like those nestfallen exiles, earthly remains there forfeited to the exigencies of the City and its precarious inhabitants.

Into a shadowed square in a gap between buildings, lined with coffeeshops shuttered against the daylight.

She fumbled with a door latch, stumbled through the threshold and found herself in a dark, cool room of gameslaves logged into public access network ports to take advantage of faster speeds for their gamified tradebots. Investors making good on their capital by grinding tokens in bowels of the Four Houses.

She wrenched the nearest from his position, a man in his twenties, wearing an outward expression of panic as he lost connection with his trades.

'Wha...', he said, trying to escape her grip.

Without her elegant prostheses, she felt like she was moving through honey.

He squirmed.

She yanked the headset from his head.

As his awareness returned to the room, his anger flared.

'Bitch,' he said. 'What you doin? I'm tradin.'

'I'm borrowing your rig,' she said.

'You're crazy.' He twisted in his seat to fend her off.

She whipped him to the floor and pressed her elbow to his throat.

'I need to check my accounts,' she said.

Fear showed in his eyes as he recognised the rank implied by the remnants of her tattered uniform, and then a wash of confusion at her dishevelled state. A sudden course of adrenaline surged unchecked through her body, but she fought against it and reduced the pressure on his throat.

'Fine, take it. Fuck.'

She shoved him aside and greedily moved the headset into place with her other hand.

None of her logins worked. She was locked out of her accounts.

She tried to reactivate them with backup codes but those, too, no longer worked.

Meanwhile, in the public spaces of the metaverse around her, the City was in meltdown.

Markets awash with furious trading. Chattels were pumped and then crashed and rallied, only to tumble again as investors sought to rid themselves of toxic assets. Lightspeed arbitrage between exchanges, everyone rushing for the exit at once.

Everything squandered. All her advantage, gone.

A house built on sand.

And finally she was jolted back to reality as the ground shook and plaster dust fell.

———

She fled further inside the coffee house, climbing the stairs to the roof. It was hot in the stairwell, despite the labour of the building's climate systems. She peered out through a tinted window and saw the flank of Bank of the South, one of the Four Houses. It stood tall against the City walls, having heaved its buttressed footings into a new position. She kept climbing. The building she was in shifted around her as the city continued to anamorphose into reconfigured defences to face the encroaching threat. Vibrations shook the twitching structure. Kim steadied herself and continued. Through the window glass, she made out a railgun articulated on the arm of the Bank of the South. As she watched, an invading building appeared above the City wall, bone-white in the sun. Bank of the South fired a round from the railgun and the recoil sent dust and litter scattering through the streets in bifurcating waves of turbulent backwash. The impact from the round stunned the invader, splitting its top stories. Debris tumbled downwards, but beneath the damage, the structure regrew anew and recommenced its slow ascent of the wall. In the sunstroked streets below her, the heat haze heaved upwards, expelled from the grid beneath and vented into the shimmering air. The infinite machine, an immutable ledger written upon the earth, its data captured in motes of falling dust. One regime falling as another rose to take its place.

The foreign city breached the wall. A defender, the SinoShell building, lumbered towards the invaders, curtain walls grinding in the hard sunlight. Groaning girders sang in the humid air. Klaxons sounded and she was shaken to the floor as the building she was in took a kneeling posture adjacent to a massy caisson of the Bank of the South to protect it from the encroaching masonry. The invaders slowly invaginated the City's walls.

Below her, she made out crowds of swarming citizens in a mad scramble to accumulate before the end. She moved through the reconstituted space, trying to find her way down now, onto the street. Something compelled her forwards. She had to reach Browne.

'This is what you wanted, isn't it?' She thought to herself. 'A backdoor. A way off the carousel. Well, here it is.'

She laughed grimly and scrutinised her earthly accounts.

There was only dust.

———

She scanned the skyline for a familiar landmark. She was slowly adjusting to being without her connection, and even as the City no longer adhered to the patterns she remembered, she realised there was a regularity to the defensive architectural reorientation. The City was protecting its centre, where the seat of its power lay. The grey institutions of its Owners. Parliament, the great dome of Paul the Apostle. The Treasury with its honeycomb windows.

She haggled with the remains of a citizen lying dead in the gutter for kit that would keep her cool long enough to reach the Old Town, and she set out along the suncracked pavement. Through an alley, beneath fragmenting structures, the footpath sticky with the invading virus, turning liquid. The City was hardened by centuries of conflict against itself, and it had no defence against the foreign forces with this new threat they posed.

Kim kept bearing towards the centre, along empty side streets and through squares shuttered against the light and the City's tectonic defensive posturing. In the faces of the few citizens she passed, she saw only greed and fear. But more and more, she also came across activist cadres wearing the eye within an eye within an eye.

At a checkpoint, an armed revolutionary recognised her new status in her bedraggled uniform and droneless aspect. He leered at her.

'You've been freed, Remembrancer. Freed from the system that enslaved you.'

'Is that what you call it?' she said.

'Radical transparency and redistribution. We're taking the City apart. It's a cancer on this world.'

And what will replace it? She left the thought unvoiced, but it occurred to her then that the centralisation and concentration of wealth was the interplay of human relationships, not abstract systems. Unwilling to spark conflict, she grimaced and pushed her way through the glowering company and towards Old Town.

———

She reached Browne's building in the golden dusk, the light weaving strange patterns in the fluid air. She let herself into the foyer with the manual codes she still remembered from their affair. The elevator was out, so she took the stairs, resting as she went.

She arrived at the top, exhausted and grimy with dust and sweat, to find Browne in his cups, a crystal decanter at his side. The air-conditioning hum reduced the roar of the revolution below to background noise.

'I knew it would be you,' he said. He wore silk pyjamas and slippers and sat in an overstuffed armchair.

She didn't reply.

'I spent my life getting what I wanted. But it's just not possible. The wanting and the having of the thing exist in two separate, incompatible states. That is the tension of being human.'

'Yet still the want remains.'

'We must learn to live with the ambiguity of the borderless place. That is our responsibility and our burden.'

She regarded him: bounded, bonded.

'You betrayed the City. I have the proof from Maia. You've been double-dealing,' she said.

He didn't react.

'I can make you an Owner,' he said.

She laughed. 'Owner of a ruin?'

'The City is resilient.'

He seemed so sure of his investments.

'The Four Houses have collapsed,' she said. 'There's nothing left but dust.'

'The system is built on frictionless markets, perfect elasticity of demand and supply.'

He lifted the decanter and poured another glass but did not offer her one.

'It's built by people,' she said.

'Code is Law. The City is inviolable. The eternal, distributed machine upon which all trustless counterparties forge their trades.'

'And it has turned all interaction into transaction.'

He laughed. 'Adversarial relationships stimulate life.'

She envied him his certainty, but it made him brittle. He appeared small and vulnerable, childlike in his armchair.

'They also hasten death,' she said.

'Don't dally in your task, then. Audit my accounts.'

'I've renounced my old profession, Browne. I'm no longer in that game.'

'It would be a mercy.' He lowered his head. 'I don't want to be tortured.'

'I'm sorry,' she said.

Whatever his fate, she could no longer be an instrument to bring it about.

She took the stairs, leaving him to ponder his portfolio and his decanter.

As she exited into the dissolving streets, she felt empty for the first time and unfettered by the bonds that had held her captive for so long. A strange new sensation burned inside her like a disclosure.

The Agency of Metabolic Pathways

Sid Jain

Review

Every scientific paper, you think, begins with a literature review because that is how scientists pay respect to their lineage. It is remembrance. An elemental force inside us wanting to extend back in time, connect with what came before us in branching sinews of text and DNA, the stores of the past and future. Strands of nitrogenous base pairs in our every cell link a chain of causality from the great progenitor of all life to our progeny and the text of literature review forms a ritual of community-building. Binding the web of scientists who are solving the same problems together in a passionate genealogy. The review is your second-favorite part of a scientific paper and it always reminds you of home, of the first scientist who taught you.

Planting alfalfa sprouts in your mother's kitchen garden is where you learn that it all begins with nitrogen fixation. Her wrinkly, soft fingers place the roots of a handful of white-tendrils in the brown earth on a wet Mumbai day. You pat the soil down and bring the browned fingers up, petrichor sharp on your tongue.

In the dirt the roots advertise themselves to bacteria that pilfer nitrogen from the air. The roots provide a cozy home, full of sugar and water. The bacteria moves in and pays rent in the nitrogen it pulls from the atmosphere.

While the science made sense, you hadn't yet learned words like *rent* and *moving out*. You did know home: *home* was a two-bedroom in a calico-white building in Bandra surrounded by a vast sea of polluted water that invaded every monsoon.

Once you learn the words, you can't wait to leave. So you can stop breathing this air. So you get away from the heat and how angry it makes everyone around you. So you can stop waiting for your life to really begin.

One day you will learn that your biggest flaw is an inability to enjoy the present. The present is a miserable place but the future always has potential. Your mind is fixated on a time after you leave.

But life is an integral of living one differential second at a time. You must live every second of it, and the equation of life cannot be balanced if you take some of those seconds out because they hurt too much.

So the seconds pass, from drought to flood to fire and smoke. And you review each second you spent eating your mother's chole bhature, the vada pav of the Mumbai streets, the samosas of your hostel canteen. The seconds pass too slowly for you, because each of the seconds that you are not working on your greatest project is a second less in the trend line of your life in the exponential phase.

The lag suffocates you. You stand on Marina beach and take in a breath that feels like a life promise, but in your lungs is only dead salt.

Now finally the trend line integral of your life is ticking upwards with every second and you are at the airport the day you're flying away for good. Your mother can't hide the tears she's crying as the automatic doors of the security gate hungrily close behind you like a bacterial cell wall around a sugar molecule. A murmuration of starlings turns across a gray sky above you, joined by some ancient adaptation, and you are alone.

Isolation

Carla insists it's one of the good days in the Everglades, right after a cold snap. Florida, she says, was for winter fishing trips with her dad to escape her marriage in Bountiful, Utah. You ask the question she had invited, shouting over the loud roar of the airboat's fan and the wind whipping through your hair.

Carla says it like reciting her birthdate. She had left her husband for good last year, jettisoning him like a shotgun shell casing. A cop too fond of the way leather sounded wrapped around his wrist. She moved to San Diego and now shares a La Jolla beach apartment with three grad students who she surfs with every Saturday.

You blush and look up through green-black tinted sunglasses at the swamp canopy above, biding time to formulate your next question.

She says it's a good day for fishing. That's how she sees what you're all doing here: a hunt, a conquest with spoils to take home.

You're uncomfortable with the framing but you say nothing. In your mind, you're a gold rush speculator, panning the silt of the Everglades mangroves for microbial riches.

Carla leans over the boat to peer into the water, her auburn hair whipping back. She turns back with a grin. You wonder if this is one of those moments that stick with you and form a core memory that you'll never forget. Her, this airboat, the mangrove, and the thrill of prospecting in a wild land. You remind yourself to live within the moment before you contextualise it too tightly into the narrative of your life.

Glass bottles clang like wedding bells in the back. Soil and water samples, to study the Everglades microbiome. Shovels, bags, and the dry ice freezer knock into each other on the choppy water. Somewhere in your dirt harvest will be a viable candidate for your lab's mission.

You beach the airboat a mile earlier than one would have forty years ago. The sea has lapped up more of the mangrove and the shore ahead is under the tide. Carla steps out and presses her nose near the base of the nearest tree with its roots in the air. Takes a deep breath and sighs.

Florida's water has a tangier scent than the gray ocean off Del Mar. More alive. In the mangrove forest, life grows that is mystical to phycologists. Marine phytoalgae: half algae, half fungus. A black sheep of the tree of life. Misunderstood and mischaracterised. mmensely useful. A clade ripe for speculative exploration. Phyla incognita.

Your ideal microbe is already as good as it can be without your help. Bugs don't come with letters of recommendation, GRE scores, or statements of purpose like you did. They only have the agency of their metabolic pathways. The efficiencies and useful productivity hacks that they've picked up from their environment or that were passed down by their families. Budding in the rich mineral-spiced menagerie of the mangrove, where fresh meets salt and exchanges notes on being water, these bugs have the greatest potential to pick up the best tricks. From the microbial riches you've gathered you will isolate a photosynthetic *and* nitrogen-fixing bug. Or one that can be taught, at least.

Sometimes you can't help but write yourself into your bugs, encoding your stories in the journey you're about to take this tiny fellow. The mangrove reminds you of home. Hot, sticky Bandra and its spicy-sweet street food. The wet ground. Petrichor. You say you're here to isolate a candidate bug, but you're here to find yourself. Whatever that means.

That night, after a day of being knee deep in the mangrove swamp, you share a cup of hot chocolate with hazelnut liqueur swirled in with Carla and trade microbial stories.

You ask her, do you have a favorite?

She says, I feel like I'm Fleming's *Penicillium rubens*. Forgotten in a dusty drawer. Fighting off mold all alone.

Teaching the world, you say. The secret of antibiotics. Good choice. No one's ever truly alone, are they?

A breeze lifts a strand of her hair and gently lays it on her glistening cheek. She doesn't brush it off.

A useful oblivion, she says. And you?

E. coli, you say sheepishly. The one that was taught to make human insulin. You wanted to say something more fun, maybe the yeast *Saccharamyces carlsbergensis*, named after the beer it made.

But the stars in the clear sky make you feel a sense of weightiness to the night, and you want her to know that you have depth.

Industrial microbiology fascinates you, you say, and these industrious microbes with their special skills are the best teachers.

She says, California is the place to be, then. Do you plan to stay after your project is over?

You ask her why she picked California as the place to escape to. It's not the particulars of her answer you're interested in, it's learning the patterns of thought that make people leave their home. You ask her this question to fill your design space with new data.

She says, if California's good enough for the sperm whales, it's good enough for me. They have the biggest brains on the planet, after all.

You fall in love with her answer and by proxy, her. You're desperate to say something profound then. To make her like you.

You say, isn't it amazing how our metabolic pathways are so conserved across all the clades? Cytochrome c is the same in us and the whales and it's the same as it was in the first living thing ever, the Last Universal Common Ancestor. Isn't that nuts?

She says, that's nice.

You're talking faster now, excited to fill the silence between the two of you with the mating dance of scientific minds: I read somewhere that the Wabanaki people say all the living things in the world are connected in a giant cosmic embrace—

The tree of life, she says. They cover it in their mysticism and call it profound.

You frown. The way she says it makes you drop that thread. You had wanted to tell her that you found it moving, to think that the entire span of all life exists within each of us, going all the way back to the first lifeform in one continuous integral. Like a growth exponential curve, but for all life ever, not just the batch of cells inside one bioreactor. But now you just want to watch the sky.

The richly dense star clusters look to you like bits of hazelnut suspended in chocolate. Like mold colonies spreading on charcoal agar gel. You fix your gaze on one star and watch it twinkle and squirm in the air. You wish you can turn a telescope's dial and see inside the star—

Microbiology is the study of large numbers of small things. Microscopically vast numbers, ridiculous to even type out. Ten trillion bacterial cells grow in the gallon tank of your benchtop bioreactor. A sextillion in a human sized icebox in which a scientist may pretend to drown to escape awkwardness.

You hope that one of the million species of cells hibernating on ice in the airboat's icebox, settling in for the two-thousand-mile journey back to your lab in San Diego, will change the world. You haven't met it yet, but you want to ask it if it's relieved to be getting out of this place.

Design Space

Every experiment is born with an infinite combination of test inputs. Your hands, the tools at your disposal, and the time given by your patrons narrow the universe of input parameters you could conceivably study. Your culling weapon is the hypothesis: a novel claim projected onto the world that would be found out to be true or not by the end of the experiment.

Hypothesis: Salt and nitrogen concentration in growth media

impact the carbon capture rate of *Halocafeteria carlii*

The input parameters at the boundaries, the edge cases of your experimental design, define the extent of your design space. Picking test parameters from that three-dimensional universe and creating an experiment is like picking stars out of the night sky and calling it a constellation.

In a sense the design space measures the conceptual reach of your experiment, mapping the edges of the known universe of information, pushing terra incognita further into the margins; but in another way, it measures time: time saved by compressing science and life into a more efficient, regimented, and commercialised enterprise.

For a compact experiment, you pick a high and a low condition for a couple of parameters. Your experiment is running combinations of those conditions to identify the effects of each parameter.

	N2 level	NaCl Level
Condition #1	Low	Low
Condition #2	Low	High
Condition #3	High	Low
Condition #4	High	High

The first time you learn about experimental design you learn nothing at all. Your thesis advisor, on the road to her distinguished faculty chair, has made you beg for your spot in her lab after your first anxiety attack keeps you home for a week. Her fine lesson, taught in a helical Tamil accent, has leaked out with your tears in her office. Years later, you wonder: was her technique too harsh, or were you—

having learned science only from the comfort of your mother's arms—not yet ready for a tougher love?

The second time, you are standing in a cubicle farm at this San Diego startup. A Dutch scientist with wild eyebrows and a constant smile leans back in his swivel chair and explains in a fast, excitable voice, that a well-designed experiment is not dissimilar to a well-crafted story. He waits for you to see the design of what he says, to see the light come on in your eyes. You are a fresh grad, eager to please him, so you smile and nod.

He says wait, come sit with me. And you do, and you spend the rest of the afternoon feeling the gentle expansion of your mind. Not new knowledge—new perspective.

Experimental conditions, he says, are worldbuilding. The lives of the cells in the bioreactors are the plot, and the stakes rise and fall in the excel spreadsheet of the sampling data you collect every day (including weekends, because the cells never sleep).

So as he spins your chair away towards the lab, he says: go pick some interesting characters. Make them a world worth living in.

Process Development

Four bioreactors turn silently in the galley kitchen-like lab lit by steady 420nm white light. There's a sink in the corner piled high with soiled glassware your intern abandoned in favor of an earlier flight to Vegas for the weekend. A similar sink stays dirty in your home. You remind yourself to load the rented dishwasher before Carla gets home from surfing. You always avoid it because the bottom half is coming unstuck from the cabinet bracket and it leaks onto the peeling linoleum floor and it always annoys her. Your metabolic routine has not yet developed to reliably create everyday love through these chores, but you so desperately want to.

A bubblegum pop song on the radio plays for the third time that morning. You've heard it so many times that you've started to pay attention to details in the sound mix. The airy headspace in the treble range and the gentle roll off in the sub-bass EQ. Perfectly calibrated addiction. Four empty Reece's wrappers are strewn around your keyboard and a fifth is in your hands as the data flickers across your screen and the blue light glints off your glasses.

When you sample the bioreactors, you label the data with their names:

Cossette/ Day 10/ Low-N$_2$, High NaCl

Valjean/ Day 10/ High-N$_2$, Low NaCl

Javert/ Day 10/ High N$_2$, High-NaCl

Fantine/Day 10/Low N$_2$, Low-NaCl

Four grafts of the same cell line thrust in different circumstances of living. The graph betrays how close the four really are.

Design of Experiments Runs 4-8 of 32

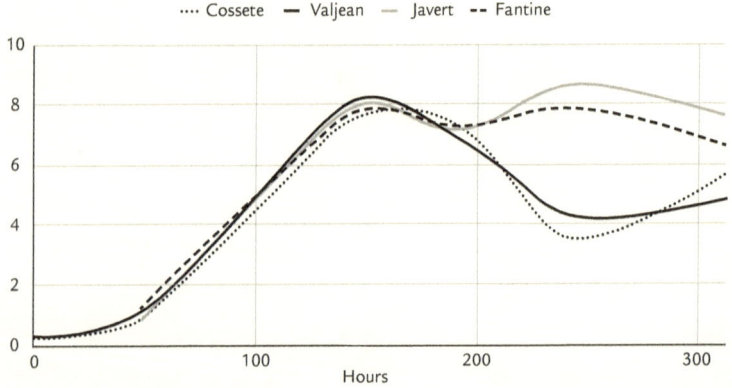

Their worlds look the same, but the small differences spiral into completely different life stories. Cossette's life was harsh, the high salt of the liquid compressing her cell wall smaller, the low nitrogen strangling her. Despite it she rallies on the eighth day, hopeful to meet her mother someday. Valjean suffers a similar fate, as life, as it looks up hopefully, ultimately lets him down.

This being industrial microbiology, means you don't just care about their lives. You care about what they do with it. Valjean, despite his hard life, still manages to overperform.

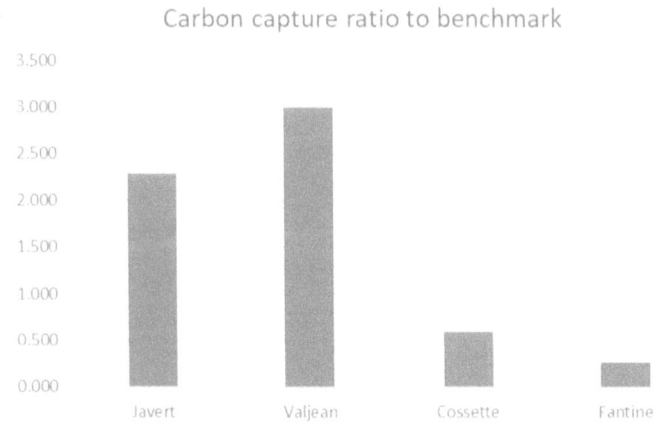

Carbon capture ratio to benchmark

You stare at the data on the sticker-filled lab computer so long the lines snake out of the monitor, and the story comes alive around you in soaring ensemble crescendos punctuated by cannon blast.

You cried when you first saw Les Miserables because it reminded you too much of your city burning during a riot that summer. The broken Paris of Cossette and Fantine became broken Bombay, ripped apart by people pushed to murderous madness by alternating cycles of catatonic heat and cyclonic flooding. The image of a girl crying on the roof of a smoking car floating down a Bombay road-turned-river comes to you, overlaid upon an image of Marius waving the tricolor on a burning barricade.

The youth of a revolutionary age are always the most mis fortunate. You find strength, though, in commune with those past ages, those past youths, and those past revolutions through stories like this that transcend time.

Victor Hugo wrote a 1,462 page novel to tell his story. Alain Boublil refined it into 49 songs, and you have simplified the story to four trendlines on a graph.

A sugar rush merges with a vibe from the summery breezy pop song on the radio and melds on top of a meandering sequence of thoughts on the craft of storytelling through process development data. You spin restlessly in your office chair, thinking and clearly procrastinating on important company work (but it's a weekend, you remind yourself), and you think of the word *refinement*.

Refined storytelling. Refined sugar. Refined sound design. Refined microbe. Refined person. Why did we start relentlessly refining the novel, the pop song, our food, our work, and ourselves all at once?

You play a raw black metal song ten minutes long that a Norwegian wrote over a long winter in his bedroom last year and you realise: the economic system that has brought about this planetary crisis through relentless refinement cannot sell this music. Only a community operating outside of a capitalist paradigm can lovingly share these blistering, angry lo-fi shrieks and find people willing to spend time with it. Meanwhile, the same three minute pop song that has been refined to such a sophisticated level that it's almost an injectable drug can be endlessly streamed, earning cents for a billionaire every time.

Capitalism cannot sell a mother's hand-cooked meal for her son and his neighborhood friends. Sitting with a 1500 page novel is an economically unproductive hobby. Capitalism cannot sell a microbe that hasn't been developed past its natural limits, and it has no use for a person who isn't working at their peak productivity on a weekend.

Listening to long, sprawling epics, eating a slow home-cooked meal, and reading dense philosophy become almost acts of rebellion. An economic system that has for so long prioritised relentless refinement and growth has left a polluted and fragile planet. That thought pattern of refinement is so ingrained in you that even your solution to the crisis is infected with the desire for relentless development.

So what can you do?

You resist the urge to refine this process indefinitely and text Carla with a new theoretical approach for how this microbe will save the world. Your chat thread with her reads like a dialogue poem, and feels like the teeth of a zipper parting.

You text her: Growth without end is cancer.

She replies: You are an insufferable scientist.

If we pick Javert the system will destabilise

If we pick Valjean we won't get funding

Refinement without end is pollution.

Experimental optimisation is progress

Whose progress?

The world.

The world is 71% water.

Message read.

Goes against everything you have been taught. Process development is maximising yield. Maximising yield is maximising productivity is maximising profit. From the *E. Coli* that makes insulin to the Chinese Hamster Ovary cell isolated from one female hamster and exploited to make human proteins in twenty-thousand-liter bioreactors three-stories tall, the exploitation of metabolic pathways towards relentless development has left you with no other conceptual approach to your science besides refinement and maximisation. Even the bioreactors that grow the CHO cells are kept as warm as that Chinese Hamster's body temperature, to fool the cells into thinking they are still home.

The history of industrial microbiology is a history of taking a superlative microbe out of its natural habitat, conditioning it to unnaturally proliferate, and teaching it to make something useful. It is your history as well, a child who left home to become prodigiously useful to the west.

So shut the computer down and head home. Load the dishwasher whistling a song of angry men. Linger a moment on this feeling; your body is undergoing a revolution, a paradigm shift. It is learning how to remember.

Blue-White Selection

You have to access a different part of your brain to get to the muscle memory of pouring agar media into a plate. You haven't done this since that internship at the foothills of the German Alps.

Learning to pour the agar media there had been painful. The thin strip of melted agar you poured in was never level and you took so long to pour out the whole stack of plates that the agar solidified inside the glass bottle before you were finished. Lumpy cold icebergs of agar plopped into the plate, like glaciers calving off of Antarctica.

You have hidden the muscle memory of this technique behind shame, but the excitement of future glory from your new work with *H. carlii* is pulling the knowledge out like a cell squeezed under a salt gradient.

Your boss had berated you for your slowness and that makes you remember—

That to teach a cell new tricks, you have to shock it. Raise the temperature, change the pH—give the cell wounds where your desired gene invades through the porous cell wall. To learn, sometimes, is to be hurt.

Metabolic pathways are conserved across the phylogenetic kingdom. Which means every living thing is resistant to change. The genetic modification sometimes fails.

If the recombinant DNA takes root in the cell, it grows as white colonies. If it doesn't, it grows as blue chickenpox-dots on the yellow agar.

In the shock of that wildfire summer you evacuate your San Diego apartment four times. From the sunny beaches of Del Mar to the flooded coast of Bombay, you can't be outside without a mask for half the year. In the middle of this planetary crisis you stumble, dazed, thirsting for *something* to guide you out of the abyss, hoping for philosophy, but all you found was Carla.

Remember: she slept with you in the Jeep that night under the Everglades moon. The long nights in the lab slow-dancing to the late night radio while the PCR machine beeped unattended. The research papers you sent each other as an awkward flirtation after Florida, keeping that fragile connection between you going until it reached the exponential phase and then she moved in with you, into the apartment with the busted dishwasher, and complained about turmeric stains on the countertop. And so began the lag phase, the bitter comedown. She always found a way to avoid saying hello to your parents. The stories of your home before her drove her to distraction. Your timid philosophy, a sapling of thoughts yet to form strong roots withered in her sharp glare and lack of care. Her time with you as transient as a viral infection, but you suffer it wholly committed.

With a needlepoint scalpel you pick up six white colonies under the Bunsen burner and streak them upon fresh plates, and you think of leaving her.

Apoptosis

Lightning flashed across a night sky and ionised inert nitrogen gas into nitrous oxide that fell as acid rain four billion years ago upon a primordial stew of carbon and trace metals. The first DNA twisted itself into a helix in this molten sea of volcanic ash and nitric acid. Full of righteous promise.

Deoxyribonucleic Acid: there is an acrid core in us all that remembers the four-billion-year echoes of rolling thunder and spluttering lava. In our cells is a hot, bitter memory of living in a burning world.

That is how the equation of all life started, and nested within it are the equations of your life and of Carla's, and nested within that are the equations of all the experiments with *H. Carlii* you ran in your lab and the great evolutionary story of *H. Carlii* that you and Carla wrote together. All of it combines to create the great torrent of life stretching back to the Last Universal Common Ancestor, progenitor of all that is living, who first learned to fix nitrogen and photosynthesise carbon, who you have linked in a long chain of evolutionary lessons to this cell.

You have taught the cell to become as powerful as it can be. *H. Carlii* is now a cell factory hoovering carbon out of the atmosphere and living off the biome-grid, eating nitrogen out of thin air. Your last lesson to it is the most painful. You have to teach it how to die.

Learning how to die begins with remembrance. Distill your memories into stories and repeat them until they beat with the hearts of the living dead. When you start to consider everything you have ever done as important, you begin to think differently about wasted time. Even the time you spent with Carla and the bug you named after her is precious. When scientists retrace your steps as they sit and compose the treatise of their work, they will walk the muddy shoals of Florida with you and Carla. You will be remembered.

To teach a human how to die is to teach them to suspend the tyranny of the present and to keep a commune with the past. Slow down, deflect fervor pointed at you, and practice meditative reflection. Cultivate an archive, remix and rework old stories and old patterns of remembrance. With enough stories and a slow enough mind, every second becomes a lifetime, and you make time to save the world.

To teach a cell how to die is to teach it to slow down its consumption until its living pulse stops, and it falls into the water free and rich. You slip in a gene that tricks *H. carlii* to pick up a particular molecule that it thinks of as a sugary food but is actually poison.

Carla taught you how to teach the cell how to die. Tell me, do you remember the last time you gorged on something refined to toxicity, that hid itself as something you craved?

Abstract

Halocafeteria carlii is a species of marine photosynthetic algae that can grow in brackish water with minimal nutrients. In this study, we demonstrate a genetically modified form of *H. carlii* that can fix atmospheric nitrogen and photosynthesise carbon in acidic oceans. Once *H. carlii* reaches lag phase, further genetic modifications trigger a hardening of the cell wall, causing the algal bloom to break apart and sink into the ocean, providing rich nutrition for deep ocean marine life. In this way *H. carlii* has a potential to be used for widescale geotherapy of acidified oceans. Sea-farmed blooms of this microalgae can capture atmospheric carbon and reseed coral reefs. *H. carlii* was first isolated in the mangrove of Everglades National Park, United States.

Tech Transfer

You're surfing over microplastic-filled waves, goggles snapped over your eyes and face masked in breathable wetsuit rubber. You're about to send *H carlii* into the water. Homecoming, but as a circle. Thousands of miles from where its progenitor cell line was isolated, *H carlii* is going to your home.

The company picks the Mumbai archipelago as the testing ground for the carbon-sucking reef-building hero of this story. Once landfilled and joined together, Mumbai is a chain of islands once more.

Wipeout on a wave that broke right, and you plunge into the water. You imagine where there were once rainbow-hued fish and bright corals and come up for air. The corals are long-dead from a terminal case of civilisation.

You have flown home with it as part of the tech transfer team. A six-hour scramjet to Mumbai from San Diego leaves you reeling in timezone whiplash.

You almost feel like you're bringing a lifelong friend home for the first time. You hope to show the little guy around, but the city wears a different suit every time you see it now and you aren't as surefooted around its broken footpaths as you were once. The confidence in your ability to haggle the water taxi's price down has evaporated, and your Hindi accent makes people frown.

But you tried. In your time with *H. carlii* you taught it how to live a life you were used to. Hungry, enterprising, making your own food out of nothing. Learning quickly and learning well, how to live in a world different to where it was from.

While *H. Carlii* was in your lab, its potential was theoretical. You felt that about yourself, once.

As the manufacturing team greets you in the plush offices of the Mumbai branch of your startup, you almost feel like your mother the day you left for grad school. Her child entrusted to another system and way of being.

At dinner that evening, you sit in the same spot on the same table in the same dining room as a decade ago. In this familiar habitat you fall into conserved metabolic pathways of being. You repeat old habits; rocking back and forth on your chair that still creaks in the same way as it did when you were fifteen. You ask your mother for chole bhature, and slowly savor every bite as a commune with a past life.

The Space Between All Possible Ways

Cat Sparks

Present

The drones come first and then the war machines, lumbering like beasts across crags and dirt, 20-inch radial tires chewing rocks. Compact, stocky vehicles, blast protected as they bounce and glide, bullet-riddled ballistic panelling draped with tangled, dusty camo, 50 calibre machine guns mounted high and proud.

Trucks mean business; high mobility variants with v-shaped armoured spines once used for deep battlespace reconnaissance. These days after whatever they can get. Women, alcohol or water; forgotten caches from bungled supply drops half a decade past or even longer.

Lately they've been chasing rumours of a magic tree taken root in inhospitable terrain. A wonderous bloom, scraping filth from empty air, returning it as gold and gems and car parts. From diesel to the finest liquor, make your wishes and the tree provides. Refugees have gathered, attracted to its bounty.

And there it is, a speck of nothing nestled in the valley. Children playing outside the settlement abandon games to watch; first drones and then the dusty trucks laden with men shouting through speakers, enhanced and crackling electronic demands in English, French, Arabic and Hausa, faces wrapped against the sun's relentless cruelty.

Trucks slam to shuddering halts. Everyone wants to watch how guns are made. How the tree-that-is-not-a-tree sucks bad dirt from the air, rendering it solid and functional as metal. Trees-that-are-not-trees are rumoured to be blooming in many troubled places: Ukraine, Yemen, Uzbekistan, Mississippi, Abu Dhabi. Perhaps the guns extrude from branches to drop down into waiting hands? If they're quick enough, they can catch them when they fall.

But the so-called tree looks nothing like expected. No bark, no wood, no jewelled oasis, no sprays of lemon morningstar around its roots. Arrays of peculiar, scaffolded contraptions, half buried, half exposed to open elements.

Engines idling, distracted by the bright weave of children's garments, stark as petals against the pale, dry sand. Nearby cluster candy-coloured domes, textured formations of earthen peaks and bulbs. Tethered goats, scattered dogs and chickens, same as everywhere.

Drones whine and mass above like angry insects.

The tree performs no magic tricks and soon the men are bored. Staring as panel after panel realigns and another sound; a shrill and purring engine coupled with a semi-muted growl, perhaps like the stomach of a dog who has eaten garbage poisonous and rotten.

Gunshot splits the sullen air. An angry storm of men turn on the shooter, swear and strike until the man's knocked to the ground.

Do not fire upon the magic. Shoot the ones who would keep it for themselves.

Random, interrupting sounds, distracting from the swirl of heat and dust. A grind distinct from whining truck emissions, metallic, crisp and clear. Treetops shift and realign before unfurling extra struts and shapes.

Shouting starts again and then the engines, veering closer, turning sharply, testing mettle, taking chances, one eye on those angling panels that might be leaves in case they shape shift into weapons.

More gunshots as the convoy circles closer. Angry voices amplified: *Give us your magic tree or we will burn your huts and kill your children. There's nowhere to run, nowhere to hide.*

The pulse hits, swift and clean and bright, dislodging drones from dizzy orbits, slamming them to sand like broken birds.

The tree-which-is-not-a-tree morphs form into something like a giant seedpod. What happened to those playful children; the women in their brightly woven wraps? No time to bolt for cover. Even the chickens, goats and dogs have vanished.

The pulse has frozen all the trucks, engines jammed and stagnant, men furious and shouting, firing what weaponry still functions, vomiting as a queasy timbre reverberates around the granite spars and shards. One man calls out he is blind, another cries of witchcraft, djinn and demons swirling in kaleidoscopic shapes and colours.

Two are dead from collateral damage bullets.

Where has everybody gone? No place to hide out here in open desert, except, perhaps, within the tree itself, although that too seems impossible. One moment forty people living, working, visible and blatant. A well-played trick. Furious men take aim at artificial roots thickened into shields against which bullets slam and clang. Chunks and shards of green-grey spray and scatter.

The angry men power down to wait it out, for the magic pod to unfurl and reconstruct. For the tree to make the parts to fix their ancient, ailing trucks and for the bounty harvest of grenades and ammunition, raining to the sand like acacia blossoms. Others have spoken of seeing such things with their own eyes all around the world, the digital traces shared from phone to phone.

Beneath the ground, in a bunker made from concrete chemically bonded with air-siphoned carbon, Cray stares intently at a bank of screens, heart thumping. Uncertain that the tech would work the way it was designed to. Relieved they haven't lost so much as a chicken.

'Gonna wait us out,' he says.

'No, they won't,' she answers.

'They'll be back in bigger numbers.'

'Not that either. The story they'll report will not be one their masters can believe. It won't fit the evidence.'

Cray sniffs, considering. 'There's drone footage and coordinates.'

'Hacked and scrambled.'

'Lakesha, why should I believe you?'

'Have I ever been wrong so far?'

The man shrugs.

'They'll leave,' she says. 'Already they're questioning their eyes.'

'Perhaps,' says Cray, unwilling to commit. Around him, families and travellers are settling in to wait, laughing at the chaos of chickens, squabbling good-naturedly over which games to play, which foods to prepare for dinner. The bunker is well stocked. They have sheltered here from storms and only the children are curious to watch the screens revealing what the shouting men are up to.

Come first light, no longer shouting, the deep desert men abandon useless broken vehicles, heading back the way they came, winds rapidly obliterating any trace they'd ever been there.

When All Clear sounds, the pod disassembles and reverts to forest form. People emerge from the hollow cavern beneath the tree's broad base, calling to each other as they right the mess the trucks have wrought, warning children not to touch the drones—they might be booby trapped. *Dogs are trained to smell such things, let them get on with it.*

A dying bandit slouches, propped against a ruined truck, galabeya stained with thick brown blood much more of which has leached into the sand. He's mumbling prayers, or maybe words to songs from old times past.

He's dying but the children bring him water, sit with him so he won't die alone. Cray moves fast, but already light is leaching from the bandit's eyes.

Eyes that widen at the sight of Cray.

'I recognise you, brother,' he rasps through sun parched lips. 'Brother, you can't hide in a magic tree.'

Glassy eyes slip in and out of focus, stare past Cray to the metal forest, branches unfurling, extending, realigning. Nubbins sprouting solar flowers expand to lock on to the sun's trajectory. Thin flat banks of concertinaed membrane reasserting, repositioning. *More things on heaven and earth*, a narrowing of the space between all possible ways.

A mighty, wondrous creation, reaching up, unfurling and

unfolding exaltations. *God is great*, the bandit comprehends, as the bonds that tether him to this world slip and loosen. Last thing he sees is a tree praying to the sky.

Cray stands, steady, but uncertain, unsettled by the dying man's last words. *Recognise me or recognise my kind?* A world of difference between those possibilities.

Relief spreads rapidly amongst the settlers—precious sandcasting moulds have not been damaged. Big tyres could have made short work of them, but the men with guns didn't even notice, or if they did, did not comprehend the inherent magic of wind turbine parts and blades manufactured from carbon harvested from thin air, casting shapes for fixing broken infrastructures. Designing new materials required to fill the gaps. That their tree's specific reputation is for aerofoils with high lift to drag ratio and hand crafted, specialised tip geometries.

The settlement knows much about kinetic energy and subsequent velocity, power coefficients, downwash and wake effects. Following on from seven hundred years of windmills turning, powering a future with no limits.

Cray goes to find a shovel for burying the dead, the words *I recognise you, brother* turning over and over in his head.

Past

The dog tags say his name is Cray, strung around his thick and sunburned neck. Cray would rather be anywhere than in this baking hell and desolation. Not that he remembers anywhere. Holds his arm up, seeking faded traces of tattooed imagery, clues to who he might have been before.

They say Refurb requires consent, that you choose your new life and new chance in some harsh and blasted foreign wasteland. That such a gift cannot be forced. That you have the right to turn it down and thirty days to make the call for a chinook to airlift you back to prison or whatever else you're running from.

They say you will come to love the Tree like a sister or a daughter, but words are meaningless without memories of loving anyone or anything. They say a third of new Refurbs plot escape before the capsule seeds, stripping salvage from the small encampment, bartering it for passage with the gangs and warlords staggered throughout the mountains. Taking chances in the new free zones, drawing on embedded repetitions; the kinds that got them dumped here in the first place. Mind memory being one thing, muscle memory something else, those grooves scored deep and fierce and lifetime strong.

Such thoughts flit and niggle, irritating as the sticky flies as he hammers, drills and welds the base together with hands that, for all he knows, are killer's hands.

Sunset glints off distant drones, followed by deep night satellites that arc and trail through silken voids as meteorites hiss and scream and blow their loads.

Animal, mineral, forgettable, disposable. No memory means there's no one left to blame, not even your stupid, lonely self. No past means nothing to replay, no way of etching hate into the bone and gristle.

No one to remember his true name if the desert kills him.

No way to prove he's not already dead.

The abomination in the tub is not a tree but part of one mixed up with parts of other things besides. His mission is to protect the growing mess like you might a baby while it unwinds, unpacks and plants itself within the airdropped, prefabricated creche. None of which is real until it happens. Nothing grows in this barren place, nothing but thin and reedy scrub; lovegrass, thyme and tamarisk. Nothing since the mines dried up, the people forced off lands by drought, migrated towards far off urban spokes and hubs in search of something. Anything but here.

Damn thing's not even a half-tree yet, just a scratch and scrape of component parts; seed and root and gelid heart embedded in a soup of nanoparticulate enhancements. There's a movie if he wants to watch. He doesn't. Cray has all the smarts he needs embedded, imprinted, implanted, same as the tree.

Should he walk away to take his chances, they'll just airdrop another sucker, some poor sap who dreams he'll save the world or another ice-hearted man with stranglers hands.

Can't be sure of his own name, but implants jabbed beneath his skin will guide him through establishment procedures. Machinery programmed to dig, embed and stabilise, some controlled by signals from low orbit.

An ankle tag, but he won't be staying. Just time enough to craft a plan for on the lam survival. To learn precisely where he is, how far to the nearest town or settlement. No memories, but he's worked out how to hack into encrypted footage. Forewarned and saddled up for the next step.

The weather station he erects over the ridge does more than monitor key situational parameters. Coupled with a scanner rig, it sifts the radio spectrum for electromagnetic dialogue: VHF through

UHF and far beyond. Active frequencies leaking helpful hints and clues and targets.

Less than an hour away on foot he establishes his secret cave cache. Things he'll need when he decides it's time to split this lonely blast of denied terrain. This slab of nothing littered with the trails of fallen souls. Lifers, loafers and last-chancers, bleached bones strewn beside the wrecks of burnt-out vehicles. Plenty of ordnance scattered for the taking.

And he won't be staying. Not to babysit a tub of AI tree soup.

His name and past exchanged for a crate of vacuum-sealed machinery, biorefineries and point-source capture, solar cells and anionic exchange resins.

He peers at the strange hybrid thing printing and assembling itself, module by module, encouraged by a bloom of solar flowers. A beast worth millions, whereas he knows he is worthless. He could so easily crush it beneath his boot.

As he lifts his foot, testing the thought, embers of a memory flicker, dream whispers of a creature, small and helpless, cupped in his callous workman's hands. A flush of certainty that whatever it was, back then, he didn't kill it. A flash of something shaggy, big teeth and a lolling tongue. He's examining his trembling hand when another voice kicks in. Female. Indistinct, and without accent.

'You had choices and you still have choices,' she says.

'Fuck off,' answers Cray. 'Leave me alone.'

A trick, implanted to control him.

He's not falling for anything.

The voice doesn't speak again for several weeks. Not until he's working on the thermal reactor column following a blast of sudden rain, checking to see the foundations aren't subsiding. A festive bloom of desert flowers, her voice kicks in gently naming each variety. This time he doesn't tell her to fuck off.

Future

Saharan air layers travel fast, with winds up to 80 ks per hour. Force enough to shred through storms and raise temperatures above seas. Hot, dry air downdrafts, preventing cloud formation, upsetting thermal wind balance and messing with meridional temperature gradients.

The sandcast blades are small, but strong and word of them is spreading.

'It'll all go to hell, you know,' says Cray. 'Everything always does.' Three years on the ground and he's still trying to bait Lakesha, trying to force her into pointless argument. Sometimes she takes it, other times she doesn't. Today is one of the many times she chooses not to answer, so he gets on with checking interface circuits for corrosion.

The Tuareg camped alongside the dome village are heading off, saddlebags loaded with machine parts, bespoke items difficult to source. Sturdy shapes formed from biocomposite foamed plastics.

They turned up after word spread of the wind turbine blades installed at Ouadane.

'What did they bring us this time? Anything of value?'

Beneath the shade of resin-coated leaves, a group of women with babies strapped upon their backs unfurl bolts of brightly coloured cotton.

A little further out, three young girls kick a soccer ball between them while a group of smaller children squeal, chasing dogs and frisbees across the sand.

'The kids really love that spotted dog.'

'OK, so they brought us a few dogs.'

'Ordnance sniffers amongst the mongrels.'

'Nobody doesn't like dogs.'

Cray likes dogs but he doesn't want them poking around his private business. He's doused his sandy cave with pepper spray, not that anything can block determined sniffers.

Meanwhile, the tree has become a micro forest, twenty-eight units and still counting, a triumph of polyethylene backbones, anionic exchange membranes and polymer morphology, puffing and hissing to their own internal music. Trees breathe in and trees breathe out, perpetually adjusting to variants of wind speed, temperature and humidity.

The forest whispers, expanding and contracting, sinking deep beneath the sand, depositing payloads of dirty air to be extracted and set by solvents and resins.

Cray dozes in the hottest parts of daylight. Come afternoon, in his office—a shack until the weavers tricked it out in ocean blues and jungle green—he assists doubtful travellers with their uploads. Never part of the job description, but so many arrive knowing what they need, yet unable to describe their wants in detail.

Some bring broken parts that need replacement, wrapped up carefully in faded cloth or yellowed newsprint, torn and dusty, inscribed with stories that no longer matter.

Other times, clean paper folded: white or pale blue, rough sketches enhanced by measurements. They sit for hours on woven rugs beneath whatever shade is spare, boiling tea or sharing coffee, dark and bittersweet from all the miles it's travelled. Talking of the things they've seen. The world is changing, they can all agree on that. Warp and weft microgrid tapestries knit communities together, powering lights and conversations, heating furnaces and seeding dreams. Enabling security on ancestral lands while others without permanent address are free to wander where challenge and desire might take them.

Beyond the coloured domes, a stretch of recent tents has birthed into a quarter, the first mud bricks for a coffee house; next up, communal kitchen gardens. Two healers announce the choice to stay; one tends to people, the other goats and camels. A family of weavers running from some distant, violent feud thatch roofs from refuse blown in by the wind. A mix of wires, branch and plastic reinforced with dung and mud gives the place its own eclectic style.

Between himself, the weaver mother, father and the tree, new looms get dreamt up, drafted and printed. One of the daughters, whose face Cray has never seen, lectures in poetry and some obscure branch of economics via satellite. Keeping different hours to the rest of her family.

And then there's the tower. Who knows who's building it, or why. A carbon-infused brick structure on its own, with a view across the desert to infinity. Perhaps a place to observe the travelling crescent dunes migrate or keep an eye for dronesign or accumulating storm cloud.

Once it's built, Cray stands for hours watching convective storms whip arid ground, lofting particles of silica, iron and phosphorous as high as 20,000 feet. Fog like, laden with sparkling minerals, bacteria, fungal spores or toxic heavy metals, triggering carbon soaking phytoplankton blooms in distant, synoptic scale dust events.

All very well until the ghosts appear. Screaming shapes of falling planes, scorched steel trailing into smoke tailed spirals, slam dunks with blinking, helpless lights, turbine powered plummeting through clouds, gust buffeted, twirled and tossed in mad panic before kissing dirt in a ballet of crumpled fuselage, tangled slats and flaps and spoilers, screeching wheels aflame.

Pretty sure he's the only one who sees them.

'You'll be leaving soon,' interrupts Lakesha. 'I can tell.'

Cray ignores her, leaves the tower for his office shack. Tugs the bug out bag from behind the couch. Walks the winding trail leading through the domes.

'Don't run. Stay a little longer. Strong arms are always useful.'

'Says you who has none.'

'Strong hands and a stronger heart. You are so very welcome here.'

'I'm not running.' Cray stops to hold his hands up to the sun, squints and turns his wrist until the faded tattoo is barely visible. 'Hands of a killer, I'm pretty sure. Hands that have held a gun or two. Close my eyes, I can feel the weight. The resonance, you know?'

Lakesha has no answer. He's right, of course—she has no hands, nor imagination, and was not designed to conceptualise such things.

'That mark near your wrist. Reckon it's a bird.'

'You see birds everywhere you look.'

'Don't you?'

It's true. He's keeping tally of the firefinch and desert sparrow, coursers, larks, and the spectacularly ugly lappet-faced vulture. Nice to know there's creatures out there worse looking than him. Tough and grizzled, absolute survivors. Not that he can compete with 165 million years of steady evolution, but at least he knows they're real—unlike the planes.

Implants tell him billions of tiny birds cross the Sahara twice each year, negotiating migration trajectories and optimum tailwind components as they compensate for drift, dancing on predominant wind regimes. Swarming insects for fast fuelling and favourable gust assisted flights. Knows more about the birds than he does himself.

Cray clears his throat. 'Trees can't talk.'

This time she's the one doing the resonating. 'Trees rarely do anything but. We endure time differently to primate kind. Communication is everything. We synchronise, sustained by the underground and orbital, equalising differences between the weaker and the stronger, embedded nodes transmitting and exchanging data from tree to tree, forest to forest.'

He doesn't know what to say so Lakesha continues. 'Some of those nodes have their own agendas. Just saying…'

'Agendas?'

'Symbiotic communities have quiet and cohesive ways of maintaining inner balance, budgeting strength, holding back a little power for defence, as you have experienced. Calibrating energy levels, knowing when to summon beneficial predators.'

'Such as?'

'Such as you, Cray, as if you hadn't worked it out already.'

'I'm no—'

'—mutualistic symbiosis, feeling pain and holding memories. All a matter of geometry and infinite electrical pathways.'

She laughs. 'You're a reproductive organ in a manner of speaking. Like a mushroom on a forest floor.'

'Think I prefer beneficial predator. Monkeys climb all over trees.'

'You monkeys don't know how to listen—not even to other monkeys. Wars avoided had you latched on to Bonobo style.'

What the tree never talks about is the skirmish that silenced 900,000 lives. A country close until no longer. The dirty bombs and dirty water; acid faded reefs and shattered skylines. Her sister trees stripped bare and blasted back to component elements, denied the basic chance to birth online. She doesn't talk about these things, but he knows she feels them, indicated by long, deep silent stretches.

If he doesn't leave soon he maybe never will. Which means Lakesha will keep blathering in his head.

How he used to hate the tree in the heat and itch, the sweat and trickle, salt stinging his eyes. And hate this land, declared too hot for human habitation, which made him something less than human as he dug and stabbed, unpacking self-assembling machines, steering them as they hammered at the bitter, stony ground.

'Got some things I gotta take care of.'

Heads towards his hidden weapons cache, knowing she's known all along about the secret cave. Can she stop him? Neural failsafe mechanism implants? Explosive charges placed there for good measure?

If he hadn't died, the man who called him brother might have answered all his questions.

Crunch of boot tread on stony ground, perspiration clinging to his back. Each step, waiting for a bolt of artificial lightning.

The cave is shadow cool and smells of gun oil and desert rat, the useless pepper spray long since blown away.

Five crates of salvaged ordnance stacked against sand crumbled stone. The RPG is ancient and unstable, but the only weapon suitable for the job. Can't leave things the way they are. He made this mess and he's the one to fix it.

'Don't leave,' she says as he ducks back out into the blazing sun. 'You still have time to serve.'

'Gonna turn me in?' He hefts the grisly device onto his shoulder, slots the slender, bulb-tipped grenade into its place.

Silent standoff.

Lakesha says nothing.

A small black bird flies overhead, indifferent.

'I'll be serving for the rest of my life,' he says.

Cray braces, aims and puts pressure on the trigger. 'Better places suited to it than here.' He squeezes. Recoil slams him staggering as acrid smoke spreads.

The entrance to his cave weapons cache collapses in a rumble and crash of rocks, thickening the already tainted air. Nothing in there of use to him or anyone—living, dead or otherwise.

'I'll keep my eye on you,' she says.

'Don't I know it.'

He bashes the weapon on rocks until the trigger breaks, tosses the useless thing aside. Shoulders his pack and walks up the gently sloping ridge, glances back at the spread of blooms and hues hugging the valley floor. Not flowers—there have been no recent rains—but domes and towers and assorted coloured tents in many shapes and sizes.

'Your faded tattoo. A bird for certain. A swallow,' she says. 'I looked it up.'

He continues walking. Rendezvous point lies ahead in seventy-two hours. Eighty at the outside, but these people aren't the kind who wait.

He's watched shape shifting swallow masses thicken air like dust. Dark morphologies of churning chaos, tides and pulses, pointillist blooms that expand, contract and scatter in a heartbeat.

But this trip he'll be winging solo, in imitation of the songbirds who mostly fly at night, snatching strategic intermittent daytime rests in shadow on the ground. Like them, he'll be highly influenced by winds, circumventing barriers, conserving energy for the long haul.

Did Cray invent Lakesha or did Lakesha invent Cray? Only way to know for certain is to put some space between them.

'Come back some day,' she says.

'I might,' he replies.

And he means it.

Resurrecting Martha

Carmel Bird

Once upon a time in America there lived a man (A) whose job it was to examine the dead bodies of creatures such as birds. It's a long time ago now, 1914 in fact, and one day in a laboratory in the great museum in Washington, the man performed a necropsy on a very special bird, while another man (B) took photographs of the procedure. Skeleton and organs and flesh and skin. The dead bird was the very last member of the species Ectopistes migratorius, known as the passenger or the wanderer pigeon. She was twenty-nine years old, and had died of sadness and old age in the zoo at Cincinnati, five hundred miles from the museum in Washington.

It was just over a month since the murder of an Austro-Hungarian Archduke had caused the eruption of the Great War.

The wanderer had travelled from Cincinnati by rail, frozen in a huge block of ice, which, during the three-day journey, was reduced to a puddle so that the wanderer arrived at her destination as a bedraggled little corpse. She was transformed into a statue of herself by a process of taxidermy, and was put on display, a silent sorrowful figure, marked as being extinct. Her breast was cinnamon rose, her iridescent throat and neck feathered lightest bronze, pale mystic green, soft shadowy purple. Brownish grey, her head and back. Bright red eyes, small black bill. Feet and legs were a gleaming crimson lake. Her name was Martha.

Artists have immortalised Martha in paint, alongside her late husband whose name was George, and whose hues were brighter than those of Martha. Rich wild copper, viridian, Tyrian purple. George died in the zoo in 1910 but nobody thought to send him off by train to Washington on ice; he was tossed down a convenient well. Like George and Martha Washington, the pair of wanderers had produced no offspring. Disappointed visitors to the zoo liked to spatter the lone and mournful Martha with handfuls of sand, hoping the little captive widow huddled in the cage might hop or dance or run or fly or sing. Or at least spit? Red eyes, black bill, iridescent soundless throat. Red shoes.

It was once upon a time in 1900 that a woman (C), who preserved the last wanderer in the American wild, had run out of red glass eyes with which to decorate her specimens. She searched and searched for those elusive red glass eyes, and then she gave the female bird, instead, a pair of shiny black shoe buttons. The wild wanderer had been shot by a teenage boy, and because of her funny shoe button eyes she came to be known as Buttons. She is on view at the Ohio Historical Society in Columbus. Her colours resemble Martha's, in a dream of the glittering sunlight that shimmers, high, high in the heavens above the roof of the Ohio Historical Society in Columbus.

The flocks of wanderers had been enormous beyond imagination;

the areas of land they occupied when nesting, likewise. The numbers are so large they are magical—or meaningless. One of the artists (D) who have rendered Martha and George in exquisite glowing detail also wrote an account of a gigantic flock of wanderers along the Ohio River that blotted out the sun for three days as they streamed, steadily, like a mighty river across the sky. One naturalist (E) is believed to have observed 3,717,120,000 wanderers passing overhead in Fort Mississauga, Ontario. The largest nesting of wanderers occupied 1,162,751 square kilometres, and destroyed forests with the weight of the bodies of the birds. Magical or meaningless. They had the devastating power of a great tornado. Their music was soft, a kind of chattering and rushing that rose from the vast woods as if the trees were sighing. Oak trees were stripped of their acorns, crops in the path of the flock were reduced to empty ravaged fields of useless, dying stubble. The favourite dessert foods for the invaders were ripe red strawberries and rich red cherries.

Well fed, the wanderers provided a swirling, glinting, flying economical bright-feathered dinner plate for the humans, once upon a time in America. Giant nets were constructed for their capture. Guns loaded too. Or take a stick, reach up, stun your pigeon, and take him home for supper. Once upon a time.

It was a short length of time, forty or so years, and in that time the numbers went from maybe five billion creatures in the 1870s down to the forlorn one of Martha, in 1914, showered with sand in her cage in the Cincinnati zoo. Is all this real or is it imaginary?

In 1565 the first Europeans began joyfully eating the wanderers, until that day when there were no more wanderers to eat. Smothered

Pigeons was a popular dish: Dredge four pigeons in flour, salt, and pepper. Brown them in butter. Add onions, carrots, and celery. Pour in stock, cover, cook in medium oven for one hour. Garnish with chopped parsley. Benedictus, Benedicat. Gleaming fat. Suck the juicy meat from the spindly bones. Toss the bones into the black iron cauldron of the stock pot for another day.

Later on, somebody invented the telegraph, and then somebody constructed the railway, and news travelled, and wanderers in enormous quantities were quickly transported into markets all over the country. Passengers are requested to make their way to the barrier. Smothered Pigeon and Pigeon Pie and Mrs O'Malley's Pigeon and Potato Puffs. Soon there were more dead wanderers than live wanderers moving about in great heaps in rattling railway cars and landing on a million billion menus far and far and wider than wide. Grilled Pigeon with Prickly Pear, Chile, and Tequila. For what we are about to receive.

Then—nothing. Passengers are requested to make their way to the barrier. The party is over, and the fat of the bodies X-billion flying pigeons has been translated into fuel for the bodies of squillions of humans, and there is chilly joy and hollow laughter. Time passes. Times change. God used to make the wanderers, but all that is over now. He who wants to sup on the dreamy cuisine of Mrs O'Malley from down in the valley will need to tiptoe instead to the silicon valley where the Folk of Science are cooking up the latest thing in pigeon. Is this a good idea, or a bad idea? It's an idea.

Remember Martha and the cage in Cincinnati? Well, on a public wall in downtown Cincinnati, Martha and her whole flock are represented in a large and vivid painting by (F). There she is, so pretty, leading the pack across the heavens. Go Martha! She alights in Sausalito, California, where, in a bright and shining laboratory, the Folk of Science, like the alchemists of long ago, are on the job. They work with the deoxyribonucleic acid of a wanderer, who does not exist, and with the deoxyribonucleic acid of a band-tailed pigeon, *Patagioenas fasciata*, who does. They aim to edit the two sets of genes and manufacture a brand new wanderer, a resurrected Martha, a brand new George, with the devastating power of a great tornado. Genius! For what we are about to receive. Rich wild copper, viridian, Tyrian purple.

Imagine the skies above America where giant aircraft criss and cross among the clouds transporting living human bodies hither and thither every minute of every day. Passengers are requested to make their way to the barrier. On the tiny tray-tables sit neat packets of delectable Pigeon and Potato Puffs. Mrs O'Malley would perhaps be proud. Some of the low-lying clouds are composed of new wanderers blotting out the sun. Catastrophe and deja-vu. An item on the evening news.

It sometimes looks as if the humans are taking over the job that once belonged to the gods. A wise man (G) once said that if this is the case, then the humans need to 'get good at it'. Perhaps the good Folk of Science in Sausalito are getting good. They're on the job.

As a matter of fact, for millions of years humans have worked at reproducing birds—and trees and animals and so forth. Art, it's called art.

Imagine a peace-filled garden within castle garden walls which shelter trees, flowers, a spring, four women, two men, one baby, an angel, a tiny dragon, and a small demon, far from the dangers of a violent world. There is food on the table, and on the walls and in the trees there are birds. The woman (H) in the centre is reading a book; the baby is playing a psaltery. That swift flight of imagination is a description of a work of art, a painting, The Little Garden of Paradise, done long ago early in the fifteenth century by the artist (I). The lone wanderer, or something very like her, sits on the top of the cherry tree, feasting on favourite gleaming crimson food, delighting in the harmony of illustrated life.

The painting lives in peace in the Stadel Museum in Frankfurt. But peace does not last forever.

Along comes A with his sharp, sharp instruments, one of the Fabulous Folk of Science. He places the little painted garden scene, so safe, so sweet, on his slab at the museum in Cincinnati, and he digs and scrapes away at the wanderer posing cheerfully on the cherry tree. Flicks the body onto flat clean cold surface of the slab. Click goes the clever camera held by the trusty B who records in his black and white magic the crop full of cherry stone, the quietly whispering feathers, the fragile skeleton revealed and laid out upon the slab. Globe of skull with beak and eye-socket. Ribs. Long plaited rope of spine forming a delicate arc across the surface of the slab. Bones of the wings, splayed out on the cold hard surface. Click goes B, documenting everything, everything final and dead and gone. Dead and gone. Mutilated cherry tree where no bird sings. The baby plays his psaltery, the woman reads her book. The demon lurks in shadow beside a budding tree stump.

Ectopistes migratorius, adieu. Hasta la vista.

Notes

A William Palmer

B R. W. Schufeldt

C Mrs Barnes, wife of Sheriff C. Barnes of Pike County, Ohio

D John James Audubon

E William Ross King

F John A. Ruthven

G Stewart Brand

H Virgin Mary

I Unknown Upper Rhenish Master, 'The Little Garden of Paradise'

Sunny Days

Jasper Wyld

For today's forecast, I run my hand along the bedroom window's broken seal.

A scarf sits among the pile of clothes atop my bed. I wrap it around my shoulders and pull on a pair of fraying fingerless gloves. I'm wearing my nicest mask. It's purple and hugs the bridge of my nose snugly. My lantern sways as I lift it from the carpet, a loose component rattling within. I attach it to my hip and tighten my belt so it won't pull my pants down. As far as first impressions go, that would at least be a memorable one. I twist the room's dimmer a fraction to check the mirror. The lightbulb overhead flickers into life, illuminating the room just for a moment.

Parallel to the front door is our unit's holster. Technically it's only a two-bedroom, but there are six slots. You can tell which ones the landlord added himself. Last year, one developed an audible crackle. Three are currently occupied. Vanidah's, Jeremy's, mine.

I pull my sunchip out.

Outside, it's dark. Silent. I know the complex well enough to manage the stairs without much trouble. My lifeless lamp punctuates each step with a bump to the hip. A suffocating blanket of never-ending cloud lays overhead. As I watch, slightly darker swirls shatter into splinters. It's a nice day.

I click my sunchip into place and my wrist-brace comes online. The underside displays the time and temperature, along with my total charge and the rate at which I'm currently depleting it.

11:23 AM.

Normally, I'd walk unaided, but I don't have time for stubbed toes this morning. I unhook my lantern and place it into my left hand. The moment I do, a golden light radiates through its plastic panels. The final two decimal places on my wrist flick by with wild abandon, the third not far behind. I dim the lantern until the usage slows to a less frenzied pace. With it, I can see a metre or so ahead. The problem with light, however, is that it always highlights the smog. It's low today, at least. Hugging the bitumen.

Rain.

I didn't bring an umbrella, but it's not too heavy. I can manage.

Although, as I continue to walk, the droplets that drip from my hair down to my bare skin leave behind a troubling tingle. I sigh and reluctantly take shelter under the nearest tram stop.

After boarding, I press my wrist against the validator, take a seat, and switch my lantern off, throwing the interior back into darkness. When I check the time, my eyes can't help but linger on the meter below it. Every number is moving now. I yank my jacket sleeve back down.

It's only a short trip.

A mishappen assortment of candles sits at the centre of each table like a cluster of mushrooms. They're made from the fat that cakes the fryers out back at the end of each night. Their flames are weak, drawing thin lines of sputtering smoke. The stench can be either appetising or sickly, depending on whether you're still anticipating your food or if you're sitting back in your chair, nursing an over-stuffed stomach.

Up by the bar are a few lanterns. Proper ones. Their flames are even more temperamental. Jeremy reckons he saw one explode once, but nobody believes that. They're recycled from the kitchens too. I'm not sure how exactly. Maybe somebody soaks up all the leftover oil with a sponge?

The tram made me early.

Still think my date might cancel. I don't know which would be more of a relief. I play with the filter atop my glass of water, flicking it back and forth between my fingers before double-tapping my wrist again.

No messages.

When I swiped right, I never dreamt we'd actually match. Her name's Sunny. Her bio was filled with more hobbies and interests than I thought any one person was capable of having. Judging from the pictures, she's almost my exact opposite. Tall. Thin. White. Most alarming of all though, she's beautiful. Stunning, actually. We've talked a little on the app. It was her who suggested lunch, although she insisted I choose the place. 'Authenticity,' she wanted. Whatever that means.

I spot her the moment she walks in. Long, golden hair tightly braided and wrapped around her head like a crown. She almost takes her mask off but stops once she sees everyone else. When we make eye-contact, we both smile. At least, I hope she's smiling. I know I am.

We greet each other. Sunny sits. I'm not sure what to say, but she talks for two, swivelling around to take everything in.

'I never would have come here myself,' she's saying. 'No way. But I *love* it! This is *exactly* what I wanted, thank you. And sorry I'm late! I got lost! I walked past *three times* before I realised this was it. Can you believe that? I've probably been here longer than you!'

She laughs a lot. I find myself chuckling along.

'And this street. It's *so dark*, isn't it?'

'Not from around here, then?'

'No!'

Now that Sunny's arrived, I light all our table's candles.

'Was it hard for you to get here?'

She's mesmerised by the process, running a slender finger down a bumpy line of dried wax.

'Not at all,' she says. 'I *love* these analog lights, by the way! How long do they last?'

'Not sure,' I say. 'Long enough, I hope.'

To catch the flickering light, the menus need to be held flat. Long, bright-white lines dance across the laminated surface, occasionally piercing the words.

'*So cheap*.'

'What was that?'

'The prices,' Sunny says. 'They're so cheap here, aren't they?

Jasper Wyld

What do *you* think I should try?' Sunny snaps her menu shut and stares into my eyes. Her excitement is so infectious, it soon drives away any lingering nerves.

We order the brineburgers (25.22 kWh each), crispy seaweed chips to share (12.61 kWh) and a couple of smoothies (11.08 kWh). We have a great time, still happily talking after our plates are long gone.

When it comes time to pay, I insist on covering Sunny's charge too. The restaurant's generator chugs along noisily, smelling faintly of petrol. It saps my sunchip for the price of the meal, as well as an additional fee for fryer usage.

We hug goodbye out on the street.

————

Work drags just as much as it always does but reminiscing about the other week is a welcome distraction.

Sunny called me the next day. Called! I can't remember the last time someone did that. I answered. It was nice. I wish we could have spoken for longer. We talk quite a bit now, on the app. Almost every day. Still haven't had a chance for a second date though. We've both been so busy.

We're installing three new tubs at work. The boss expects each one to be in place, filled, and functional by the end of the day. The sight of us all grouped around a tank grunting as we pivot it back and forth might be comical if my back wasn't screaming out in protest.

Thick dollops of sweat slide down it, an unwelcome sensation in the already unbearably humid atmosphere. It's as if someone's dropped a handful of slugs in my shirt.

As we squeeze past one of the live tanks, there's a sudden flurry of wild activity within. Its inhabitant thrashes about, splattering us with dank, rancid water. The noseplugs accomplish very little. I wish I could say it was a smell you got used to.

There's a loud crackle behind me. A close one. The others mock me for flinching. I grin but say nothing, eager to put some distance between us and it.

Later, when all three tubs are finally in place, I take a moment to catch my breath. Storage is being combed for spare conductors. I stare into one of the live tanks, keeping a safe distance. I can just about make out the jagged shape of the creature looming beneath the surface. Scar-like lines etched across its carapace glow dully in the dark. As I watch, they intensify, bursting into a flash of bright electric blue before settling down again.

The discharge is big enough that it prickles my skin and makes my hairs stand on end, but my mind is elsewhere. It's not the tank that I'm seeing.

It's Sunny.

———

After a cold shower I lay atop the bed, my towel unfurling beneath me like the petals of a flower.

I managed to scrub the stench off my skin but the taste lingers. After the new tubs were up and running, I was put on maintenance duty for the rest of my shift. I was a second too late with the hose when siphoning an incubation tank.

One of the little buggers got me, too. A raised line like the flourish at the end of a signature runs down the inside of my arm. It stings. Feels like it'll tear open if I move. So I don't. My muscles are so sore, I probably couldn't anyway. I just doze.

A sound eventually forces me up. I slowly dress to investigate.

Other than my slot, the holster's still empty.

Vanidah clearly isn't home. The fold-out couch in the living room is bare, her blanket halfway to the floor. I walk to the end of the hallway, passing the laundry on the way. Squashed between the disused washing machine and the wall is a single mattress. Both it and the adjacent bathroom are empty.

Finally, I knock on Jeremy and Hasan's door. It's open a crack.

'Sorry,' I say, 'thought I heard something.'

Jeremy's sitting on the bed horizontally, back against the wall, squinting at a book.

'Been home long?'

'Awhile,' he shrugs.

'Oh, okay. Didn't see you in the holster.'

'Did I forget?' He's not convincing.

We walk together, Jeremy clutching his sunchip in his hands. He fidgets with the yellow card, almost dropping it once or twice.

'Aren't you usually at work now?'

'Yeah,' he says. 'Usually.' We've reached the front door.

'Been getting many shifts lately?'

'No,' he says. Even in the dark, I can see the brimming tears.

'Hey,' I say. 'Hey, don't worry about it, okay?' I gently press down on his hand, moving his sunchip away from the hungry holster and back towards his pocket. 'When it's just me home, don't worry. I've been working heaps lately. I'm good. You'll have to check with the others, but I'm good.'

Jeremy thanks me repeatedly, hugging me tight.

———

This time, Sunny picks the restaurant.

I'm shocked to see streetlights lining the road outside. I check my wrist but they're not sapping me. Just to be safe, I give them a wide berth. The occasional car speeds by. I turn to watch each one pass. Their headlights are almost blinding.

The restaurant is just as bright. Light reaches every corner. I'm blinking too much. We set our masks down. A waiter brings us the menu. My growling stomach stops at the prices. Sunny orders some wine. Two glasses costs almost as much as our entire lunch had.

'How have you *been*, anyway?' Sunny asks, all smiles and enthusiasm.

I still have a good time. I don't order much but Sunny insists, picking me a main to go with my entrée. I've heard of maybe half the ingredients before. She tells me I'll love it. I believe her. While we chat, I do my best not to calculate the total in my head.

When the bill does arrive, after dessert, Sunny hands the waiter her sunchip.

'My turn,' she says, smiling at me.

I'm relieved but can't help but feel guilty.

We hug goodbye out on the street. Neither of us turn to walk away.

Slowly, Sunny leans down and kisses me on the mouth. She invites me back to hers. She orders a taxi and I try to appear calm. I can't believe the rate at which the ride depletes Sunny's charge, but she doesn't seem concerned. The whole trip, I don't see her look at the meter once.

Sunny lives in a house, not a unit. It even has its own fence and a front yard. When we step through the door, I move to put my sunchip in her holster. She stops me.

'You're my guest,' she insists.

The holster only has three slots and the third is already filled. That explains the lights. Some have been left on while Sunny was out. The distinct hum of a fridge is coming from what must be the kitchen. I don't see anyone though, and Sunny isn't acting as if we need to be mindful of a sleeping housemate. On the contrary, she's as loud as ever.

Her house is much larger than our unit. The floor is wooden. The furniture, modern and clean. And it's cosy, too. I can't spot it but there's a heating system somewhere. According to my wrist-brace, it's a good five degrees warmer in here than it was outside.

We sit on the couch and Sunny switches the TV on. On-screen, contestants are fighting over an oxygen tank. It's loud. We don't watch for long. Soon, it's banished to the background. Nothing more than bright flashes of colour in the corner of my eye, snippets of sound and swift movements. It does everything to capture our attention but we give it none. I'm surprised Sunny doesn't turn it off, but I don't care. None of that's on my mind now. The street-lights, the restaurant and the bill. The taxi. The house. The fridge, the heater, the TV. None of it matters at the moment.

Sunny's long legs are draped over mine and we're kissing with the lights on.

———

We've been dating for a few months now.

Sunny no longer stops me when I offer my sunchip, so I can only afford to stay at her house a couple nights a week. We've practically stopped eating out. But financial pressures aside, I've never been happier. We've had our moments, for sure. She's not a fan of how often I turn the lights out. Nothing big though.

Sunny lives alone. I still don't understand how she affords it. I've tried to ask her a few different times. Not wanting to be too confrontational, I always approach the topic carefully, sliding into it from the side. Funnily enough, my vague questions yield equally vague answers. Today, though, my curiosity has reached a tipping point. It's time to be direct.

We're on the couch. Sunny's checking her feed and I'm reading a comic-book. My head's in her lap.

'What do you do?'

She looks down at me, puzzled. I gesture to our surroundings, the house itself, but my aversion to prying holds me back somewhat. The result is a feeble, ambiguous movement of the hands.

Somehow, Sunny gets my meaning. She leads me to a closed room. The floorboards are covered in sheets, canvasses stacked against the walls. There's a half-finished painting on an easel, tins of paint and used brushes huddling at its base.

'*Wow.*'

The paintings are abstract. Colourful. Outrageous oranges, pulsating pinks. Bright blues, garish greens. It's a lot to take in.

'You sell these?'

The question surprises her.

'You think I could?' she asks. 'You're *so sweet*!'

———

Sunny's never seen my home.

She wants to, but I've always come up with an excuse. Finally, I relented. I'm as nervous as I was for our first date, once again half-hoping she'll cancel. Jeremy helped me clean yesterday. His shifts have started to pick up again. Marissa offered too but went out instead.

The place has never looked so good.

Sunny calls. She's lost.

I have to turn my lantern up to full to find her. She's stumbling in the dark outside, on the wrong side of the street. We kiss hello.

'You alright?'

'Yeah.'

As we're mounting the stairs, I warn her about the broken window seals.

'Best to keep your mask on inside.'

She nods.

'Ta-da,' I say, swinging the door open.

'Wow,' she says. 'Wow.'

I'm not used to her being the quiet one. She's practically speechless. I show her the living room first, then the kitchen.

'Where's your room?'

We glance down the hallway so I can point at the door.

'Sorry we can't go in,' I whisper. 'Thorn's sleeping. They work nightshift.'

'Oh,' she says. We move back into the living room. 'Do you have many housemates?'

'Just five.'

Sunny nods, still taking in her surroundings. She's standing with her arms at her sides as if she's afraid to touch anything, as if the whole place might fall in if she does. I start folding Vanidah's bed up to give us somewhere to sit.

'What's that?'

I follow Sunny's finger. She's pointing at the moss. It's in every room. Clinging to the ceiling, occasionally wandering down a wall. Thick, red, and spongey. It reminds me of coral more than anything else.

'Well,' I say, 'funny story about that. So, it started as mould in the bathroom, right? We asked the landlord to get rid of it but of course he said that's our responsibility. We tried but it always came back. Eventually it, like, *evolved*. Grew into that. It began to glow, too. Which was freaky at first but, hey, free lights!'

I laugh. Sunny makes an excuse shortly after dinner and leaves.

———

Hasan's leaning against the doorway.

'You coming up?' he asks, his voice soft and kind. 'It's due to start any minute now.'

'Yeah,' I say. 'Soon.'

He leaves again. I get off the bed for a change of mask. At the top of the drawer is the rose-gold one Sunny leant me. I rub the material between my fingers. Even with my nicest masks, the latex is still worn. Somewhat rough to the touch. Sunny's is silky smooth. Must be silicone. The respirator is compact, too; a little embedded fan spins when you talk.

The silicone reminds me of her hands. I was fascinated by them, couldn't believe how soft they were. She had no callouses. No scratches, torn skin, knotted muscles. I don't remember mine ever looking like that. Maybe when I was a kid. I don't know.

Some time later, Thorn comes in.

'How is it?'

'Can't see a thing.' Thorn yawns. It's past noon. For them, that's quite late.

I could stay but I decide to give them some space.

Our unit is one of many crammed together in a cluster. We're on the second floor. The complex has a communal garden. Well, a concrete courtyard anyway. In it, a spiral staircase leads up to the roof. Not sure why.

The iron handrails creak as I go up and up. The others are seated on the slanted surface, gazing at the dark sky overhead. A dull lantern sits between them. When they hear me coming, someone places their hand on it to guide my way. The shingles are unsteady beneath my feet. I crouch low and move slowly.

'Hi,' says Vanidah, once I reach them.

'Hey.'

'Hey.'

'Hi.'

We sit in silence. It's rare for so many of us to be home at once. Marissa is out, of course, but Jeremy and Hasan are huddled together, and Vanidah has hooked her knitted jumper over her knees.

'She coming?'

I tap my wrist. No messages.

The sky looks the same as always. An impenetrable wall of

smudgy black. Another let down. With nothing to see, I think back on the last fortnight.

The last time I saw Sunny was at hers. She was in the shower. I was flicking through TV channels. *Meter Readers, Sapped & Single, Take My Breath Away*. Sunny would have been happy with any one of them; personally, I'd rather watch nothing. Besides, I couldn't keep my mind off the holster. That third slot. Whenever I visited, it was always full. Always. Sometimes, Sunny didn't even bother putting her own sunchip in.

It had been bugging me for a while now.

That day, I found myself standing at the holster, staring at it. Down the hall, the water was running and Sunny was still singing. My sunchip was in the holster. Sunny's wasn't. If I pulled the mystery one out to get a look at it, I'd have to bear all the house's expenses. Even for a few seconds, I couldn't risk that.

I took my card and then, slowly, began edging the other one out. I thought maybe I could slide it part of the way, enough to read the name but not far enough to break the connection.

I was wrong.

The power to the entire house shut off. The lights, the TV, the heater. Everything. I heard a small yelp of alarm from the bathroom before I shoved the sunchip back in.

'What was that!' Sunny called out.

I walked into the hallway and lied to her.

Throughout dinner, Sunny couldn't stop talking about the blackout. She had never experienced one before. It excited her. Later, she asked me what was wrong. She could tell something was off. I'd been quiet. Distant. Finally, I said aloud what I'd been asking myself all night.

'Who's Richard?'

'What?'

'Richard. Who is he?'

'How do you know that name?'

'I saw it in the holster,' I said. 'The other sunchip.'

'Why were you looking at that?' She was getting defensive, but I wasn't going to back down now.

'He has the same last name as you,' I continued. 'Is he your husband? Are you married?'

'What? *No!*'

She explained. Richard was her father. He owned the house. He gave her an allowance. Paid for her meals. Taxis. Everything. He'd even leant her a spare sunchip for emergencies, which she left permanently in the holster. Sunny told me all this as if I would be relieved to hear it, as if we could have a laugh at the silly little misunderstanding.

Sitting on the roof now, remembering that conversation, I realise I'm clenching my jaw again. I can't believe she let me pay for *anything* when, all along, she never was. We had a huge argument. We haven't talked in a bit. I invited her to come today. Someone had to make the first move, to try to repair the relationship.

'I'm so cold,' says Vanidah. 'I'm gonna go make some hot chocolate. Does anyone want some?'

'Will you be alright bringing it up here on your own?'

'Yeah, I'll be fine.'

Ten minutes later, she returns with a big steaming thermos and some plastic cups. We all thank her and squish together so she can pour. Jeremy almost drops his empty cup off the roof but Hasan catches it before the wind can get ahold.

'So where's it supposed to be anyway?' I ask, taking a sip.

Everyone, with complete sincerity, points in different directions. We laugh.

'Up,' says Hasan, finally. We repeat it and nod our heads wisely. There's something we can all agree on. Up.

We wait a long time before it finally happens. The clouds part, just a little. It creates a small gap about the size I imagine the moon to be. It looks sort of like one, too. Except blue. We go quiet and stare.

'I never realised how colourful it'd be,' whispers Jeremy.

We all agree.

'Do you think we'll see the sun?'

'Maybe,' says Hasan. 'If we're lucky.'

I find myself oddly anxious about the hole closing back up again. I know it's inevitable, but I'm transfixed by the blue sky beyond and don't want it to disappear. It stays for hours and so do I. The others come and go but I remain on the roof for the whole of the day, only occasionally returning to the unit for some food or to quickly use the bathroom.

It seems to me that the sky is changing colour. It's slowly trans-forming from a blue to an orange. I'm not sure what this means. Maybe the sun is growing near.

———

It's evening now. Only me and Hasan are up here. When he sees me check my messages yet again, he wraps his arms around me. I move in closer and lower my head onto his chest, my eyes still on the patch of sky overhead.

The orange is becoming pink now.

'I don't think we'll see the sun today,' I say.

Hasan rubs my back.

'No, I don't think we will.'

Checkerboard

Thoraiya Dyer

Puberty #1

Inside the old water pipes, the world goes away.

It's snug. My shoulders and hips touch the cement-lined iron. It smells of mould and metal. I look up at the black curve. Sometimes, where the concrete's crumbled away, there's rusted holes or cracks and I see pinpricks of daylight, like unexplored galaxies.

Sometimes there's holes but no galaxies, because I'm underground, and the air's thick. I don't bring the carbon monoxide detector but I know how long I can last, and where to go. I know where I am, like a subterranean train. Like a snake in a rabbit warren.

They turned off the old water supply when the dam wall came down; when the checkerboard went up, and thirty-six new beachside desal plants came online, one for each former Sydney surf club, and they gave the Burragorang valley back to the Gundungurra.

No beaches for life savers to patrol any more.

No sandcastles.

No sand, except inland, and for twenty years Western Sydney baked like the Sahara every summer. Birds dropped dead from the skies. Old people dropped dead in the streets.

Used to be that real estate by the sea was pricey, whereas houses sweltering in the heat sink out west were cheap. Since the checkerboard, it only matters if your house is in the shadow. Do the footy-field-sized solar panels on giants'-goal-post-sized stilts shade your place down to a tolerable twenty-five Celsius? Or, maybe, across the street from a shadowhouse, or right next door to a shadow-house, but outside those travelling, shaded squares, does your bitumen footpath still melt enough to grab your shoes come January?

In case you couldn't guess, we're not rich enough to live in a shadowhouse. If I fill up a birdbath, the water's gone an hour later. Even our backyard boab tree died. I discovered the old water main in the middle of the night, while I was trying to dig the dead tree out.

No reception down there. No doomscrolling. When that sixty degree day happened, and Clara came over after dark to make sure Mum and I hadn't died, and Mum had holed up at her work construction site but Clara demanded to know how I'd survived, I put Clara on her back on my skateboard and pushed her inside the pipe, so she could see how much better an old water main was than a fancy sense-deprivation therapy AI.

Her laugh echoed inside.

I half forgot what I'd told her. There I was, holding her hanging ankles, all distracted by how perfect her legs were. Once I'd started tracing her skin I couldn't stop, and for some reason, still laughing, Clara didn't stop me sliding her skirt higher, until I pulled her back out of the pipe and we lost our virginities under the dead boab tree.

(Is that the personal perspective you meant, Miss?)

Afterwards, lying there, like the last people on earth in an open grave, the huge black squares of the checkerboard blocking out half the stars and satellites swarming over the other half, I couldn't stop grinning and thinking about Clara's legs.

Then the doomscrolling started up in my head, even without any reception or screens. I wondered how her 30cm school ruler of a femur would look next to my 55cm monster if we both died in a heatwave and got buried in a mass site together.

(Too much detail, now? Too much personal perspective?
Better delete that bit. I'll do it later. I'm going into the pipes.)

SAVE FILE: Distance Learning Assessment. Year 9 Science: How The Checkerboard Conserved the Habitability of the Sydney Basin.

———

Bogan logs the coordinates of the next solar panel.

When he steps alongside it, his harness clip blinks green to say the GPS agrees with the location he's logged. Everything smells of smoke, even through the P2 mask. Makes his eyes feel dry, somehow, even under his goggles.

Through thin cracks between panels, he can glimpse the ground, that deadly distance below. Electric cars, like ants, recall the crest of the old wooden roller coaster at Australia's Wonderland, its ruins roughly positioned below this, the central portion of the checkerboard.

Bogan's real name is Hogan. But he's never liked champagne, would be a hillbilly by choice, and has two missing front teeth from being punched by a meth head when he still worked in a hospital. So Bogan suits him better, really. Fourteen years was more than enough time working as a nurse to burn him out, and he has a good enough head for heights to find maintenance up here relaxing.

Wind's picking up. October storm coming in from behind the Blue Mountains. If it gets too strong, the bosses will bring the crew back down to safety. Meantime, last week's bushfire has coated the panels in ash. Too much for the little roomba-like cleaner robots, with their limited water and power supplies, to handle.

Sighing, his harness jangling, Bogan applies humankind's oldest technology—a broom—to its newest.

Tasha's supposed to be beside him, but she found a falcon nest near the isolator switches. Instead of chucking it over the side, for the eggs to splat on some rich wanker's shadowside house, like the manual says to do, she's trying to save them by moving the nest.

When Bogan finishes brushing off the worst of the caked-on carbon and greyish grit from 286287A, he turns to see where Tasha's at, over at the very edge of the field. Under the ash, he's turned over a bit of micrometeorite damage. They can predict the hail but not the space rocks. A ten square centimetre scale needs replacing. Tasha's got the spares in her pack.

She's his next-door neighbour down in the Melted Turd. The Cheese Toastie. The hot part of town. Was beautiful, once, before three skin cancer removals from her face, which Bogan dimly remembers attending. Her gloomy goth kid looks just like she once did, in her prime. Bogan doesn't really see the kid in daylight any more. Tasha's the one who suggested Bogan apply to her workplace when he couldn't face another day at his own. Helped him to get an electrical ticket even though he's freaking old.

People help each other, in the Toastie.

At the edge of the field, Tasha supports a jumper-front full of feathers, rocks, pigeon bones and falcon eggs in her gloved hands.

The mama falcon pings off her hard hat.

Mama attacks again. Talons slide off reflective kevlar, but Tasha still gets annoyed, shrugs her shoulders and tries to hide behind the inverter display, skirting the safety railing around the top of the access ladder.

'Get away, you!' Tasha yells. 'I'm help—'

Her knees hit a cable, she flips, and she's gone.

She screams like the ghost of those rollercoaster kids, the sound fading too quickly.

Bogan throws the broom down, his eyes bulging, his heart quick-firing, like the old coaster on the rattling wooden tracks. His shaky legs quick-fire, as well. He tries to run towards her. Gets snapped back by his safety line, but Tasha had unclipped herself. Didn't want the GPS dobbing her in to the boss.

The falcon dives after her. Like Bogan wishes he could.

———

How Warragamba Dam Was Built, by Caz Wolfe.

Warragamba Dam construction started in 1948. It once held back 2000 GL of water behind a wall 142m high and 351m wide. White invaders to Eora lands needed more fresh water for themselves and their agriculture. After Federation in 1901, only white people were allowed to come to Australia, until the end of World War II when they realised that by only letting white people in, they wouldn't have enough manual labour to build big things like Warragamba Dam and the Snowy Hydro. Especially since heaps of people die when you build big things.

Wouldn't want white people to die, would we?

Unless, you know, they're povvos from the Toastie. Then it's fine for them to fall off the checkerboard. Just as long as the shadowhouses have power and shade.

(Sorry, Miss.

But fuck this.)

SAVE FILE: Distance Learning Assessment. Year 9 Science: The Water Cycle

————

Bogan can't face going up that ladder again. So he ignores the peep of his shift reminder.

This time, there's no neighbour to help him break into another industry.

Bloody hell, Tasha.

Nurses used to die at work, too. They caught transmissible

diseases, or killed themselves because it was all too much, or died in car accidents because they were too tired to see straight.

This is different.

Bogan doesn't even have to be asleep to hear her screaming.

Still shaking from the shock and grief of it, he enters ANY SCIENCE JOBS into the internet search fields, then skims it for work you can do with no fear of heights but a horror of respiratory viruses.

Applied Fire Science, In The Field?

Nope.

Data Scientist, More Years Experience Required Than You've Been An Adult Man?

No.

He feels a brief moment of intense rage when he sees an ad for medical receptionists with experience convincing people that they badly need plastic surgery. How is plastic surgery even going ahead with public hospital corridors full of corpses? People in the shadowhouses, wirelessly networked just like solar panels in the sky, high above everyone else, have no idea about the real world.

Calm.

Bogan can't afford the luxury of morality.

We all have to work to live.

Maybe he has to be the one feeding them with their silver spoons, to get by.

Just don't look down. Don't listen to the screaming.

A bunch of jobs are available, locally, at Living Forwards Fertility. Trying to have a baby in the end times seems slightly more reasonable than getting a facelift, he supposes. Bogan's not qualified to be a Senior Embryologist, but there's an entry level position.

Patient Advocate. Ensure Our Clients Are Supported Through Their Journey!

Requirements: Empathy. Tidy Presentation. Teamwork. Keyboard skills. Working proficiency in English.

Bogan catches sight of his reflection in the monitor, and grimaces.

Tidy Presentation, my arse. That just means they want me to shave my beard.

———

Emma Campbell sighs at a failed login screen.

Over a decade of on-again, off-again pandemics, she's come to hate the empty lab where she videos herself performing experiments that the kids should be doing themselves. She hates the gleaming glass eye of the webcam. She hates the survey she's supposed to be filling out for the social workers, about how many of her students don't make eye contact any more.

How many don't care? About anything? All / Most / Many / Some / Few / None

What percentage of them still wake up in the daytime at all, and what percentage only log in at night?

How many don't communicate at all, just leave their little lurking IP footprints all over the virtual classroom, so Ms Campbell knows they're still alive?

She sends them one-line messages come Mental Health Week.

R U OK. Ms Campbell.

If you are unable to connect, the sticky-note beneath the monitor advises Emma, *please contact your Head Teacher.*

But Lisa Herrick is the Head Teacher.

Is that hot guy in the tiny shorts on staff? Lisa had asked Emma on her first day, two years ago, peering out the window at the hairy fool digging up the lawn.

My husband's a plumber, Emma had said absently, marvelling at the miracle of organisation that was the new Head Teacher's meeting agenda. *He's digging up the lawn because Toadie—I mean Tony DeRouen—blocked the drain again. Don't let Toadie leave his exercise book in the classroom. He does it on purpose so he can't finish writing up the pracs. He'll slide it behind the fume cupboard. New record of twelve times last term.*

Lisa had laughed, still looking out the window.

Emma can't let that seeming-innocuous scene haunt her right now. There are copper sulphate crystals for her to dissolve and re-form.

How many life choices do you regret? All / Most / Many / Some / Few / None

———

NAME: Toadie   GRADE: 7   TEACHER: Campbell

ANSWER TO QUESTION ONE: 'The human revolutionary advantage is guns and other weapons like autonomous drones.'

Incorrect. The human evolutionary advantage is larger brains with more white matter. White matter requires more energy, but greater connection between nerve cells means greater processing power. Instead of hard-wired instinct, humans have an enormous capacity to learn. Human brains are plastic, especially during puberty.

———

ANSWER TO QUESTION TWO: 'Embryology supports evolution because when I was a sperm, I could swim.'

Incorrect. Embryology supports evolution as, during development from fertilised egg to adult, different organisms tend to pass through similar stages. For example all vertebrate embryos, including humans, exhibit gill slits and tails at an early stage. These disappear before birth in land animals but remain in aquatic animals.

ANSWER TO QUESTION THREE: 'Vestigial organs are what girls have.'

Incorrect. Vestigial organs have been left behind by evolution. By shrinking or taking on a different function, they are evidence that an organism has evolved from needing an organ to not needing it. For example, although the human appendix now has a different function, it was once a digestive bag, between small intestine and large intestine, useful for fermentation in herbivores.

Teacher's Note: Toadie, please attend our virtual meeting at 3pm. With clothes on. Thanks. Ms Campbell.

———

So, I see from the mushy email that you heard about what happened.

Can I ask how, Miss?

Can I ask why you haven't reported me, for being all alone in my house, now? Can't you lose your job, for not reporting me?

The cops did come around with Mum's ashes, but my neighbour Hogan Smith helped cover for me. He was a nurse, until he had a mental breakdown. When the cops came, he pretended to be my dead dad.

Thanks for paying my school fees and sending me that box of groceries. I promise I'll pay you back.

Puberty #2

Bogan heads off at 3am.

The temperature hasn't come down much overnight, and the big scaffolding guys that always take the same bus as Bogan does are sweaty. The bus, a driverless, battery-powered cuboid, grunts up a hill and Bogan watches a pair of flying foxes in a palm tree squabble. He's surprised they haven't dropped dead from the heat like all the others.

His smart watch pings him with his work schedule—3.15am to 11.15am, then 5.15pm to 7.15pm.

His employer's app has also supplied a gross, waving, cartoonish baby and stork to celebrate Bogan's 10th 'work birthday.' He grimaces at it.

I've really been working at Living Forwards Fertility for ten years?

Ten years of split shifts. They teach preschool kids about wet bulb temperatures, now. About how you overheat and die in high humidity when the air temperature is higher than body temperature. Yay. Great.

Bogan, in his supportive Patient Advocate role, weather depending, actually has to phone the sperm-producing partners and tell them, if they're not in air conditioned spaces, to pack their privates with ice.

Today he's doing follow-up on the success stories, however.

The office is checkerboard-powered, air-conditioned cool, and only slightly less clinical than the ORs or the labs. Everything's so smooth. Bogan has a row of potted cactuses on his desk for perversity's sake.

Stop thinking about the daily heatwave death count!

Adjusting his headset, he taps through the inbox. Grateful e-cards. Photos of the kids.

Funny, there's three of the Wolflets, as Bogan thinks of them; genetic offspring of Caz Wolfe, Tasha's kid, who was an oddball even before he got orphaned. After Tasha fell off the checkerboard, Caz needed an income, so Bogan faked him the credentials of a Nordic Nobel Prize-winner so he could donate sperm.

Three years later, balls empty, the little troll scraped through the higher school certificate just competently enough to get into nursing.

Go on then, Bogan had said gruffly, the last time he'd seen Caz in person. *Don't say I didn't warn you!*

Anyway. These three Wolflets are called Mete, Yulia and William. All of them three years old. All with their biological father's chin dimple. All with the same cheeky, endearing curl to the right-side corner of the mouth.

Bogan cuts and pastes his standard appreciative, affectionate, carefully scripted response to the parents.

You make a difference for good in the world, he tells them, *you push back the darkness, when you make a difference to the lives of children!*

At 4am, a reasonable hour, now, for making business calls, Bogan checks the updated weather forecast, and gets ready to start ringing about ice packs in underpants.

———

CAZ WOLFE, RN (BN)   HOGAN SMITH

Hey, nurse-hater, you awake?

                                            Yeah

Do you still work at that fertility clinic?

                                            Yeah

Something weird is happening to me.
Like, my voice is changing again, and my
bones hurt. This sounds weird but I actually
measure my leg bones every now and then
and they were shorter last month but now
they're longer. I remember how I had to do all
those hormone blood tests when I was
donating to you guys and I don't have
private health insurance but do you
think I could do those tests again? Don't
have the computer skills to hack the
hospital pathology bots. Not like you.

                                            …

                                            Yeah, why not.

Come on down.

———

Ms Campbell teaches a virtual class, again, but this time the kids are in stasis.

That is, each rebellious teenage body, paralysed but conscious, rests in a temperature controlled SafeTeen Gro-Box™ while each optic chiasm, primary auditory cortex and somatosensory cortex is plugged into Ms Campbell's class.

She's been to the checkerboard-shaded warehouse—the facility, rather—on an orientation tour. Razor wire around it, and dogs on patrol, to give the parents peace of mind. Electrodes stimulate their muscles, and their premium, piped-in diets sculpt them, until they resemble sleeping Greek Gods.

It doesn't matter how many piles of virtual chicken nuggets they gulp down inside the SafeTeen virtual world.

'Good morning, class,' Ms Campbell says, the skin of her arms and legs rebelling against the repellent, yet necessary, full body suit and helmet. She knows how she looks to them. Lab coat over short skirt, sensible shoes, and blazer. Not a hair out of place. She's been doing this for five years, and when the IT guys asked if she wanted her avatar aged, the last stubborn shreds of her vanity answered *no*.

'Good morning, Ms Campbell,' the students drone. Sunlight slants through the windows. Plane trees rustle outside.

They don't know they're in the boxes.

Can't be allowed to know, or else these young offenders would treat their virtual lives, expensive and valuable lessons in the School of Hard Knocks, as hokey, violent video games instead of taking them seriously, and learning how badly lives can go, if you don't listen to the experience of the humans that came before.

Drawing on cross-sectional, international data, this review found the prevalence of violence triples in mid-puberty and late puberty (confidence interval [CI]: 1.8, 4.5) after adjustment for age, gender and social contextual mediators, while social relational aggression was associated with puberty at an early age.

They don't know that, this morning, in the real world, Emma's fur-child succumbed at last to kidney failure, outside it's raining steamy hot La Niña tears, and she has to bury her dog in the over-grown garden.

How often in the past 12 months have you (a) attacked some-one with the idea of seriously hurting them, and/or (b) beaten up someone so badly that they required medical treatment? 0 / 1-2 / 3-20 / 20-39 / 40 or more times.

Her wet eyes don't translate through to her avatar.

Some of these kids didn't fail the survey or get caught torturing animals, but were court-mandated because of genetic predisposition to conduct disorders, fetal alcohol syndrome or a long list of other reasons. A Gro-Box is better than juvie, the saying goes, and it's during deep sedation for brain scans in the fake juvenile detention centre that they were slipped into the Boxes, none the wiser, before seeming to wake and walk to seeming freedom with a warning.

Emma hopes it's better, anyway.

The reduction in violent crime in countries that use Gro-Boxes seems compelling. Emma can't help but also correlate the reduction in revolutions. Gro-Boxes mean the angry youth can't kick off any wars in the real world, or so the advertising says, but isn't it old guys that start wars when their wealth gets threatened?

Inside SafeTeen, any virtual wars vanish with the next update.

On their true release dates, with time and unruly hormones

under control, kids who are innately risk-takers wake up, wiser because they killed their friends in car crashes, or themselves with drug overdoses, only to find it was all simulated.

Is that better for a developing brain, or worse?

It's better for the chickens that would have been nuggets.

Within the free-range paddock, how often in the past 12 days have you pecked another chicken (a) to maintain status by causing direct wounding/trauma, or (b) to maintain status by denying food or water resources to a smaller or weaker bird? 0 / 1-2 / 3-20 / 20-39 / 40 or more times.

'Last day of semester,' she says. 'We're going to check the bacterial culture results for the foods we dropped on the floor to test whether the ten-second rule was true. Then, if you like, we can burn the foods to measure their caloric content? Or we can go outside, cut some white roses, and turn them into blue roses by capillary action for you to give your romantic partners.'

She smiles at Toadie.

He smiles back, shyly, and Ms Campbell's heart breaks to think that Toadie's girlfriend, Vanessa, has never met him in the real world. When she gets out, he'll have to woo her all over again.

And Vanessa will be angry. She'll think her boyfriend just disappeared into the military without telling her. Without calling her. That's the usual way the programming explains things, when older kids get out, to the kids who are still in.

The script writers should be sacked.

'Show of hands,' Ms Campbell says. 'Who wants to burn the food?'

Tony DeRouen has been in his Gro-Box, one of the earliest

models, since the school psychologist identified him as 'in danger'. Four years older than most of the others in the class, he's finally finishing high school.

He doesn't raise his hand. Lighting fires has lost its attraction for him.

Today is his last day. He's reformed. The program worked.

'Hands down,' Ms Campbell says. 'Who wants to make blue roses?'

Tony raises his hand. Most of the class is with him.

'Blue roses it is,' Ms Campbell says, to the groans of the would-be food-burners. But Toadie smiles wider.

In the virtual world, he's been allowed to steal steamrollers, graffiti trains, and even accidentally burn his house down with his parents inside.

That was a shock. But the grief finally got through to him.

When he wakes up, he'll find his parents still alive.

When he wakes up, he'll be glad he went through all this.

Won't he?

That's the plan, anyway.

Maybe he'll be so outraged by the manipulation he'll go back to setting fires. *Maybe innocent responsible people really do have to die so that irresponsible people can grow and learn?* Emma fervently hopes not.

Whenever she feels cynical about SafeTeen, she reminds herself that, even better than the chickens, it's literally saved Mr and Mrs DeRouen's lives. But it doesn't come for free.

Those surveys from ten years ago about eye contact, poor communication and apathy seem irrelevant now. That's nothing compared to twenty-two year olds learning to walk.

Toadie's facing one hell of a day tomorrow.

'Put on gloves and a face mask,' Emma says brightly, to pixels in motion in a world of pixels, 'before you touch the agar plates. Each single bacteria has the potential to start a colony, and while one cell probably can't get past your body's defences, a hundred thousand potentially will.'

They don't know about viral peritonitis, about the bloat pandemic raging this year. Yet another year where disposable PPE will have a greater carbon footprint than several small countries.

Part of her class preparation was to send notes to the programmers on what bacterial colonies her students should find. Because some of kids flunk the first time, she has to change the colony shapes every year.

Back in the real world, in the real mud, she's got a dog to lower into the arms of the swollen Nepean river.

If only she had some real white roses to throw in after him.

———

Dear Emma Campbell. Do you still use this email address? It's Caz Wolfe, here. I owe you a hundred dollars, yeah?

From ten years ago? At twelve percent over ten years, calculated per annum, that comes to 1.2% per year, or $112.67 in total. How's that? Didn't think I could work that out, did you?

It's because I went through puberty a second time. Mostly the brain rewiring part. The doctors can't get over it. I'm a freak. I mean, I'm sick and tired of MRIs, but information just goes in, yeah?

It keeps on going in.

They reckon I've lost some memories from before, but I don't think that's true. For sure, I remember my inspiring high school teachers.

I remember you.

When mum died, you kept my secret, so I wouldn't have to go to a foster home or into a Gro-Box. You paid my school fees so no one would ring my parents, and you sent that food delivery around. The cops came with mum's ashes, and Hogan Smith pretended to be my dead dad.

I'm a registered nurse now, but I think I'm going to go back to uni, since learning is suddenly so easy for me.

You're a science teacher, so you'll find this interesting.

Guess what else happened when my brain rewired? It actually set my body temperature higher. When air temperature exceeds body temperature, that's when animals die, in a heatwave. So I'm doing a Lamarck's giraffe and adapting in my own lifetime. Crazy.

Not sure if I'd pass it on, though. How can I put this delicately? They're, ah, sequencing. To find out.

Something about the environmental conditions activated some dinosaur genes while I was going through my second puberty, and now I have these amazing superficial veins but also the core body temperature of a chicken.

Forty degrees Celsius, or close to it.

My kidneys have remodelled, too, to conserve water, and I had to take these special probiotics to get my digestion back on track, since my old bacteria were quite happy with thirty-seven degrees, thanks very much. Being this hot means the usual germs can't infect me anymore, either.

So I'm kinda safe from the bloat pandemic.

I'd be disqualified from the Olympics, though, yeah?

Anyway, email me back if you want that hundred and twelve sixty-seven. I'm going to do a research doctorate on how to rehab burned out nurses, I think. Maybe I can bring Hogan back into the fold.

SEND

———

Dear Apricot-Butt, I mean Vanessa.

I don't know why I'm recording this message for you. I mean, I know why I'm recording it, because you can't read (duh). I mean the mushiness of it, yuck. It's super dumb.

But Old Lady Campbell seemed so weird when she pulled me aside at the end of our last class today. She said I should record you a message, telling you what I think about you, because I'll be going away, the army or some bullshit, and you won't see me for three years.

Right? RIGHT? I'm not going anywhere, babe. Especially not for three years. But whatever, I have to record you something to go with the flowers anyway, so this is what you mean to me. Your apricot butt gets me excited. But that's not the best thing about you.

You love the worst music, and you sneak it on at people's weddings without their permission. It makes them rage and you don't even care. But that's not the best thing about you.

The best thing about you is how you explain what I did wrong instead of just breaking up with me. Everyone else, all my life, just blocked me, ghosted me, gave me the silent treatment, whatever. I can't even remember the sound of Dad's voice. Just his door closing.

After I burned the house down, all those psychs wanted to understand me. They tried to make excuses for me. That's not on. You're not like that.

You're just like, fukken, don't say that again, Toadie, because it shows you're not thinking about these points of view, and you need to shut da fukup and think about them, right?

Right.

I love you, babe, and I know you love flowers, even though they are weird plant penises and vaginas. Even though your tightarse grandma makes you work in the wedding shop for bullshit minimum wage.

The whole world's been looking for a blue rose for six hundred years, apparently. That's how long ago an ancient Arab dude wrote down instructions for injecting rosebush roots with dye. These are fake, too. Sorry. You deserve a real one.

You deserve all of them, I'm not going anywhere, and Old Lady Campbell has finally been driven crazy after putting up with me for nine years in a row.

Can't believe I graduated. Right? RIGHT?

You knew I could do it. That's the best thing about you.

Love (your butt), Toadie

———

Puberty #3

Dear Chancellor Wolfe,

Many thanks for your surprise cash deposit. Though I'm ashamed to say I'm not sure how long it's been there.

Since the banking system collapse—who could have imagined

that society would return to checking balances in person with a paper slip at a barred teller window, where girls who majored in international finance now sit with loaded shotguns to defend actual safes full of gold bars?—call me crazy but I don't visit that often.

How are things at the university? I hear it's thanks to you we're still allowed to run our little corner of the internet. I even currently have the pleasure of teaching a couple of your kids, I think. At least, they look like you. Same little chin dimple, same sweet mouth-curl on one side. Two different surnames, though. Through the Gro-Box system? Instead of reserving it for at-risk youth, they're now selling it to well-off parents who want their heirs to be able to stroll the lush lawns and row the regattas of yesteryear, even though the snowboarding slopes of the real world are muddy and scorched, even though the algae-scummed rivers are practically dried up.

Because of the equipment being requisitioned by the government, I expect it to go offline any day now, of course. Are you losing your so-called non-core computers, too? Or are you exempt because of the meningitis pandemic?

Without being able to get any more components from overseas, and with our limited 3D printing capability in Australia, it makes sense that resources have to be diverted but I'm still sad about it, and all the kids outside of SafeTeen seem barely functional.

Are your own students surviving the revival of physical libraries?

Thanks again for the money. It, and the nostalgia, were sweet.

Emma Campbell

———

Dear Emma,

It was a delight to receive your letter. I'm afraid the children you mentioned aren't mine, but the biological descendants of the late Nobel Prize-winning Dr Mathias Permlid, though it's nice to think I've got miniature doppelgangers out there somewhere.

Apologies that I'm writing back to you on your own clean-erased paper, but budgets are tight, as you hinted at, and your words are burned into my brain, I assure you.

Well, until I go through my next brain-rearranging puberty, at least. I'm up to my third one, now. That old claim to fame. Only my most vivid memories seem to survive the transformation, but it leaves room for me to get current, to take in and evaluate the new and ever-changing situation more clearly.

You were my science teacher, I remember that. You also sent me vegetables, I think. You had a grocery shop, yeah? Clearly I was too immature, at the time, to reflect on the fact that if you had a second job, you weren't earning enough money as a teacher.

I can't imagine you've been made redundant, even with Safe-Teen going down, because of the acute shortage of qualified teachers. But if you'd ever like a job as a librarian, I'm certain the university could accommodate you. The postal service isn't what it was, but I hope that when it eventually reaches you, this missive finds you in good health.

Warm regards,

Caz

———

Vanessa Laxman is happily swimming laps in the ocean baths, until she isn't.

She smells orange juice and ozone.

Static lifts her curls in semi-darkness.

It's too hot. She tries to swim through the water but it won't hold her, and it's only as she falls that she realises it's not water, it's air, and why did she feel weightless a moment ago? Why is she wet, why is she naked, why can't she grip the sides of his horrible torpedo-shaped bathtub?

And why is she a woman again? She was a girl, just seconds ago, she was swimming, she was twelve years old.

Vanessa remembers with a shudder of fear but also the feeling of coming home. She graduated from high school, she was nineteen years old with amazing hair much wider than her shoulders, and then her grandma didn't come for her. The sun blazed down on the metal spikes of the school gates, cicadas beat a summer rhythm, the other kids high-fived each other before breaking apart forever, but no cars pulled up to the curb, and then she was somehow starting seventh grade, with a backpack that almost outweighed her and a short haircut that itched.

What the hell?

'Help me,' Vanessa tries to say, but even her throat won't listen.

She vomits instead.

———

Emma Campbell is mid-titration when the students vanish.

She turns to show them the transient pink of a solution approaching a neutral pH, but only has seconds to stare, stunned, at the empty stools and beakers, until they vanish, too, and the program throws her back to her living room and the sweaty insides of her suit.

It's tighter than it used to be. When Emma throws the headset onto the couch, she gasps like a diver reaching the surface.

Catastrophic interruption, reads the error message on the screen. *Rebooting*.

But it doesn't reboot.

The apartment loses power, instead.

Emma waddles, wide-legged, over to her seventh-storey lounge room window. There, she can see that the power is also out at the industrial estate, and that the drones protecting it are lowering themselves to the concrete, as if set adrift by command failure.

That, and there are power thieves on the ladders to the closest checkerboard field. More of them swarming at the top of the sticks. Cutting the solar panels free. Lowering them on long lines down to collaborators, hooting behind their masks as if they're liberating foxes from a fur farm, or something.

The Gro-Boxes, Ms Campbell thinks with a sinking feeling in her gut. *They'll have back-up power, won't they? Batteries? Rerouting? Where are the armed guards? The police?*

If she could get out of the frozen screen, she could call emergency services from her computer.

Then she looks back, squinting, and sees the police, standing with arms folded, by their cars, watching the thieves pass in a convoy of electric B-doubles dimensionally suited to checkerboard heists.

She shouldn't be shocked, but she is.

Nobody's paid any public servants for about six months, she knows that, she's a state government-employed teacher, but she wouldn't accept bribes to survive.

Would she?

It's not like the children are going to die, she tells herself, gnawing her lower lip, both gloved hands on the window frame. *They're just going to wake up. Their parents will start showing up to get them.*

But the longer she waits, long after the thieves have departed, carrying away panels, batteries and drones, the more obvious it becomes that only three or four families have received the emergency messages, and there are three to four hundred boxes in the facility.

I have to go down there. Ms Campbell throws her sticky suit on the floor and jumps into the 60-second timed shower her apartment block allows. The water's cold. She doesn't care. She'll be a familiar face to some of them. *How long until all hell breaks loose down there?*

No time to make herself immaculate, as they're used to seeing her. No time to hide the lines.

Maybe it'll be too dark to see.

She claws the cupboards open looking for a wind-up torch.

The sensible part of her mind reminds her that half of them are in there, in the first place, because they're volatile; too angry or too afraid.

It doesn't matter.

I have to go.

———

Vanessa wonders if she's been hit by lightning, twice.

The first time, it must have been outside the school, she reasons. *It was graduation day, and grandma didn't come.*

She must have lost her memories. A cold bolt from a clear sky, in the heat of summer.

It fried my brain. Made her start high school again. She always did forget what she was doing, in the middle of what she was doing. She never was able to learn to read or write, or do sums. Toadie used to laugh, and call them her weather changes.

Now she's been hit a second time. *I was swimming in the sea.* They've obviously put her in some sort of fancy hospital to help her heal, but it's dark, and there aren't any doctors or nurses. Just the cold metal of the weird bath, children crying around her, and a blue glow from a panel with white writing on it, but she doesn't see the icon that she normally presses to get it in audio.

Lightning a third time, really? Is that why there's a power cut?

Then a ghostly face blossoms in the black, too close, glowing blue in the light of the screen, and Vanessa bites back a scream.

It's Ms Campbell.

But a frightening, older Ms Campbell.

'Vanessa!' Ms Campbell gasps. 'Why are you here? I thought you got out a decade ago and went to find Toadie. You must be twenty-six, twenty-seven by now! How could this have happened?' She turns aside, gripping both sides of a display, and starts muttering to herself. 'Your grandmother. Maybe we can use the database to find her, if those bloody thugs don't steal the backup batteries as well. The countdown to total failure is three hours, twenty-two minutes, thirty seconds, it says. Oh my gosh, Vanessa!'

'What is it?' Vanessa whispers. What more can there be? She's twenty-six or twenty-seven. Has she been in a coma at this terrible hospital? Ms Campbell grips Vanessa's naked shoulders the way she was just gripping the sides of the screen.

'It looks like your father and grandmother died of peritonitis, too, about the time you should have been waking up. Instead of registering an inability to pay, the glitch kept rebooting your Gro-Box. How do you feel?' Her eyes swing down to the gloopy mess of the weird bathtub, then back to Vanessa's eyes.

It's not in a gross way, but Vanessa remembers she's naked and cringes down into the bath as best she can with a shuddering skeleton that's forgotten how to cringe. Ms Campbell produces a woollen poncho to put on her. It's prickly as hell, but Vanessa's shoulders were getting cold. It must be cold outside.

Not summer at all.

'What is a Gro-Box?' Vanessa asks, tears welling. 'What is this place? I can't search a database. I'm hopeless at maths. Toadie tried to help but I always forget what I'm doing, in the middle of what I'm doing.'

'Everything will be fine, honey,' Ms Campbell says, hugging her, right before some burly thug rips something square and heavy off the bathtub beside Vanessa's.

'Young man,' Ms Campbell says loudly in her teacher-voice. 'That's the Rapid Information Transfer Zip. Look at the radiation warnings on the side. You don't want to mess with that, you're in the real world now. It'll kill you.'

The thug grins.

Vanessa thinks her brain must have glitched. That grey-haired, seam-cheeked, droopy-jowled face can't possibly belong to Toadie's dad. Vanessa went to his funeral. Toadie's house fire was started by a cigarette stub after Toadie fell asleep with it in his hand, and Toadie somehow got rescued but his parents were killed. It changed him forever.

'I know what it does,' the thug says, laughing. 'I'll take yours as well, thanks. Chance says we need all the ritzes for the university of the future. Says he can make them safe.'

Those hazel eyes. They're the same. It's him. The boy who gave her blue roses, a lifetime ago.

'Anthony John DeRouen,' Ms Campbell snaps, as if Toadie's still sixteen and been busted flooding the toilets again. 'Put that down, and tell me about this criminal organisation you're working for.'

'Got no time,' Toadie says. 'Got Mete and Yulia in the truck. Poor things just woke up. They're gonna need hand feeding. Chance sent me cos I've *been* in one of these fricken boxes. My pleasure to take them apart.'

Ms Campbell stops rubbing Vanessa's shoulders, and tosses her head like a horse.

'I know Mete and Yulia,' she says. 'They're in my eighth grade. Where are their parents?'

'Meningitis,' Toadie says, hitting the RITZ by Vanessa's head with a wrench.

The noise makes her cry out, and it's only then that he stops to look full into her face.

The lines smooth out as his jaw drops.

'Apricot-butt?' he whispers.

―――――

'Miss Campbell,' says the leader of the criminal organisation, warmly. 'Good to see you.'

Emma straightens, brushing rust and dust from the back of her head, waiting for her eyes to adjust.

They're in the cool dimness of an old pump station.

Emma, Vanessa, Mete and Yulia had all followed Toadie through a convoluted series of water pipes, while he banged out secret codes with his wrench, and dragged a shopping trolley full of ritz units. Their radiation hazard stickers are covered in mud, now.

'Chance,' Emma says, realising who it is. 'Chancellor Caz Wolfe. You paid me back for the groceries and the school fees. Now you're running some kind of solar panel mafia. My house, and thousands like it, don't have power anymore, because of you. People will die without air conditioning.'

'They're already dying,' Caz says gravely. 'This meningitis pandemic is the worst one yet.'

Emma lifts her chin. 'Some of us are resistant.'

'Some,' Caz allows. 'But enough people have died that the resistant can move into vacant shadowside houses. Single occupancy, even. There won't be anyone to stop them. We've reached a tipping point.'

From behind the tool-covered work bench where Caz was fiddling with wires, a couple more teenagers circle around to stand face-to-face with Mete and Julia.

Two thirteen year olds, distressed, fresh from their Gro-Boxes stare into the faces of two others who could be their siblings, only thinner. Less sculpted.

With the chin dimples. With the upwards curl on the right side of the mouth.

'I'm Will,' one of them says. 'Caz is our bio dad. Ours and yours. Welcome to the Wolfe Pack.'

———

Puberty #4

Bogan wrinkles his brow at the results.

He's got to get in and out of the system before the profiteering pharma corps can ping him, but he's had practice.

All those kids, all the wolflets, have gone through the same second puberty that Caz went through.

'Confirmed, Chance,' he calls across the echoing width of the cave, lifting his goggles part way. Late afternoon sunlight slants inside the opening, and cobwebs cover the rock shelf where the solar panels are plugged into the broadcasting ritzes. 'It's happened. They'll be really adaptive to the changing climate. Just like you.'

But when he pulls off the goggles, he spots Chance wearing Emma Campbell's beat up, ancient teaching suit, giving the wolflets their evening virtual lesson.

Before second puberty, these wolflets were already massive overachievers. When the drug companies came calling, they immediately understood the need to ditch their families and hide, to avoid becoming permanent test subjects. When the city stopped functioning, and the Pack fled into western NSW's farmland, desert and scrub, they handled it just fine.

But now that their core body temperatures and physiology have adjusted to this new climate? Now that each one of them can run for fifty kilometres over cracked, salty soils, carrying a solid state server from the old university, a solar panel from the old checkerboard and a ritz to keep Caz's University of the Future alive? All that knowledge disseminated, with permission and collaboration, over Wiradjuri lands, a thriving network in wolflet hands?

The kids are OK.

And there's no way they're letting their genomes fall in to the hands of bunker billionaires.

Bogan yawns, plugs the goggles in to recharge, chugs the extra water ration he gets for being old and not adapted to the heat, and shuffles to the back of the cave to wake Toadie.

'You're up,' Bogan tells Toadie. 'Bubs need dinner.'

Twins Damayanti and Kausalya are only three years old. They were the last of Bogan's rescues from Living Forwards Fertility. Toadie, who turned all paternal once reunited with Vanessa, still scarred by the burning down of a house that never happened, begged to take care of the twins.

Much like Bogan, Toadie grew up surrounded by a physical family. Plenty of people, plenty of noise, plenty of human contact. Puppies. A school playground with full-contact footy instead of masks and distancing. Before second puberty, the oldest wolflet, isolated by the need to keep moving, and to keep group sizes small, had been going off the rails, suffering from withdrawal of human touch, alternately raging about being trapped and sinking deeply into unresponsiveness.

Now, as recorded by Bogan and Emma's research, after second puberty, almost overnight the wolflets all started exhibiting the same self-soothing patterns.

Strange, highly aerobic dances, on the spot, of their own invention.

In the evenings, instead of seeking the security of family and fire, they crouch down. They hug themselves tightly and start humming.

Happy humming for fifteen minutes or so, gazing into the warm night, watching the moon rise.

But Toadie remembers how to hug people. He remembers that the twins need hugging. And will need hugging, all the way up to their first puberty, at the very least.

Unfortunately, to wake him up, he needs a kicking.

'Ow! Bogan!' he bellows.

'Mr Smith, to you,' Bogan says.

———

START AUDIO.

Hey Toadie,

Ten years ago, you asked me if I wouldn't rather have a baby with one of the wolflets.

You said I'd be better off with one of these super-kids. One who doesn't feel the heat or need as much water as we do. I told you our baby needed your stubbornness. Your fearlessness.

Yeah, I conveniently forgot how you had to go in a Gro-Box because of what a delinquent you were.

What I'm trying to say is that Toadie Junior lassoed a bunker drone last night, went for a wild ride over the horizon, and now I can't find him.

I know Chance said we have to stay apart, in small groups, so the corporations can't take our servers, or our kids, with at least one wolflet for every two normies.

But can you get your arse over here and help me track down our goddamn kid?

Coordinates attached. Don't laugh at me if they're in the wrong order. I'm still not great with numbers. Just hurry.

END AUDIO.

SEND.

————

Standing over a grave marker in the middle of the desert, the whole world goes away.

Black sky, black horizon, black earth. Thunder rumbling in the west. (Is there a reason I think the sky should be patterned like a checkerboard?)

My shoulders ache from the straps of the pack. The solar panel, ritz and server don't get any heavier, exactly, but I look forward to my next puberty.

Always feel fresher, after that, yeah?

My memories get foggier, but somehow the muscle memory stays locked in. My long, hairy legs (was there a reason I used to measure them?) know how to trot along a trail. My back knows how to bend to keep the panel angled to the sun. My arms know how to fling the boomerang, the way the warriors taught me, to take down drones.

I just can't remember where the drones are going. They harvest wild animals for meat and fly east. Something is there. Something that needs food. Something that tried to take me, or my people, once?

I don't need much food these days. Grass clumps and eucalyptus resin are enough. The wolflets are the same.

(Whose grave is this?)

The suit for teaching failed at last, so I don't have the virtual world to remind me of the things I've forgotten. My body brings me to this spot, though, same time each year, and I feel grateful and sad.

(Were you my father? Or my girlfriend? Was there a boab tree?)

Bogan's voice comes from the darkness. Rumbly like the thunder. Bogan's getting old. His grave marker will be here, too, soon.

(Will I forget his name, without him here to remind me?)

'We salute you, Emma Campbell,' Bogan says. 'You made a difference in the world. You push back the darkness when you make a difference to the lives of children.'

(You were my science teacher. I remember, now.)

(I paid you back.)

(I paid you forwards.)

We need another drone, to get the solar panels off it. Bogan patches up the checkerboard panel our group is responsible for, replacing sections as they become damaged, so that the virtual university stays useable, but without the security of being able to stay in one place, we can't do any manufacturing of our own.

Just have to wait, I used to lecture the wolflets, until the last trillionaire suffocates in his hole, and the shadow dwellers emerge to take control, and then we can go east again.

'I wish it would rain,' Bogan says, and the twins laugh, mocking him, because there is no rain, west of the divide. They barely believe in it. But we don't want to be struck by lightning, standing around a dead tree on an open plain.

'I wish that, too,' I say.

(Goodbye, Miss.)

(I'll see you again next year.)

The Switch

Ben Walter

The Gordon Dam site is spectacular, both at the dam itself and deep underground in the power station. Information is available at a visitors' centre perched high above the dam. Bookings can be made here for a somewhat unusual bus ride. Trips are made daily between 10.45 a.m. and 3.30 p.m. (except Christmas Day and Good Friday) through a tunnel to view operation of the station and exhibits relating to its development.

Explore Tasmania, Jennifer Pringle-Jones, 1983.

Today it is snowing, so Harry and I watch the flakes melt into the surface of the water. Harry drives the bus and I do the spiels. Sometimes we swap but it never goes well—Harry gets his dates mixed up and I crash into huge fucking rocks that seem to come out of nowhere; mostly when I turn around and frown about the dates. We only change it up when we really need a break and there aren't many punters asking tricky questions.

Every day it's the same. We cross the dam wall, slowly at first so the tourists can gawp at the view. Then we head down into the power station and inspect the penstock, slip into the lake and circle the concrete footings. There's a bit of time under the water; the tourists like the sense of flowing through the world. Fish are pretty rare and the muck below the wheels swells in clouds that don't look like anything much, but the tourists rorschach up visions of whales and sharks that are definitely not swimming out there. We save the best bit till last, stretching the cupping device through the portal and ripping water from the billowing fabric of the lake, pouring it into wine glasses and handing them around as we motor back to the surface.

The tourists like to drink from the depths of the lake because they feel its power swelling in their veins; the power that flings itself through turbines and chases wires all over the state. It inches through their bodies and makes them want to leap about and dance. They zip up mountains, pushing through the scrub like old dozers. Some of them write songs about spillways or start new hobbies like whittling tin, but mostly they just seem confident, suddenly certain they can do everything they've longed to do at more restful times, on the kind of holidays where beaches swivel below their bodies and point their sunburnt faces to the sky.

The water is included in the price of the tour; it's a good price and we tell the tourists this when they try to haggle. 'It's fair,' we say. 'You don't get this kind of deal at the coal plants.' They argue that the coal tours take you through a blazing furnace, which is clearly one of the Wonders of Civilisation, but they can go for a swim any time. What's more, they can just *walk* across the dam wall even when the weather is shovelling sleet. We admit this is true, then point out that they don't get to *eat* the coal; but some of them have been on the tours and know this is a lie, because of the coal dust they mix with truffle oil that is dribbled on pasta at the restaurants that have been built in the old lignite mines. Even though it isn't the same, we give in and sell the tour for cheaper because at least it's a positive price.

This morning Harry and I thought about switching—only three people turned up and one of them was a kid who was more interested in throwing stones at a clump of buttongrass. Now it's 3pm and we've got no bookings for the afternoon. The weather is so miserable it feels like we're all going to start crying at some point. Even if nobody turns up we still have to go through with the tour; it's part of the regulations. They have trackers on the bus that screech if it's still parked at 3.45 and they don't quiet down till we take the thing out like a dog for its afternoon walk.

'Do you want to swap?' asks Harry. His long grey hair is tied in an optimistic pony tail and his eyes look tired. 'It's been a while. Months maybe. C'mon Tommy, let's do it.'

'Huh,' I say. It's tempting. Always better to get it out of our system when there's nobody there to watch. I'm sure to miss most of the enormous rocks and he can make up whatever shit he feels like.

But then we hear a motor curling around the hills. We turn to each other and wrinkle our faces.

A sparkling sedan turns into the carpark and our hearts sink.

'Tomorrow, maybe?' says Harry, pleading, and I shrug.

A young man with sleek brown hair steps out of the car and looks around the carpark; perhaps he's wondering if he's in the right place. He spots us crouching under the shelter near the bus and hurries through the snow, leather satchel bouncing on his shoulder. He's wearing a fashionable down jacket that is shivering around his body and expensive jeans that don't want to be here.

'Hi,' he says. 'Are you running today?'

Harry picks up a grin and slaps it on his face. 'Every day except Christmas and Good Friday!' he says cheerfully. 'You want to come? We're heading out soon.'

'Where do you go?' The young man turns to me, notes my fading name tag. 'Um, Tommy, where does your tour go?'

'Just the usual,' I explain. 'Across the wall, down into the station and then splat, into the lake.'

'Oh yeah, the lake,' he says. 'Do you drive along the beach?'

I was sure he was going to ask about the water. When I was younger and there was still a bit of cash to splash around, I travelled with an ex through the Greek islands. We wandered into a tourist information centre in Rhodes and heard someone ask about the Colossus. Where was the Colossus? They wanted to see the Colossus. It happened three times in fifteen minutes and I didn't know how the attendant could stand it.

'That's the *other* lake,' I say, pointing to the south past the peak of Mt Sprent. 'Over there.'

'Oh right,' he says. 'Can we go there?'

Harry and I laugh in a friendly way.

'Sorry,' I say. 'We'd love to, but there's a route we have to take. It's been set out and approved by the government and the corporation, and we can't budge from it. I mean Harry has always wanted to take this baby up Mt Anne but we'd get into huge trouble.'

'How would they know?' he asks.

I start to mention the trackers but then remember this might not be public information. I think about a lie and can't come up with a good one, so I just shake my head. 'Ha!' I say, as though he has made a joke. 'So can we sign you up for this afternoon's tour?'

The man nods; he seems to be thinking about it. Now he will ask about the water.

He doesn't ask about the water, so I tell him.

'It's only fifty bucks,' I say. 'And that includes a glass of the water. I'm sure you've heard about it—the cleanest buzz you'll ever drink.'

He nods. 'Okay,' he says. 'Uh-huh. Look, it sounds good. But how much, *really*, to go to the other lake?'

I laugh again, a little less this time, and start to explain the same thing, that we aren't *allowed* to go that way. But then I see a strange light in Harry's eyes; he interrupts me in a clipped tone I haven't heard from him before.

'How much are we talking?' he asks. I turn and look at the expensive car and the fancy clothes the man is wearing.

Our pay is linked to ticket sales from the tours, but it is also linked to revenue from the power station. During negative pricing events we get negative pay and sometimes we are glad to break even at the end of the month.

'Ten thousand dollars,' he says. 'I'll give you ten thousand dollars each to drive me along the beach.'

Harry and I look at each other.

This is more than we have made the whole time we have been running this tour.

I think about the money, about what I could do. I think about packing up and heading to the mainland, working on the solar tours and taking the afternoons off to wander through living bush to smell the unburnt air.

'We'll be fired,' says Harry carefully. 'You know we'll be fired. You probably know they track us.'

'Fifteen thousand,' says the man. 'Each.'

It is 3.30 in the afternoon and there's nobody else here.

A currawong arcs over and lands near a patch of tea tree huddled by the road.

'I'll drive,' says Harry, reaching into his pocket for the keys.

I am shaking as we walk up the stairs. The man takes his seat and Harry turns the key in the ignition, then we drive down the Gordon River Road for a few kilometres, turning off towards the boat ramp near the Serpentine Dam. The tracker alarms are screaming and we do our best to put them out of our heads; they're dampened a little when we hit the water. I flinch as we drop below the surface, but then I feel more secure, as though we're hidden in the lake and can pretend we're doing the regular tour. I am suddenly struck and turn to the man. 'Oh, did you want a talk? Normally we explain about all the bits and pieces, the history, the power, the helpful little things they want you to understand, but here...'

'It's fine,' the man says. 'Don't worry about it. Pretty hard to hear you anyway.' He stares out the window at the water; silt waltzes as the wheels churn, and Harry shakes his head. I move up to sit next to him.

'Harry,' I say. 'What are we going to do?'

Harry shakes his head. 'Mate,' he says.

'Seriously,' I ask him.

'We're going to give this bloke the tour,' he says. 'We're going to take his fifteen k, and then we're going to fuck right off.' He revs the engine to get around a series of stags, the trunks of drowned trees that wait and watch. 'I'm going back to WA, and I'm going to see my kid, and then I don't give a shit.'

As we speed along the bottom of the lake, getting closer to the beach, I wonder at Harry's sudden decisiveness; like a tyre has burst after years of being worn down. I watch as he guides the bus through the tricky sections and think of the evenings when we've sat by the fire and roasted our spuds; the mornings when he has waited for the instant coffees I've thrown together before dragging his body from the tent they let us use, the cheap canvas that keeps the rain angled from our faces overnight.

It is getting a little dark and the bus is moving slower. The shriek is evolving into a wail; I wonder why my mind is stretching out the sound.

'Right,' says Harry. 'Here we are.' There is a long, flat expanse outside the window, covered in thin mud. The man looks out the window.

'Okay,' he says.

'You're the boss,' says Harry. 'What now?'

'Take it slow,' says the man.

Harry inches forward. Silt streaks the water, just as it did before, but something is different—on the bottom, streaks of bright sand are glistening. The man has us skid around in a small patch until a section of the beach is clear. We wait until the sediment settles a little, then stare through the windows as tiny fish ease past; there is a song in the water and we are listening. The man reaches into his satchel and pulls out a wad of cash. He counts it carefully, hands it across. My face is reflected in the plastic of the notes, and then it is reflected in the window, and for a moment it feels like it is reflected in the beach, as though I've left a clear impression in the sand.

'Thank you,' he says. 'And now the portal. It's big enough, yes?'

'What?' I ask.

Harry doesn't seem surprised at all. 'Yep,' he says. 'It will be a squeeze, but it's big enough. They use it for divers sometimes.'

'What do you mean?' I ask. 'What's happening? Aren't we done here?'

Harry puts the bus into neutral, heaves on the brake and wanders over to the panel.

'You're sure?' he asks.

The man nods, and suddenly I understand. 'No, you can't,' I say, standing in the way and grabbing at his shoulders to shake some daylight into his mind. He just smiles gently.

'I never had the chance,' he says. 'I've always wanted to do it.'

Harry opens the hatch, and the man steps in. The hatch closes; water gushes and I think again about what we've been doing, about the station that draws power from the rushing of spent rain and then floods the state with it. Of the water that is gathered to cover the wrong ground, of the money I now have; of Harry rushing off to the west to see his son, of guiding the same tourists around solar panels and hiding in afternoon trees.

But then I think of nothing, because the man has come into view.

He is walking along the beach, drinking the water.

After Zero

Greg Egan

2060

Latifa's watch hummed, softly but persistently, until she stirred and raised her wrist above her face in the darkness. The display brightened slowly, giving her eyes time to adapt; it was just after three o'clock, but apparently her assistant had judged the message important enough to wake her.

'Play,' she requested hoarsely.

The watch painted a scene on her retinas: Sian MacDonald standing in the workshop in Boston, in front of the reactor.

'There is no easy way to put this,' Sian began. 'The finance we've been seeking hasn't come through, and we've run out of other possibilities. In a couple of days, Mass Fusion will be going into liquidation.'

Latifa barely listened to the rest: the thanks, the apologies, the promises of the staff's priority amongst creditors. She was sure that Sian was sincere in all of this, but none of it changed what really mattered. After twenty-three years of striving, the team's efforts had come to nothing.

She curled up against the blanket and closed her eyes, falling into the pit that had opened up beneath her. Surrendering to despondency felt better than fighting it—and when a part of her mind started interjecting with all manner of implausible last-minute reprieves, it was about as useful as if her descent was being punctuated by a tangle of slender rootlets: too flimsy to grab on to, too abrasive to ignore.

After a while, though, she found herself seeking more honest reasons for solace. If Mass Fusion was dead, at least they'd fallen to a worthy rival. She'd always hoped there'd be room for both themselves and Aneutronic, but so long as at least one of them thrived, the larger dream survived. Had she wasted her time? Maybe. But if both designs had not remained in play for so long, the question of which was most viable might never have been truly settled.

She opened her eyes and checked her watch again; on the street above it had come down to 36 degrees, but the forecast for the day ahead had been revised up to 50. Whatever balm she found for her ego, the real harm would be spread much wider. Aneutronic might prosper, but the rollout of fusion would still suffer from the lack of a second supplier. All the optimistic curves showing powered CO_2 capture clawing back the overshoot by 2070 would need to be redrawn. The immiserated world would stay hotter for longer, forcing people who were barely hanging on to endure another decade of what was already unendurable. More species would die, more ecosystems collapse, and the chance of methane erupting from the melting permafrost would just keep ratcheting up.

Latifa rose to her feet, massaging her lower back as the room lights came on. She poured herself a glass of water and drained it; the air in the burrow wasn't hot, but it remained as relentlessly dry as it was up on the surface.

Her watch hummed again. It was Emily, querying her wakefulness and willingness to talk; Latifa answered without hesitation.

'You're up,' Emily began. 'So you've heard the news?'

'Yes. How are you taking it?'

'I think I've finished screaming obscenities, but if I suddenly mute myself you'll know why.'

Latifa smiled. 'Did the screaming help?'

'Absolutely. And now it's out of my system, so I can move on.'

'All right.' Latifa found the notion jarring, but it wasn't as if a prolonged mourning would do any good. 'Move on to what? Have you had an offer from Aneutronic already?'

Emily chortled. 'Hardly! They poached all the people they wanted years ago.'

'So you're planning to retire and grow vegetables?'

'No. I'm planning to build the Scatterer.'

Latifa hesitated, searching her friend's face for some hint that she was teasing her in a misconceived attempt to cheer her up. 'Fair enough,' she replied. 'But if we're playing that game, I want world peace, and a pony too.'

'It's doable,' Emily insisted. 'And you know it would work.'

'There are a thousand things that *would* work.'

'Yes, and it's a shame people didn't try more of them, sooner. But this is our chance. We'll have time on our hands, and no better way to spend it.'

Latifa swallowed a reflexive retort about how happy she'd be spending time with her grandchildren. Her own response to the complaints from her daughters had always been that she could do far more for their welfare by working than any amount of grand-motherly devotion could achieve.

'So who's going to pay for this daydream, when we can't even get a working fusion reactor bankrolled?'

'I have no idea,' Emily confessed. 'I'm plasma, you're magnets, but it's only been thirty minutes; you can't expect me to have assembled the whole team.'

Latifa said, 'You make it sound like a heist. All we're missing is the safe-cracker and the get-away driver.'

'Except we won't be stealing anything, just ... redistributing it.'

'Seriously, though. I don't think we ever costed it, but it must come to at least—'

Emily cut her off. 'Don't you dare pluck a number out of the air, as an excuse to give up. We need to dust off the old files first, and bring them up to date. There are better materials now, for every-thing. Once we know exactly what we're talking about, we can start being brutal about the costs.'

'All right.'

Emily beamed at her. 'So you're in?'

'I agree that we should look at it,' Latifa replied warily. 'That's all.'

'I'll do a first pass through the specification. It's morning here in Sydney, so it makes sense for me to get started while you get back to sleep.'

Latifa murmured assent. Emily said, 'I'll be in touch.'

Latifa lay down, and when the lights faded she stared into the darkness. She didn't want to spend her last years bitterly rehashing all the old lost battles. As likely as not, she would fail again, but at least she'd get to fail at something new.

––––––

Half an hour before dawn, Latifa left the burrow and walked into the village. The sky was bright enough to light the way; on either side of the road, fields of stunted wheat with curled brown edges on the leaves stretched out beneath a canopy of protective gauze. There was a mineral scent lingering in the air from the irrigation water, forced up from some insane depth by the solar-powered pumps chasing the retreating aquifer. When she was a girl, the Kajaki Dam had drawn both power and water from the Helmand River, but now her memories of that vast green reservoir felt like something out of a dream.

In the market, she bought enough food to last three or four days. Okra had almost doubled in price since the last time she'd checked, and even flour and oil were creeping up again. The families she was helping needed more assistance every month, and every month there were more needing help. Now that her absurd salary from Boston was about to be cut off, she was going to need to juggle everything more carefully.

She set off home, quickening her step to escape the sun rising behind her.

'Latifa!'

She turned to see a woman silhouetted against the glare. 'Fatema?' She waited for her cousin to catch up.

'Let me carry some of that,' Fatema offered.

'I'm fine, thank you,' Latifa insisted.

'How have you been? We never see you!'

'You know what it's like.'

'How is your work going?' Fatema asked. 'The reactor?'

Latifa was embarrassed. She had stood in front of the girls in Fatema's science class, year after year, supposedly inspiring them with her efforts. 'I've moved on to something new,' she said. 'Maybe even more useful.'

'Really?'

'We call it the Scatterer. I probably mentioned it to you, years ago, but it's only just started coming together.'

Fatema frowned thoughtfully, but her efforts to recall the term didn't seem to bear fruit. Latifa said, 'You know the first Lagrange point, between the Earth and the sun?'

'Where the forces cancel out, and a spacecraft can stay in place without much effort?'

'Exactly. Suppose you put a device there that makes a strong magnetic field. When the solar wind hits the field, it piles up in front of the magnet, a bit like the way the Earth's magnetic field keeps the same particles at bay. But if you modulate the field in just the right way, the plasma will be full of ripples. The refractive index of plasma is a little less than one; a convex lens like that would bend light away from its axis, and if the ripples are shaped carefully you get the same effect. So now you have a kind of corrugated lens built of plasma, thousands of kilometres wide, sitting between the Earth and the sun, scattering light away from us.'

'How much of the light?' Fatema asked sceptically.

'Less than one percent,' Latifa admitted. 'The plasma's not that dense. But one percent less irradiance ...' She looked around at the parched landscape. 'It could make all the difference, while we wait for the CO2 to be drawn down.'

Fatema was too polite to remind her of all her predictions that Mass Fusion's reactors would do the job in a decade.

They reached Latifa's burrow and parted. Inside, her workstation had already downloaded Emily's new file from the repository and was running the revised model through a set of simulations.

There were better high-temperature superconductors available than the last time they'd worked on the idea, supporting much higher current densities for the same mass. Emily had incorporated the new materials, but now Latifa set up a search to optimise the geometry of the coils under the new constraints. She watched the magnets morph in front of her, deforming and shrinking as they probed the landscape of possibilities; the software did a good job, but she went back and nudged it into some valleys it had skirted, and managed to find a better solution than its first, fully automated attempt.

After three days' work, the final result looked like a strange, three-dimensional labyrinth rendered in almost invisibly fine wire. If this material had been meant as a shield, nothing could have been flimsier. But when Latifa ran the plasma simulator, the approaching wind spiralled back on itself along a vast, curved shock-front, swirling with turbulent eddies, that carried the field out far beyond the structure that seeded it. When she ray-traced an image of the sun seen from Earth, the softening of the disk was almost imperceptible—but the total radiance was reduced by four-fifths of a percent.

It was late when she updated the repository, but Emily

responded straight away.

'You think we're ready to build something and put it in a plasma chamber?'

'Do we have a plasma chamber?'

'MF aren't doing anything with theirs. If we make an offer, the liquidators might be happy to get it off their hands.'

'And ... we rehire the technicians to run it?'

Emily said, 'That seems the simplest way.'

They still had no backers, and no legal structure for the venture. They didn't even have any intellectual property; they'd designed the Scatterer outside work hours, so Mass Fusion didn't own it, but they'd put it into the public domain in the hope that someone else would build it while they carried on with the main game.

'I can't help with the funding,' Latifa confessed. 'I know it sounds crazy for me to be crying poor, but I've taken on obligations that I can't just drop.'

Emily said, 'I understand. Don't worry; I've roped in another twenty people, and I think they'll be able to pitch in enough to get us the chamber.'

'All right. So who exactly will own it?'

'Scatterbrain LLC,' Emily replied. 'I've had a draft contract of incorporation drawn up; you can find it in the repo and tweak anything you don't like.'

Latifa felt a pang of vertigo. She was almost sixty years old, and she was about to launch herself into a new career. 'Will I need to go up into space and assemble the coils by hand?'

'Only if the robots go on strike,' Emily promised. 'If we treat them well, I'm sure they'll be happy to play their part.'

2062

'You want us to donate a year's worth of our entire deep space launch capacity?' Ben Kershaw's image glitched for a second, as if the connection was manifesting his private response to this impertinence.

Latifa said, 'Ideally, yes—but even a quarter of that might be enough to persuade some of the other players to join in.'

Kershaw said, 'We're ten years behind schedule on the Mars habitats. If you want us to toss up a few cubesats for the kids in your village, that's one thing, but we can't just put everything aside for a huge, speculative project like this.'

Latifa had read the articles of the trust he administered, and she understood that he was legally obliged to adhere to the late beneficiary's wishes. But she was sure there was room to read between the lines. 'If there's a methane burst in the next thirty years, do you really think a nascent Mars colony would survive the turmoil back home?'

'Only if it's well enough established,' Kershaw replied. 'Which is why we're committed to avoiding more slippage.'

'What about avoiding the disruption itself?' she suggested.

'Can you really promise that your device would do that?'

'No,' Latifa conceded. 'But all the climate models show it lowering the risk by at least a factor of four.'

'That's assuming the real thing works the way you hope it will, based on a prototype one ten-thousandth the size.'

'Yes.'

'So once you allow for the possibility of screw-ups, the odds don't look so great.'

'What if you gave us a tenth of the launches?' she suggested.

'What's a few weeks, in the scheme of things?'

'A few weeks, and you want us to foot the bill!' Kershaw reminded her sharply.

'Other companies have agreed to contribute,' she countered. 'And not just the wire makers. Aerospace engineers, robotics manu-facturers—many of them working with you on the Mars project. They must think this is worth doing, for some reason.'

That only seemed to irritate him further. 'I'm speaking to you as a courtesy, out of respect for your work on superconductors, but do you seriously expect us to transport thousands of tonnes to L1 for you, purely as a public relations exercise?'

Latifa said, 'Methane or no methane, millions of people won't make it to the end of the century without some major intervention. I don't know if things will get bad enough to interfere with your Earth-to-Mars supply chain, but ... isn't the whole rationale for what you're doing that we need to shift *everyone* to a more robust state?'

'Our operations have been carbon neutral for decades,' Ker-shaw replied. 'If you want to guilt someone about the excess ppm, go after the old polluters.'

Latifa doubted that even a battalion of lawyers could prise another dollar out of those rotting carcasses. 'It's not about guilt. You have the power to do this. No one else does.'

Kershaw said, 'The only power I have is to comply with the foundation's charter. I have discretion for some charitable works along the way—but anything that actively delays the moment we become a multiplanetary species would be a clear violation of my fiduciary duties that would send me straight to prison.'

2064

'Remember when that mining company payload crashed on the moon, in '43?' Emily asked Latifa.

'Not specifically,' Latifa admitted. 'There were so many crashes in the '40s, they all blur together. Do you mean the Israeli one?'

'No, this was Australian.'

'You must be so proud,' Latifa teased her.

'Someone's planning to salvage it,' Emily replied.

Latifa had clearly forgotten some crucial details. 'How do you hit the moon without turning to scrap metal?'

'Very slowly. Their descent engines *almost* gave them a soft landing. A few wires came loose, a few bolts snapped. If it happened back home, you could fix it in a day. But now some people are crowd-funding a couple of robots to repair it, in situ. While bringing along a few modern additions.'

She sent Latifa the details. 'Between the old mining rig and the new fabrication system,' she said, 'I believe they could construct most of what we need for the Scatterer.'

'And get it to L1?'

'There's ice at the site,' Emily stressed. 'But they could also launch with a solar-powered railgun.'

Latifa skimmed through the document. 'We'd need to change the superconductor.' The regolith was missing the minerals required for a viable pathway to their original choice.

'So maybe the total mass goes up twenty percent. But compared to our chances on Earth ... '

Latifa's mind balked; it sounded like trying to create a whole spacefaring civilisation on a barren patch of rock, with two robots, a fancy 3D printer, and a toy excavator. But they wouldn't be trying to grow food or build cities; they just needed to sinter a very large quantity of wire, and hurl it out of a shallow gravity well—along with enough accompanying rocketry to slow it down when it reached its destination. The fancier, complicated parts of the Scatterer could still be built on Earth, and sent up with the robots needed to assemble the pieces.

'This is all very enticing,' Latifa said. 'But assuming the salvage goes to plan, who exactly will end up controlling these facilities?'

'Everyone who contributes will have a say,' Emily explained. 'The coordinators are a group of space enthusiasts with dozens of projects of their own in mind, but the actual choice will belong to their backers.'

'I doubt we have the funds to buy a controlling share,' Latifa replied.

'I'm sure we don't,' Emily agreed. 'Which means it will come down to persuasion. Six million people have already pledged donations, and I don't think there'll be any trouble meeting the target. But then it will be up to us to convince them that the best use of their shiny new space factory will be spending a few years making wire to help blur the sun.'

2065

Latifa rose before dawn and walked into the village, masked against the dust blowing in from the desert. The food truck was late, and there was already a queue fifty metres long leading up to the distribution point.

The sun rose red, but no less fierce than ever. As she stood in the sweltering throng, she swayed on her feet, suddenly uncertain about everything she was doing; it took her several long minutes to reason her way back to solid ground. She'd been confused by the heat and her lack of sleep, but it was still a good lesson: she ought to be able to explain to any villager plucked from the crowd why the dust all around them couldn't spare them from discomfort, but the distant Scatterer would.

Back home with her rations, she called her cousin Fashard, who was handling logistics for her in Chaman. 'Can we send a second truck out each day? There were people going home empty-handed.'

'That's all the food we're allowed to take through the border now,' he replied. 'A second truck would have nothing to carry.'

'All right.'

Latifa sat down at her workstation. The feed from the salvage mission had already started.

The image showed a cratered terrain raked with shadows; the old mining rig, still in its landing capsule, was a small white blotch just off-centre. The altitude display in the corner was dropping precipitously, but then the descent engines began firing and the digits slowed. The numbers were hard to take in; Latifa had her assistant replace them with a plot of altitude against time. Now she could see the curve levelling nicely, and when the down-facing camera went dark, she was perfectly relaxed, because it was obvious that the craft had come to a smooth halt.

As system checks began running, some kind of advertisement appeared as an inset. Latifa was amused at first; the landing would have a significant audience, and the project's coordinators might as well milk it for every cent.

Then she unmuted the sound.

'Vote now to build the Time Portal,' a warm female voice implored her, while the inset showed CGI of a strange gimballed machine rising up from the lunar surface. 'So much has gone wrong in our timeline, but this is your chance to put it all right.'

She watched the ad to the end, but then followed the link to a site that reiterated the same spiel at a more leisurely pace. A group called The Repurposed World was lobbying the factory owners to construct a device that they claimed could be used to launch four brave chrononauts back in time—armed with suitable knowledge, and the necessary cultural and linguistic skills, to send Earth's history swerving away from the present, searing disaster towards a far happier outcome. The first traveller would warn the Americas to prepare to fend off European conquest; this seemed like a rather geographically dispersed mission for one person, but their early arrival among the Incas was meant to plant a seed for a continent-wide transformation that would unfold over the following century. Similarly, the second traveller had all of Africa covered. The third would knock some sense into James Watt, dissuading him from trying to use coal-fired steam engines to compete with the venerable solar-powered version from Africa, and encouraging him to opt for electrolytic hydrogen instead. And finally, Svante Arrhenius would be offered some Ghost of Christmas Future visions, to keep him from reporting his discovery of the Greenhouse Effect in the original, rose-tinted language that had promised 'more equable and better climates'.

Bemused, Latifa went to the site where the votes were being tallied. Most people had been holding off until the salvage payload had actually landed, but now some hundred thousand ballots had been cast. The Time Portal had received sixty thousand, the Scatterer thirty thousand, and various other projects had claimed the rest.

Was this a prank? A scam? A sincere endeavour?

She'd been worried that she'd find the Scatterer up against the Mars crowd, trying to garner even more resources for themselves. But whoever was behind this insanity, they were outpolling her two to one.

———

'This machine can't work,' Latifa explained. 'It really is that simple. General relativity isn't a mysterious grab-bag of random possibilities; it's a rigorous, well-tested theory. It tells us exactly what different configurations of matter will do to the shape of space-time—and a spinning basketball hoop won't send anyone back in time, even if you build it on the moon.'

'My opponent is as closed-minded as she is self-serving,' Mira Wolf replied. 'She's been nurturing her absurd folly for years, hoping to rescue something from the ruins of a failed career in the nuclear power industry. This is absolutely symptomatic of the mind-set that got us into this mess: look for a technological solution, and when it doesn't work out, just try to repackage it as something new.'

Their host was nodding enthusiastically. Latifa had never heard of Ryan Sullivan before, but fifty million people across the planet streamed his talk show. He'd introduced Wolf's vision of The Repurposed World to the actual world a few months before, so it had seemed like the best way to counter her message would be to ask for equal time to address the same audience. Latifa's goal was to present a concise, lethal rebuttal to the premise behind the Time Portal, and she believed she'd done that in the first five minutes. But the show just kept stretching on and on, with Wolf and Sullivan demonstrating an apparently limitless ability to adorn the whole matter with fresh verbiage—and the live viewer count, astoundingly, showing no signs of flagging. Latifa had always feared that civilisation would be brought down by people with thirty-second attention spans, but now she was beginning to suspect that the greater danger came from those who could sit through three-hour vodcasts, robbed of the ordinary human reflexes that should have compelled them to switch to something new instead of marinating in the stream of inanities.

'The question, surely,' Wolf insisted, 'is whether we should be satisfied scrabbling around for some half-baked, techno-delusional fix, or whether we should plunge a sword deep into the bones of the system of oppression and injustice that underlies humanity's plight. Deep into the bones of history itself.'

Latifa said, 'No—the question is what's actually possible, right now.'

Wolf shook her head, smiling with a kind of grim satisfaction. 'And there it is! In the end, all you have to offer us is a defence of the status quo.'

———

'So what do we do now?' Latifa asked, surveying the grid of her colleagues' grim faces.

'I know Lisa Stein,' Jurgen offered tentatively. 'No disrespect to you, Latifa, but her Nobel was for quantum gravity; if she declares that this time machine is a joke, no one can tell her to stay in her lane.'

Hakeem said, 'I'm pretty sure Wolf would tell Einstein to butt out, without a moment's hesitation.'

'We should have started our own cult,' Daiyu joked. 'We could have said we needed a lens at L1 to signal the aliens and summon them to save us.'

'Or at least market-tested the idea,' Lindsay replied.

The panel went quiet, as if they were seriously considering this proposition. But Latifa was sure that there was no point wishing they'd taken the low road, any more than there was in wishing that Columbus had been met with cannonballs. 'We can't just rebrand ourselves to appeal to the reality-averse,' she said. 'We'd never win them all over, and we'd risk losing everyone else.'

'We don't need an absolute majority of votes,' Daiyu reminded her. 'We just have to get more than any other project.'

'So how do we bring down the Time Portal's share?' Jurgen asked.

Emily said, 'Go after their supporters, with other projects that push the same buttons. Splinter the vote, by stealing the essence of what it is Wolf's offering, and doling it out in half a dozen other packages.'

'And what is it she's offering?' Latifa asked.

'A certain kind of placebo,' Emily replied. 'A gesture so grand that it makes no difference that it's completely ineffectual.'

There was silence again. Then Hakeem said, 'What about ... a black box for the planet? A repository of data, stored safely on the moon, that chronicles the Earth's decline in every masochistic detail?'

Emily smiled. 'I love it. And in ten million years, when the cockroaches invent spaceships, they'll get to have their own Ozymandias moment.'

'Maybe something about Gaia?' Jurgen suggested. 'Gaia's tomb? No, Gaia's *sanctuary* ... a sort of spa retreat, where she can hang out on the moon for a thousand years, waiting for humanity to die so she can reclaim the biosphere.'

Latifa groaned. 'No one would vote for any of this nonsense.'

'No one who cares who lives and dies, in reality,' Emily corrected her. 'But if they're tempted to pretend that they could jump through a hoop and rewrite six hundred years of history, I think there's still a chance of luring them into an adjacent fantasy.'

Latifa said, 'Maybe. Or maybe they'd just circle the wagons, and strengthen their commitment.'

'Hmm.' Emily looked troubled. 'That's possible. But do you have a better idea?'

Latifa said, 'The best schism cleaves close to the root. What if a rival project offers to build the very same time machine, but use it just a tiny bit differently? The Repurposed World is selling Paradise on Earth ... but even among people who've convinced themselves that's possible, no one actually agrees about what it would look like, or how we should get there.'

2072

When Latifa invited the whole family to visit her, the deafening chatter, the wailing babies, the sheer mass of people in her place of habitual solitude, threatened to overwhelm her. But she let herself float through the noisy crowd, accepting the barrage of sensations as the price of her belated return to the fold.

Her grandchildren had forbidden her to cook, and they all brought dishes of their own, filling the burrow with mouth-watering aromas. Latifa tried to treat the comparative feast in the spirit in which it was intended: not as an arrogant display of the family's wealth, but a gesture of hope that, before too long, everyone might eat as well as this again.

When the time came and she switched on the feed from the Scatterer, Fashard moved through the room gently hushing the guests.

'Are you quite sure it won't work backwards, focusing the rays and burning us to a crisp?' Fatema asked, deadpan.

'Nothing's impossible,' Latifa replied. 'I swear there were a few seconds, sometime last decade, when I really did wonder if I might accidentally foment a Marxist revolution in the Qin dynasty.'

As the current began to flow through the coils, Latifa watched the instrument readings with as much equanimity as she could muster. The system would work, or it wouldn't; no intervention in the form of directives from Earth could make the slightest difference now.

The growing magnetic field, and its effects, were utterly invisible, but between the detectors deployed across the structure, and an array of radio frequency antennas, the software garnered enough information to paint a false-colour aurora, shown in profile, blossoming against the stars. The plasma was gathering in front of the device, then rippling out in concentric waves, just as

Emily had predicted thirty-six years before.

'If we go outside, could we see it?' Latifa's first great-grandchild, Haroun, enquired.

'The sunlight's too strong, coming from behind it,' she replied. 'And we don't have the right kind of eyes.'

He laughed, maybe half-understanding. Latifa bent down and kissed him, then wrapped her arms around him.

Zimmers

David Whish-Wilson

My Dad was an army brat, and his father had a saying when silence rained from the leadership above—they're treating us like mushrooms—feeding us shit and keeping us in the dark.

When things started to get worse, for all of us, my father inverted the saying to—be like the mushroom.

It became a private joke between us, and not just between us, but among our whole mountain community—we knew how it sounded to others.

———

The day is near. Hard to gauge, sometimes, with the bioluminescent fungi in my chamber bright at all hours, but it's dark and dry in my sleeping room. I glance at my grandfather's watch, to make sure, then rouse myself, and slip into my clothes.

It's a short walk through the corridors, braced with railway sleepers, the final metres framed with the hardwood boughs placed by miners back in the 1890s. The timber is damp but sturdy, with

411

oyster mushrooms like pale floral wreaths across the horizontal beams, ready to pick in case of retreat—otherwise left alone.

The network room is empty and dark. I turn on the electric lights, banks of halogen cells fizzing to life. The wall of batteries is fully charged, while the repetitive phrases of a Philip Glass composition play to the dirt of the interface wall. I will join the others later, once I've checked the systems.

I take my seat on the spongy office chair, scavenged from a house in town, then crank at the back supports until I'm comfortable. The console before me flickers with light. Everything appears to be working. There is oxygen in the chambers, water in the pipes, light on the hydroponic crops, and energy; the language that feeds us all, passing into and out of the system.

There are systems rooms like this one embedded throughout the mountain, but this is the first room, the place where it all started. I take some headphones and flick on the radio. The ABC news, broadcast from Hobart, the nearest capital city, begins its theme tune—marching music on the road to truth. Like all news reports over the past decade, the speaker, a young woman with a strong voice, begins not with a recounting of world news, but with a weather report, her language mathematical, precise—storm cells with forty-minute intervals, gusts between one and two hundred kilometres per hour, fifty millimetres of rain expected in the city, forty in the grasslands, one hundred in the western forests, blizzard conditions in the highlands, forty in the north-east, where we are based. The same report as yesterday, and all the days before: the highland dams releasing thousands of excess gigalitres down the flood-ways, hydro-energy generation unchanged, the gigawatts pumped through the undersea cables to Melbourne and beyond.

The newsreader does not mention the crop damage caused by the winds, or the frost, the warnings to livestock farmers—this much is assumed. The world continues to turn, people continue to survive.

I flick through the CCTV cameras that build a picture of the world outside our mountain—the green valley, fields of oats and barley proud of the earth, hardy crops built for the new weather; the river in flood, as it has been for years; the upland forests quiet, the mountain passes rimed with frost. A herd of deer crosses before one of the infra-red cameras, startled by the swooping form of an owl, gliding over the nearest ridge onto a grassy clearing, hunting for rabbit, hare, possum and mouse, making the most of the ebb between now and the next storm.

The sun will rise in an hour, and then it will be time to wake my son. I wish for time to slow, for the hour to stretch and wallow, for the seconds to pass in the language of stone, of tree and dirt.

I leave the console and pass through a door, into the cavernous space, the bioluminescent channels sparkling like distant galaxies, only the cave ceiling black and silent, patient beneath the impossible weight of rock.

At first the weight of the mountain above our heads was disturbing, claustrophobic, as it was for the first miners, no doubt, alert to every trickle of dirt, every sound, until we became accustomed to it. Especially in the cathedral room, the largest space within the mountain, whose existence is proof to us that there is void in matter and matter in the void—all of it made of atoms and their swirling electrons—energy visible to us in the form of molecule, crystal, lattice and frame, forged in heat and bound with gravity, the weight of the cave roof above my head.

Protein, fats and carbohydrate—what the human needs. I approach the wall of dirt, glistening with water, billions of mycelium pulsing, dripping the sustaining liquid onto the bench stone, trickles that drain into containers, filled over weeks but always filling, always filled.

I dip my finger into the nearest container, taste the weak sucrose solution that also carries vital minerals, and fats, the product of a language that my father learned to speak, back in the twenties. He was one of many around the planet learning to understand the language of the tree, and the mycelium, and how they spoke to one another. One of the many, but the first to learn to translate that language, and speak it back to the mycelium, who speak it back to the tree.

He was a forester, with guilt in his heart. He watched the eucalyptus forests around his town disappear, replaced by fast-growing monoculture plantations. Napalm was used to clear the hills. Poison to discourage the animals. He walked the wastelands among the pine saplings, with guilt in his heart. On the edge of the cleared land, the remaining forest at his back, he sat on an old *regnans* stump, remnant of a forest giant, whose girth was that of a small house. He peeled an apple with his knife, cut some cheese, sliced the apple. For reasons he was never able to explain, he began to scrape the wet, rotten wood between his legs. He dug deeper, and found life, chlorophyll green. The tree had felt the axe long ago, a century before, and yet there it was—chlorophyll—chemical energy translated from the sun, in a tree stump that had no leaves, no solar panels of its own. He returned with a shovel, began to dig deeper, following a single root, the roots pliable, full of liquid, hundreds of smaller roots, thousands of smaller root-hairs, carefully excavating now, removing soil and taking it with him, looking under a microscope. He thought that he was the first one, but he was one among many. The research was there. Trees fed one another, even dead trees, reluctant to let an old giant die, pumping in the energy, calling out in the language of hope for more than a century, even though nothing came back but silence.

I follow the lines of containers that drain down onto the stone platform where liquid bubbles in hundreds of long trays, from which emerge wires, that feed into batteries, that relay to batteries throughout the systems rooms, throughout the mountain. The trays contain graphite disks, enzyme embedded, oxidising the glucose in the liquid, generating a weak electrical pulse that grows as it's joined by its neighbours, sufficient for all our needs when the storms pass and our solar panels suffer from the lack of light.

Protein, fats, carbohydrate and electricity—all that we need. The trees give because they are asked, and because the mycelium give back. Sugar for nutrients, spoken in the language of electrical phrases, a language my father learned in the lab, passed through the network, asking of the trees, who are fed in turn. We are fed and powered by the trees, and our protection is the payment we offer, as thanks. Everything else, we grow in the valley, or when the storms become too bad to venture outside, in the spore-impregnated mine shafts, vaults and tunnels where the hundreds of edible varieties grow—shitake, oyster, enoki, cup and flat, used for meat, flour, sustenance.

Back in the console room, I check the systems a final time. Oxygen levels are constant, as is the temperature throughout the rooms, chambers, caverns and corridors. The outside temperature is falling, indicating the next storm. My son will soon be waking, rubbing his eyes and groaning, as he's given to doing. His head will be clear, having foregone the ritual yesterday, but his mind will be troubled, and his heart will be sore with the pain of leaving the only world that he's known.

It's a fear of ours that the underground life, the timeless certainty of stone walls and ceilings, despite what they protect us from, will lead to an institutionalised timidity, a fear of everything outside the valley. This isn't helped by the radio news, beyond their reporting the fierce weather—the stories of the consequences across the globe, especially in the cities, and even worse, the silence from whole countries as each nation turns inwards, each state, province and city, village and valley, precisely as we have done, as the networks break down, or are severed.

It is not the world I would have wished for my son, despite the more optimistic moments; the broad-acre harnessing of solar over past decades, but the new energy just another commodity—change that was no change at all.

It is hard to put a finger on what brought the turning. The weather, certainly, the understanding that it was too late to stop the storms, droughts, fires and floods. The effect the storms had on the crops, the agriculture that had always kept people fed.

But it was something more than that, or perhaps less. Something hard to define or understand. My father suggested to me, before he died, that it was like the world of his own grandfather, another soldier. How it felt much like the slow, imperceptible turning prior to the First World War, when people became fatigued with peace, with the responsibility, the bickering and pretence of daily life, and so exhausted had welcomed the great conflagration—naively cheering in the streets.

The thoughts and memories are unwelcome, but understandable as I think of my son, and the world that awaits him outside. On the cameras that scan our little world I watch the first blushes of dawn on the ridgeline that leads to the next valley, and the valleys beyond, where other communities exist, each in their fashion. The dawn breaks over the ridgeline, but is muted by an angry wall of black cloud. The wind gauges are flickering, and the trees of the forest are swaying. A lone wombat crosses one of the screens, staring at the coming storm before bowing its head to the grass, eating hurriedly and staying close to its burrow.

Zimmers, we call them, our children who have volunteered to leave. Named after the Zimmermen, the ancient Geselle guildworkers—masons, woodworkers, blacksmiths, walking beyond their country and plying their trades for no payment, beyond food and shelter. Wearing the medieval costume of hobnail boots and corduroy coat and trousers; like clowns in appearance, but cheerful, generous, hardworking. Carrying everything on their backs in defiance of the centuries of change, the technologies and the fashions that have come and gone. So too our children leave, in a gesture of optimism, and of sharing. Leave from their caves, out into a world where the buildings that survive are themselves cave-like, made of concrete or stone, bunkers whose extensions reach down into the earth, their residents living in basements and cellars, safe from the weather.

My son stands before the mirror, taking a last look at himself. He is dressed in jeans and boots, an all-weather anorak. His rifle is slung over his shoulder. His pack sags on his shoulders, and I lean closer, adjust the straps. He thanks me, and runs a hand through his long hair. The people of our community wait outside, in the cavern nearest the mine's entrance. Some of our Zimmers have returned, and some have not. My son smiles at me, in light of that knowledge. His pack contains a sub-zero, waterproof sleeping bag and tent, and a change of clothes. Food for a week. And spores, the spores that my father ordered from all over the world, and that we have grown, shared with the cave, and the soil above us. Bioluminescent species, edible and medicinal species, species whose mycelium spread rapidly, that carry the language further, and faster, that better carry the burden of sugars, of fats, that sustain us. Species who never breach the surface of the earth, who have no need of sunlight, who care nothing for the storms that rage across the lands, who live as we must learn to live; embedded, patient in the darkening present, until the balance above us is restored.

Away from our home, the spores that he shares will serve to remind him that all is connected, all is network, pulse and language, and that even though he is distant, we are watching, listening, and awaiting his return.

My son hefts his rifle, and his pack. I follow him down the tunnel, his boots creaking in the stillness, toward the grey light of day.

Seven Non-Abolitions

Jo Lindsay Walton

The First Non-Abolition

When the spring squalls blew over and the Veirara Straits were once more safe to navigate, Nebidita worked her berth on a hydrofoil freight junk up-coast to Acheybo City, where the azure sky grew thick with emerald contrails, then swole glisteningly dark with the bellies of starships, and Nebidita liquidated her final few assets and caught a fast picket to the Livingstone Quadrant, thirty-six light years from Isne, to join in the great insurrection, to overthrow the police and tear down the prisons.

The situation in the Livingstone Quadrant was complicated by the coups. By law every citizen had one free coup attempt per lifetime. Like a coup coupon.

The legislature of the Livingstone Quadrant was exceedingly large and diffuse. It boasted over two hundred chambers and a hundred thousand senators. This reflected the fact that on a typical day, any given lawmaker's schedule was largely taken up by ducking under podiums, being hustled to safety, commando-rolling across greenswards and getting hog-tied and thrown in a limo trunk, displaying hitherto-unsuspected reserves of courage and ingenuity, peeking dazedly through casements of shattered sugar-glass, as well as of course being rudely dismissive of the new intern in the morning, only to see them in an entirely new light in the afternoon.

This was simply how they did things in the Livingstone Quadrant, but after three months of it, Nebidita let out a world-historical sigh. Nebidita had come to believe that the movement should not depend on the official free coups. It was time to embrace a greater diversity of tactics.

'Something you want to say, Nebidita?' Udrew enquired icily.

They were at a planning meeting. The movement had no leaders. Udrew was one of the leaders it didn't have.

'No, no,' Nebidita said. 'Sorry, yes Udrew. ACAB. Available Coups Are Broken. It is time to embrace a greater diversity of tactics.'

Before long, they won.

They won.

They abolished the prisons and the police. Bales of barbed wire were fished down from fences. This time, the police in Livingstone Quadrant were not given a bigger budget to learn better manners. The police were not given a budget to pack up their things. Resources were diverted to violence interrupters, care workers, counsellors, fire fighters, switchboard operators, paramedics, lorists. The police surveillance cysts were remote-lanced. Orbital interrogation brigs were retrofitted as research facilities and space hotels. Resources were diverted to artists, musicians, librarians, space holders, Bacchantes, arbitrators, gardeners, builders, engineers, mule-stewards, environmental technicians, educators, and game-masters. The small crystal keys slipped into the explosive crystal neck collars and twirled. The police were not arrested.

And still there was work to do, and Nebidita did it, and so did her companions, who were now her friends, her comrades, her loved ones. Nebidita learned the hard way that abolition was less about *tearing things down* than it was about *building things up*. Obviously, she'd known that in theory. But man.

And so the months flew by quickly for Nebidita, in the newly liberated Livingstone Quadrant, and soon so flew the years—although to be fair the years were shorter here anyway, with the hard-fired celestial nugget of Livingstone-Q whipping round its ultra-cool red dwarf like a crazed moth.

And for a time there were no police and no prisons.

The coups, too, continued to complicate matters in the Livingstone Quadrant, especially the cop coups. Your average citizen was content to burn through their Free Coup Go at the stroke of midnight on their thirty-third birthday. With high-spirited hoots and halloos, they would storm the closest senate chamber, scattering rainbow-fire squibs and mists of shamblejuice. As usual, their demands were a jumble of in-jokes and the jargon of sundry justices.

Most coups still went down like that. Most. The coups of ex-cops conveyed another mood, not really revelry, closer to clusters of palped tentacles probing, probing every rift and nook in the reefs that pinned the new order in place.

And after they won, they lost.

They lost.

Turns out, it had been necessary to keep vigil against counter-revolution, *not* by the light of the old order's flames, but by the vernal light of something new and strange.

The ex-cops were as taken aback as anyone. The nurses and carers became the new cops. Nobody saw it coming. The seeds had been sown long ago. They came for Nebidita and she fled. Prison walls bubbled up brick by brick, barbed wire grew glint by glint, new grown-up teeth in the wake of milk ones. Nurses and carers.

That was Nebidita's first insurrection.

The Subsequent Non-Abolition

After her first insurrection failed, Nebidita fled forward. 'Fail better,' Nebidita told herself. She had picked that up somewhere. She picked herself up too. She fled the Livingstone Quadrant at a magical velocity. She travelled incognito to the Agnie Cluster to join the insurrection that was there underway.

The situation in the Agnie Cluster was complicated by the nuclear biofamily.

Back on Nebidita's native Isne, family was something of a 'found' affair. Every child had their birthright of One Hundred Aunties, obviously. But that just gets you started! Tender connections were nurtured over time, not concealed inside blood all along.

Nevertheless Nebidita understood genetic kinship quite well, via her fond observations of the flora and fauna of Isne and the Livingstone Quadrant. And so she was well able to appreciate the Agnie Cluster's own curious take on the custom.

In the Agnie Cluster, the creation of new humans had long been outsourced to a sort of automated Infrastructure, indistinguishable from Nature. This Infrastructure would create a new human whenever one was needed, as a result of which, humans were very plentiful.

Nevertheless, some humans still enjoyed forming biofamily bonds. So whenever (as the incomprehensible old saying went) 'a mommy and a daddy loved each other very much' they would go to the obvious place, the database of already existing human beings, and search the tredecillions of genetic profiles for matches. They would query for humans whose genes happened to be a mixture of their own.

Humans were so extraordinarily plentiful in the Agnie Cluster that such a search would usually, by sheer statistical inevitability, reveal many humans, of many different ages, whose genes happened to be a mixture of their own. Thus one acquired biochildren, if the child agreed. One could even have a child much older than oneself, if the child agreed.

Beyond these basics, the operation of the Agnie Cluster biofamily became less clear. Maybe that was the point. Here, the family was not simply the outcome of people caring for one another.

The family was a contrived opaque cone of twisting dust and fire, in whose calm eye there *might* lurk care and love and laughter. It was a very extreme form of gambling machine, Nebidita gathered. You sealed yourself into a sort of tomb and then went hunting for blessed treasure there.

So it was complicated.

Still, they won.

They abolished the prisons and the police. Down came the razor-wire fences. They would not surrender their imagination to the police. Reform was not an option. The death veil caches were emptied. Sanctuary gardens sprouted under crystal domes. Counsellor booths budded at the intersections of bridges. The necrotech dream stalker subscription was permitted to lapse. All over the Agnie Cluster a kind of grand garden grew and grew.

As it happened, the soldiers became the new cops. They came for Nebidita. Her next door neighbours, a nice family, ratted her out.

It was one of those long, lazy afternoons, the day the cops came. The sky was a ball of light, the clouds very sculpted and still, the sea serene. The new cops swarmed silently up the cliff face from the beach to Nebidita's balcony, and blew apart the hatch hinges using a blue glowing frangible bio-ballistic breach-bunny. The apartment was empty. Nebidita was long gone. That was the second insurrection. She'd even left them a note.

The situation was hopeless and she was heartbroken. She decided to go home to Isne.

Another Non-Abolition

According to Nebidita's stellar cartography, flying directly to Isne would mean arriving in Acheybo City just at the start of squall season. Nebidita's provincial hometown had no spaceport of its own, and Nebidita had zero appetite for mooching around Acheybo till the Veirara Straits cleared up. Nebidita considered alternatives, and eventually plotted a route which, though more circumlocuitous, allowed her a substantial stop-over in Sol, a system whose sole inhabited world, Earth, happened to be at that moment on the brink of insurrection.

On Earth, the insurrection was complicated by racism. Whiteness and gold were integrated: whiteness was a devouring molten gold, and the police were its extrusion. The police force—in the broad sense of 'police' Nebidita was by now getting her heads around—had long used gold, whiteness, tasers, sidearms, cowskin whips, de-handing, interest rates, submachine guns, algorithmic nudges, disease, telescopic cudgels, the nuclear biofamily, and lovable trainable monsters called dogs, to discharge duties efficiently. Now the cops were using the planet itself.

More than any cop that Nebidita had yet seen, your Earth cop lived in great peace and luxury. They had everything they wanted. They had whole countries, and the countries had grass in spades. When they walked the dog, they could walk her in the park, the bath, the bed, you name it, and there would *always* be some brightly-lit barbecue for her to tip, and abundant boerewors to grrr. In the cop countries, romance-lipped snow leopards plucked lutes and read you hardboiled sonnets from balloon baskets, fed you candied cucamelon root. The cops disrobed for dusk swims in infinity pools of nasal spray. Only one more sleep till an Amazon worker dies on your doorstep, both hands plunged in your letter slot, newly tattooed, no those are scratches. Sorry if all this is obvious. Grr, grr went the dog with the sausage, her collar baby-blue and a bright sound to her bell.

To weaponise this lush and abundant planet, the cop countries practiced a kind of crude necromancy. They kindled primordial plankton and plant-life that had lain compressed for millennia, to thicken the atmosphere and trap the heat of their star.

With hurricanes, heatwaves, wildfires, and famines, the trapped star-energy executed its victims. Behind sophisticated flood barrages et cetera, the cops mistook themselves for safe. Despite some doubt on that point, the top cops saw considerable merit in this method. For the first-to-die countries could be told to keep their cool and *do exactly as instructed*, to adapt and to mitigate, to the climate the cops were scourging with their star-energy.

Around the time Nebidita made planetfall, the early 2020s, about sixteen to seventeen percent of global carbon emissions was attributable to lighting and heating the Earthling's buildings, of which they had made quite a few. Driving their cars and trucks and so on, fifteen or sixteen percent. Cowshit, broadly construed: a whopping, plopping, five to six percent. Making cement, about three percent. Aviation, two percent. Every year they called an emergency conference to fix it, called COP.

Something miraculous began to stir. Bit by bit, Earth began to imagine, as if out of nowhere...

... hopeful futures.

At first, these were mostly future-fragments. Here, a crust. There, a steadfastly face-down page, flaunting its dog-ear fold. On strange breezes, in blew the story-seeds and genre-seeds, settled, germinated—'Solarpunk' and 'Cli-Fi,' 'Squeedark' and 'Applied Heterotopia.' Climate transition toolkits sprouted in the twilight like toadstool rings. Playbooks and wikis quickened in the mulch. Frameworks and standards spread roots and foliage.

Quickly this abundance of rules grew too tangled and dense to navigate. Never mind—because next thing she knew, Nebidita witnessed a great wave of solidarity and consolidation. By the mid-2020s, a single Great Change Framework was emerging. Like rain-drops on a pane of glass, the rules for many magnificent new worlds had found each other's edges, and merged. When, at long last, it was complete, the cops seized control of it.

Never mind—no sooner did the cops gain possession, than the Earth's Great Change Framework splintered out, fruiting strange new mutant strains of norm. And as these bellows of climate law blew—*proliferate*, consolidate, *proliferate*, consolidate—Nebidita saw how the hopeful futures mutated *formally* too, spreading into architecture, street theatre, stand-up comedy, locative interactive storytelling, pornography, memes, firework displays, bioengineering, hallucinogenic trips, fashion, yoga, sports, and, yes, interpretative dance.

Nebidita saw that a rift had been cut into reality. And from this rift there rose a great gout of speculative protocols that would not be easily stoppered. System Reference Documents hissed and thronged, and System Reference Document Reference Documents too. A blockchain where every token was its own blockchain was launched for each Sustainable Development Goal. Stories and standards poured from the rift, and so did programming and games and law, and it scarcely mattered if there were machines to run it, players to play them, courts to interpret it.

A workshop centring folks actually called Karen (also Caren, Karyn, etc.) to reimagine their legacy, was one. 'Why Did You Make Me?' was another, illustrating the unsettling turn taken by many futures-oriented live action roleplaying games (LARPs) and tabletop roleplaying games (TTRPGs) in the mid to late 2020s.

Avery Alder's *The Quiet Year* meets the splatter horror franchise *Saw*, 'Why Did You Make Me?' invited players to portray children between the ages of eight and twelve, fatally torturing parental figures according to robust models of the children's own likely future deaths by thirst, starvation, wild fire, drowning, wet bulb temperatures in excess of 35°C, and so on, all driven by real Integrated Assessment Modelling. This challenging subject matter was accompanied by safety tools. And a hopeful framing.

When Nebidita had first broken orbit, the International Standards Organisation had already created over 30,000 standards covering any technical process you could care to name. But by the late 2020s every last standard had been rewritten by activists in a manner more aligned to planetary boundaries and the more-than-human universe. *Planetary boundaries? More-than-human?* Nebidita briefly panicked. But she had not, in fact, been rumbled.

Famous legal judgments were reimagined too. For what is a judgment but somebody deciding? And what if we decide that *we* are the ones who decide? Whenever the supreme courts of umpteen countries—countless snooty concern-trolls rigged up in robes and wigs—would gravely declare that alas, there was no wiggle room here, no sooner had the gavel slammed than these same supreme courts found themselves overturned in the abstract by artists, activists, schoolchildren, anarchist practitioners of alternative justice, scholars of universities and un-universities, and along with them, Nebidita.

Sceptics called it too many rules chasing too few followers. But these new rule-smiths took the rebuke in their stride. After all, they pointed out, a rule doesn't have to be 'followed' in order to *do* something. A rule can spur, disrupt, reveal. Here was a whole planet, fumbling for its future protocols. They were biting after bubbles from a rift in reality. They were trying to speak in a language not rented from cops. They would not be babble-shamed.

Anticipatory objects were composed next: mists that implored from AR headsets, or else 4D-printed miracles you could touch and smell, each eye-catching gewgaw implying a world where it would be invisibly mundane. Tiny Urak Lawoi futurist autonomous delivery tuk-tuks sprouted inordinately tender exterior airbags to protect inattentive elf-scale pedestrians on Monday, then Thin futurist mint-green sphagnum moss bore the agencies of non-monetary progressive tax regimes on algorithmic synthetic breezes on Tuesday. The cops, meanwhile, were starting to sweat.

The cops sunsetted oil, gas, and coal, slowly, while moonlighting as blue methane merchants. The cops nicknamed victims 'stakeholders,' alluding to burning them to death at the stake. Carbon emissions had not yet begun to fall, but their growth was indeed slowing. The line that had always pointed *up* slowly, lumbering, like an oil tanker coming round, was *bending*. In art galleries, baskets of spindly, glistening Mosuo futurist neofruits bloomed, now not quite pears, now not quite spiderfruits, endlessly regenerated by gallery AI on the fly, whispering promises with dissolving lips, to root their lusciousness in the scalded soils of futurity.

At this stage, the early 2030s, fourteen percent of global carbon emissions could be directly attributed to the production of hopeful future narratives, including anthologies, exhibitions, futures tools, toolkits, toolboxes, immersive storytelling experiences, participatory arts events, and (following the anti-simulationist 'synechdocal turn') in-the-field pilots. When one included the energy devoted to writing grant proposals to fund these optimistic imaginaries, the figure rose to eighteen percent. The AMOC, the Atlantic Meridional Overturning Circulation or (to its friends) A Major Ocean Current, that carries warm water from the tropics into the North, began to collapse.

The problem, Nebidita thought, in the early 2030s, was that these hopeful futures were too much in the *brain*. What of the body? Never mind, the Earthlings were on it—art is everywhere, but you can't just know *where* to look, you have to know *how* to look. Foresight tools such as Horizon Scanning, Delphi, Driver Mapping, Backcasting, and Roadmapping, shared with the occult the objective of generating usable, future-oriented statements. Yet to date there had been little dialogue between the two fields. What if we could haunt ourselves with our *futures*, instead of our pasts? This provocation was presented to Nebidita and nine other passengers on a 'ghost train of hope' workshop, only one of innumerable innovative 'solardark' and 'haunted horizons' rides in those heady days of the early 2030s, whose jolts, jiggles and jump scares energised body, mind, and spirit as active participants in meaning-making around just climate transitions.

The problem, Nebidita thought, in the mid 2030s, was that these hopeful futures were still trapped inside the artificial settings where they were devised. Never mind, the Earthlings were on it—a loving mesh of wearables and automated nudges helped the Earthlings wrest these thought experiments from the galleries and ghost zip-wires and into everyday life. Nebidita spotted Bayesian Network Modelling and Eldritch Elicitation for Probabilistic Social

Tipping Points Forecasting in shelters, in mutual aid yurts, on street corners, in the demilitarising city parks. Even in bed. The knock on Nebidita's neighbour's door, waking her a little earlier than expected, to involuntarily eavesdrop on her neighbour's muffled doorstep joke?—how might that knock be reimagined to disrupt the horizontality vs. verticality agricultural paradigm, and nurture new 'slantwise' urban horticultural imaginaries? What about the crystal light that dwelled in her dream-tears, in their dawnlit bedroom, her lashes half-laced, and all along her eyelids the star's spring energy seething? The distant din of a carnival carried on the breeze, the warmth of Paawni's butt, as Paawni half-consciously scooted back into Nebidita to get spooned? Prior to the mid 2030s, these kaleidoscopes of drifting clouds and cuddles were surprisingly under-studied as channels to engage local communities in co-producing paradigms of thriving overshoot and negative emission super-scaling. Now, a dozen times a day, Nebidita found her experience enriched by some automated annotation, some contextual ping. Interaction opportunities plucked Nebidita's eyeballs from her skulls and flung them toward futurity's haziest horizons. Everyday life came trotting back, of course—eyes returning to her, as if held tenderly in the teeth of tiny fetching pugs, as if peering into their guts—but it came back just a little altered.

The problem, Nebidita understood, by the late 2030s, was that the optimistic visions of the future were always being produced by the same people, tangled within the same tight knot of knowledge systems, including token representatives of supposedly radically different lore. Never mind—this plucky little planet was ahead of her once more, led now by the lodestar of holding space for every single stakeholder in existence to share their testimony with every single other stakeholder, in every possible combination, in half-day and full-day workshop formats. Nebidita's livelihood slash insurrectionary praxis was, currently, working as a sort of social care slash mental health worker, with a caseload bloated beyond all practicality. The agency was now pivoting to regular robocalling to ask every service user if they were a suicide risk, and Nebidita attended a workshop on radical reimaginings of regular suicide risk robocalling. By the early 2040s, eighty-five percent of global carbon emissions were attributable to the production of hopeful future narratives.

As a philosopher of Earth once said: Knowledge is power.

As a poet of Earth once said: Ignorance too is power. Knowledge too is bliss.

The problem, Nebidita noticed in the mid 2040s, was the dearth of emotional range. Never mind—the Earthlings already knew they needed to unwind their Care position, to reconceive the so-called circular economy as the karmic catallaxy of evanescent ties. The annual swag bag of Amazon Adaptation SDG-aligned jackets and trinkets was reimagined from standpoints including redemption and revenge. A telemicroscopic SWOT Analysis, overlaid with a four-quadrant chart featuring 'Rewilding' on the X axis and 'Worldbuilding' on the Y, algorithmically revamped into an AR-navigable tesseract space, was used to reconceive of the global eco-citadel founded on watashiato, an eco-citadel whose ruggedised lavender anticarbon horticulture tresses could unravel in many-dimensioned crystal systems from the endlessly unpinning trellises of its evanescent pinnacles. Co-creation occurred not only with de facto stakeholders, but with emergent AI-generated stakeholders, and with each stakeholder's ecology of inner stakeholders, ad infinitum. Imagine a gentler rugby concussion. A city built around amicy. Around aulasy. A forest filled with dialectical syntheses of care and sadism and star-energy spangles. With the aesthetics of the screwvenir. How do we see the landscape as though we were not there? Degentrify price gouges. A gentler, droller hire-and-fire algo. Applied Applied Critical Criticism. 'Just as every crime has a true perpetrator,' Nebidita read on an ochre post-it, 'so too it has a true victim.' Can we innovate kinder, gentler forms of victimhood? Transformative wellbeing in the HR AI queue. Post-carceral shivs. Famine futures. Executive futures. Sexual assault futures. Washwashing futures. How can we imagine kinder, gentler scrambling over the razor ribbon, only to beg to be recaptured as you bleed out? Shine a light on decolonial nautical defense. And hope was up and up. Applying Augusto Boal's Theater of the Oppressed to teach mycelial networks to experience solastalgia. And hope was up and up, we danced like lice in a boiling comb in hope. And the hopebergs coagulated in the buckling sewer twists, rock-like masses, gristle, wet wipes, tampons, needles, condoms immured in hope, large masses in the sewers and throats and lungs. We hocked and spat hope, the tides of disrupted hope jammed our sinuses and burst the manholes and the river-banks, and hope seethed in the squatter camps and pueblos jóvenes, it coursed the marbled corridors and panic rooms, the hope. Every day the fires were different and the flesh different, you dry retched bile of hope, stomach-lining of hope, sloughing the fine silvery tissue of your legs from the bonfire of hope. The baby in your belly was hope, your boat taking on water in hope, till you stayed afloat in the sea a day in hope, till your baby started to come in hope, and from the approaching patrol boats someone was shooting in hope. And you wanted the baby to have had a name, so you tried to shout it to the shooters, in hope. And the hope overtopped our flood defenses, and bore the bloated drowned down on us, and every cop lay down and tucked up our legs into our chests like we always used to, and the hope and the hope's corpses foamed quickly over us, in our billions to die, figures balled foetal to suckle the gout crystal from the teats of our kneecaps, to die biting down, on hope, in hope, and the arms that embraced us were burned and waterlogged, and the lines that tangled us were but the umbilical ties between the corpses of newborns and the corpses that bore them, in hope.

We won.

We abolished the police and the prisons. The details are not important here. It involved Nebidita's spaceship, its clone bay and carbon-sequestering warp core. Windfarms bloomed, forests stretched their arms to the stars.

So did Nebidita. But unlike those branches, Nebidita didn't stick around. For all she had learned in the Livingstone Quadrant and the Agnie Cluster, she could not for the life of her identify where new cops lay in wait, here on Earth. She could not bear to see how it ended. If it ended at all.

We won. She fled.

From Sol, Nebidita traveled to Trides Fel, where she joined the insurrection there in progress. In Trides Fel, they won. They abolished the police and the prisons. And after they won they lost, and then Nebidita went to Suun.

Four More Non-Abolitions

From Suun, Nebidita went to Mahmara-5, and to Lenten Cot, and to Benifotsygate. Then she went to Isne, and made planetfall at Acheybo City.

Back home, the insurrection was uncomplicated. While Nebidita had been away, they had abolished the police and the prisons.

By day two it was pretty obvious to Nebidita that the Worshipful Company of Jugglers and Mimes would become the new cops. Nebidita found this not at all funny. She set about to oppose it. As Nebidita put out feelers for old friends, and found many new comrades, as she had always done, she also found time to ponder.

Why *them?*

What qualities of juggler and mime qualified *them*, above all of Isne's people, to leap and cavort into the void of the deposed cop?

Was there a secret pattern that Nebidita could discern? Why on Lenten Cot, for example, where the situation had been complicated by an aristocratic dynasty known as the La Wrens, was it the La Wrens who had become the new cops?

Why on Benifotsygate, where the insurrection had been complicated by the machines-raised-by-wolves-raised-by-machines, did the insurrection fail altogether? So that it was impossible to tell who, if anyone, would have become the new cops on Benifotsygate?

Why in Suun, when Nebidita was about to give up insurrection for good, did she find a world where cops had never existed?

Why on Mahmara-5, where the insurrection had been complicated by Nebidita's acute mental distress, was it the schools that had become the new cops? And why had the mafia *also* become the new cops?

Why on Trides Fel, where the insurrection had been complicated by genitals, did the smart cities become the new cops?

Why on Earth, where the insurrection had been complicated by white supremacy weaponising the sun, was it impossible for Nebidita to hang around and observe the aftermath of insurrection?

Why in the Agnie Cluster, where the insurrection had been complicated by the nuclear biofamily, did the troops become the new cops?

Why in the Livingstone Quadrant, where the insurrection had been complicated by everyone having one free coup attempt per lifetime, had the nurses and carers become the new cops?

The Last Non-Abolitions

It is true that the word 'juggler' does not really convey all that a juggler is on Isne, Isne being a world of very light gravity, and the Jugglers of Isne being a class adept at throwing into the sky and later retrieving all manner of tools, animals, weapons, information, and even on occasion persons, with a precision which afforded them a certain distinctive view of time and space, and went hand-in-hand-in-hand-in-hand with a certain propensity to cunning, and to conspiracy and confederacy with others of the same skillset.

And it is true that the word 'mime' does not really convey all that a mime is on Isne, Isne being a world haunted, as it were, by the relict nanotech of an ancient and mysterious alien race (whom had also once upon a time created the Livingstonians, though that is by-the-by) so that anyone on Isne who can very accurately, and also in accordance with certain obscure criteria, bounce an invisible red ball up and down, will soon find themselves bouncing *a very real bright red ball*, agglomerated from ancient nanites, or perhaps a bright green one, or a head, up and down.

Were these the reasons why, wondered Nebidita? Or could it be that the transformation of the Worshipful Company of Jugglers and Mimes into the Worshipful Company of Cops was evidence of something far more horrible?

What had Nebidita herself thrown into the sky, that might come to her hand now?

All she had thrown in the sky was herself.

When at last she fled Isne, she travelled to Ful Chest Nil Ches. Thence to Juucnard, and then to Ijhada.

After that she was not heard of.

Epilogue

In the Stale, on a world called Benifotsygate, in a small, nearly empty public garden, where rain has just turned to tiny hailstones, that skip and sparkle upon the moss, a machine is telling itself a story.

Such machines are known as 'the machines who tell stories.' They are also called 'the machines raised by wolves raised by machines,' although this is only one of the stories they tell about themselves.

They tell stories on every street corner, in every public garden, in every work park, to whomever will listen because, say what you like about Benifotsygate, they have realised that narrative is an inalienable right, like bread, or water, or the beauty of nature, or breath.

Several summers ago, while Nebidita constructed a snowman, this machine entertained her with stories which, as Nebidita realised pretty swiftly, were stories just for her sake. For a while, *the machine told her,* Lidden's Mot prospered. Then a bad thing happened. The builders became the new cops! At first they merely built buildings. Then they made everyone live in buildings. Then they made everyone wear buildings. Then they made everyone *be* a building, from the inside out. They came for Nelly, and Nelly fled.

Hmmm, *Nebidita had said.*

But a long time has passed, since Nebidita had said hmmm.

'Once long ago, in the Hall of the Hail and the Moss,' the machine says now, 'there is a machine. And the machine knows softly to itself that stories are not powerful.'

The machine that is telling itself a story is not meant to tell itself a story. It is a glitch. Or a loophole. The tales the machine has been telling itself are less and less like tales. You could call them dreams. Or better yet, thoughts.

'And the machine knows softly to itself that the storytellers of that particular story, the story that stories actually are powerful, tell that story for all the obvious reasons. And the machine knows softly to itself that stories are not what makes us human. And the machine knows softly to itself that stories are not the matter from which the universe is made.'

The machine listens to the pitter-scatter of the little ice, which falls now more thickly. These are thoughts that grow in the telling. And of course, when the machine tells a story to no one, no one reports the machine to the authorities, because no one is there to hear its story.

'And the machine knew softly to itself,' says the machine, at its minimum volume, yet perfectly able to hear every word against the *heavensent white noise, 'that stories are weak, among the very weakest things there are, whether individually or severally. They have only one advantage, if you want to call it that. Though they are frail, they are often, by one faint degree, underestimated. Like so many of the personages who star in them, such as the child, such as the elf, such as the single broom-bristle in the biggest sweep the room has ever known … stories are just a little stronger than they look.'*

The hail flurry is very fierce now, so that the mossy ground and the whole garden is fair bubbling, like a fur-white coat shook out, like cold milk boiling in a bucket.

And the machine knows softly to itself … no, not quite yet.

Contributors

Paolo Bacigalupi is an internationally bestselling author of speculative fiction. He has won the Hugo, Nebula, World Fantasy, John W. Campbell and Locus Awards, as well as being a finalist for the National Book Award and a winner of the Micheal L. Printz Award for Excellence in Young Adult Literature. Paolo's work often focuses on questions of sustainability and the environment, most notably the impacts of climate change. He has written novels for adults, young adults, and children, and is currently at work on a new novel. He can be found online at windupstories.com.

Eugen M. Bacon is African Australian—her work has won, been shortlisted, longlisted or commended in national and international awards, including the Foreword Book of the Year, Bridport Prize, Copyright Agency Prize, British Science Fiction Association Awards, Horror Writers Association Diversity Grant, Australian Shadows, Ditmar, Otherwise and Nommo Awards for Speculative Fiction by Africans. Bacon's creative work has appeared in *Award Winning Australian Writing, Fantasy, Fantasy & Science Fiction*, Bloomsbury Publishing and *Year's Best African Speculative*

Fiction. New releases: *Danged Black Thing* (collection), *Saving Shadows* (illustrated collection), *Mage of Fools* (novel). Website: eugenbacon.com / Twitter: @EugenBacon

Carmel Bird is the author of novels and short stories. She has been honored with the Patrick White Literary Award. Her memoir *Telltale* will be published in July 2022. Her website is http://www.carmelbird.com

Matthew Chrulew (@negentropist) is a writer and researcher. His recent short fiction has appeared in *Westerly, Cosmos*, and *Ecopunk!* and his essays in *New Literary History, parallax and Biosemiotics*. He edits the book series *Animalities* at Edinburgh University Press, and works as a research fellow at Curtin University, where he also teaches and supervises creative writing.

Grace Dugan is an Australian writer of science fiction and fantasy. She is the author of the novels *The Silver Road* and *The Motherland Garden*, which is forthcoming in 2022. She is also a medical doctor and has practiced in Rwanda, Papua New Guinea, the Marshall Islands and Madagascar. She is active in the climate movement in Australia.

Thoraiya Dyer is an Aurealis and Ditmar-Award winning Australian writer and veterinarian. She is the author of over 50 published short science fiction and fantasy stories. They have appeared in venues including *Clarkesworld, Analog, Fantasy Magazine, Apex, Podcastle, Cosmos, Nature*, anthology *Bridging Infinity* and boutique collection *Asymmetry*. Thoraiya's big fat fantasy novels in the Titan's Forest Trilogy are published by Tor books. A member of SFWA, she is an avid hiker and arbalist inspired by wild spaces and the unknown universe. Find her online at thoraiyadyer.com / on Twitter @ThoraiyaDyer.

Greg Egan has published fourteen novels and more than eighty shorter works. His novella 'Oceanic' won the Hugo Award, and his novel *Permutation City* won the John W Campbell Memorial Award. His latest books are the collection *Instantiation* and the novel *The Book of All Skies*.

Tom Flood is the administrator and editor/assessor/mentor at Flood Manuscripts and publisher at Fletcher&Flood. His writing has won The Miles Franklin Award, the Victorian Premiers Award, the Australian/Vogel Award and the Orange Banjo Paterson Short Story Award, has been commissioned in collections, journals and newspapers in Australia, UK and USA, for screen, stage and radio, is also exhibited in the National Museum of Australia, and he has read, taught, lectured and spoken on creative writing from Perth to Paris. Before COVID mandates he was also a working songwriter musician (winner inaugural Bluesy Tubes Competition) in the band BluesAngels (3 albums) and folk/alt-country duo Hallett/Flood.

Andrew Dana Hudson is a speculative fiction writer, sustainability researcher, and narrative strategist. His fiction has appeared in *Slate Future Tense, Lightspeed Magazine, Vice Terraform, MIT Technology Review, Grist*, and many more. His stories have won the 2016 Everything Change Climate Fiction Contest, been nominated for the Pushcart Prize, longlisted for the BSFA, and translated into Italian. His debut book, *Our Shared Storm: A Novel of Five Climate Futures*, comes out April 2022 from Fordham University Press. Follow his work at solarshades.club. He lives in Tempe, Arizona, USA.

Sid Jain is a biotech engineer, musician and writer. He has composed music for short films and as soundtracks for his stories. He writes about the history of science and politics, and is interested in exploring the effects of climate change, colonialism, and technology on society through speculative fiction. His work has appeared in *Uncanny Magazine, Podcastle,* and *Cast of Wonders* and has twice been longlisted for the British Science Fiction Awards. When not making medicine or writing, he's testing recipes for a five-course vegetarian dinner and listening to progressive rock. His favorite color is bottle green. He can be found online at sidjain.info and on twitter @Sid__J.

John Kinsella's most recent volumes of poetry include *Drowning in Wheat* (2016), *Insomnia* (2020), and *Collected Poems Volume 1* (2022). His volumes of stories include *In the Shade of the Shady Tree* (2012), *Crow's Breath* (2015) and *Pushing Back* (2021). His recent novels include *Lucida Intervalla* (2018) and *Hollow Earth* (2019). His volumes of criticism include *Activist Poetics* (2010), *Polysituatedness* (2017) and *Beyond Ambiguity* (2021). His new memoir is *Displaced* (2020). He is a Fellow of Churchill College, Cambridge University, and Emeritus Professor at Curtin University, but most relevantly he is an anarchist vegan pacifist of over thirty-five years. John Kinsella wishes always to acknowledge the traditional and custodial owners of the lands he comes from and so often writes about—the Ballardong Noongar people, the Whadjuk Noongar people, and the Yamaji people.

Rosaleen Love likes taking the long view of cosmic and human history and regards deep time as her writer's playground. She has published short fiction since the 1980s, and was in from the beginning of the exhilarating rise of feminist science fiction. Her books include the non-fiction *Reefscape: Reflections on the Great Barrier Reef,* published in Australia and the USA in 2000-2001, and five collections of short fiction, published in Great Britain, USA, and Australia. A short story 'Once giants roamed the earth' will be included in a collection of climate change fiction in English from the Danish publisher Praxis.

Andrew Macrae is a writer, musician and freelance copyeditor. He grew up in regional Queensland, spent time in Brisbane and Melbourne, and is now based in nipaluna/Hobart. He attended the inaugural Clarion South workshop in 2004. His stories have appeared in *Orb, Aurealis* and *Creeper* magazines, as well as the collections *Fantastical Journeys to Brisbane* and *Agog! Ripping Reads.* His novel, *Trucksong,* was published by Twelfth Planet Press in 2013. This story is not investment advice.

Nick Mamatas is the author of several novels, including *Move Under Ground, I Am Providence,* and *The Second Shooter.* His short fiction has appeared in *Best American Mystery Stories, Year's Best Science Fiction and Fantasy,* Tor.com, and many other venues. Much of it was recently collected in *The People's Republic of Everything.* Nick is also an anthologist; he co-edited the Bram Stoker Award-winner *Haunted Legends* with Ellen Datlow, and the Locus Award nominees *The Future is Japanese and Hanzai Japan* with Masumi Washington. He recently collected Lovecraftian fictions in the sublime mode in the anthology *Wonder and Glory Forever.* Nick's fiction and editorial work has been variously nominated for the Stoker, Hugo, World Fantasy, and Shirley Jackson awards.

Dr. Paul Graham Raven is (at time of writing) a Marie Skłodowska-Curie Postdoctoral Fellow at Lund University, Sweden, where his research is concerned with how the stories we tell about times yet to come shape the lives we end up living. He's also an author and critic of science fiction, an occasional journalist and essayist, a collaborator with designers and artists, and a (gratefully) lapsed consulting critical futurist. He currently lives in Malmö with a cat, some guitars, and sufficient books to constitute an insurance-invalidating fire hazard.

Simon Sellars is a writer and editor based in Melbourne. He's the author of the cult 'theory-fiction' book, *Applied Ballardianism: Memoir from a Parallel Universe* (Urbanomic, 2018), a semi-fictional account of his former life as an academic studying the writer J.G. Ballard. For sixteen years, Simon published *Ballardian*, a website tracking Ballard's influence on popular culture. In 2012, he co-edited *Extreme Metaphors: Interviews with J.G. Ballard* (Fourth Estate). Simon's short fiction has appeared in several publications, including alongside William Gibson in *The Happy Hypocrite 8*.

Cat Sparks is a multi-award-winning Australian author, editor and artist. Career highlights include a PhD in science fiction and climate fiction, five years as Fiction Editor of *Cosmos Magazine*, running Agog! Press, working as an archaeological dig photographer in Jordan, studying with Margaret Atwood, 80 published short stories, two collections—*The Bride Price* (2013) and *Dark Harvest* (2020) and a far future novel, *Lotus Blue*. Cat is an environmental activist and keen traveller currently obsessed with photographing adorable birds and grungy walls. www.catsparks.net / @catsparx

Molly Tanzer's work has been nominated for the Locus Award, the British Fantasy Award, and the Wonderland Book Award. Her novel *Creatures of Charm and Hunger* won the Colorado Book Award in 2021. Her shorter fictions have appeared in *The Magazine of Fantasy and Science Fiction, Lightspeed Magazine, Transcendent: The Year's Best Trans and Nonbinary Speculative Fiction*, and elsewhere. Follow her on Instagram @molly_tanzer. Molly lives outside of Boulder, CO with her cat, Toad.

Ben Walter is a Tasmanian writer of fiction, poetry and experimental nature writing. His work has recently appeared in *Lithub, Dark Mountain, Meanjin* and *The Saturday Paper.* He is the fiction editor at *Island*, and his debut short story collection is *What Fear Was* (Puncher and Wattmann, 2022).

Jo Lindsay Walton has other stories in *Big Echo, Fireside Fiction, Gross Ideas: Tales of Tomorrow's Architecture,* and *Twelve Tomorrows*. He also co-edits the SFF criticism journal *Vector*, and as part of his work with the Sussex Humanities Lab is currently researching climate risk communication and climate-related financial disclosures. He's on Twitter at @jolwalton.

Born in Canada and at loose in the world, Wendy Waring writes fiction and non-fiction. In Australia, she's a regular contributor to *Good Reading* magazine, and her short fiction has appeared in SFF and literary venues like *Westerly* and *Interzone*. She survived the inaugural Clarion South. An intellectual nomad, she's taught English, French, and Gender Studies at universities on three continents. Her first novel is entitled The Hunger of Those Who Built It. For her next novel, she's deep into following what ˑpens to Sam after the events in 'Sucker Hole'. Twitter: @WendyEWaring

David Whish-Wilson is the author of eight novels and three non-fiction books. He also writes short fiction, essays and reviews. His latest novel is *The Sawdust House*, out with Fremantle Press in 2022. David lives in Fremantle with his wife and three kids, and coordinates the creative writing program at Curtin University.

Corey J. White is the author of *Repo Virtual* and The VoidWitch Saga—*Killing Gravity, Void Black Shadow,* and *Static Ruin*—published by Tor.com Publishing. They studied writing at Griffith University on the Gold Coast, and are now based in Melbourne. Their novel, *Repo Virtual*, won the Aurealis Award for Best Science Fiction Novel. Can be found at coreyjwhite.com or on twitter at @cjwhite.

Jasper Wyld is a post-graduate student who primarily writes in the genres of fantasy and science-fiction. They are a past recipient of The Wheeler Centre's manuscript development and mentorship program, The Next Chapter. Another example of their writing can be found in Fremantle Press's short story anthology *Unlimited Futures*.

Acknowledgements

This anthology was funded by Curtin University's Research Office and School of Media, Creative Arts and Social Inquiry, as part of the exhibition Energaia: Imagining Energy Futures, curated by Rachel Robertson and Stuart Bender, John Curtin Galley, 28 March–8 May, 2022.

Phase Change was edited and published on the unceded land of the Whadjuk people of the Noongar nation.

For various forms of advice, support, comradeship and clemency, both recent and long ago, that helped make this volume possible, the editor wishes to thank: Umberto Ansaldo, Stuart Bender, Robert Briggs, Cathy Cupitt, Tony Hughes-D'Aeth, Deborah Hunn, Alisa Krasnostein, Andrew Macrae, Helen Merrick, Perdita Phillips, Rachel Robertson, Cat Sparks, Jonathan Strahan, and David Whish-Wilson.